LEARNING TO SWIM

Clare Chambers

ARROW

Published by Arrow Books in 1998

3 5 7 9 10 8 6 4 2

Copyright © Clare Chambers 1998

Clare Chambers has asserted her right under the Copyright, Designs and
Patents Act, 1988 to be identified as the author of this work

First published in the United Kingdom in 1998 by Century

Arrow Books Limited
20 Vauxhall Bridge Road, London SW1V 2SA

Random House Australia (Pty) Limited
20 Alfred Street, Milsons Point, Sydney,
New South Wales 2061, Australia

Random House New Zealand Limited
18 Poland Road, Glenfield
Auckland 10, New Zealand

Random House South Africa (Pty) Limited
Endulini, 5a Jubilee Road, Parktown 2193, South Africa

Random House UK Limited Reg. No. 954009

A CIP catalogue record for this book is available from the British Library

Papers used by Random House UK Limited are natural, recyclable
products made from wood grown in sustainable forests. The
manufacturing processes conform to the environmental regulations of the
country of origin

ISBN 0 09 927763 8

Typeset by SX Composing DTP, Rayleigh, Essex
Printed and bound in Great Britain by
Cox & Wyman Ltd, Reading, Berks

For
Christabel, Julian and Florence

LEARNING TO SWIM

Clare Chambers was born in Croydon in 1966 and read English at Oxford. She wrote her first novel, *Uncertain Terms*, during a year in New Zealand, after which she worked as an editor for a London publisher. She married one of her schoolteachers, lives in Kent, and has three small children and no hobbies whatsoever.

Praise for Clare Chambers' previous novels:

'Delightful' *Sunday Times*

'A moving as well as a very funny first novel' *Evening Standard*

'Lingers in the mind long after it's been put down' *Company*

'A funny book which slips in some acute and painful observations on the side' *The Times*

'To warm the heart and chill it is a rare ability' *Evening Standard*

'A funny and moving story with a great deal of style' *Sunday Telegraph*

'A great read' *Time Out*

I

I

Loyalty never goes unpunished. My father said that once when he was passed over for promotion at work and I've never forgotten it. I went to visit my parents on the Saturday afternoon just before I was due to play in a big charity concert, having received a summons from my mother. She was having a clear-out ready for the decorators and could I come and pick up a box of my belongings or they'd end up in the church jumble sale? My mother likes to invent a practical purpose to my visits so she doesn't feel she is making frivolous, self-indulgent demands on my time.

She was in the process of sifting through a cardboard box of old, uncatalogued photographs when I arrived, and had clearly been at it for some time. All around her lay empty packets, slippery strips of negatives and neat piles of pictures sorted according to subject matter, date and quality.

'Blurred, blurred, duplicate, awful bags under my eyes, don't know who that is,' she intoned, tossing a series of rejects into the bin. I reached past her and picked up an old school photograph from the box. It was of the netball teams. There I was, standing on the end, second reserve for the B team. And there was Frances, captain of the A team, seated, holding the county trophy on her lap, that usual defiant expression on her face. I was assailed by a sudden, overwhelming sense of nostalgia – my memory has a trigger that's easily sprung – and I started leafing through the loose prints in search of other ghosts.

'Don't rummage,' mother said crossly. 'I've been at this all morning.'

'One thing I always hated,' I said, looking at my thirteen-year-old self, long hair scraped back off my face into a ponytail, my spindly legs ankle-width from plimsolls to knickers, 'was being the thinnest person in the class.'

'You weren't thin,' she said defensively. 'I would never have underfed you.' My mother can take the oddest things personally. She twitched the photo out of my hand. 'That's never my Abigail,' she said, screwing up her eyes, and then, realising that this line of argument was not going to be sustainable, said with a snort, 'Well, I don't call that *thin*.'

❧

In the kitchen, my father was unpacking a new toy: a large, shiny black and chrome cappuccino machine which took up half of one work-surface. Ever since he gave up smoking his pipe – after realising that he could no longer keep up with mother's cracking pace around museums and art galleries without wheezing – he has become increasingly addicted to modern gadgetry: anything that keeps his hands busy.

'Hello,' he said, blowing dust from the glass jug, before setting it on its stand. 'Can I get you anything to drink?'

'I'm dying for a cup of tea,' I said, without thinking. 'Coffee, I mean.'

'Colombian, Brazilian, Kenyan, Costa Rican, Nicaraguan or decaffeinated,' he asked, producing half a dozen unopened foil packets from the shopping bag in front of him.

'Whatever,' I said, and then thought, oh don't be an old spoilsport. 'Colombian.' And I watched him meticulously measure out the beans into the grinder with a little plastic shovel, and crank away at the handle.

'Have you got a concert tonight?' he asked, spooning the grounds into the metal funnel and tamping them down, a rapt expression coming over his face.

'Yes. A charity do. The Arid Lands, or something.'

'Very poetic. Where would that be?'

'Er . . . Senegal, I think.'

'I meant the concert.'

'The Barbican. Want to come? It's only a hundred pounds a ticket.'

His eyebrows shot up. 'A hundred pounds. That's one whole wall plus ceiling and mouldings. Besides, there's still all

4

this clearing out to do – plus the packing.' They were off on holiday while the decorators moved in: Florence, this time. They never took me to Florence. It had been left to others to introduce me to the pleasures of the Continent.

Over the sound of hawking and spitting from the coffee machine father talked about the trip, which had been planned to the last detail. They would be staying in a cheap hotel – a former convent – some distance from the centre of the city, but it had its own restaurant, so they wouldn't need to venture out after dark. During the day there was a punishing regime of galleries, churches and palazzos to be followed. They were going to *do* the Renaissance if it killed them. 'Apparently all these museums and so forth are free for geriatrics,' he said, putting a jug of milk under the jet of steam and frothing it to the consistency of uncooked meringue. 'We'll save a fortune. Here.' He handed me a tall cup containing about an inch of coffee topped with a stiff peak of milk. I could see my thirst was going to remain unslaked. 'Oh, wait. Let's do the thing properly.' He took it back again. 'Cinnamon? Nutmeg? Grated chocolate?'

I glanced at my watch: I still had to pick up my sub-fusc from the dry-cleaner's. 'Whichever's quickest.'

As I left, carrying my box of salvaged possessions – mostly old schoolbooks, elementary sheet music for the cello, letters, badminton and tennis racquets, and a collection of wooden, glass and pottery elephants of different sizes, amassed over many years – I noticed a pile of library books on the hall table. Background reading. Where normal people might take *Where to Eat in Florence*, my father had Machiavelli, and Giorgio Vasari's *Lives of the Artists* as his guides.

I nearly didn't make it to the concert because of a burst water-main at Blackfriars: on such mundane contingencies our fates hang. Part of Embankment and the underpass was closed and the traffic was gridlocked. I was forced to abandon my car on a double yellow line and take the underground – something I would never normally do because of the rough treatment meted out to my poor cello by other tube travellers, but it was just that bit too far to carry the thing on foot.

It was crowded on the platform and I could see that no one was going to give an inch. I was already dressed in my performance gear – a precaution in case I was late – and I had to keep hoisting my long skirt up to stop it getting trodden on. When a train blew in there was a surge back and then forwards like a wave breaking and I found myself being sucked through the doors with the crowd and shoe-horned into a corner, my feet straddling the cello case.

By the time I emerged at Barbican I was convinced the poor instrument had been reduced to firewood. A few flakes of snow were starting to fall. I must be getting old because I immediately thought, Oh bloody hell. *Snow.* I've caught myself out like that once or twice lately. A few months back I had a desperately unflattering haircut but I found I was completely unperturbed. In fact I tipped the hairdresser handsomely. And at the last party I went to which was in Bristol, when the prospect of a hundred-mile drive home at 2 a.m. was beginning to look intimidating and it was suggested I might like to 'crash out' on the sofa, I suddenly realised how very far I would be prepared to drive to sleep in my own bed. Finally, the other day I used the expression 'all the rage' in all sincerity. This wasn't even acceptable currency when I was at school, but I couldn't think of any modern equivalent. The person I was talking to didn't seem nonplussed. Perhaps it's come round again. Perhaps it's all the rage.

I hardly had time to do more than check that my cello had survived the journey, and was in my seat a matter of seconds before the first violinist swept on to the stage. Grace, next to me, shot me a questioning look as we tuned up, and I raised my eyes ceilingwards. I could feel sections of my hair working loose from the clip at the back of my head. It doesn't matter, I thought, as another hank swung down in front of my eyes. No one will be looking at you.

There was a reception afterwards. Most of the orchestra went straight home: a lot of them have young families and they tend not to linger after performances. There was no reason for me to rush off. I've always hated that moment of entering my flat alone last thing at night and will put it off if I can. Grace said she was staying: she knew one of the organisers at the charity end and felt she ought to show her face. I like her because she's a born enthusiast, but her endurance is low. She always has some new fad to promote. This season it was celibacy, which she claimed to have been 'practising successfully' for three months. I didn't like to tell her that I had been similarly disposed for the last couple of years without needing to practise. The difference was I tended to view it as a predicament rather than a hobby.

I hadn't had time to eat before the concert, having rushed home from my parents' via the dry-cleaner's, and thought I might be able to pick up a *vol au vent* or something. I'm not keen on charity galas generally. The audience aren't necessarily music lovers; they've come to gawp at the royal patron. They clap in the wrong places and seem reluctant to return from the bar at the interval. Tonight they were a well-behaved crowd, but disgruntled no doubt because the minor royal had been replaced at the last minute by a lesser breed.

I found Grace drinking champagne and reading one of the display boards illustrating the charity's work on an irrigation project. There was a sequence of photographs of some aid workers and local villagers digging a well, and some rather patronising text.

'Not exactly hard-hitting images,' I said to Grace.

'Well –' she indicated the bejewelled hordes – 'we don't want to rub their noses in it.' In our long black skirts and high-necked blouses we looked like a couple of governesses who had wandered in from the servants' quarters. One woman had already tried to give me her coat. Grace's friend, Geoff, approached us looking hassled. He was about six foot six and thin with it, and held his arms bent at elbow and wrist as if he was being operated by strings. Grace introduced us and when he offered me the feeblest of handshakes I noticed that the cuffs of his dinner jacket were frayed and exposed a good three inches of shirt. He smelled of stale cigarette smoke. He won't remember my name, I thought.

'Lovely music,' he said, stooping to kiss Grace. 'Bloody Duchess.' He scratched his head violently, making his hair stand up in tufts. 'I suppose she can't help being ill,' he conceded.

'Do these events work?' asked Grace.

'Oh yes,' he nodded emphatically. 'I know it's easy to dismiss these people as . . .' he looked at the guests milling around in their finery, 'socialites, but they do in fact come up with the money.'

'Is this what it's all about then? Digging wells?' I asked, indicating the posters. 'Do you have full-time engineers out there?'

'If you're interested I can introduce you to the chap who's been running the project in Senegal for the last five years. Or were you just being polite?'

'No,' I said politely. 'I'm interested.'

He disappeared into the crowd and after ten minutes still hadn't returned. I picked up a glass of champagne from a patrolling waitress and thought about my car by now sitting in a pound on some bleak industrial estate off the A3 with a price on its head no doubt. I discreetly hailed another waitress who was holding a large platter of what Grace insisted were called *de luxe canapés* in catering circles. Certainly there wasn't a sausage roll or a Ritz cracker in sight. Someone – man or machine – had taken the trouble to remove the yolks from hard-boiled quails' eggs, mix them up with something creamy and pipe them back in place in little rosettes. Everything was so tiny, so beautiful, so delicately done, you could eat all night and never be satisfied.

'Oh, there you are,' said Geoff. 'Abigail Jex. Marcus Radley.'

Marcus Radley. I had rehearsed this meeting, or variations of it, a thousand times in my mind, but in spite of all this preparation failed to deliver any of the brilliant and devastating lines I'd practised over the years. Instead I said 'Hello "Marcus",' putting the faintest emphasis on his name and savouring its strangeness. His appearance was just as I had planned it: my imagination had aged him automatically so that in my mind's eye he was always two years older than me. His hair was the same – dark and curly and badly cut – as was his frown, which the uninitiated took to indicate disapproval but which occasionally signified concentration, and his eyes, which registered the shock of recognition before reverting to neutral.

'Hello Abigail,' he said, quite composed now. 'Jex.' He considered this for a second. 'Good name for Scrabble.'

Geoff, whose mind was on other things and who evidently hadn't absorbed from this exchange that we weren't strangers, said, 'Abigail was playing the cello here this evening. She's interested in hearing about the project.'

'Marcus' looked at me sceptically.

'Excuse me,' said Geoff and hurried away again, unaware of the minefield he had left us to negotiate. Grace wasn't nearly so obtuse and said, her eyes narrowing, 'Do you two already know each other or something?'

Flippancy was what was needed here, I decided. 'I'm afraid so. Marcus once branded me on the forehead with a red-hot poker. Although he wasn't called Marcus then.'

'Abigail sent me her hair in an envelope,' he said, almost smiling. 'She wasn't called Jex then.'

Grace looked at us in turn with raised eyebrows. No casual acquaintanceship this, clearly. 'So how long is it since you last saw each other?'

'Thirteen years,' we replied simultaneously, without needing any time for totting up. The ghost of a smile was gone. We were both remembering the occasion of our last meeting: the heat in the chapel; the schoolgirl soprano breaking the last of us down; the windy graveside. There was a moment's awkward silence, then in a determined effort to get the conversation back on to safer ground, he said, 'You're a professional cellist now, then?' I nodded. 'That's good – good that you kept it up.'

'There are worse ways of being poor,' I said.

'You'll have seen most of them,' said Grace to Marcus.

'What about you?' I said. 'I gather you're not a professional . . . er. . . philosopher.'

'No,' he laughed. 'Not even an amateur. I never finished my degree.'

'Ah.'

'I've been out in Senegal for the last five years. I've only been home a month; I'm still adjusting.'

'Why did you come back?' asked Grace.

'I'd been there too long. They need someone young and enthusiastic.'

'You look young enough to me,' she said, emitting signals like a Geiger counter.

'Also the longer you're away the harder it is to settle in back home. No doubt after a couple of weeks in the office drafting public awareness surveys and arguing whether we need a new soap dish in the staff bog I'll be wishing I was back there.'

In the background I could see Geoff weaving through the crowd towards us, stopping to acknowledge people left and right. 'Marcus, can I borrow you?' he called when he was within earshot, beckoning with a skinny finger.

'Excuse me,' said Marcus. 'Someone else must want to hear about my drains. It was nice to meet you again.'

'You haven't changed a bit,' I said, then cringed at the cliché.

'Oh I have though,' he said with a half smile, before following Geoff into the heart of the party.

A hovering waiter offered us more champagne. 'Well,' said Grace, tilting her glass towards mine and winking. 'Here's to the Arid Lands.'

I examined my fingernails, waiting for the inevitable interrogation.

'Okay, in your own time.'

'I don't know what you mean,' I said, innocently.

'Oh, come off it. I've never seen such a shifty reunion. Talk about painful. What's the story?'

I just laughed, enjoying her curiosity.

'He's not one of your old boyfriends, is he?' she asked, too casually.

'Why? Are you interested?'

'I might be. He's good-looking enough. Nice body too. I bet he works out.'

I gave her a pitying look. The Marcus Radley I'd known would readily walk ten miles to get somewhere, but he would never, ever *work out*. 'I thought you were supposed to be celibate.'

'I am. But I don't want to get fanatical about it.'

What's the story? Every time I thought I'd found a starting point I'd remember some earlier incident on which the later one depended. However far back I took it I couldn't seem to reach the source. If only I hadn't gone back to the house on the day Lexi left; if only Anne Trevillion had been better at tennis; if only they hadn't taken on a new German teacher at my father's school thirty years ago. Finally I had said, 'I used to know the whole family. I practically lived with them when I was at school. But we lost contact.'

This is what I didn't tell her.

II

2

I was christened Abigail Onions. I was meant to be Annabel but my father, in a state of heightened emotion when he went to register the birth, misremembered the very name he and my mother had spent a full nine months debating. He blamed this lapse on the fact that he had been listening to *Nabucco* the night my mother went into hospital, and the name Annabel and that of the wicked sister had become transposed in his mind. It was a long and difficult labour and an element of confusion is understandable. I suppose I should be grateful he wasn't playing *Götterdämmerung*.

After a few tears my mother resigned herself to the new name and as I grew into it she began to prefer it to the original, which she mysteriously came to decide was 'cheap', in her book the very worst thing a name – or anything else for that matter – could be.

All of this meant little to me of course. Beside the horror of my surname – ammunition for a thousand puns and paralysing introductions – the slight variation between my intended and given names was immaterial. 'Abigail' was unembarrassing – a quality I admired above all others.

We lived in a large, inter-war semi in suburban Kent. The garden, which was divided from its neighbours by knee-high fences, backed on to a railway cutting. The line was an underused commuter line operating four trains a day, and mornings and evenings would see me hopping up and down at the end of the garden waving at the dozen or so passengers as they clanked past on their way to and from work. When I was four this childhood ritual was rudely curtailed: a man in a carriage on his own exposed himself at one of the windows and when I told my mother she burst into tears and forbade me to wave at any more trains. 'Robbed of an innocent pleasure by some filthy *pervert*,' I heard her rage to father. I didn't tell her that for some weeks I had been showing the commuters *my* knickers.

My mother was the gardener of the family. She used to talk of landscaping, as though she had mountains and rivers to tame instead of a tablecloth-sized lawn and some flowerbeds. Father was assigned various menial duties – trudging up and down with a rotary mower sending up a glittering rainbow of grassdust; digging over the vegetable patch; fetching and carrying bags of compost, and pruning anything large and spiky and liable to snag.

Roses were mother's department. All winter the stunted skeletons squatted in their beds like a reproach and a reminder of the battle that was annually waged over their tender blooms between mother's arsenal of powders, pellets and sprays on the one hand and greenfly, mildew and black-spot on the other. Her efforts were not unrewarded though, as each summer the bushes would sprout and thicken and finally erupt in a velvety mass of colour and scent. Picking the flowers was strictly forbidden. I received my first dose of corporal punishment for pulling all the heads off Baroness Rothschild as part of an experiment in perfume-making. The hand that was too gentle to crush a petal left a four-fingered bruise on my bottom through two layers of clothing. I had hoped to be vindicated by the success of my project, but the jam jar of water and rose petals turned overnight into a foul-smelling brown mush and had to be thrown on to the compost.

Our road was a tree-lined cul-de-sac, lollipop shaped, with a round green at the top from which dogs, children – indeed any creature whom it might have afforded some pleasure – were debarred, and it was used as a turning area by drivers who had overshot and missed the Bromley road – a fact which caused my mother considerable dismay. I would sometimes find her standing at the window, arms folded, staring through the net curtains, following the progress of some offending vehicle. 'Turners,' she would explain, tutting. Apart from incursions by the Turners it was a quiet road: front gardening tended to be done in silence, and neighbours communicated across adjoining hedges and walls with nods and inflexions of the eyebrow rather than words. It was quiet inside the house too. The thick, spongy carpets seemed to swallow sound the way blotting paper takes up ink, and mother's rule about the removal of outdoor shoes meant that the three of us padded around in our socks as silently as cats. Even the cuckoo clock, a souvenir from my parents' Swiss honeymoon, had gradually lost its voice, and the little bird would emerge every hour from behind its shutters with a silent grimace instead of a chirp. Mother sometimes listened to classical music on the record player, but only with the volume on its lowest setting: oboes twittered like canaries, cymbals clinked like teaspoons, and great, roaring symphonies were quelled to a whisper.

I suppose this is why the following incident stands out so clearly in my memory. It seems strange that I can remember something that happened when I was only two in such detail, but I know I can't have been any older because I was in my cot at the time and it is well-documented in family lore that the cot collapsed when I was two and a half, trapping my fingers, and was deemed dangerous and given to the Scouts' jumble sale.

What I remember is this: some time after I had been put to bed I was woken by the sound of my mother crying, sobbing in fact. Through my open door I could see light from my parents' bedroom striping the landing, and my mother emerged dragging a suitcase. A moment later there was the clump of footsteps on the stairs and my father appeared, also crying. Then there followed an exchange of angry voices and a struggle for possession of the bag, which my father naturally won, and a tremendous crash as he flung it down the stairs. It was the only act of violence I ever witnessed under that roof and my frightened wails soon brought my mother hurrying in and she cuddled me, fiercely, to sleep. To my knowledge they never raised their voices again. It was a very civilised household.

There were also medical reasons why quietness was so revered at Number Twelve, The Close. My mother suffered from terrible migraines which would incapacitate her for days at a time and which could be triggered by bright light, heat, noise, emotion and a variety of innocent-looking foods. She would resist their onset for as long as possible, dragging herself around the house, white-faced, her eyes pinched shut and a packet of frozen peas pressed to her forehead, until she was finally driven upstairs to seek refuge in a darkened bedroom. The ice compartment of our fridge was stocked with frozen vegetables for just this eventuality. The packs had to be circulated regularly as the white-hot intensity of mother's headaches could melt one in twenty minutes. She never complained. At frequent intervals father and I would tiptoe to her bedside and change the ice-pack or apply a wet flannel to her brow, and she would smile weakly and promise to be down soon. Occasionally I would be called upon to scrape her scalp with a metal comb, according to the principle that if the pain could not be relieved it could at least be varied.

During these periods of withdrawal father and I would be left to fend for ourselves downstairs. Refusing merely to muddle along, father would rally, fetch out cookery books from the study, drive for miles in search of obscure in-gredients and produce something elaborate and quite unsuit-able for a child's palate – squid, perhaps, or a fiery curry – which I would force down valiantly, all the while praying for my mother's swift recovery.

Sometimes father would think it his duty to entertain me, a situation which would cause anxiety to us both. Once when I was five he took me to a matinée of *Love's Labour's Lost* through which I slept soundly, and on another even worse occasion to a circus where I had to endure both the spectacle of grown men in clown costumes making themselves ridiculous and that of my father beside me writhing with boredom and embarrassment. 'Did you think I'd enjoy that, Daddy?' I asked him kindly afterwards, a story which he would often tell against himself when I was older. After these disasters father refrained from suggesting excursions for a while and confined himself to more homely entertainments –

teaching me to play backgammon and rummy, or merely sitting alongside me on the couch while we read our separate books and waited for the migraine upstairs to pass. One occasion, though, stands out from all the rest.

❦

There has been an atmosphere in the house all morning. Not an argument, but a sense of things simmering. Our regular Saturday visit to the butcher's and the greengrocer's has been conducted in silence, and by eleven o'clock mother has retired to bed with a headache. For me this is an early stage in my growing awareness that my parents are not particularly happy – at least not simultaneously. I have begun to realise that although they don't shout at each other like couples I have seen in the Post Office, for example, neither do they show any special signs of affection. They kiss, cuddle and tease me, not each other.

While mother withdraws to her bed and father to his study, I am in the back garden playing with Margot and Sheena. By this stage (I am six) I have acquired two imaginary friends, Margot, who is slightly older than me, pretty, dark-haired and very bossy, and Sheena, who is younger, fair, pretty of course and not quite so confident. I prefer Sheena, but it is Margot who gets things done. We are practising our ballet. Margot executes a series of pirouettes culminating in a leap and Sheena and I applaud enthusiastically. Margot is already using pointes, whereas we are still in soft pumps: our feet are not sufficiently developed, is Margot's reasoning, and if we attempt to move into pointes too soon we will end up deformed and very probably crippled.

'Your turn,' she commands, and I begin the routine which I have been polishing for some days now. It is, I think, superior to Margot's, because it tells a story: it concerns a young girl who befriends a nightingale which then flies away leaving her bereft, and it is performed with as much pathos as I can manage. Sheena is very moved.

'Do you like it?' I ask Margot.

'Yes darling, very good.'

'Was it as good as yours?' I persist.

'No darling,' says Margot kindly, 'not quite.'

I am still recovering from this when I see father at the window. He is standing between the net curtains and the glass and gazing into the middle distance. I wave at him but he doesn't see me. He is still in the same position when I get indoors, and I creep up beside him, under the net. He absent-mindedly puts a hand on my head and ruffles up my hair, which I promptly smooth down again.

'Daddy?' I say. 'Why are you and Mummy sad?'

He jerks his hand away as though he has put his finger in a live socket and says, 'We're not sad, sweetie. How could we be with such a beautiful daughter?' And fighting off the net curtains, he swings me up and gives me a kiss on the nose. 'I'll tell you what, we'll go out, shall we? We'll go out for lunch.' This idea is very exciting to me as I've never eaten outside the house before.

As father is reversing the car out of the gate, the bedroom window judders open and mother appears holding a plastic bag. 'Haven't you forgotten something?' she says coldly, and father yanks on the handbrake and strides back down the drive. A moment later he re-emerges with the bag, which seems to contain a brown paper package, and stows it in the boot.

'What's that?' I ask as we are finally on our way.

'An errand,' he says, in a tone that discourages further questions.

I am sitting, legs stretched out, on the back seat – it is apparently dangerous for me to be in the front, but all right for father. This makes conversation difficult, but father is not a great talker anyway and the journey continues in friendly silence through street after street until after nearly an hour we pull up outside an extraordinary house. But for this house the road is unremarkable – two rows of tall redbrick houses, no gaps between them, small front gardens, and two ribbons of parked cars. On the corner though, set back from the road at the top of a crescent-shaped drive, squats this monster with a turret room on each side, like a pair of hunched, bony shoulders, and windows of uneven sizes, giving it an alarming squint. The garden, a forest of unmown grass and brambles and vast rubbery bushes choked with purple flowers, is surrounded by a high wall and on top of the gateposts are two terrifying carvings. One is the head of a wolf, snarling, and the other is of an eagle or vulture – a ferocious-looking bird anyway – with a hooked beak and glaring eyes which seem to be fixed on me. While I cower on the back seat, trying to avoid their gaze, father retrieves the parcel from the boot and hurries up the driveway. His business at the front door is obscured by one of the purple bushes, but a moment later he reappears and we set off once more. His errand behind him, father seems more inclined to talk, and he tells me that he is taking me to a lovely place, one of his favourite places, a holy place called Half Moon Street, and that he hopes I am wearing comfortable shoes as there will be some walking involved. I look down at my feet. Taking advantage of my mother's indisposition I have put on my white patent leather sandals which I am only allowed to wear indoors, on special occasions. Father can usually be counted on not to notice such details. I tell him that they are extremely comfortable, which is true, and pray that there will be no mud.

We have lunch at a village pub. We sit in the garden as it is a sunny day and as children are not allowed inside. Father is extremely scrupulous about observing this sort of prohibition, and won't even let me use the pub loo; instead we have to trail around the village until we find a Ladies.

We both have steak and kidney pie and chips. When I have finished father picks over my scraps and eats the tinned peas which I have steered to the side of the plate, and the chunks of meat which I have discarded as too tough or gristly. I have my first taste of clear lemonade. How, I want to know, can something that looks like water taste so lovely? Father starts to explain about flavourings and chemicals, and then seeing my face remembers himself and asks if I would like another glass. He lights his pipe, and as the first plumes of smoke drift skywards the people at the next table pick up their plates and decamp to the furthest corner of the garden. Sighing, father taps out his pipe into the ashtray. It is warm enough for me to have tied my cardigan around my waist, but father is still wearing shirt, tie, jumper and jacket. He always wears a tie. His wardrobe is modest and although none of his clothes are casual, none are exactly smart either. He feels the cold, too, which is unfortunate as our house is virtually unheated: any trace of warmth can bring on one of mother's heads.

Half Moon Street is reached through a tunnel of sunken lanes. The trees, newly in leaf, arch above us, blotting out the sky. All around us is the sharp acid green of spring. It is like burrowing into an apple. We have to park some half a mile away in a pub car-park and approach on foot; the path becomes a dirt track, and I have to be careful to avoid puddles. Occasionally father has to carry me across great swathes of mud. We descend into a hollow, round a corner and there it is: my first sight of Half Moon Street, not a street at all but a moss-green lake surrounded by a coronet of trees, with a tiny redbrick cottage and a jetty on one side. The garden, a waterfall of bluebells and forget-me-nots, reaches to the water's edge where there is a small wooden boat tethered to a sign which reads NO BOATING NO FISHING NO SWIMMING. The cottage is evidently inhabited as the upstairs windows are open and I can see curtains fluttering. There is a tub of wilting daffodils outside the front door and a flaking green chair with a patchwork cushion on the seat and a book hanging astride the arm. 'Last time I was here the cottage was empty,' says father. 'I'm glad it's got a tenant. It seemed such a waste.' Out on the lake a duck and some ducklings are swimming. Only their hairpin trails disturb the symmetry of the trees' reflection. It's so beautiful it isn't real.

'It's a hammer pond,' says father, and starts trying to explain about water wheels and iron smelting, but my mind has soared out of reach and I soon stop listening. I'm planning how I will live here in the future, with a friend perhaps. I already know that it is going to be one of my special places. I haven't even asked father how he discovered it. It doesn't matter; it's mine now. We make a circuit of the lake; father walks and I run, weaving in and out of the trees and down to the water. A sign nailed to a tree reads BEWARE ADDERS, and seeing it father tells me to watch where I'm treading.

When we get back to the car an hour or so later I notice that my sandals are black with mud. Wiping them with a hanky proves fruitless – dirt is ingrained into the stitching and the leather has been grazed by twigs. They are ruined. After a few deep swallows I burst into tears and blubber out a confession. Father is sympathetic. Compared to his own shoes, which are plastered with mud, mine look quite respectable, but he knows that little girls and indeed grown women set some store by smart footwear. Besides he will be held partly responsible for their deterioration by mother and therefore remedial action is called for.

'Where did you get them?' he asks. Between sobs I tell him: it's a cheap chainstore and he is confident that we will be able to find a branch on the way home and replace them. Dorking has them but only in the beige. Reigate doesn't have my size. We finally run a pair to ground perilously close to home and the relief is immense. The old pair and the packaging from the new are discarded in a litter bin and a vow of secrecy is sworn. Father tries to make light of the deception, while hinting that he would rather it was maintained. 'We both know Mummy wouldn't really mind, but there's no point in making her cross when she's got a headache,' he says, somewhat illogically. The excitement at allying myself with father against mother is diminished by a sense of unease. I am inclined by nature to be truthful.

By the time we return, mother's headache and bad temper have evaporated and she is downstairs making a chocolate sponge – a great treat and concession, since chocolate is one of her prohibited foods, and therefore her pleasure in it will have to be entirely vicarious. She and father and I greet each other cheerfully, and after stowing the treacherous sandals in my room I am hugged and petted and allowed to lick the cake-mix spoon. In the evening, after tea, instead of retiring to his study to mark schoolbooks, prepare lessons or work on his Project – some monumental and eternally incomplete commentary on Greek drama – father joins mother and me for a game of cards. There is some piano music playing, quietly, in the background, and we have hot milk and cake with our rummy, which we are playing for matches. We are happy, all three of us, in the same place at the same time.

3

My father had his own equivalent of the untreatable headache: the unexplained absence. Since mother had never learned to drive, father was Lord of the Vauxhall Viva and would disappear off in it for hours on end, usually on some minor errand, like buying a washer for the tap or paying his library fines. (As Latin master at the local Grammar School, he had unlimited access to its library and was therefore used to protracted lending times.) He never gave any warning about his excursions, but would, apparently absent-mindedly, wander out of the house, and only the revving of the car engine would alert us that once again he was Off. Occasionally he would return with some purchase or other which might legitimise four hours' absence: an obscure spare part for the car, or a stack of books in a Foyle's carrier bag. But sometimes he would come back empty-handed. To my mother this behaviour was one of those endearing eccentricities grown hateful over time, but which having gone so long unchallenged could not now be remedied. (Certain rules, like father's being allowed to smoke his pipe only in his study or in the garden, and the removal of outdoor shoes on the threshold, had been established early on and could therefore be enforced with rigour, and after a dozen years of marriage almost came naturally to him.)

He used to enact a small-scale version of his truancy within the confines of the house itself, absconding to its furthest reaches just moments before dinner was served or we were due to go out.

'Don't disappear, I'm dishing up,' mother would say, inverting a pan of vegetables into a colander in a cloud of steam as father hovered in the doorway. But by the time the food was on the plates he would be gone – ferreting in his desk for some suddenly remembered document, or making a hurried amendment to his Project.

I caught him out once. It was the Saturday before Easter. Father had slipped off just after lunch; mother was weeding the front garden. I had finished my comic and tidied my room and had decided to cycle to the shops for sweets. Cycling without support was a relatively recent accomplishment of mine, and my reward for this endeavour had been a new, red bicycle with a basket on the front and a saddle-bag on the back, to replace the rusty jumble-sale model on which I had learnt the art. Riding round and round the perimeter of the untouchable green at the end of The Close had become my preferred form of entertainment, and as I flew along the bumpy pavements to the newsagent's that morning with 10p in my pocket, I felt that sense of complete, unambitious happiness that as an adult I've rarely experienced.

Inside the shop I paused by the freezer cabinet, debating whether I would be able to get an ice cream home before it melted, when I saw father at the counter. I was on the point of accosting him, for there would surely be sweets in it for me, but stopped just in time as I saw the newsagent descend from his step-ladder and hand father a huge Easter egg in purple foil. Instinctively I dropped down behind the rack of magazines, realising that the egg must be for me, and that if I intercepted the secret I would be guilty of something, though I wasn't sure what. From my squatting position I could hear the rattle of the cash register and father saying thank you, and then to my dismay I saw his shiny black slip-ons come round the corner and advance towards me. I kept my head well down, pretending to be engrossed in a copy of *Bunty*, holding my breath for the moment of recognition, but it never came.

'Excuse me,' father said, vacantly, brushing the top of my head as he squeezed past, and was out of the door before I had even looked up.

The next morning, Easter Sunday, I woke with a vague sense of dissatisfaction and couldn't remember why. Then it came back to me: no surprise to look forward to. I had quite unwittingly done myself out of that gambler's delight in confronting a wrapped present: it's bound to disappoint, but just for a second hope triumphs. When I came down to breakfast, however, I found the parcel next to my cereal bowl was not remotely egg-shaped. I tore off the paper to reveal a chocolate bird's nest containing several brightly coloured sugar eggs and a marzipan chick. An expression of bewilderment must have clouded my face.

'Don't you like it?' mother asked, put out by this display of ingratitude.

'Oh yes, it's lovely,' I said, remembering myself, and to prove my thorough satisfaction with the gift I began to line up the sugar eggs alongside my plate and make a great fuss of the marzipan chick.

I never saw any trace of that shiny purple Easter egg and the incident puzzled me for some time. It was only when I was a little older that it occurred to me as a possibility that father might simply have bought it for himself, since he had a sweet tooth and mother couldn't eat the stuff. The idea that a grown-up – my father – might nurse the same petty desire as me to hide himself away and gorge on unshared chocolate felt like a shocking discovery.

4

It wasn't until I reached junior school that my status as an only child became an issue. I suppose I must have noticed that other children and characters in books had brothers and sisters, but when you are young you accept your own situation as normal, whatever it may be. It didn't strike me that I was somehow defective until Sandra Skeet, into whose gang I had failed to ingratiate myself on the first day of term, called me an Only in the playground.

'What do you mean?' I demanded, blushing under the gaze of six pairs of hostile eight-year-old eyes.

'You're an only child – you've got no brothers and sisters. It means you get spoilt,' she replied, linking arms with her courtiers to form an unbreachable barrier of blue gingham.

'Sticks and stones –' I began bravely, reciting the infamous lie that mother peddled whenever I reported some instance of playground name-calling, but Sandra had already finished with me.

'You've gone all red,' was her parting shot as the chequered wall swung round, ready to advance on some other pariah.

From this time onwards my onliness began to preoccupy me: I was reaching the age where it no longer seemed so important to have my parents all to myself. I wanted someone to play with, to talk to after lights out, to giggle at over the tea table, but most particularly to invoke as a protector and ally in the face of the school bullies.

There were several of us in the class who had been marked out for treatment by Sandra and her friends. My surname was enough to do for me, and various other children with the misfortune to be fat or feeble, or especially dim or clever, were similarly targeted. I would suddenly become aware that I was being shunned by various sections of the class; the desk next to mine would remain empty; people who the week before had been my friends would ignore me when I spoke or discuss me with each other as if I wasn't there. When I walked into the cloakroom the conversation would die and then unnaturally begin again on a new theme. And then, just as suddenly, without any warning, it would all stop, and Sandra would be saving me a seat at lunch, sharing her crisps with me and telling me her secrets, and for a few days life would be sweet again. It's strange that we victims never thought of getting together and forming a rebellious gang of our own, but the fact was we hated one another. And Sandra's methods were too subtle to allow for insurrection: only one person at a time was bullied, and when that person wasn't me I was so grateful that nothing would have induced me to make myself conspicuous by standing up for that week's scapegoat. In fact I was so spineless, cowardly and demoralised, that on those occasions when Sandra did make overtures of friendship in my direction I would abase myself thoroughly, even to the point of colluding with the treatment being handed out to a fellow sufferer. But those times were less common than the times when I was on the receiving end, or so it seemed; walking down an infinitely long corridor past a column of smirking girls, or sitting alone at my desk day-dreaming of the imaginary sister whose loyalty would be absolute. Break times were the worst, as we would all be turfed out of the relative safety of the classroom into the cheerless wastes of the playground, where a solitary teacher with a whistle round her neck was all that stood between me and any number of unimaginable atrocities. Skulking in the loo was out of the question as the Girls' Toilets were used as a sort of headquarters by Sandra and her gang, and wandering in there would have been regarded as an act of provocation. By denying myself drink at breakfast and lunch I had managed to train myself not to need the loo all day. On occasions when that proved impossible I would ask if I could be excused during lessons – itself a humiliation – which earned me a reputation with the teacher for having an unreliable bladder.

My parents were powerless in the face of my enduring despair. Every Sunday evening would see me labouring to manifest the symptoms of a new disease which would suffice to keep me at home on Monday.

'Can't you find some other nice friends?' mother asked one night as I sat in bed snivelling into my cocoa – a low point, I remember.

'No. There's no one left. When Sandra starts ignoring me they all do.'

'What about the other girls she picks on? Can't you pal up with one of those?'

'I don't want them as friends. I want normal friends,' I sobbed.

'Doesn't the teacher put a stop to this sort of thing?'

'She doesn't notice.'

'Well, why don't you tell her? This Sandra girl shouldn't be allowed to make your life a misery. And mine,' she added.

But tale-telling, I knew by some instinct, without ever having been told, was the worst crime of all for which Sandra would already have devised the ultimate punishment.

There was one person however – a girl called Ruth Pike – who was even more unfortunate than I was. As well as being dim, she was also afflicted with terrible eczema, which smothered her hands, face and legs in red, flaky patches, so that there was hardly a thumbnail-sized patch of undamaged skin left. As if this wasn't bad enough she had serious asthma, which meant she was always wheezing and puffing on a little plastic gadget. Her alarming appearance made her a natural object of ridicule, and she was often to be found hiding behind the coats in the cloakroom, sniffling and trying to make herself invisible. Needless to say, the pity I felt for her didn't extend to friendship. Try as I might, I couldn't like her. Because of her various ailments, and probably because of her unhappy experiences at school, she was often absent, and the sight of her navy mack with its mittens still sewn childishly on to the sleeves with tape, hanging on her peg, would fill my cowardly heart with relief at the thought that she and not me might be the day's sacrifice.

One Monday morning in spring, after a particularly bad week in which I had cried myself to sleep every night and mother had only been dissuaded from complaining to my form teacher by desperate entreaties from me, I arrived at school to find that the weekend had wrought a miraculous transformation and the sunshine of Sandra's favour was smiling on me once again. She was sitting at the spare desk beside mine, brushing the nap of her furry pencil case and looking up at me from under her fringe. For someone with such power she was oddly harmless in appearance, being small for her age, with very pale, almost albino skin and white blonde hair which she always wore in two thin pigtails to her waist. Her pale blue eyes with their colourless lashes gave her a slightly washed out, unfinished look, like a painting that needs some outlines. Her sister, Julie, who was at the High School, was supposed to be even more dangerous. A rumour was currently running around the class that she had held some girl's head down the loo and pulled the chain because she hadn't shown the proper respect – a punishment known as *bogwashing*. My avoidance of the Girls' Toilets had never seemed so wise.

'Hello,' said Sandra. 'Nicky's off sick today so I'm going to sit next to you. I've got some new pens. Do you want one?' She shook out the pencil case on to her desk to reveal half a dozen plastic propelling pencils which smelled of fruit.

'Really?' I said, cautiously, in case it was a trick.

'Yes, go on, have this one. Pineapple's the nicest.'

We were in the process of sniffing them all and comparing flavours when Ruth Pike came in and sat down. She had one of the few single desks at the side of the class, occupied by the disruptive or the terminally friendless, and she lifted the lid hastily when she saw Sandra and pretended to be busy sorting books, a strategy familiar to me.

'My mum says if you've got what she's got you can't wash properly because you're allergic to soap,' said Sandra loudly. The shuffling behind Ruth's desk intensified. I felt myself blushing with pity and shame. Sandra blinked at me with her pale lashes. 'You can copy me in the spelling test if you want,' she added, which was really an invitation for me to leave my own paper uncovered: she was a hopeless speller – *buisness* and *Febuary*.

At break time, after a test in which Sandra and I alone of all the class had scored full marks, a result which earned us a good hard stare from Mrs Strevens, Sandra swept into the playground and enthroned herself on the only bench on the site, displacing the previous occupant on the grounds of a full year's seniority with a cool 'Off you get, I'm here now'. Her acolytes, including myself, hovered close at hand. The girls were always squeezed out to the edge of the territory by the boys' football games which dominated the central space. Sometimes there would be as many as seven different matches taking place on one pitch, with seven hard tennis balls ricocheting around at head height. I could see poor Ruth Pike skirting the perimeter fence in a doomed attempt to infiltrate our group and remain invisible at the same time. Every so often she would realise she was observed and tack off again in the opposite direction. She was holding a packet of biscuits. Her mother had probably in desperation recommended this as a way of winning friends, or perhaps offered them as a bribe to get Ruth to school. I recognised that tactic too. As the bell went and we started to straggle back across the courtyard into class I found Ruth at my side. 'Do you want a biscuit?' she asked, holding one out between her fingers. It was a proper bought biscuit with pink icing and jam in the middle, a luxury to me, used to mother's gritty flapjacks, and I had just taken it from her and exchanged smiles when Sandra suddenly appeared, grabbed my other arm and shrieked, 'Don't eat that!'

'Why not?' I stammered, looking from Sandra's white face to Ruth's stricken one.

'Because you'll get what she's got – eugh!'

Ruth instinctively put her raw hands behind her back, but said defiantly, 'No, she won't. It's not catching.'

'Drop it,' Sandra urged me, with real concern in her voice, and – craven heart – I did as she said, and watched her grind it into the concrete with her heel. As she frog-marched me back into the building, I saw Ruth looking at me with utter disbelief and reproach in her brimming eyes and I felt as small and hateful and despised as the smallest crumb of biscuit under Sandra's shoe.

❧

'Why haven't I got any brothers or sisters?' I asked my parents over supper that evening, as if that was the source of all my troubles.

Father looked up from his lamb chops nervously, deferring to mother.

'Well,' she said, uncomfortably, 'having children isn't as easy as all that, you know. They don't just arrive on the doorstep fully formed. Anyway,' she said, quickly, in case my questioning took an obstetrical turn, 'you can't always choose: things don't necessarily turn out quite as planned.' And here she gave my father a glance that wasn't entirely friendly. That was all the explanation I was getting.

'If I had a sister I wouldn't care about Sandra. We'd just go around together and talk to each other,' I said.

'You know, sweetie, I think it's time you stood up to this Sandra,' said father mildly.

'I think it's time I went up to see the headmistress,' said mother with some asperity.

'No, no,' I insisted, covering my face with my hands. 'If you do that Sandra will *really* get me.'

The truth of this principle was proved some weeks later.

I had been sent to the medical room to lie down after feeling dizzy during P.E. It was one of mother's days at work (she was a doctor's receptionist, part time) and the school secretary was having some difficulty contacting her, so I was left to languish on the sick bed, authentic ex-hospital issue with an adjustable backrest and abrasive grey blankets. The medical room was in the same corridor as the headmistress's study. From my vantage point I could observe through the half-open door the passage to and fro of various miscreants, and hear the sighing and fidgeting coming from the vicinity

33

of the wooden chair on which offenders, like prisoners on death row, were obliged to await their punishment. The first visitor to pass the doorway was Peter Apps, the school layabout, a recidivist in his final year who was caned on a regular basis. The door creaked open to admit him and clicked shut, and then there was a minute or two of silence before he was ejected and slouched back up the corridor rubbing his bottom.

The next to pass into my field of vision were Ruth Pike and her mother. Their conference with the headmistress lasted at least a quarter of an hour and ended in the corridor with much handshaking between the two women, apologies on one side and thank-yous on the other. Five minutes later I heard a familiar footstep on the tiles; I would have recognised the slip-slop of Sandra's sandals anywhere. She sat on the chair outside the head's office holding on to the seat with both hands and swinging her legs from the knee. After some time she was admitted, and for all my concentration I couldn't catch so much as a syllable of what went on inside. She certainly hadn't been awarded the school prize, as when she did emerge her pale face was whiter than ever, apart from her eyes which were pink and puffy with crying.

Just before lunch the school secretary poked her head around the door. 'I'm afraid we still can't get hold of your mother, Abigail. Is there a neighbour we could call, or are you feeling better?'

I was no longer feeling ill by this time, and besides the blanket was becoming almost unbearably itchy, so I decided to rejoin the class. The midday bell was ringing as I made my way back to the form room to retrieve my sandwiches, swimming upstairs against the tide of bodies that surged down to the dinner hall. Classrooms were out of bounds during breaks. The only exception to this rule was the monitor who was allowed to stay behind at the end of the lesson to clean the blackboard and tidy the chairs. This duty, which was much coveted, happened this week to have fallen to Ruth Pike, who would happily spend the entire lunch hour rearranging the furniture, lining up the scissors and pens in their racks and wiping every speck of chalk dust from the board rather than face the savagery of the playground.

As I reached the top of the stairs I could hear a commotion coming from the classroom. Through the panel of glass in the closed door I could see Ruth Pike lying on the floor, surrounded by a pack of girls whose job it was to restrain her. Sitting astride Ruth's stomach was Sandra Skeet who was in the process of slapping her about the head, face and arms with the blackboard rubber, which sent up clouds of filthy dust with every blow. Ruth's dark hair was grey with the powder, and her raw skin was cracked and smothered. She was making a strange choking noise.

'Stop it!' I shouted – my voice emerging as a squeak – as I threw the door open, and was brought up abruptly, as Sandra glanced over her shoulder at me and then carried on oblivious. For a second I stood there, helplessly, as if I had done my bit and there was really nothing more I could do, and then from nowhere I felt a tremendous anger rise up in me like boiling milk, and before I could stop myself I had marched over to the scissor rack and seized a pair. If they hadn't been round-ended safety scissors I would surely have drawn blood, but as it was I grabbed one of Sandra's spindly blonde plaits and chopped it off about two inches from her scalp. It wasn't a clean cut either, but Sandra was so stunned by my assault that she only realised what was happening after the first snip, by which time I had a firm grip on the hair and her writhing and screaming were to no avail whatever. I was still standing over her, pigtail in hand, when Mrs Strevens erupted through the door, scattering conspirators, while Ruth lay twitching and gasping on the floor, a little puddle spreading beneath her skirt.

I never saw either Sandra or Ruth again. Sandra didn't come back to school after that incident – a pity, as I was looking forward to seeing how she would disguise her lopsided haircut – and gossip swiftly confirmed that she had been expelled. Ruth was taken off in an ambulance: a combination of terror and the lungfuls of chalk dust she had inhaled had brought on an asthma attack. Despite the headmistress's assurances that the chief culprit had been permanently excluded from the school Mrs Pike decided that Ruth would be better off taking her chances elsewhere. I was severely reprimanded for the amputation of the pigtail, which in the commotion of the moment I had been left holding and had finally stowed at the bottom of my desk, where it lay coiled like an anaemic viper. I was saved from expulsion by my previously unblemished record and the fact that I was acting in defence of Ruth. My parents felt obliged to make a show of disapproval of my behaviour to satisfy the head, but although my mother was concerned at this previously unsuspected streak of aggression in my character, their principal feeling was one of relief.

'After all, she only cut off *one* pigtail,' my father offered in mitigation.

5

My part in the deliverance of the class from the tyranny of Sandra had unexpected consequences. Her former attendants, floundering without their leader, began to transfer their allegiance to me. Not because they liked me or felt guilty about past unkindnesses, but because they were now frightened of me. It was as if the class was waiting to see what I would do next. This situation seemed to me hardly more appealing than the one it had replaced. The thing I had hated most about being bullied was the visibility; now I was more conspicuous than ever. 'That's the girl who cut off the other girl's hair' ran the whisper around the school walls wherever my shadow fell.

It was fortunate for me that something else soon arose to occupy my time or I might have abandoned myself to the role of School Bully Elect.

'Do we want Abigail to learn a musical instrument?' father said one evening over tea, reading from the school newsletter. 'Do you want to learn a musical instrument, Abigail?'

'Yes, we most certainly do,' said mother. 'How much does it cost?'

'It's free. We just have to tick this box. Are you sure you want to, Abigail?' father persisted, his propelling pencil hovering above the paper. 'It means lots of practice.'

'Of course she does. I've always said she was musical,' said mother, as if the fact was already proven. 'Choose something like a flute that's nice and quiet and easy to carry.'

'A cello?' There was a hint of concern at the edge of mother's voice.

'That was all they had left,' I said. 'Cellos and Tubas.'

'Well, thank heavens for small mercies,' said mother, eyeing the canvas-clad beast at my side.

'Mrs Allen's class is right next to the music cupboard and they went first and took all the flutes and violins and by the time it came to our turn there was only big stuff left.' Strange to think my career should have turned on such an accident. 'We can do other instruments if we want, but we've got to buy our own. I'd rather learn the flute.'

'The cello will be fine,' said mother firmly, and she put on Jacqueline du Pré playing Elgar (quietly) in the background while we sliced runner beans, just so I would know what I was aiming at.

How I hated that cello – dragging it to school like a corpse each week; hauling it on and off buses, blushing and apologising as I left a trail of skinned ankles and bruised shins in my wake; walking with a list to one side to keep it from scraping along the ground, my free arm stuck out as a counterweight. Physically we were such an odd couple – me: small, fair and skinny as a flute, and the cello: huge, dark and broad-hipped. It was by no means a new model either, but well used and slightly chewed around the waist so that I got splinters in my legs and had to have a special dispensation to wear trousers to my lesson, a further indignity. Nevertheless I resolved to bear this burden, did my practice for twenty minutes each day as instructed by the teacher, Mrs Ede, and subjected my parents to recitals of scales and demonstrations of my pizzicato technique which they endured with fortitude. After two months the little white tapes which had marked the elementary positions on the fingerboard were removed, leaving faint traces of glue which I used as a guide for weeks to come. Although I moaned and whined about doing my practice, and put it off until just before bedtime so that the shadow of it darkened the whole day, once I had actually begun to play I found I was enjoying myself and was unaware of the time. In my end-of-term report Mrs Ede praised my 'natural ear' – the first complimentary remark ever made about my ears – and I began to take the whole enterprise more seriously. By this stage more than half of those children who had elected to learn instruments in the first place had proved uninterested or incapable and had thrown in the towel: the music room was once again plentifully stocked with flutes. But, encouraged by Mrs Ede's cheering words, I remained loyal to The Monster, as it became known at home. I even began to treat it with more respect, wiping the resin from the strings with a saffron-coloured duster, polishing the wood with Pledge until I could see my own frowning face in its shiny back.

After two terms of sawing away dutifully at scales and arpeggios and three easy pieces I passed Grade One with distinction and my vocation announced itself. As a reward and a spur to further endeavour, my parents offered to buy me a Big Present. I chose bunk-beds, and slept in the top like a princess in a tower, with the cello, my surrogate sister, on the bunk below in a nest of cuddly toys.

6

'She walks in beauty like the night
      Of cloudless crimes . . . chimes . . . it's no use,' said
Mrs Gardiner, 'I can't see a thing without my specs. You'll
have to read, Monica.'

Wednesday night was poetry night. My mother had once
belonged to the local choral society which met once a week
to rehearse an unchallenging repertoire of popular works for
performance in the parish church to an audience composed
of friends and relatives of the choir. The advent of a new,
young conductor who wanted to introduce an element of
modernity into the programme – adventurous pieces full of
percussion and discords and unnerving silences – had caused
rumblings of dissension within the ranks. He had finally
overreached himself with the intimation that certain of the
second sopranos were having trouble with the top notes –
were not in fact sopranos at all, and might like to switch
voices. My mother and half a dozen other women, already
aggrieved at a recent hike in the annual subscription, resigned
in a body. They were suspicious of modern music, resentful
of being talked down to by someone just out of college, and
they were *damned* if they were going to sing first alto: give up
the tune after all those years, no thank you.

To fill in the chasm that this act of insurrection had left in
their cultural lives, my mother and the other rebel sopranos
decided to turn their attention to another branch of the arts.
In pursuit of poetry, as of music, they preferred to hunt in a
pack, and every Wednesday evening would see them
gathered in whosoever living room the hospitality rota
decreed, sherry in hand, thrilling to the forthcoming chase.

One of the women, Mrs Davis, who worked as a librarian
and had once had a poem of her own published in the *Lady*,
acted as chairwoman. Her job was to introduce the poems to

be read with a few words about the life of the poet, the historical background and the movement to which he belonged. Poets, I gathered, did not come singly but in waves.

My father, who was rather fond of poetry, would retreat to his study with his pipe the moment the first arrivals crunched down the gravel drive. I was allowed to sit in or not as I chose, provided I was quiet. I usually joined in, as I always liked to be included in anything that was going on, and besides there were better biscuits to be had on a Wednesday night.

On this particular evening, though, I left at half-time because my granny, mother's mother, who was staying with us, was starting to fidget with boredom. She was not keen on poetry, having been forced to learn reams of the stuff at school – Gray's 'Elegy' and 'The Charge of the Light Brigade' – and was anyway rather deaf, so kept missing bits and tutting which made the readers nervous. Another source of discomfort was the lack of heat in the living room; Granny's house in Bognor Regis was centrally heated to a ferocious degree, and she found my mother's aversion to warmth impossible to understand. To be fair to my parents, they had not left her to freeze, but had furnished her room with a three-bar electric heater which made a twanging noise and smelled of scorching dust, and it was to her room that we retreated with tea and biscuits for a game of cards.

'I'm not a great one for poetry,' Granny said as she shuffled the pack. We were sitting either side of her bedside table; I was perched on the bed, she was in the armchair. 'I've always preferred novels, myself. Have you read much Thackeray?'

'No,' I said. I was nine years old.

'Well, you should. I'd read all of Thackeray by the time I was your age. Used to read all night under the bedclothes by torchlight at school. Caned for it regularly. Ruined my eyes of course. The reading, I mean, not the caning. Wouldn't you like to go to boarding school?'

People often remarked how dissimilar my mother and granny were – an observation intended to flatter my mother.

There was some truth in it: my mother tended to disapprove of things silently; my grandmother vocally. Granny had acquired at an early age the air of a woman thwarted. As a young girl her ambition to study law had been obstructed by parents reluctant to sponsor the education of a mere female. Instead, she had watched them squander their money on putting her three less intelligent brothers through public school and university where to a man they failed to distinguish themselves. She had however absorbed some of the lessons of her schooldays – she would rather starve than use the wrong knife and fork, for example – and could at least claim that thanks to Thackeray and Co. her nights had been spent profitably. Her marriage to an older man from the village was not happy. My grandmother was not suited to marriage, and my grandfather was not suited to my grandmother. Domesticity did not come naturally to her. She had some modern notion that motherhood was not necessarily women's work, and if you had been bathed by her as an infant in two inches of cold water with wedges of hot ash from her cigarette dropping on to your bare skin you tended to agree. Determined that her own daughter should not be similarly penalised, she budgeted and saved and went without to send her to a good school. But she had reckoned without the vagaries of human nature. What my mother enjoyed by way of material advantages she completely lacked in ambition, wanting nothing more than a quiet family life and a little job to bring in some pin money.

I did love my grandmother, as children often do, but I was frightened of her too. She was a fine storyteller, and could be relied upon to take my side in any dispute – just as a way of evening things out and prolonging the argument. But her outspokenness and lack of tact were legendary. 'What's that appalling noise?' she once demanded, and when told that it was the sound of me practising the cello, laughed and said, 'Good Lord, I thought a cat had got stuck up the chimney.'

Visits to her house in Bognor were an ordeal, too, as we would be obliged to go down to the beach for the afternoon, a pilgrimage which inevitably exposed me to public scrutiny and embarrassment. While other families seemed to get by with a few towels, our luggage had to include an ice-box, hamper, towels, spare towels, deck-chairs and wind-breaks from which father was required to build a bedouin-style encampment. While normal people undressed, Granny would add more and more layers – coat, scarf, rugs – and sit grimly facing out to sea as if it was all a test of character.

'No, not there, Stephen, there. Not too close to those people. They've got a wireless.' Her voice would echo across stretches of sand like a drill-sergeant's across a parade ground. Mother and father instead of hiring a beach hut used to get changed, with much hopping about, inside a home-made orange towelling tent with a drawstring neck which was worn like an oversized poncho. Designed with self-effacement in mind, it rendered the wearer visible for miles. As a mere child I was expected to be exempt from finer feelings like modesty and to manage with just a towel. The last time we had been to the beach together I had wriggled out of my knickers and vest and half-way into a one-piece swimsuit under cover of a small towel which I was holding up with my teeth, when granny, provoked beyond all endurance by this display of prudery, snapped, 'Oh for heaven's sake, what does she need that for? It's not as if she's got any bosoms!' and snatched the towel away to expose the truth of this to the whole beach.

On this particular evening, while the ladies downstairs were laying Byron out on the slab, we were playing Beggar Your Neighbour, which my mother always called Beat Your Neighbour, because, she said, beggar was a swear word, or very nearly. Granny was a formidable opponent; there was no question of her letting me win, and after two hands she suggested we play for money. 'We usually play for matches,' I said, but she dismissed this with a wave of her hanky.

'Go and ask your father for some change, then we can play properly.'

'Come in,' came father's voice from the study in response to my timid knock. I peeped round the door – I didn't often venture further than this into his sanctuary. My role was usually one of summoner, calling him to lunch or supper. Occasionally, of course, I crept inside while he was out, but the carpet was so covered in papers, schoolbooks, marking, piles of typewritten pages, notes on this, translations of that, that it was almost impossible to cross the room without disturbing something. It always looked like the scene of a recent break-in.

'Can I have some change? Granny wants to play cards for money.'

'You're not listening to the poetry then?'

'We stayed till the interval,' I said. 'Granny got cold.'

He nodded. He was wearing, over his regular clothes, an all-in-one flying suit made of dark brown sheepskin, fleecy side out – obviously designed for Antarctic flights in open-topped aircraft – which gave him the appearance of a large teddy bear. There was a gas fire in the room but he never lit it, refusing to claim for himself any comfort which mother had relinquished.

He searched his pockets for a moment before trying to stand up, realising he was hemmed in by boxes of papers, and subsiding again. 'I don't seem to have any on me,' he said. 'Try my jacket – it's somewhere in the bedroom.'

It had been hung up on the back of the door, no doubt by mother. One pocket contained nothing but chalk – a few broken sticks and some grey powder which lodged under my fingernails as I scrabbled for coins – the other held father's wallet, which like the study was full of bits of paper but no money. Although it was obvious at a glance that the wallet was too flat to contain any change, I browsed idly through the contents. I didn't consider this to be snooping as father had more or less given me permission. There were library cards and bank cards, stamps, old receipts, and some pieces of blue paper with numbers on and words like NET and GROSS and TAX. And tucked in a pocket at the back was a square black and white photograph of a tiny baby in a cot. A baby who was not me: on the back in blue ink in unfamiliar handwriting were the words: *Birdie aged 18 days.*

7

I was helping mother to set the breakfast table the following morning when I brought up the subject of the photograph. We were doing things properly because Granny was here: toast in a rack, butter in a dish, sugar in a bowl. Father, oblivious to our ministrations, was hidden behind *The Times*. Granny was fussing about in the kitchen trying to find her knife and fork. (She always brought her own silver cutlery from home because she said our stainless steel tasted funny.) I was distributing boiled eggs, covering each one with a hand-embroidered felt cosy. They were the sort of thing we were encouraged to make during needlework lessons as they were simple and didn't require too much material. I used to dash them off so quickly mother now had a drawerful; if she ever found herself needing to insulate twenty-four boiled eggs at a time she would have been well prepared. At just the moment when mother was bringing in a tray loaded with cereal bowls, milk jug and teacups, my mind must have made the unconscious connection between eggs and birds, and I said, without any preamble, 'Who's Birdie?'

Crash went the tray as mother let out an 'Oh' which burst in the air like a bubble. She dropped on to her knees and started mopping up the milk with her apron, scraping shards of blue and white china into a ragged hill. My father looked up from his paper, white-faced.

'Where did you get that from?' mother said indistinctly from the floor, her head well down. Father covered his face with his hands and said 'Oh God.' I started to cry.

'What have you done with my table napkin, Monica?' Granny demanded, walking in on us and stopping mid-stride as she took in the scene.

'I just f-f-found a picture in Daddy's wallet. He said I could look for some change. I didn't mean to do anything naughty,'

I sobbed as mother struggled to her feet and rushed blindly from the room. 'Oh no. Oh *God*,' said father, going after her, crunching heedlessly through the broken pottery leaving a trail of milky prints behind him. There was the sound of pounding footsteps on the stairs and then agitated voices.

'Darling, please, you've upset Abigail now.'

'*I've* upset her!' And then more crying as the bedroom door clicked shut.

'Now look here, ducky,' said Granny, putting a hand on my shoulder and shaking me gently as if trying to wake me. 'What's this all about?'

Through a film of mucus and tears I gasped out what I'd said. At the mention of the name Birdie she said, 'Oh dear. Oh dear,' and sat down rather hard next to me, using my shoulder as a prop. She pulled out a large man's hanky, embroidered with my dead grandfather's initials, and wiped my face, then put her arm around me and gave me a squeeze, an utterly uncharacteristic gesture. 'Shall we leave Mummy and Daddy upstairs for a moment and go out in the garden, eh?' she wheedled. I nodded and made a grand effort to reduce my sobs to a whimper as she led me out through the french doors. The lawn was still wet with dew and our shoes left green trails on the silver grass. After a few circuits of the garden we sat down on the bench between the rose beds: the first leaves were just appearing. Granny traced the outline of her lips with one finger for a few minutes. She seemed to have forgotten I was there. 'What are you doing?' I asked.

'Thinking,' she said. 'Will you be very good when I tell you what I'm going to tell you? And very brave?'

'Mmm-mn,' I said, clamping down my bottom lip with my teeth to stop myself crying.

'Of course, what I tell you is a secret. And that means you must never breathe a word of it to anyone. You've had secrets before, I suppose.'

My experience of the currency of friendship was still very limited at this stage, but I said yes anyway.

'Well . . .' She took a deep breath. 'When you were just a baby yourself you had a little sister, but she died.'

'Was that the baby in the picture?'

'Yes.'

'Why did she die?'

'Er . . .' She paused for a moment and glanced up at the sky as if the answer might lie there, before saying, 'No one knows. It was just one of those things.'

'How old was I?'

'Much too young to remember anything about it. But of course your mummy and daddy do remember, and that's why you must never mention the name Birdie again, or ask about her. Do you understand?'

'Why didn't they tell me about her before?'

'Because you'd no need to know. Sometimes it's easier to get over things if you don't talk about them or think about them too much. And they wanted to do whatever would be best for you. So you just go on being the Abigail we all love so much and forget all about this. Do you promise?'

I nodded, dry-eyed. There was no room for negotiation. But I didn't forget; how could I? In the space of a few minutes I had gained and lost a sister, the friend and companion I had dreamed of for so long, for whom my bunk-beds and my tennis set, and my cupboard full of games waited in vain; who should have grown into my clothes; who would never hear me play my cello or walk to school with me, or wait outside the unlockable Girls' loos with one foot under the door, or keep the secrets I would one day surely have. I thought about her often; last thing at night when I lay in my top bunk I imagined her hand reaching up from the bed below to hold mine. I thought about her on all those rainy weekends when mother had a headache or father was working in his study with the door closed and the silence in the house became a roaring in my ears. And whenever I heard my mother sigh, and I knew she must be remembering, I thought about you then, Birdie. But I kept my promise and never asked about you or mentioned your name, or heard it mentioned until that night nine years later when my life as an adult really began.

III

8

In the summer of 1977 I left Saint Bede's with one friend, my Grade Two cello certificate and two dozen hand-made egg cosies. The friend was a girl called Karen Smart and was the only other member of the class to have passed the Eleven Plus. This was the sand on which our friendship was built. While we were funnelled off to the girls' grammar to receive an education, our classmates were destined for the local high school for an early introduction to smoking, fist-fights, and having their heads forced down the toilet by Sandra Skeet's sister. Or so the prevailing demonology had it.

I only got to know Karen in my final term when I realised we would be going to the grammar school together. She lived a couple of roads away and we started to go to each other's houses to play. Karen was horse mad: the walls of her room were papered with pictures of ponies; horse-brasses on leather straps hung from her mirror and she had acquired a sizeable collection of rosettes. This was doubly impressive as she didn't even own a horse. I wasn't actually all that keen on horses, but I sensed that this was a deficiency on my part and did my best to hide it. In her garden there was a high wall built of breeze-blocks screening the smart end by the house with its stripy lawn and weedless flowerbeds from the scruffy play area beyond. We would throw folded blankets over the wall for saddles and use a couple of her dad's leather belts for stirrups and reins and spend hours on end riding the wall, and practising mounting and dismounting. Sometimes Karen used to rig up some jumps using broom handles and other garden implements balanced on bricks, wheelbarrows and watering cans and we would gallop, horseless, around the course, timing each other and counting faults. Unlike Karen, I never managed to get a clear round. She could play this game all afternoon without getting bored. Sometimes, when

I really couldn't take any more, my horse would run amok, sending broom handles and buckets flying, and Karen would ask if I wanted to put him back in the stable.

Although we had not been the best of friends at Saint Bede's Karen and I clung together like survivors of a wreck in the swirling sea of blue blazers that was our first experience of secondary school. She saved me a locker in the changing room; I saved her a place in the dinner queue; she saved me a seat next to her in French. French. This was new terrain. *Philippe est dans le jardin. Marie-Claude est dans la cuisine.* Truly, opportunity was all around.

Everything was new and strange. The timetable at first seemed unfathomable. Where previously we had sat in the same place all day, we were now continually on the move, herded along from room to room every half-hour like driven cattle. The building smelled different from Saint Bede's – not of poster paint and disinfectant, but floor polish and old books, a combination that was at once clean and dirty. The uniform took some getting used to: the blue felt hats with elastic tight as a garrotte, used as frisbees in the playground, were regarded as valuable trophies by marauders from the high school, in the way that a rhino's horn might tempt a poacher. And the itchy polo-neck jumpers which were supposed to free us from the tyranny of the tie rode up under our tunics to form a tight sausage around the chest. At break time the loos were always full of girls hoisting up their tunics and tucking these exasperating jumpers back into their knickers.

It was useful to have a ready-made ally in the face of all this novelty. So many of the other girls had come up to the school together that it was easy for singletons to find themselves stranded on the margins as the class began to shake down into its component parts. Karen and I might have become good friends. She was pleasant enough, and the sort of polite, innocuous girl my mother would have chosen for me if she could. But fate – that wicked jade – had settled otherwise.

Some people can look back at their past and can identify certain pivotal moments where a meeting, an action, a decision, or even a failure to act or decide, has proved critical and altered the course of their life. I can think of three such moments in my life. The first of these happened just a fortnight after I had started at the grammar school and was contingent upon a number of trivial factors: Karen Smart's swollen glands, the incompetence of a firm of North London solicitors, and the failing health of Miss Mimosa Smith.

※

One Monday morning I arrived at school to find Karen was off sick. I already knew all about her 'glands', which she said were liable to swell up like golfballs without warning: Karen was often to be found examining the back of her throat in a pocket mirror, and feeling the sides of her neck with finger and thumb to check for any sudden expansion.

We always sat at a double desk in the same position in whatever class we were in – about half-way back and off to the left. There were usually a couple of spare desks in each room, so if one's partner was away there was no need to share, and on this particular day I had sat through morning lessons unaccompanied. When afternoon school began and we took our places in the history room – well named, given the antiquity and decrepitude of the furniture – a stranger was sitting in Karen's seat. She had very thick, very dark brown hair and was wearing an odd variation on the school uniform: her jumper, tunic and cardigan all approximated to the prescribed kit but were not quite the same. I learnt later that her mother, appalled by the prices at the bespoke outfitter's to which we had been directed, had trawled the chainstores in search of cheaper versions: she was not the sort to be intimidated by school rules.

'Who are you?' I asked, hovering uncertainly next to my usual chair.

'Frances Gillian Radley. That woman' (she meant Dr Peel) 'told me to sit here. My brother's just invented a five-move checkmate.'

'Oh. Are you new?'

'Yes. Obviously.'

'Why didn't you start at the beginning of term like everyone else?'

'Because we were moving house so that Auntie Mim could come and live with us, but it all got held up and Mum had to go down to the solicitor's and have a row. We were stuck in Highbury till last week. Rad – that's my brother – still goes to school up there. He gets the train and tube every day. It's fourteen miles.'

'Rad's a funny name,' I said. (I was interested in anyone with an affliction similar to my own.)

'It's short for Radley. His first name's *Marcus*' – she whispered it – 'but you can't call him that or he'll hit you.'

'Oh.'

'He doesn't like girls anyway.'

'Oh.'

This was my first introduction to Frances; the first time I heard the name Rad or a mention of the curious Radley establishment. I was to hear plenty more about them in the weeks to come.

The following morning I hung around anxiously in the playground waiting to see whether Karen would be back to claim her seat. The truth was I already preferred Frances and was hoping to sit next to her again and wondering how I could arrange this without hurting Karen's feelings. As the class filed in for registration, however, it became clear that neither of them had turned up, and my anxiety had to be deferred to another day. Half-way through the first lesson, which was history again, there was a noise outside the door and I could see Frances, her face slightly flushed, bobbing up and down behind the glass panel, gesticulating and nodding and jerking her head in the direction of the teacher, who fortunately had her back turned and was writing on the board. I frowned at Frances and mouthed, 'What are you doing?' A few of the other girls were beginning to notice and giggle. Dr Peel looked round sharply as a tremor of fidgeting ran around the class like wind through a wheatfield.

'Ssh,' she said sharply, and carried on writing.

Frances abandoned her pantomime outside the door and pushed it open. She was half-way to her desk when Dr Peel turned round.

'Yes?' said Dr Peel in a sarcastic voice.

'It's me, Frances,' said Frances.

'I can see that,' said Dr Peel, pursing her lips. 'What are you doing?'

'I'm just going to my desk,' she said, pointing at me.

Dr Peel started to bristle. 'What I meant, Frances, was what are you doing strolling into my lesson twenty minutes late?'

'Oh,' said Frances, full of apologies now, 'I'm sorry, I've only just got here. I had to take our dog to the vet.'

'I see. You've brought a letter from your parents, I suppose.'

'No – they're not there. That's why I had to take him myself. He's got a growth,' she added.

'Yes, well, perhaps you'd better see me at the end of the lesson,' said Dr Peel, momentarily nonplussed.

'He's not actually *our* dog,' Frances conceded, as she slid into the seat beside me. 'But we're going to adopt him.' There were some titters from the rest of the class, who were enjoying this diversion from the Enclosures Act. Dr Peel's hand came down flat on the desk with a crack like a gunshot.

'Thank you, Frances.'

'What's up with her?' Frances said in a stage whisper until a frown from me silenced her, and the lesson was able to proceed without further interruption.

The next day she failed to turn up altogether, and I began to wonder whether I hadn't in fact imagined her, but on the Thursday morning father and I passed her in the car on the way to drop me off. There she was, toiling up the hill in her funny uniform – her blazer slightly darker than the regulation blue, her tunic a paler grey, her hat obviously bought second-hand from a careless owner as, instead of being stiff and flattish on top, it was domed and floppy and made her resemble some species of mushroom. I asked father to pull over so that I could walk with her the rest of the way, and waited for her to catch me up.

'Where were you yesterday?' I asked accusingly.

'I had to take five bags of washing to the launderette,' she explained in a matter-of-fact tone. 'Our washing machine hasn't been fixed yet and we've all run out of clothes. There was so much I had to make two journeys with Auntie Mim's shopping trolley. I got it all done by lunchtime, but I didn't want to come in late again in case I got into trouble.'

'But you can't take a day off school just to do washing,' I said, flabbergasted. Who had ever heard of such a thing?

'I had to,' she said, surprised at my indignation.

'But what about your mother. Couldn't she do it?' Mine would have done – well, she would never have let five bags of washing build up like that in the first place.

'No. She leaves too early in the morning for work. She's a market research co-ordinator. Dad's working nights, so he was asleep; Rad has to go to school because he's taking Maths O-level this year – two years early, and Auntie Mim couldn't do it – she can't do anything, that's why we had to move in the first place. Anyway, I said it didn't matter if I missed a day at school because I'd got this brilliant friend I could copy off.' And she gave me a winning smile.

'Did you bring a letter from your parents this time?' I asked, already nervous at the possibility of witnessing another clash between Frances and Dr Peel.

'No, Mum had left before I got up,' she said, then seeing my dismayed expression added, 'Don't worry. I got Rad to do one – he's got Mum's signature off to a T.'

Dear Beatrice

I started at my new school today. I didn't think I'd be nervous but I was. I'm in 1T – Mrs Twigg's class. She's all right, but she's got this funny way of shutting her eyes when she's talking and not opening them again for ages. I don't think she'll be much trouble. The history teacher, Dr Peel, is rather fierce. She made me sit next to this girl called Abigail – wait for it – ONIONS, who is a bit stuck up but quite nice. She's got long hair, a crooked tooth, a pointy sort of nose and really neat writing. She said I could borrow her books to catch up all the work I've missed which is a good thing because after history we had French, and I didn't know what was going on! When I got home Mum was working late and Dad was out I don't know where, so I did a bit more unpacking till Rad came home then I made us a fried egg sandwich for tea and we played chess till Mum got back. I lost sixteen–nil. She'd brought in a Chinese takeaway so we ate that too.

Frances was a serious diarist. She would even bring her 'journal' – a large maroon leather volume – to school and every so often would ostentatiously produce it from her bag and start writing, one arm protectively shielding the page. Then she would make a great show of locking it and stashing the key in her purse-belt. It was unnerving to be in the middle of a conversation with her, only to have it terminated as she dived for her diary and scribbled down a few words. It made you rather inclined to watch what you said. After a couple of weeks and much wheedling on my part she allowed me a glimpse of the above entry and my curiosity was justly rewarded.

'Oh!' I gasped as I read her appraisal of me, blushing to the tip of my pointy nose. 'Why did you let me read that bit?'

'What?' She looked over my shoulder. 'Oh, did I say you were stuck up? Well, it doesn't matter. I wrote that two whole weeks ago. I don't think that now.'

When Karen's glands had once more returned to their regular dimensions and she reappeared at school I was forced to reconsider my loyalties. Of course I ought to have told Frances that Karen would be wanting her seat back – there were unspoken rules about territorial disputes of this sort. But it was Frances I wanted as a friend, and so a compromise presented itself. We would take it in turns, the three of us, to sit in a pair, so that none of us would feel left out for long.

Frances accepted this arrangement, as she accepted all life's inessentials, with complete equanimity. Karen was dubious at first, feeling that she had been outmanoeuvred behind her back, but when she saw in what esteem Frances was held by the rest of the class for her sheer oddness she relented. This caused me even greater anxiety as I began to worry that they might discover a common interest which would exclude me, and I tried to engineer my periods of exile at the single desk so that they coincided with a lesson with one of the stricter teachers who demanded absolute silence, so that I knew no confidences were being exchanged.

Three girls can't be friends for long: the pairing instinct is too strong. And so it proved with us. Although nothing was said, perhaps even thought by the other two, gradually, inexorably Karen began to be squeezed out, and this unspoken allegiance in an unwilled but still genuine unkindness only served to bring Frances and me closer together. For me, who had never had a sister or a proper friend before, it was like a miracle.

How can I express the strength of her appeal to my eleven-year-old self? Maybe it was that in a strange way she reminded me of my old enemy, Sandra Skeet, but without the malice. They both had confidence and the ability to command loyalty, yet in Frances' case those same qualities were deployed unselfishly. Perhaps it was her lack of timidity that I liked. Almost nothing embarrassed her, whereas I would blush merely in response to passing someone in the corridor. Or perhaps it was just that she was more interesting than me: she was always regaling me with new stories about her family, throwing in names and references without any explanation as if I already knew them all intimately, which after a few weeks I felt I did.

'Last night Lawrence was supposed to be coming round to supper —'

'Who's Lawrence?'

'One of Mum's old boyfriends – but he was late and the lamb was getting more and more burnt, and then Fish and Chips started their banging–'

'Fish and Chips?'

'Our next-door neighbours. They're not really called that, but Dad's always bitching about them and the walls are quite thin so we have to say Fish and Chips in case they're listening.' Apparently Fish and Chips, a mother and son, were keen home improvers and the sound of drilling and hammering would issue from their side of the party wall at unneighbourly hours.

'Last night the noise was so bad we gave up and went out to a restaurant and didn't get back till twelve – that's why I'm so tired. Anyway, Growth was pleased because he got the lamb.'

'Who's Growth?'

'Our dog – his real name's Buster but he's got this big lump on his side and Rad started calling him Growth and it sort of stuck. We've adopted him because Bill and Daphne couldn't look after him properly.'

'Who are Bill and Daphne?'

Events in the Radley household often conspired against Frances getting a decent night's sleep. She frequently came to school yawning and bleary-eyed. Friends of her mother would arrive without warning and need to be put up for the night, and Frances would have to surrender her bed and sleep on the sitting-room couch. This would entail waiting up until the early hours for the guests, who were invariably conversationalists of some stamina, to make a move upstairs. As far as I could gather from these and other stories her parents seemed to spend almost no time together. Her mother's hours at the market research bureau were very long, and the job often involved playing host to panels of volunteers testing and discussing new products. At our house women assembled on Wednesdays to discuss Robert

Browning; at the Radleys' it was more likely to be gravy browning, but their gatherings sounded livelier, somehow. Her father worked nights – at what, exactly, I wasn't sure; Frances was evasive about the details. During the week she and Rad existed on a diet of school dinners and in the evenings fried egg sandwiches, and another staple, 'the Greasy Dog' – a sausage and a rasher of bacon rolled up in a slice of bread and fried in butter, on the strength of which Frances was slightly on the plump side, though extremely fit. She was easily the fastest runner in the class and could hit a rounders ball right out of the school grounds into the back gardens beyond. Unlike me she was a confident swimmer, and while I loitered in the shallow end, kicking around on a polystyrene float with the other defectives, she practised the front crawl in the Olympic pool.

'You're a brilliant swimmer,' I said, enviously, as we peeled off our white rubber hats which made us look like so many boiled eggs bobbing in the water.

'I'm not as good as Rad. He once rescued a girl from drowning in Cornwall when her canoe capsized. He had to drag her in to shore and give her the kiss of life – which was doubly amazing because he hates girls.'

When we picked teams for netball she was always first to be chosen. If she was captain she would pick me first out of loyalty, even though my natural place in the ranking was well down. I returned this kindness by allowing her to copy my homework on the frequent occasions when she failed to do it. Academic discipline was beyond her: she could only understand subjects where an element of the personal prevailed. For this reason she was rather good at English where her gifts for autobiography and embellishment were effortlessly deployed.

My parents were delighted that in spite of their fears I had turned out to be capable of making and hanging on to a friend and that at last there was some prospect of my being normally happy at school. They urged me to invite Frances to tea so that they could meet her. I hesitated. Keen as I was to establish a further bond of friendship between us I was cautious about bringing her home. Whether I was worried that my parents and I would be exposed as the drones of convention that we doubtless were, or whether it was fear that Frances' rather free way of addressing adults might offend a stickler for manners like my mother, I wasn't sure. I didn't examine my feelings too closely in case they revealed something about myself that I didn't want to know. Besides, an invitation to The Close, as far as I was concerned, was only a means to that most pressing of ends: a return visit to the home of the Radleys, where I would at last meet the characters whose habits and exploits I had come to know, and where something interesting would surely happen to me.

9

At the end of that first Christmas term the upper school
mounted a production of *The Mikado*, in which leading roles
were taken by sixth form and staff and a few lesser parts
filtered down to the younger pupils. It was rare for anyone
below the third year to be considered, but Frances, as well as
having a clear soprano voice, had the sort of black-haired,
pale-skinned looks which could be made suitably oriental
without further stretching the resources of the wig department, and she was duly dragooned into the chorus. As one of
the few cellists in the school I auditioned successfully for the
orchestra and found myself playing – or at least miming, until
I had memorised the trickier reaches of the score – alongside
much older girls, girls who wore tights and eyeliner and high-
heeled shoes, and who seemed marvellously unafraid of the
teachers.

This, we were given to understand by Mrs Twigg, was an
honour and a privilege far in excess of our deserts and, rather
than distracting us from our work, ought to spur us on to
greater endeavour. These remarks were directed principally
at Frances, whose initial interest in the production had been
awakened by the discovery that final rehearsals were to take
place during lessons. Frances was also, it emerged, in competition with Rad who, as well as being a boy genius, chess
Grand Master and champion swimmer, was also a distin-
guished actor. I had no ambition to be up on stage, but was
happiest in the twilit obscurity of the orchestra pit; partici-
pating but out of sight. The older girls, when they saw how
timid I was, and how grateful for their attention, looked after
me, fussed over me and made fun of my blushing. The girl
whose music I shared, a prefect and therefore an object of
some awe, turned a deaf ear when I strayed into unwritten
keys, indicated where we were in the score when it was clear

I was adrift, and smiled encouragement when, on familiar territory at last, I set to with any conviction.

Although I was content simply to be in the presence of Art, an additional incentive offered itself to the older girls in the form of a detachment of half a dozen boys from the local independent school drafted in to take the key male roles. Competition for their favours was fierce, and come rehearsal time a better turned-out collection of townswomen of Titipu it would have been hard to find. In the hot-house atmosphere backstage romances blossomed and died in a matter of days. Ko-Ko, the best looking of the boys, seemed to be working his way through the entire cast. There was always one puffy-eyed girl being comforted by friends in the changing rooms, or glowering from the wings at Ko-Ko and his latest conquest.

I had two reasons for looking forward to the performance – which was to run for three nights in the last week of term; the pleasure of being involved in something so far beyond my individual abilities, and the fact that Frances' family would be coming to the opening night. At last I would get a glimpse of the legendary Radleys.

On the morning of the dress rehearsal I awoke with a sore throat and a shivery, dizzy feeling which was unmistakably the beginning of something nasty. Refusing to acknowledge these symptoms I put on an extra vest and staggered down to breakfast. Mother looked at me suspiciously as I sat at the table stirring my uneaten cornflakes, my teeth chattering.

'Are you feeling all right?' she asked, laying the back of her hand against my burning forehead. That settled it. 'You've got a fever!' she exclaimed, clattering around the medicine cupboard for the thermometer which a few minutes later confirmed her diagnosis. 'Up to bed!'

'I can't – it's the dress rehearsal today,' I said urgently, my hot face getting hotter. 'I can't miss that or I won't know what's going on tomorrow in the real thing.'

'If you don't get up to bed now you won't be well enough to be in the real thing,' mother said sharply. 'Go on and I'll bring you a hot water-bottle.' Water-bottles and ice-packs:

there was no illness which could not be treated with the application of extreme temperature. I started to cry.

'Come on, treasure,' said father gently. 'If you spend today in bed you might be better by tomorrow morning.'

'And if you go in today,' mother threw down her trump card, 'you'll probably pass on your sore throat to one of the soloists, and then you'll be popular!'

If prayer could heal I would surely have been cured by lunchtime. I lay sweating under my sheets applying all my concentration to getting better. Mother had urged me to try and sleep, so I clenched my eyes shut and willed myself to drop off. When that failed I stared straight ahead hoping boredom would see me off. After a while the patterns on the wallpaper started to disintegrate and re-form themselves into recognisable shapes. How could I not have noticed until now the smiling face of Jesus looking down on me from above the bookcase? Or that curious snarling dog?

At lunchtime mother brought me some chicken soup and toast on a tray. She ate hers sitting on the floor beside my bed, and then when she had washed up she read me the first chapter of *Jane Eyre*, and we played rummy. Mother was always much more sympathetic to my maladies if they happened to fall on her day off. By evening time my temperature had gone up by a degree or so and I was starting to ache. My head felt as though it was filled with sand, one minute I was hot and dry as if cooking from within, the next cold and clammy. The water-bottle was alternately tossed out of bed and retrieved as this pattern repeated itself throughout the night. When morning came I was so weak, so wretched, so steam-rollered by flu that I had resigned myself to missing not only the show but Christmas itself. I was too ill to care.

While my fellow performers were being made up with five and nine and black eyeliner, I was being sponged down with lukewarm water; while they were deferring to the Lord High Executioner I was raving deliriously that there was a sea-horse in the bottom of my bed. The third day brought a slight improvement: I now had the energy to mope and grizzle and shuffle around the house in my dressing gown and slippers feeling mightily sorry for myself.

Mother continued to ply me with easily digestible food, weak drinks and hot water-bottles or cold flannels. She often came to sit with me when I was awake: we were fairly galloping through *Jane Eyre*.

One afternoon, the day of the final performance and the last day of the Christmas term, I was sitting in bed trying to cheer myself up by making paper chains to decorate the sitting room. It had dawned on me that I wouldn't be seeing Frances, or anyone from school, until the new term – until 1978! – and that I had missed the opportunity to send or receive any cards. As I licked and stuck the last link in the chain and tried to disentangle the rustling coils on my bed without crushing the paper, mother called up the stairs, 'You've got a visitor', the door opened and in walked Frances herself.

'Hello,' she said, pleased at having taken me by surprise. 'I thought I'd better drop in on the way home – not that it is on the way – and see how you are. This room's tidy. Where do you keep all your stuff?'

'What stuff?' I had a wardrobe, a desk, a bookcase and my bunk-beds. On mother's advice I was occupying the bottom layer in case I threw myself out in a fit of delirium. I shuffled the paper chains on to the floor so she could sit down.

'Oh, you know, bits and pieces.' She plonked her school bag on my feet and produced from the turmoil within it a small parcel wrapped in red tissue paper and fastened with a strip of Elastoplast. 'Happy Christmas,' she said, handing it over.

'Thank you,' I said, delighted, careful not to probe the packaging in case I guessed what it was. 'I'm sorry I haven't got you anything, but I haven't been out.' I laid the parcel gently at my side.

'Well, aren't you going to open it?' demanded Frances, disappointed.

'I can't open it before Christmas,' I said, as if this prohibition had the full force of the law behind it.

'Oh, all right. It's nothing much anyway.'

'It's really kind of you.'

'No, it was only cheap. It cost 10p.'

'Don't tell me what it is.'

'I'm not going to. They were two for 20p so I got one for Mum as well.'

'Well, don't give me any clues. I'll go and put it under the tree now.' But there was no gagging her.

'Don't put it near a radiator or anything or it'll melt.'

'Oh Frances, you've given it away now.'

'No I haven't.'

'You've said it'll melt – it's pretty obvious that it's chocolate.'

'No it's not. Actually . . .'

'Well, don't tell me.'

'. . . it's a candle.'

'Oh *Frances!*'

This exchange was interrupted by mother bringing in two cups of tea and some home-made biscuits – tooth-cracking peanut brittle and ever so slightly salty shortbread. Frances cleared the plate. 'Oh great,' she said. 'We never get anything like this at home.' Through a mouthful of crushed nut and toffee shards she brought me up to date with the progress of *The Mikado*.

'The first night was really good, although the audience was a bit dead, and so the next day everyone who hadn't been in it was wishing they had. And then last night there was a bit of a hoohah because Yum Yum forgot one of her lines and was just standing there waiting for a prompt which never came because the prompter was chatting up Ko-Ko in the wings. The audience was starting to fidget so finally Pitti Sing sort of hissed the line at her and Yum Yum said "What?" and the audience fell about. So now none of the other upper sixth girls are talking to the prompter – she's a bit of a leper anyway because she's just *lower* sixth – I don't think they care about her making Yum Yum look a berk, they're just jealous because Ko-Ko fancies her.'

'Have your parents seen it?'

'Mum and Rad came the first night. Dad was on an early

shift so he couldn't, but he might come tonight. It was really distracting with them in the audience, though. I could tell exactly where they were sitting because they came in late and the whole row had to stand up, and Mum's got this sort of loud guffaw and I kept hearing it in really odd places which aren't supposed to be funny.'

'What did they think of it?'

'Pretty good. Even Rad, and he's got very high standards.'

Mother poked her head around the door. 'Er, Abigail, can I have a word?' she said with determined casualness. Puzzled, I followed her out of the room, leaving Frances sitting on my bed wiping up the crumbs on the biscuit plate with a wet finger. Once in the corridor mother whispered, 'Is she staying for dinner? Because I'll have to put extra rice on if she is.'

'I don't think so,' I said.

'No, I can't stay for anything to eat, thanks,' came Frances' voice from the bedroom. 'I've got to get home and cook something for Rad.'

'Oh,' said mother, thoroughly abashed. 'How are you getting home, dear?' she asked at last, venturing to address Frances to her face.

'Buses I expect.'

'Oh, but it's dark outside. Abigail's father will run you home. Ste-phen!'

'Don't worry, I'll be all right.'

'Yes, she'll be all right,' I agreed. I was a little nervous at the prospect of unleashing Frances on my father whom she was quite likely to address as 'Squire'.

Mother shot me a cross look before going back downstairs to ferret him out.

'Extraordinary girl,' I overheard him say to mother on his return from this errand some half an hour later. 'I rather like her. Never stopped talking. She kept saying, "Just drop me at the end of the road", but I insisted on driving up to the door and when I said I'd wait to make sure there was someone in, she said, "Oh, there won't be anyone *in*", and then offered to make me a fried egg sandwich.'

'Good heavens. Do you think she's got a bit of gypsy in her?'

I buried my laughter in the pillow.

As we had said our goodbyes Frances had asked what I was doing for Christmas. 'Nothing much,' I said. 'There'll just be the three of us on Christmas Day, and maybe my granny.' I failed to suppress a little groan. 'And then on Boxing Day we usually go next door for drinks and peanuts. They haven't got any children, but they've got some tropical fish so it's not too bad. What about you?'

'Oh God, millions of people descending. It's our turn this year, although I'm sure I remember doing all the sprouts last Christmas. We'll probably go out for a meal on Christmas Eve up in Highbury with Uncle Bill and Auntie Daphne. That's Mum's brother. Then there'll be about eighteen of us for Christmas dinner. Last year on Boxing Day we took a picnic over to Hampstead Heath, but I suppose it'll be Bromley Common this year.'

My eyes were beginning to smart with envy. 'Your Christmas sounds so much more exciting than mine.' She didn't make any attempt to deny this. I tried another tack. 'I wonder if your family look anything like I imagine them,' I hinted.

'Oh, you'll have to meet them,' she finally conceded. 'I would invite you over, only, only, I don't want to introduce you to my family because they'll try and take you over – they always do.'

'What do you mean?' I said.

'I can't explain. They'll start acting as if you're their friend as much as mine. As if they discovered you.'

I had never before considered myself an object of discovery, and I lay awake that night in a state of pleasant agitation, trying to envisage that moment in the foreseeable future when I would, in some mysterious and magical way, be *taken over*.

On Christmas Eve, the first day I was well enough to go out, father and I paid a visit to the newsagent's where all those years ago I had caught him buying that Easter egg. I was looking for a present for Frances; her red package, which, now that she had let it slip, felt and smelled overpoweringly candle-like, was sitting on top of a modest pile of presents under our artificial tree.

The shop windows were spattered with spray-on snow and a line of loopy writing which proclaimed A HAPPY XMAS TO ALL OUR CUSTOMER'S.

'Customer's what?' said father. Coloured fringes of metal foil and fairy lights flashed along the edges of the shelves. Behind the counter an assistant was stickering packs of Christmas cards and Advent calendars with half-price labels. A thick bunch of mistletoe was hanging over the door and the newsagent was frisking around pretending to kiss any girls that came through. The doorstep was covered with trodden berries. Giftware was somewhat scanty, and after dithering over an address book – the sort of thing I was often given, though I had no addresses to put inside, except my own which I was unlikely to need to look up – I settled on a keyring in the shape of a fried egg. This seemed appropriate. Frances at least had her own door key. Father bought a large jar of peanuts and some chocolates 'for the tree'.

After tea we left mother in the kitchen peeling chestnuts for the stuffing, and drove round to Frances' house to drop the present off. She lived a good fifteen minutes away in a slightly less salubrious part of the borough, although Balmoral Road, the busy main road on which she lived, looked smart enough, with rows of three-storey Victorian semis.

Although a light was on in the front room and there was a car in the driveway – a dirty yellow Triumph Spitfire with a torn black hood – the doorbell's metallic rattle was answered only by distant barking, followed by the clatter of paws on floor tiles and much louder barking. When I pushed open the letter box, which was at knee height, a white muzzle with a black nose and two rows of sharp teeth rammed itself into the slot. Growth. I withdrew my hand swiftly. Peering into the living room I could see a real Christmas tree festooned with lights and thick, snaky tinsel. High though the ceiling was, it could not quite accommodate the tree, whose topmost branch was bent over, pinioning a plastic fairy to the plaster moulding. On the floor beneath was a landslide of brightly wrapped presents reaching half-way across the room. The mantelpiece and window sills were crowded with cards. In the centre of the floor was a coffee table on which were at least a dozen used mugs, a large bowl of nuts and an even larger heap of nutshells. The gas fire was roaring away as bright as neon. I could almost feel the heat coming through the window: I didn't fancy the chances of that other candle.

Growth wandered in from the hall and picked his way through a litter of fallen nutshells to the hearthrug where, impossibly close to the fire, he flopped down. A gentle hooting from the road reminded me that father was waiting on a yellow line. I pushed the keyring in its green and gold wrapping through the letter box which sprang shut like a trap, bringing Growth scampering back to the door. And to the sound of growling and ripping paper I returned to the car and our own quiet Christmas.

The invitation did not come until the following spring. Frances had by that time been over to my house on several occasions and had thoroughly charmed my father, who pronounced her 'spirited'.

'She's a very confident young lady,' was mother's verdict, delivered in a tone of voice to leave me in no doubt that confidence was not necessarily something to aspire to.

Frances made her offer at the end of the last lesson on a Friday afternoon as we were sorting out our books for the weekend's homework.

'Are you doing anything tomorrow?'

'No,' I said, hope fluttering.

'Do you want to come over, then? We could go to the woods with Growth, or just hang around at home.'

'Will your family be there?'

'Probably, worse luck. Still, you'll have to meet them sooner or later. Don't take any notice of my dad. He'll try and be funny all the time – don't laugh at his jokes. Rad is bound to be out, but he wouldn't bother us anyway. Auntie Mim's deaf so you won't be able to talk to her; she stays up in her room mostly. Mum's the only one who matters really – and she's completely normal, so that's okay.'

So it was that on Saturday afternoon father drove me for only the second time to the house in Balmoral Road. He had instructed me to telephone him when I was ready to be picked up and had given me 10p to leave in payment for the call.

'Don't wait,' I said ungraciously as I slammed the car door, and then I stood on the doorstep making shooing gestures until he finally took the hint and the car crawled off at a snail's pace until the front door opened to admit me.

'Hello, come in, GET DOWN GROWTH.' Frances turned on the brown and white Jack Russell who was yapping and dancing around her ankles and springing up at me, his teeth bared. I kept my hands in my pockets. On his left side was a lump the size of a golf ball. 'He's in a vile temper today. I think he's getting a cauliflower ear.'

The passageway in which we were standing was long and narrow with a black and white tiled floor and an uncarpeted staircase leading up to a landing and more stairs above. The walls had been stripped to reveal patches of flaky paint and plaster and stubborn little flecks of wallpaper like cornflakes.

'Are you in the middle of decorating?' I asked.

Frances, silencing Growth with a dog biscuit, looked puzzled. 'No. Why?'

'Oh nothing,' I said, blushing, as she ushered me into the front room with the words 'This is my mum.'

My blush hadn't even had time to recede when it flared right up again. Frances' mother was in the middle of the room, ironing, surrounded by piles of neatly folded laundry. Shirts and blouses were draped over chair-backs and on hangers hooked over the mantelpiece. The windows and mirrors were fogged with steam. A pile of socks tucked into themselves in little balls lay like horse droppings on the carpet. Apart from the tiniest pair of lacy black knickers, the 'completely normal' Mrs Radley was naked. This was my first real encounter with bare breasts and I flinched as if from the glare of headlamps.

'Oh Mum, you *could* have put some clothes on,' Frances remonstrated. 'I told you Abigail was coming any minute.'

'Nonsense – we're all girls. Abigail doesn't mind, do you?'

'No,' I squeaked, my eyes watering with the effort of not staring.

'There you are. I'm very pleased to meet you, Abigail. Please call me Lexi.' She leaned across the ironing board and shook my hand, her breasts trembling at the movement. I had never realised they could be so mobile. Hugging my mother, who was in any case flat-chested, with her formidable armour of elastic and mesh girdles and nylon lace petticoats, was rather like clashing with a trussed fowl.

'Come on,' said Frances impatiently, 'let's go upstairs.'

'Take this lot with you,' Lexi ordered, pointing to the piles of laundry. Frances looked at me and raised her eyes to heaven. As if in reply there came a loud crash from above our heads followed by swearing and the sound of heavy furniture scraping against wood.

'LIFT, DON'T DRAG!' Lexi bellowed at the ceiling as we swung swags of shirts over our shoulders and gathered up folded sheets and towels, still warm and smelling of the garden.

On the first landing two single beds were standing upended against the banisters, wedged firmly in place by a double bed which was on its side half in and half out of a doorway. A man's head and shoulders appeared over the edge of the headboard. I was relieved to see that he was clothed. 'Keep out of the way, you girls. On second thoughts, Frances, why don't you two take hold of this end and try and lift it past that leg.'

'What's going on?' Frances demanded. 'What are you doing with my bed?'

'We're swapping your single ones for our double, what does it look like?'

'Why?'

'Because your mother keeps complaining that I wake her up when I come in from work.'

'So I get the double all to myself?' asked Frances suspiciously.

'Yes. If we can get it out of this doorway.'

'Where's Rad?'

'Up in his room, working.'

'You've knocked a bit of the paint off here,' came another man's voice from the far side of the bed.

'Oh, hello Uncle Bill,' said Frances to the voice, relieving me of the ironing and dumping the lot, not very neatly, on the bathroom floor.

73

After some more grunting and straining from the bedroom the double bed jerked back a couple of feet, taking with it a sizeable strip of wood from the doorframe. Frances squeezed through the gap and trotted up the next flight of stairs with me in pursuit. 'That was my dad,' she said.

'Don't bother to introduce us,' he called out after us. 'I'm just the odd-job man.'

The second landing was lit by a skylight and was even smaller than the first. On the three sides not occupied by the stairs were closed doors. 'That's Auntie Mim's room.' Frances pointed at one, then gave a sharp rap at the second and flung it open without waiting for a reply. 'And this,' she said, as if showing off some interesting new acquisition at a zoo, 'is Rad.'

A boy of about fourteen was sitting at a desk with his back to us. He turned round, scowling at Frances before turning back to his work. He had thick, dark hair which fell, unruly and unbrushed, into his eyes, which were so dark it was hard to tell where the iris ended and the pupil began.

'Handsome, isn't he?' said Frances with some pride.

He certainly was, though as an only child at an all-girls' school I was no connoisseur of male beauty. I gave a nervous laugh which could have meant yes or no and concentrated on holding down another blush. Apart from bookshelves, the walls of his room were bare, in some places down to the brickwork. On the desk in a cone of light from an angle-poise lamp were a pile of books with intriguing titles: *Catcher in the Rye*, *Lord of the Flies*, *Memoirs of an Infantry Officer*, *The Myth of Sisyphus*.

'Rad's an atheist,' she whispered, confidentially, as we made our way downstairs. 'We all are actually, except for Mum. She doesn't believe in anything, but she's very spiritual. Does your mum believe in God?'

I thought for a moment. She believed in going to church: more than that I couldn't say.

To avoid being drafted into any more laundry work or furniture removals we took Growth for a walk in the woods. He went berserk at the sight of the lead, whirling around in tight circles at our feet and then slinging himself skywards, eyes rolling. Frances was trying to teach him to jump up and retrieve a Bonio from between her teeth, a trick which nearly cost her her nose, and left the lower half of her face dripping with slobber.

'Yuk, nearly there,' she said, wiping her mouth on her sleeve, as Growth tossed back his third biscuit, crunching and gagging at the same time.

He dragged us all the way to the entrance to the woods, a roll of fat bulging over his choke chain as he strained against the lead. No sooner was it unclipped than he shot off into the bushes and was out of sight in seconds.

'*The woods are lovely, dark and deep,*' Frances intoned, kicking through the bluebells. We had just read the poem in English comprehension. *Imagine you are the poet. Write a story to explain how you came to be in the woods, and where you are going.* In mine the poet was a lowly woodcutter returning to his family on Christmas Eve with a bundle of twigs for the fire. Frances' version had a wandering minstrel, the only survivor of a happy band of actors who had been savaged by wolves; there were several subplots, and the story was accompanied by a family tree.

It took hours to locate Growth. He had cantered right out of the woods to the playing fields beyond and disgraced himself by interrupting a football game, capering after the ball and finally lifting his leg against a pile of coats behind the goalpost. Frances retrieved him by whistling urgently from the edge of the pitch.

'Oy, I hope you're going to pay to get this coat cleaned,' called one of the players furiously. 'That's suede that is.'

Frances clipped the dog's lead back on and, having judged that the man was too far away to give chase, took off for the woods at a sprint with Growth flying along at her heels and me, terrified, puffing along behind. We didn't stop until we reached the front door, gasping with laughter and the stitch, while the culprit began his tail-chasing and leaping routine at our feet. The exercise, far from tiring him out, seemed to have stirred him into a greater frenzy. Frances unleashed him in the hall and he skittered into the living room and wedged himself under the gas fire which was fortunately unlit. Mrs Radley, by this time decently clad in a floor-length housecoat, was lying on the couch watching a black and white film. Frances had told me once that she used to be a child actress and I could well believe it.

'Fish popped in a moment ago and said he'd have the hose on later if you girls want to go round and be squirted,' she called after us, as if this was the most normal suggestion in the world.

Frances screwed her face up in disgust. 'No way.' Apparently frisking around next door's garden under the sprinkler on sunny days was something she had used to enjoy at the age of four or so – a tradition Fish had heard about and was eager to uphold in spite of the passing years. Lexi could see no harm in it, but for Mr Radley it was another mark against the man.

Upstairs the furniture removals had concluded successfully with only a few dents and scars to the doorframes and wallpaper. The double bed had been dropped like a raft in the middle of Frances' room in a sea of clutter – books, singles, games, jigsaws, odd shoes, clothes, paper, pens. Her dressing table was similarly crowded with trinkets and china and letter racks bristling with more paper, and every drawer was open an inch or so more than the one above, like a flight of steps.

Frances gathered up an armful of junk and, without sorting it, opened her wardrobe and stuffed it on to a pile of still more junk, which was beginning to teeter as she slammed the door and locked it. From inside came the pitter patter of rubble sliding down and coming to rest against the door.

'There, that's tidied,' said Frances, flinging herself down on the bed and extending her arms and legs, starfish style, to test its dimensions. 'Oh this is great.'

Privately I was shocked at her calm acceptance of the household's new sleeping arrangements. It seemed obvious to me that her parents' move into single beds was just the prelude to divorce. Even my parents who, heaven knew, were cool enough towards each other most of the time, still shared a double bed.

From a white chipboard unit beside her Frances produced her journal and offered to read me some extracts.

Dear Beatrice [I had already learned to my relief that Beatrice was not in fact a cousin or special friend but a device, borrowed from Anne Frank, to make the entries seem more personal.]

There was a good-looking boy in Saint Michael's uniform at the bus stop today so I decided to follow him home. I got on his bus, a 194 which I've never been on before, and pretty soon I was completely lost. He didn't get off for ages and I was beginning to think it was another stupid idea of mine when he rang the bell. I had plenty of time to study the back of his neck on the bus, which was a bit sort of greasy, his neck not the bus, so I'm not quite as keen as I thought I was. Anyway I followed him at a distance and now know where he lives, though I don't know what I'm going to do about it. Nothing, probably. I was really late home – luckily everyone else was still out. Fish was up a ladder next door putting criss-cross strips on their windows. He saw me and said 'You're late, been in detention, heh heh?' and started to come down so I shot indoors. Growth went mad when he saw me and started throwing himself up against the back door so I had to take him out for a run. I didn't want to pass Fish again so we went out the back and over the fence. I was starving when I got back and the fridge was bare so I ate a whole carton of glacé cherries out of the larder. Quite nice, though they must have been years old – I don't think anyone here has made a cake or anything like that in my lifetime. Tried a Bonio but it was disgusting.

I could see Frances was getting into the swing of this. She would roll around the bed, laughing and wheezing at her own exploits. Her laugh was so theatrical, so preposterous, that I couldn't help joining in and soon we were half-way to hysterics. Encouraged by this gratifying response, Frances rattled through a few more entries, occasionally straying into dangerous terrain and having to improvise on the hoof.

March 16th

Dear Beatrice

Mum made me wear her new walking boots to school today as she is going off on a 'ramble' with Lawrence this weekend and wants them broken in. They are pretty uncomfortable. Dr Peel caught me clumping down the corridor in them and said I'd be sent home to change if I wore them again. Honestly! It doesn't say anything about not wearing walking boots in the school rules. It says 'sensible brown shoes' which they are. Abigail was wearing her hair in a bun today. It didn't really . . . er, blah blah blah . . . Got our reports today. For Maths Mrs Taylor put 'Frances has consolidated her position at the bottom of the class.' Ha ha. Dad will love that. Abigail's was brilliant as usual . . . er, blah blah blah. Limped half the way home then took the boots off and walked the rest of the way in my socks — or rather Rad's socks, as they turned out to be on closer inspection.

Dinner was late. Frances and I were dragooned into preparing vegetables: mountains of sprouts, carrots and so many potatoes that they filled a roasting tin all of their own and my peeling hand developed a wet blister. Frances' method of preparing carrots consisted of removing the woody ends and then hewing them into unmanageable chunks like jumbo-sized batteries and tossing them unwashed into a saucepan. There appeared to be enough food for twenty. The chicken itself was the size of our Christmas turkey. I was like Gulliver in Brobdingnag. It was all so different from home, where everything was small and dainty and nicely presented and then cut into tiny pieces and chewed twenty-eight times.

By eight thirty, when red juice was still leaking out of the chicken cavity into the surrounding lake of hot oil, and the potatoes were still waxy white and hard as new soap bars I began to worry that my parents would be wondering where

I was. I crept into the front room where Lexi was curled up, still in her housecoat, reading *Vogue*.

'May I use your telephone, please? I've got to ring my father and tell him what time to pick me up.'

'Pick you up? I thought you were staying the night. Why don't you tell him you're staying, then he won't have to come out. Hmm? I used to spend every weekend with my girlfriend, Ruthie, when I was young.'

'Oh no . . . I . . . they're expecting me back.' My first thought was that my parents might not be able to do without me, but presently plenty of other admissible excuses came to mind. 'I haven't got my nightie.'

'Frances will lend you something.' There was something indefatigable about Lexi that made opposition pointless.

'Well, thank you. I'll just ring and ask permission.'

'Stay the night?' mother echoed. 'Whatever for?'

'For fun.'

There was a silence while she turned this idea over. 'I don't see why not, I suppose.' Her one condition was that I let father drive over with my night-clothes and toothbrush, which rather defeated Lexi's object of saving him the journey. 'And don't forget to strip the bed in the morning. It's very important,' were her final words.

11

Father arrived just as we were dishing up dinner. Lexi, who had changed into a black velvet dress, slightly crumpled and faded around the seat, beat me to the front door. Frances was restraining Growth in the kitchen.

'Hello, I'm Frances' mother, Lexi,' she said holding out her hand.

'Stephen Onions,' said father faintly.

'You needn't have come all this way – we could have lent Abigail some night-clothes.'

Seeing father standing there on the doorstep in his jacket and tie, overnight bag in hand, suddenly made me feel homesick. 'Won't you come in for some dinner?' Lexi was saying. 'Or a drink?'

'Oh no, I can't stop, thanks very much. Here you are,' he said, passing me the bag. 'I hope you're behaving,' and he gave a nervous laugh.

'Oh, she's been delightful,' said Lexi, crushing me to her side. 'She's cooked the dinner in fact.'

'Ah-ha,' said father, not sure if this was a joke. 'Well, thank you for having her . . .' And he withdrew into the night.

At the dinner table Mr Radley had appeared to carve the chicken while Frances shovelled vegetables on to plates. This was my first proper sighting of him. He was smaller than I had imagined – a couple of inches shorter than his wife – with thinning brown hair, beginning to go grey from the front, and very blue eyes with a little oyster of slime in each corner. He was wearing a polo-necked sweater – something my father would have considered insufferably dandyish – tucked into trousers which were belted below a modest paunch. An elderly woman in a woolly shawl – Auntie Mim, I guessed – was sitting with her back to the coal fire which was burning even though it was a warm evening. She was pouring water into six crystal wine glasses with a shaking hand. Only Rad's chair remained empty. Growth was circling like a shark around a wreck.

'What a wonderful smell from that bird,' Auntie Mim said. 'No, I won't have any, thank you.' Frances had forewarned me that Auntie Mim had existed on nothing but sprouts, potatoes and weak tea for as long as anybody could remember. As if this was not odd enough, nobody was allowed to refer to this peculiar habit, but continued to offer her chicken and carrots and gravy which she would, after some consideration, politely decline as if on a whim of the moment.

'Any stuffing for you, Auntie?' said Lexi.

'Er, do you know, I don't think I will, thank you.'

After a few minutes I began to envy her restraint: helpings were enormous. Mr Radley had given me a whole leg – hip, thigh, calf, ankle and all – which I had no idea how to tackle. I only ever had the white meat at home. I don't know where my mother bought our chickens, but they must have been reared without bones. Just as the last plate was set down, steaming, at Rad's empty place there came the sound of footsteps clumping down two flights of stairs and the latecomer walked in, a book under one arm. He slid into his seat without a word and immediately propped the book open against the sprout dish. Albert Camus *The Plague*, it said on the spine.

'For every cup and every plateful Father make us truly grateful,' said Mr Radley suddenly, in a booming voice, making us all jump. It was only when everyone else had started tutting and telling him not to be stupid that I realised he was joking. This I found rather shocking, as mother said grace in all seriousness in our house, usually at some length and invoking the starving of other lands to blackmail me into clearing my plate. He gave me a wink which made me blush, and every time I caught his eye afterwards he would do it again, enjoying my embarrassment.

'Rad, I thought we'd agreed you could read at breakfast but not at dinner,' said his mother reasonably.

'Hmmph,' he grunted without looking up from the page.

'It's not as if we eat together all that often,' she went on.

'Oh, cranberries,' Auntie Mim was saying, picking up the sauce dish. 'Wonderful piquant flavour.'

'Precisely,' said Rad.

'No, not for me, thank you dear.'

'Why should I have to fit in with an arrangement that's not even regular?'

Everyone but me was making great headway with their dinner. Frances had nearly cleared her plate, while I was still wrestling with bone and sinew. Every time I tried to dig my knife and fork into the chicken leg it would swivel round on the plate and kick sprouts and carrots on to the table. I spent as much time fielding as eating. The heat in the room was tremendous, with the coal fire, the steam from the plates and Growth lying panting across my feet. I could feel his little golf ball pressing against my ankle, and didn't dare move. The windows ran with condensation. The others, apart from Auntie Mim, were on to second helpings before I could even see the pattern on my plate. My wine glass seemed to have developed a slow puncture – every time I put it to my lips water would drip down the stem and into my lap.

Mr Radley took pity on me. 'You're not going to eat that, are you?' he said, pointing at the chicken leg, which looked even bigger now, since its mauling.

'No,' I admitted meekly.

'Good. I was hoping you'd say that.' He leant across and speared it with his fork and removed it to his own plate, leaving a trail of gravy droplets between us.

'You're all dressed up,' he said to his wife, noticing for the first time. 'Are you going anywhere?'

'Just to the golf club with Clarissa for a drink,' said Mrs Radley. Clarissa was her younger, unmarried sister who enjoyed a wild bachelor-girl existence in Sevenoaks. 'In fact,' she looked at her watch, 'she's picking me up at nine thirty.'

Suddenly it was all over. 'God, is that the time?' said Mr Radley, knocking his chair over as he leapt up. He departed for work still clutching the chicken leg. Rad took this as his cue to vanish back upstairs, and Mrs Radley was borne off to the golf club in a cloud of peppery scent leaving Frances and me to clear up. Auntie Mim was still at the table finishing her sprouts. It was good to see that there was someone slower than me.

Later in Frances' room we undressed shyly with our backs to each other. Mum had packed my least favourite nightie – a green nylon one which made me itch the moment I put it on. In the dressing-table mirror I could see Frances wriggling out of her bra. She was the only girl in the class who wore one, a fact advertised by her evident discomfort and perpetual fiddling with the straps. She peeled back the brushed nylon sheets with a ripping sound of static and a crackle of blue sparks. In my fleecy nightie I was going to stick to them like Velcro. Having spent some time brushing her teeth, Frances produced a tin of treacle toffee from the bedside cabinet, and we sat up in bed, jaws locked, trying to chew and giggling and dribbling all at the same time.

'What do you think of Rad?' Frances asked through a brace of toffee.

'All right,' I replied, blushing through the lie. After all, she had been building him up for months until I was determined that if he wasn't truly hideous I was going to fall headlong in love with him.

'*All right?*' she echoed, indignantly. 'Well, you haven't seen him at his best yet.'

Frances wrote up her journal for the day while I politely averted my eyes, and then she switched off the light, leaving the room semi-lit by the streetlamp outside and the sweep of car headlights. The traffic noise was deafening after The Close. The mattress was as slack as a hammock and we kept sinking into the middle and clashing elbows, so I lay as near as possible to the edge of the bed, clinging on with fingers and toes like a sloth to stop myself rolling back into the trench. Within minutes Frances was asleep and breathing evenly, while I counted the cars as they whooshed by outside until twelve, when I heard Mrs Radley come in and retire, singing lightly, to her single bed. I dozed off not long after and dreamed I was hanging on to the edge of a cliff. Much later I was woken by the sound of Mr Radley returning from work. There was the grating of a key in the lock, the click of the door shutting and then a crash as he tripped over something in the hallway followed by swearing.

In the morning while Frances was in the bathroom I dressed quickly and, remembering mother's instructions, set about stripping the bed. I had everything piled neatly on the bare mattress and was just peeling off the last pillowcase when Frances came back in.

'What are you doing?' she said, thunderstruck. 'Mum,' she appealed to Mrs Radley who was just whisking across the landing in a bathrobe and turban, 'she's just taken all the sheets off my bed.'

Mrs Radley took in my red face and the bare mattress and said, 'Well, that's because it's the polite thing to do.'

'I've never heard of it before.'

'Nevertheless . . .'

'I'm going to have to put them all back again now,' said Frances, aggrieved.

'No you're not. You're going to take them up to the launderette. I've got some blankets that can go in the big machine while you're up there.'

'Well done, Abigail,' said Frances scowling, and looking exactly like her brother.

'How was I to know you'd be sharing?' said mother, as I related the bed-stripping incident in some dudgeon on my return. She was in the kitchen making Yorkshire pudding batter, whisking it ferociously to get rid of the lumps. Father was off somewhere. 'Whoever heard of a girl that age having a double bed?' And she wrinkled her nose as though, even at this distance, she could smell dirty linen.

12

This was the beginning of my absorption into the Radley family. It was taken for granted that I would spend my weekends there: this was what Lexi used to do with her girlfriend, Ruthie, as she was fond of telling us.

'Whatever happened to Ruthie?' Frances asked her mother after their exemplary friendship had been invoked half a dozen times in one evening.

'I don't know,' came the unromantic reply. 'We drifted apart as soon as we left school. As you do.'

Frances and I exchanged a look. Things must have been different in those days: there was no way we were going to 'drift'.

The only people who weren't thrilled by the new arrangement were my parents. In their civilised way they did not get on especially well and needed me there as a distraction. In the absence of fights and arguments, it was hard to see exactly what was the cause of their disenchantment – I wasn't sure whether the chill had always existed and was only now apparent to my maturer self, or whether it was something recent. One bone of contention was the amount of time my father spent on his Project, a perpetually expanding work that gave him ample scope for disappearance on research-related errands or long sojourns in his study. Although my mother was no doubt happy to have him 'out from under her feet', an expression which put me in mind of a ruckled carpet, the intangibility of all his labour infuriated her: it was not like making quince jelly, which could be eaten or given to the church fête, or ironing, which simply had to be done. It rankled that what was so obviously a hobby should have acquired the status of *work*.

It was during this time that my mother's mania for cleanliness reached its height. At least that's how it seemed:

perhaps it was just the coincidence of my exposure to the Radley household where a less rigorous regime prevailed. Visitors to our house used to flatter mother by saying they could have eaten their dinner off the kitchen floor: at the Radleys' it generally looked as though someone just had.

Mother's latest acquisition in her war against dirt was a carpet cleaner, picked up at a church bazaar. It was a pale yellow plastic gadget, like a small upright hoover, which had to be filled with special shampoo and dragged back and forth across the floor, leaving trails of foam like spittle in its path. She became quite infatuated with this machine, and for a while there was always at least one carpet in the house that smelled of chemical soap and felt damp and mossy underfoot. Housework became a sort of retreat for her: where a more histrionic person, and one less prone to migraine, might have pounded out her frustration on a piano, mother resorted to the mop and duster. One morning I looked out of my bedroom window and saw her trying to sweep the front path during a high wind. There she was, teeth clenched, wielding her broom while dust and grit and fallen blossom whirled around her.

Another occasion provoked my parents' cordial version of a row. It was a sunny Sunday in May and I had returned from Frances' early to do our homework. It was safer to do both than to let Frances copy since she would either reproduce mine in every detail and get us both into trouble, or deliberately introduce such ridiculous errors in an attempt to personalise her version that it rather defeated the object of my efforts. I had just knocked off the life-cycle of the liverwort and had come downstairs for a tea-break. In the sitting room mother was ironing the newly washed net curtains and father was standing at the bare windows looking up the road.

'The room looks rather nice without net curtains,' he remarked, absently. 'You can see out.'

'And people can see in,' said mother, ironing with slightly more vigour.

'People don't often come down this road,' father pointed out. 'It's not as if we've got anyone opposite, come to that.'

As the house at the end of the lollipop, we faced the green and the length of the road.

'It would be like living in a goldfish bowl,' said mother, laying the first curtain at full length on the couch and setting to work on the next. 'Anyone passing would be able to see every speck on the wall.' As if there were any specks!

'It would be different on a main road,' father conceded.

'The Radleys live on a main road and they don't have net curtains,' I put in.

'Well, net curtains take a lot of looking after,' said mother pointedly. She seemed to have some idea, obviously picked up from an unguarded remark of mine, that the Radleys lived in squalor – an unfair impression: Frances and I often did the housework.

'They make you feel shut in somehow,' said father, as mother started threading the curtains back on to their vulcanised rail.

'Well, I've just spent the day cleaning them,' said mother, in a voice that was both mild and utterly inflexible, 'so back they go.' And climbing from the couch to the window sill with the yards of net fanning out behind her she hooked them back into position like an army raising its banner.

The one-sidedness of my arrangement with Frances offended my mother's sense of propriety. 'Why don't you ever bring her here?' she asked one Saturday as I was stuffing some clothes into an overnight bag. 'They can't keep feeding you every week.' I didn't tell her that more often than not we fed ourselves – and them, for that matter. Nor could I explain the real reason why we always went to Frances' place. It was simply more fun there. Nothing *happened* at our house, whereas at the Radleys' there was always something going on; someone arriving or departing with fresh adventures or disasters to relate.

Growth and Auntie Mim were the only members of the household who were guaranteed to be present. We would sometimes find the latter in the kitchen tending a foaming green pan of sprouts. She cooked them with so much bicarbonate of soda, Lexi said, that nutritionally they had no value whatever and it was a miracle that Auntie hadn't got scurvy by now. Rad was often out on Saturdays, playing rugby, or swimming, or competing in chess tournaments. He didn't appear to have a girlfriend, or any interest in acquiring one, a source of great mirth to Frances, who loved to tease him. 'There's only one girl at Rad's school,' she would say. 'And she only comes over for woodwork lessons. What's she like, Rad?'

'Fat, ugly and stupid,' Rad would reply, sending Frances into peals of delighted laughter.

When at home Rad tended to stay in his room. The sound of rustling from the larder might alert us that he was on the prowl and on the pretext of going to the loo I would try to engineer a meeting on the stairs so that I might be the recipient of a terse 'Hello', which would form the substance of tormented dreams for nights to come. He never showed the slightest interest in me, of course. I didn't dare tell Frances of my infatuation as she would certainly have told Rad, probably in my presence, a humiliation for which suicide would have been the only remedy.

Mr Radley, because of his odd hours of work, was usually asleep for part of the day and silence in the vicinity of his bedroom had to be observed. I had by now learnt from Frances that he had once had a proper career in the Civil Service but for some years now had survived on a series of odd jobs of brief duration, the latest of which was lobby attendant at a London hotel. When he was up and about he frequently came into Frances' room to ask her some trifling question, such as the whereabouts of a particular item of food that had vanished from the fridge, and ended up staying for hours telling us about work or cross-examining us about school. He loved us to ask him questions and would never be short of an opinion, but somehow I didn't have great confidence in his pronouncements. When my father explained something you had the sense of drinking from the top of a deep well, whereas with Mr Radley you couldn't help feeling that what you got was all there was – and some more – and if you persisted any further he'd be left thoroughly parched. I couldn't work him out: he seemed to like the company of young people, and yet according to him they were responsible for all the ills of the world. 'Youth is wasted on the young' he was fond of saying, especially when he caught us idling in front of the television, or complaining we were bored. It was he who invented a nickname for me – Blush – which caught on as only the cruellest or most pertinent can.

Lexi might spend the day enthroned in the living room entertaining a succession of callers. Clarissa or other golfing friends might turn up, followed by Lawrence, a good-looking man who was introduced as Lexi's boyfriend. Everyone not a blood relation was hailed by Lexi as a 'boyfriend' or 'girlfriend', so this was no cause for suspicion. Lawrence also seemed to be on the best of terms with Mr Radley, a further reassurance. On non-visiting days a brief but frenzied onslaught would be made on the housework. Lexi would tear through the house like a tornado, picking up discarded belongings and hurling them back into the owner's bedroom, while Frances followed behind with the hoover, which made a terrific din on the uncarpeted floors. Wooden furniture would get a quick smear with a waxy duster, and anything above eye-level would be left to fester. In the evening Lexi would dress up, curl her hair in heated rollers and float out to dinner on a cloud of musky perfume. Occasionally she would play host herself and Frances and I would be paid to act as waitresses, serving food and drinks and washing up. Mr Radley, because of his anti-social working hours, was rarely of the party.

After I had been to the house a few times I ventured to enquire about the mysterious third door on the top landing.

'It's Dad's studio. He goes up there to do painting and stuff now and then.'

'What – oil painting?'

'Yes, you know, portraits and stuff.'

'You mean he's an Artist,' I said, impressed. I must have known he was something more than an overgrown bell-boy. 'Why didn't you tell me before?'

'Well, he's not really an *artist*,' she said. 'It's just a hobby. Some of his stuff's a bit weird. Do you want a look?'

The door shuddered open on contact with Frances' shoulder to release a dry smell of wood and turpentine. The floor was uncarpeted and marked with blobs of dried paint. Along one side of the room was a wooden bench cluttered with jars of brushes and palette knives, charcoal sticks, buckled tubes of paint and rosettes of crumpled rags. In the light of the window stood an easel and a blank canvas, and in the middle of the room was a low armchair covered with a grubby white sheet. Against one wall some canvases were leaning face down. Frances started to look through them. I peered over her shoulder. They were all rather blotchy nudes: one was obviously meant to be Lexi, but the others were different people, men and women, some *old* people, in outlandish colours.

'A bit blobby, aren't they,' said Frances, critically. 'He must get through loads of paint.'

'Does he just make them up, or what?' I couldn't imagine a troupe of naked people processing through the attic room just to be rendered in tones of orange and green.

'No, you twit, he goes to life-drawing classes. All these people like Dad sit around and they take it in turns to take their clothes off.'

'No!'

'I think that's what happens. Where else would you get the people from?'

'How embarrassing! Why can't they just draw people with clothes on?' I said. 'It's not as if he uses flesh-coloured paint anyway.'

'Artists always paint people in the nude. Perhaps it's more difficult, or easier or something,' said Frances. 'Anyway,' she added in warning tones, 'if he ever offers to paint you, you'll know what to say.'

'Did your dad go to Art College, then?' I asked, as we

made our way downstairs.

'No,' said Mr Radley, emerging from behind his bedroom door, making me jump. 'I wasn't clever enough to go to College,' he said in a mock-apologetic voice that left me in no doubt that on the contrary he considered himself far too clever.

13

Living from Saturday to Saturday as I did seemed to make time travel faster, and the summer term was over, the exams sat and passed almost before I'd noticed it had begun. The rounders season had come and gone, and our despised summer uniforms – straw boaters and turquoise dresses which showed dark sweat patches under the arms – could be consigned to the back of the wardrobe. The long holiday approached, bearing down on me like an express train. I anticipated its arrival with something close to dread. By an unhappy accident the Radleys had planned their holiday for the first three weeks, while my parents were taking me away for the second three. We overlapped by a day so there was no possibility of my seeing Frances all summer. Six weeks – it didn't seem possible. Frances' composure in the face of this catastrophe was an added provocation. It was prompted no doubt by the prospect of an exciting trip abroad: Lexi was taking her to Menton via Paris, while father and son went somewhere called 'The Trenches', an annual pilgrimage, apparently.

'Poor Rad,' tittered Frances. 'Three weeks of Dad's driving. He'll be a nervous wreck – if he's not killed.' Mr Radley's reputation as a bad driver was part of family lore. He would always set off without doing up his seat-belt, and then once on a busy main road would think the better of it and fumble about looking for it down the side of the seat and tugging it across himself while the car veered from side to side. And he seemed to have an aversion to windscreen wipers – refusing to deploy them until the screen was a blur. His most dangerous habit, though, was his inability to hold a conversation with his passengers without continually swivelling round to address them face to face.

'Why do you go on separate holidays?' I asked, slightly

shocked by the arrangements.

'We always do – we just like different things. Mum doesn't want to go traipsing round The Trenches year after year.'

'What's The Trenches?'

'Something to do with some war. Lots of graves and stuff – really gloomy. Dad loves all that. So does Rad, actually. It's the only thing they agree on.' At the end of the three weeks, I gathered, the family, plus any extras collected on the way, would meet up for a night in a hotel in northern France to exchange stories before returning home together.

My chances of an exciting holiday did not look so rosy. Mother and father tended to stick to the British Isles – usually its wettest and most windblown reaches – favouring walking holidays to places of literary or historical significance. Blasted moorland or chilly cathedrals were their holy places. This year there was an added significance to the choice of destination. For Christmas mother had bought herself a stone polisher she had seen advertised in a craft catalogue. She had sent off for it, at some expense and in great excitement, with plans to decorate the house with jars of sparkling stones in which one would be able to trail one's hands in times of anxiety. The venture was not an immediate success: the machine, a small drum containing iron filings, had to be left running for weeks on end; mother stowed it in the spare room under a table to muffle the noise, but it could be heard grinding away day and night, persistent as toothache. It was mother's ignorance of geology, however, that proved her undoing. Most of the stones she had collected were soft rocks like limestone, and when at the appointed time she opened the drum, instead of uncovering a sparkling horde of treasure, she was faced with a mass of grey slurry. Even those few surviving pebbles, glossy and jewel-bright when wet, looked much as before when dry, only smaller. This summer, then, we were off to the Isle of Skye in search of igneous rock.

The night before Frances' departure I went over to say goodbye. A quarrel was in progress over which party was to take which car. Finally it was decided that the women would have the Spitfire while the men took the Estate.

93

'You'll hardly have the weather for an open-topped car where you're going,' Lexi pointed out.

'We'll need a four-seater anyway,' said Mr Radley, addressing his son in a stage whisper, 'for picking up girls.' Rad laughed. All four were in high spirits. Lexi's cases were already in the hall, the larger of the two strapped to the wheels of Auntie Mim's shopping trolley. Upstairs Frances was sorting clothes into four piles, categorised Hot Weather, Cold Weather, Smart and Scruffy, of which the fourth was by far the largest. Her journal and a blurry photo of Growth in the back garden were the only items so far packed. The house seemed quiet without Growth: he had been billeted with Daphne and Bill, his original owners, for the duration. I had almost offered to have him myself, but mother abominated all animals, and Growth, with his unprepossessing appearance and continual scratching, was unlikely to commend himself to any but the most ardent dog-lover. Auntie Mim was staying with Clarissa in case she left a pan of sprouts on and burnt the house down.

'Send me a postcard, won't you?' I said, watching Frances squash the last of her clothes into a large nylon hold-all.

'Oh no, I'll write proper letters,' said Frances. 'I've written one already actually, so you should get it tomorrow. And if we stay anywhere with an address for long enough I'll send you that and you can write to me.' I allowed this thought to cheer me a little.

The next day, as promised, the first letter arrived.

Dear Abigail

By the time you get this we'll be At Sea! We're getting the early boat to Calais and stopping at a place called Amiens for lunch. I spent all this morning hoovering dog hairs out of the Spitfire then Rad said they wanted to take it, so I had to do the Renault as well just in case. I wish you and Growth were coming too, but there's quarantine and all that, and your holiday getting

94

in the way. Dad keeps taking Rad's books out of his suitcase when he's not looking; he says they've got to talk to each other in the evenings! Rad asked in a sarcastic voice if Dad was taking his paints, and Dad got all uppity and said yes he might. Can you imagine him setting up his easel in the middle of some square? Rad will die of embarrassment. Well, I'd better go and post this now. My next letter will come from Paris.

    love

       Frances

The next few days passed with agonising slowness. I knew from careful interrogation of my parents that mail from abroad was notoriously unreliable, took weeks to arrive and sometimes didn't arrive at all. I cast around for new ways of occupying myself. I practised my cello with more dedication than usual, finished all my holiday homework within a day, and rearranged the few pieces of furniture in my room into every possible permutation. The weather during all this was hot and dry: the sunshine would clearly have exhausted itself before our trip to Skye. I helped mother in the garden, weeding and spraying and dead-heading. I went for long cycle rides around the streets. On about the fourth day I cycled further than usual, drawn irresistibly towards Balmoral Road. I don't know what I was expecting to find, but as I drew level with the house I could see the Renault still parked in the driveway and the top floor windows wide open. Too shy to ring the doorbell I pedalled home at a furious pace, careering down hills and weaving up on to the pavement to avoid traffic lights. As soon as I got home I tried Frances' phone number. After a dozen rings Rad answered.

'Hello, is Frances there?' I asked timidly.

'Is that Blush?' he said. 'They're in France, remember.'

'Yes, yes, but I was just passing the house and I saw the car and thought maybe she was still there. Why haven't you gone yet? Weren't you all supposed to be leaving together?'

'We *were*, but Dad couldn't get organised in time so Mum

and Frances went on ahead, and then Dad realised he didn't have any money in his account, so he had to go round to Bill's and borrow some. And then he found his passport had expired. We're supposed to be trying again tomorrow.'

'Oh dear.'

'He does something like this every year. I'm used to it.'

This was the longest conversation I had ever had with Rad and I was grateful for the protection of the telephone and the several miles' distance between us which prevented him seeing my burning cheeks. Sometimes I had been known to blush so violently that I gave myself a nosebleed. I was convinced that there was something pathological about my condition, but mother had dismissed my demands to see the doctor as ridiculous. In her view it would have been unhealthy for a twelve-year-old girl *not* to blush. It was one of the things she found suspicious about Frances, this refusal to be cowed.

'Just think of something cool when you feel a blush coming on,' was her suggestion. So for a while I would mutter 'frozen peas, frozen peas' to myself whenever embarrassment threatened.

The Paris letter finally arrived the day before we were due to depart for Skye. I had spent the previous weeks moping around the house, bored and fidgety, rising late and driving my mother to distraction by shutting myself indoors watching television for hours at a time instead of enjoying the sunshine.

'You'll get rickets,' she warned.

I had made one other trip to Balmoral Road on my bike but the house was locked and dark. I even peered through the letter box, half expecting to hear the sound of yapping and paws skittering on the tiles, but there was nothing.

Then it came at last, fluttering on to the mat in its airmail envelope, as light as an autumn leaf. I withdrew upstairs to my top bunk, closing the bedroom door in case the letter contained secrets that would otherwise escape. It had been posted two weeks ago: to Frances the events described would already be history.

Dear Blush

I'm writing this in the hotel room. It's boiling hot and Mum is lying on the bed with nothing on. We're having a great time – we've been to the Eiffel Tower and the Louvre and Notre-Dame where I lit a candle for you and one for Growth. It cost two francs. You have to put your money in this tin box but no one's there checking. Mum keeps expecting me to talk French. I've tried telling her we only know stuff like 'Il fait beau aujourd'hui' and 'Le chien est sous la table' which is no good in shops or anywhere. There are loads of beggars in the underground with little bits of cardboard saying 'J'ai faim' – even I understood that! I gave one a franc and he said 'Merci' and I panicked and said 'Merci' back. I'll never get used to this food – last night I ordered fish and that's all I got – just a whole fish on a plate in a bit of sauce, staring at me. No chips or anything. I think I'll stick to the steak from now on. Guess what? This morning we were in this café and guess who walked in? Lawrence. He's in Paris for a few days at some architects' conference so he's taking us out to dinner.

1 a.m. We've just come back from dinner with Lawrence. My feet are killing me. We went to this really flash place – Mum made me wear a dress and lent me a pair of her high heels. She was all dressed up of course. Lawrence speaks really good French – he didn't ask us what we wanted or anything, he just went ahead and ordered a whole load of stuff – about six courses. And he bought Mum and me a red rose each from this chap with a bucket who was wandering around the tables. I've just tried to press mine between the pages of my journal but it's gone a bit squashy. After dinner he took us to this club for more drink – I'd already had about two pints of Coke! – and you won't believe it but there were these women on the stage, sort of formation dancing, wearing loads of feathers and sequins and stuff, but nothing on their boobs or bums! *Honest! And no one except me even seemed to have noticed. Better not tell Dad about this place or he'll be down here with his easel. I asked Mum afterwards if she'd seen them and she said yes, of course, and I said why did they have those bits showing, and she said, wait for it, 'because a woman's body is the most beautiful thing in creation' and then I got a lecture about not being ashamed of my body because in the eyes of Nature even the*

ugliest woman is beautiful, not that I was at all ugly, etc etc. I
think she was a bit sloshed actually. She's fast asleep now,
anyway. Tomorrow we're off down south. Mum wants to find a
nudist beach to get an all-over tan. Perhaps I'll bury myself in
sand, or stones, or whatever they have down there.

   lots of love
   Frances

✻

There were no all-over tans to be had in Skye. In fact we had
to add layers of clothing as fast as Lexi had been shedding
them. The holiday cottage we were renting was small and
bare and bleakly furnished with cheap, mismatching chairs
and tables that no normally inhabited house would have
contained. It smelled empty – of stale air and unfilled
cupboards and a faint suggestion of gas. Draughts blew in
around the rattling windows making the curtains flutter; the
night storage heaters raged for a couple of hours in the middle
of the night but were cold as marble by morning. Mother had
pulled a face at the decor but pronounced the place perfectly
adequate 'as a base' – words which, threatening day-long
hikes over the hills, made my heart sink. Father, having
marked out his territory on the coffee table with piles of
holiday reading, guide books, local history and a couple of
Walter Scotts, seemed unperturbed. We had at least come
prepared for the cold, with extra jumpers, thick socks and hot
water-bottles.

On the living-room wall was a crude oil-painting,
executed in colours straight from the tube, of the view from
the window – the garden wall, the gate, a frothy stream, some
tussocky grass, a whitewashed cottage in the middle distance
and, in the background, the Cuillins against a violent sunset.
The day of our arrival was our only chance to compare the
picture with the original as the following morning sheeting
rain and mist swept in, turning the world beyond the
windows a uniform grey. After three days of confinement to
the house I had read all the books I had brought from home

and moved on to the odd assortment of ancient hardbacks and broken-spined paperbacks on the dresser: *Lord of the Flies*, which I remembered seeing on Rad's desk, and which mother predicted, wrongly, that I wouldn't enjoy; *Tropic of Cancer*, into which I made furtive and troubling forays when unobserved, and *The Call of the Wild*, which was to do with dogs, and less interesting.

By the fourth day it was decided that we would not let the weather spoil our plans any longer, and would go out in hail or flood. Shouldering the rucksack containing maps, sandwiches and a flask of hot soup, father led us, gloved and booted, plastic macks crackling as we walked, on a day's march to Elgol and back. In the evening as a reward for blistered feet and raw noses, he drove for miles around the island in search of a fish and chip shop, returning an hour later with three lukewarm, greasy packages which we fell on like a pack of wolves. By tinkering with the night storage heaters father had managed to get the dial stuck at Constant so that they burnt ferociously day and night. No amount of adjustment would bring them to order. The wallpaper behind them, dry perhaps for the first time, started to lift away from the plaster; wet clothes draped over them dried to a crisp in half an hour; we awoke each morning with sore throats and cracked lips; mother had a migraine, and then another.

At the end of the second week came a reprieve: after a walk to the nearest phone box to call Granny, mother returned with the news that she had fallen off a step-ladder while trying to dust the china on her topmost shelves, and hurt her back. She hadn't broken anything, except the card table on which she had landed, but was bedbound and sore. We would have to go home; mother would have to look after her. Father concealed his disappointment: the end of the holiday meant the approach of another school term. I concealed my joy, as we loaded the car, locked up the cottage, and rode the heaving ferry to the Kyle of Lochalsh, the gateway to home.

14

When mother returned from her week in Bognor Regis acting as nursemaid to my grandmother, she announced her intention of learning to drive. The inconvenience of walking everywhere to pick up prescriptions, fetch shopping and run errands, and her inability to ferry her mother to the doctor's surgery had convinced her that it was time she mastered what was sure to be a simple task. My father was horrified; the car was his refuge. In it he could slip off, without warning, who knew where. Another driver in the family would mean consultation, negotiation: it was unthinkable.

'But why?' he asked. 'You don't need to drive. I can take you anywhere you want to go. Any time. I'll worry if I think you're out on the road somewhere. It's not safe.'

There was a little flash of triumph in mother's eyes. 'Got you,' it said.

'Don't be silly,' she replied. 'It's ridiculous that I've gone all these years without learning. Everyone drives nowadays. I'd be no use to anyone in an emergency if I don't drive.'

'You'll probably *be* the emergency if you do,' said father. 'Can't you persuade her, Abigail?'

I hesitated. Although I was bothered by the apparent pleasure mother was taking in her obstinacy, I could see no good reason for her not driving.

'Think how much easier that journey to Skye would have been if we could have shared the driving,' she went on, ignoring his last comment.

'I didn't mind,' said Dad. 'I'd be more nervous as a passenger. There's no need for you to drive. If you ever want me to take you anywhere you know you've only to ask.'

'That's not the point. I'd like to be able to drive myself.'

'I can't see what you'd have to gain.'

'Freedom.' At last the word was out in the open. Two

different freedoms, and only one car. My mother won of course. Not because she shouted or ranted or had the better argument, but because in certain situations, where she could see the possibility of victory, her inflexibility was absolute. My father's protestations were like drops of water bouncing off a great lump of jade: it wouldn't be worn down in his lifetime. Sensibly he relented, even offering to teach her himself, but she was determined to do the thing properly, and twice a week the little red hatchback with its white dunce's cap bearing the driving school's insignia would glide up to the house to collect her, and bunny-hop away again with mother at the wheel. Gracious in defeat, father coached her on the Highway Code, took her out for practice drives around likely test routes, and bit back any words of advice that might be misconstrued. Her first two test failures left her rattled but not broken. After the third she said, 'It looks as though I'm not destined to drive,' devolving responsibility for her predicament upon a higher authority, the L-plates disappeared from the car and the subject was never raised again.

It was father's turn a few months later. This time it was his job that was the source of domestic tension. Having heard the chequered employment history of Mr Radley, I had never imagined that teaching Latin was anything other than a fine and admirable occupation. Nor had it occurred to me that there was anything wrong with staying in the same job for an entire career. It seemed the sensible thing to do. I was happy at school and had no inclination to leave; I couldn't see why any teacher might want to. But about the time I had left Saint Bede's, father's Grammar School had become a Comprehensive. Naturally the technicalities of this were lost on me, but I was left in no doubt by my parents' despondency and dark mutterings that this was a Bad Thing.

'You see at the moment,' father explained one morning, while laying bacon under the grill for breakfast, 'the

Grammar School only takes clever children like you – and heaven knows some of those are stupid enough.' He switched on the gas which fanned out over the bacon while he hunted for the matches. 'But when it turns Comprehensive,' he struck a match, 'we'll have to take children who are very dim indeed,' the gas ignited with a boom, 'and teaching Latin to the very dim is much less agreeable than teaching it to the clever.'

There was more to it than that, of course. Once the spirit of modernisation was on the march other changes followed. Latin and Greek, it was felt, were no longer as relevant as they had been, say, five years ago. Father and the Greek master would continue to teach the upper school, but the new intake would instead be taught a subject called Civics by a member of the History department. Father was happy to be relieved of his duties towards the very dim, but depressed all the same, and suppertimes, formerly an opportunity to recount the significant events of the day, became gloomy affairs presided over by the ghost of Civilisation, whose passing father would lament nightly.

'It seems Shakespeare may be the next to go, poor fellow,' he once said, as though referring to a member of staff. 'There was quite a long meeting on the subject at lunchtime today – I always eavesdrop on these things to pick up the latest fatuity – and the conclusion was that the English department must find ways of making Shakespeare relevant.' He sighed.

'What I don't understand,' said mother, 'is what is going to happen as each successive Grammar year leaves. I mean, there will come a time when there's nobody left doing Latin. Then what happens to you?'

'Ah,' father said. 'With each year that passes I am slowly being erased. Then what? Good question.' But he didn't have an answer, and the meal proceeded in uneasy silence.

'Tony Inchwood has got a deputy headship,' father reported over supper a few months after that conversation. 'First person to be promoted out of the place in years.'

'Tony Inchwood? What was he?' said mother.

'Head of languages.'

'So his job will be vacant then.'

'Not for long – the advert goes in the paper on Friday.'

'You could apply for it – you teach a language. Of sorts.'

'Oh, not me,' said father, cutting a wedge of white bread from the end of the loaf and dipping it into his goulash gravy. 'Wouldn't have a hope.'

'Why ever not?' asked mother indignantly.

'Too old.'

'You're not old – you're only forty-nine.'

'Fifty-one.'

'Well, what's two years?'

'It sounds worse.'

'But you've got nearly fifteen working years ahead of you. You can't be expected to hang around in the same job all that time.'

'Only recently you were worried that I *wouldn't* be staying in the job for much longer,' father pointed out, sweeping his bread around the plate, leaving a clean china trail. 'Anyway, I don't want to be head of languages – planning the German syllabus and stocktaking and running endless meetings. All that has nothing to do with teaching Latin.'

'But you must apply for it,' mother insisted. 'Surely they'd be glad to give it to you after all you've done. And it would solve their problem of what to do with you.' And before he'd finished his last swab of bread she had produced a pad of writing paper from the bureau. 'Here you are.'

'I don't need to write – I'll just mention to Roger that I'm vaguely interested. Not that I am,' he added.

'Oh no,' mother said firmly. 'We're going to do this properly.'

He didn't get it of course. Having put himself to the trouble he was more disappointed than he'd expected, but stoical and magnanimous nevertheless. 'It wasn't a complete waste of time,' he pointed out. 'I'd been meaning to get this suit dry-cleaned for ages.'

Mother's sense of justice was outraged. 'How could they?' she shrilled, furious at the implied slight and that, after all, father should have been proved right. The victorious candidate was only thirty-two.

'Looks even younger than that,' said father. 'He's been in one of those big inner-city comprehensives. Terribly nice fellow. Just what we need, really.'

'But don't all those years of service count for anything?' mother complained.

Father gave a little smile. 'Oh yes,' he said. 'Loyalty never goes unpunished.'

While my father's career seemed to have stalled permanently, Frances' parents were in the grip of change. Lexi had been promoted to something called a team leader. This meant more work and more money – money which didn't somehow translate into new carpets or wallpaper, or the sort of things that windfalls in our house would provide. Lexi did buy an antique chaise longue for the sitting room, which looked rather odd alongside the gas fire and dralon sofa, and she would recline there with slices of cucumber over her eyes after a hard day of drafting reports or analysing survey results. Unfortunately this new acquisition soon became a favoured perch for Growth, and before long the elegant yellow brocade was covered for its own protection with a hairy dog-blanket. Mr Radley by contrast had taken another step down the ladder of commercial success. He had walked out of the lobby attendant's job after a minor disagreement with the hotel manager. This was not, apparently, the first time he had left a job in such circumstances.

'The trouble with Dad is that he's got lots of principles,' Frances explained. 'And he's always resigning on one or other of them.' It was a Saturday morning and we were sitting at Lexi's dressing table trying on her make-up. 'He even resigned as caretaker of this private girls' school in Hampstead, and that was his favourite job of all. Or was he sacked from that one? I can't remember.' She applied a plummy lipstick with an unsteady hand and pouted at herself in the mirror.

'What does he do now?' I asked, unaware that Mr Radley had come into the room behind us.

'He's a sort of night watchman.'

'What does he watch?' I was craning towards my reflection, dragging a blunt eyeliner pencil under one eye to leave a thick broken line when I saw him in the mirror and started, jabbing myself.

'The clock mostly,' he said as I swung round, one eye streaming. 'Now would you two trollops kindly clear off out of here so I can get some sleep.'

Back in Frances' room we looked at our painted faces and giggled. I had two flaming bars of orange blusher on my cheeks and one bloodshot eye ringed with black. Frances had silver shadow up to her eyebrows and a wobbly clown's mouth. There was already a difference between us, though. I still looked like a girl trying on her mother's make-up; she looked like a genuine slattern.

Frances was rapidly becoming aware of her attractiveness to boys. At thirteen she already looked fifteen. This was partly on account of her figure. Although not especially tall, she was what my mother called, with a slight pursing of the lips, 'well-developed'. She didn't have that give-away skinniness which made my legs look the same width all the way down, like stilts. And she didn't hunch her shoulders, in order to try and make herself invisible, but walked upright, confidently, chest out. It wasn't just her appearance, though. Frances seemed to send out powerful signals, like radio waves, without even realising it. Whenever we went out together men on building sites or in passing lorries would whistle and leer, and she would yell 'wanker' furiously back at them before turning away with a smirk. It never happened to me when I was alone. She also had a knack of falling into conversation with strange men. There were always a few lads at the school bus-stop with whom she would exchange on-going banter, and if some new arrival should present himself she had a way of raising her voice so that it became clear that her conversation, even with me, was a performance for his benefit. I found myself falling back on my 'frozen peas' mantra all too often in those days.

From time to time Frances would arrange an assignation with one of the better looking of the bus-stop lotharios. The venue was usually a steamed up café in the shopping precinct with ripped vinyl seats and tomato-shaped ketchup dispensers on the tables, and a tea urn kept at a rolling boil all day. I would be dragged along on these occasions – rather like the second at a duel, and with similarly low hopes of a pleasant outcome. The boy in question might have brought his deputy along, too, and we would sit in a booth over our cups of scummy tea, while Frances and Baz or Gaz or Jez stirred pepper into the sugar bowl or picked the clots of ketchup from the spout of the plastic tomato and flirted with each other by the time-honoured method of trading insults and declarations of mutual contempt.

Her latest infatuation, however, was with a friend of Rad's called Nicky, who was about six foot four, with curly hair, pebble glasses and acne. It must have been his fear of her that she found attractive. Rad didn't often bring friends back home because most of them lived in North London, nearer his school, but Nicky seemed prepared to make the long journey to the southern suburbs and was soon a regular visitor to the house. Indeed Lexi soon adopted him as a sort of handyman. He was forever being called upon to fetch things down from the topmost shelves, open or close high windows, rescue spiders from the picture rails and scrump inaccessible apples from Fish and Chips's overhanging tree. He was even more afraid of Lexi than he was of Frances, so raised no objection. On his introduction to the Radleys he inadvertently precipitated a scene.

Unusually the whole family was together: the central heating had packed up and we were all in the sitting room with the gas fire full on. Even Auntie Mim had come down and was sitting on the couch in a blanket.

Lexi was looking through her address book. 'Who do we know who can fix a boiler?' she was saying. There was no question of their resorting to hired labour – petty maintenance jobs were invariably foisted on to friends, or friends of friends, or acquaintances of friends if necessary. I wasn't sure quite what reciprocal services were offered. Perhaps Mr Radley offered to paint them nude. 'I was talking to someone only the other day who knew someone who'd put in his own central heating. Who was it? Damn.'

'Your father's not a plumber is he, Nicky?' said Mr Radley.

'No, he's an obstetrician.'

'Hmm, we don't have much call for one of those any more,' said Mr Radley. 'A vet – yes.'

'My mother's a solicitor,' Nicky added helpfully.

'Solicitor,' said Lexi. 'Let me write that down – I don't think we've got one of those.'

'And Blush's father teaches Latin, so he's no use,' said Mr Radley.

'*Nicky Rupp – Obs and Solic*,' said Lexi, writing.

'I don't suppose he went into it with the aim of being useful to you,' said Rad, coming to my father's defence.

'As if you're so useful,' Frances added.

'Well, that's true enough,' Mr Radley admitted good-humouredly.

'I've got an uncle who knows a bit about cars,' Nicky put in quickly. He was not yet used to the terms of disrespect which flowed freely between father and children.

'Oh fantastic,' said Lexi. 'Does he live near?'

'Harrogate. And it's more vintage cars.'

'Well, for God's sake don't let Rad near any of them.' Ignoring agonised signals from his son he went on, 'He nearly killed me in France, swerving to avoid a *dead* hedgehog.' This statement was received with a moment's frosty silence. Mr Radley coloured slightly. Rad looked at the floor.

'Are you saying you let Rad *drive* in France?' Lexi said in a voice that was pure poison.

'Oh *bugger*!' said Mr Radley.

'Well done, Dad,' said Rad bitterly.

'You let him drive on French roads, under-age, with no licence, uninsured? How could you be so irresponsible? What if he'd killed someone?'

'He nearly killed *me*,' Mr Radley said, aggrieved. There is no indignation like that of the justly accused.

Nicky and I exchanged a look of confederacy. 'Our families are not like this,' it said.

'It was only a one-off,' said Rad. 'And it was safer than

letting Dad drive in the condition he was in.'

At the mention of this condition of Mr Radley Lexi's anger seemed to give way to extreme weariness and without a word she got up and walked out of the room. Nicky and I made our excuses and left soon afterwards.

16

At the beginning of December there were a few days of snow. Frances and I were in a biology lesson when the first flakes began to drift past the window. The weather forecast had predicted a heavy fall and the sky had been the colour of porridge all morning. Frances was in disgrace because she had refused to take part in the dissection of a rat – had almost cried when she saw its pickled body pinned out on the chopping board, and insisted the smell of formaldehyde would make her sick. So while the rest of us clustered around Mrs Armitage's desk trying to breathe through our mouths to avoid the stench of embalmed rodent, Frances was banished to the back of the room to stand near an open window and cut up a mushroom instead.

'Ahem!' Mrs Armitage stopped, scalpel poised, to admonish Frances who had thrown the window back as wide as possible and was leaning out trying to catch snowflakes on her tongue. An icy draught was sweeping through the lab rattling the pages on the benches. Already the playing fields and houses beyond were obscured by the blizzard. Frances withdrew her head and closed the window against the swirling mass of flakes which were blowing about like down from a burst pillow. It didn't seem possible that the stuff could settle: most of it seemed to be flying upwards. By the end of the afternoon, however, the school was surrounded by a pelt of snow six inches deep. As we emerged after the final bell, awed into silence like explorers setting foot on a new continent, we could see Rad and Nicky waiting by the gate. They greeted us with a hail of snowballs.

'What are you doing here?' asked Frances, spitting out snow.

'School closed early so we thought we'd come and meet you,' said Rad, lobbing a snowball into the branches of a tree where it disintegrated, bringing down an avalanche on to our heads. 'We can walk home through the woods.'

'You might as well come back to tea,' Frances said to me. 'You can do our homework there.' This decided, we set off as fast as Frances' and Rad's unsuitable footwear permitted. Nicky and I of course had come prepared with boots. The bottom of Rad's trousers were already soaked, and Frances' lace-ups were swamped within seconds. A few of the older girls looked at me and Frances with new respect as we passed. Rad was obviously an object of some interest.

We took the footpath to the woods in silence apart from the creaking of the snow under our feet. There was an unspoken understanding that hostilities would not start until we had reached the fields beyond the trees. The snow had stopped falling by now and the sky was already dark as we reached the top field. A single line of footprints was the only trail as far as the ridge of trees that divided the park from the main road. We hesitated a second and then, as if at a pre-arranged signal, ran whooping and screeching down the slope, kicking up as much snow as possible, leaving four ragged furrows in our wake. At the bottom of the dip Rad drew two lines with his foot about twenty feet apart. He and Nicky stood on one side of no-man's-land, Frances and I on the other, and at the word 'Go' we began pelting each other with snowballs packed hard as glass. Soon this disciplined approach gave way to anarchy – Nicky broke across the line, rugby-tackled Frances and stuffed handfuls of snow down the back of her blazer until she screamed for mercy. I felt slightly dizzy with excitement at the prospect of being similarly molested by Rad, but, whether from politeness or reserve or sheer indifference, he confined himself to the decorous pitching of a few more snowballs before joining Frances in her counter-attack on Nicky, who by now had lost his glasses and was easy prey. It was only when they realised that I had so far escaped injury and was looking altogether too present-able that the three of them joined forces and practically buried me alive. Nicky and Frances held me down while Rad tipped my schoolbooks out of my bag, filled it with snow and emptied it over my head. We spent the next fifteen minutes looking for Nicky's glasses which turned up, twisted but unbroken, caught in a hole in the back of Frances' blazer. He dusted the snow off them and put them back on, the bent frames giving him an even more comical appearance than usual.

With streaming eyes and raw faces we limped home. By the time we reached the main road I had lost all sensation in my fingers, and my toes felt like loose pebbles rolling about in the bottom of my boots. Every so often a chunk of snow would drop from my matted hair and slip, melting, down my neck. There was no sign of Mr and Mrs Radley in the house, but someone had lit the fire in the dining room so Rad threw some more coal on while Frances made tea and toast, and we sat in front of the hearth to thaw out. Frances was trying to flirt with Nicky, brushing the snow out of his hair and teasing him about his glasses, and I found myself squinting at him through half-closed eyes to try and see what he would look like without acne, when he caught me and demanded to know what I was staring at.

'Nothing,' I stammered, lying feebly, 'I think there's something in my eye,' and I retreated from the room on the pretext of going to investigate. When I returned they had obviously been plotting something as there was a densely conspiratorial silence. Rad was playing with the fire irons, shoving the poker into the coals until the end glowed orange. As I looked suspiciously from one face to another Rad got up and advanced towards me with the red-hot poker in his hand. I laughed and stood my ground until the tip, which had now turned white, was six inches from my face, at which point I lost my nerve and started to back away. He came at me, unsmiling. When my heels touched the wall and Rad kept coming I flinched and closed my eyes, and feeling a burning pain between my eyebrows, and hearing the hiss of searing skin, I let out a scream which brought Nicky and Frances leaping to their feet. There was a crash as the poker hit the floor and when I opened my eyes Rad was standing in front of me with his index finger still outstretched and a look of horror on his face.

'What did you do that for?' I said, tears leaping to my eyes.

'Abigail. I'm sorry. *I didn't do anything*,' he stammered. 'Did I?' he appealed to the others. The three of them crowded round me now to examine my brand, while I stood there, still too dazed to move.

'It's scientifically impossible,' said Nicky.

'Totally freaky,' agreed Frances.

It was some time before they could persuade me that what had actually happened was this: as soon as I had closed my eyes, Rad had put the poker down by his side and touched me lightly on the forehead with one finger. But there between my eyebrows like a Hindu wife's *tilak* was a perfectly round burn which, in spite of the hasty application of an ice cube wrapped in a flannel, lasted in its most vivid form for several weeks and then faded to form a silvery scar, the ghost of a full moon.

17

When I was fourteen I discovered where it was that my father went on his many unexplained absences from home. In a curious way the truth was stranger than my most lurid imaginings. For some time Frances had been entertaining the fantasy that he was a Russian spy.

'He was at Cambridge, wasn't he?' went her reasoning. 'And Latin is a useful skill for code-breakers.'

'And Latin teachers,' I said.

She ignored me. 'And he's always going off – he's probably meeting the head of the KGB in a park to pass on secrets.'

'My father's not a communist. He votes Conservative,' I protested.

'I don't suppose the communists field a candidate in north-west Kent,' said Rad, who was playing clock patience on the floor and listening to our discussion. Since Nicky's introduction to the household Rad seemed to have grown more sociable. Although he didn't exactly join in Frances' and my activities, he was out of his bedroom more often and could manage to sustain a conversation – even a frivolous one – if required.

'You don't know who he votes for once he's in that little booth,' said Frances. 'It's a perfect front – he's such a pillar of respectability not even his own daughter would suspect him.'

'If you don't mind my saying so, your dad's just as likely to be a spy as mine. I mean, he has all day to hang around meeting people in parks or whatever they do.' Her insinuations were beginning to rankle.

She looked at me scornfully. 'Dad? Don't be stupid. No one would trust him with a secret for five minutes.' There was a silence as I acknowledged the truth of this. 'Why don't you follow him on your bike one day?' she went on.

'Oh no, I couldn't do that. What if I caught him doing

something really bad – like going to a brothel?' I wasn't quite sure how I would recognise a brothel, unless it had a neon sign outside advertising itself. 'And what if he saw me seeing him?'

Frances conceded this would be difficult. As it turned out I didn't need to make any elaborate plans to catch my father in the practice of his illicit hobby.

It was a summer's evening in June, and Frances and I were on our way to a party. We had spent the afternoon trying on and discarding various costumes from her and Lexi's wardrobes. I was already kitted out in a tight black pencil skirt which my mother, with some misgivings, had agreed to make. I had only managed to save it from being a respectable piece of office clothing that a librarian might safely wear by secretly moving the pins inwards after a fitting. At Frances' suggestion I had stuffed my bra with tissues, and was now sporting a pair of hard and rather lumpy breasts under my T-shirt. Frances, who was a great frequenter of jumble sales, had settled on what was obviously a man's striped night-shirt, frayed at the collar, and was wearing it half open and belted over a low-necked vest. She didn't need any stuffing. I was practising walking in a pair of Lexi's stilettos, which were a size too large and had to have still more tissues packed into the toes to give me a chance of keeping them on. I was beginning to feel like a rag doll.

'Hmm. I think your problem is the split in your skirt doesn't go up far enough,' said Frances as I teetered past, knees locked together, eyes fixed on my feet. Years of trying on Lexi's shoes had made her a confident practitioner of the art of running for buses in high heels. 'Do you want me to alter it for you?'

'Well . . .' I hesitated. My mother's main objection to the fashion had been that a split made the wearer look cheap. And I'd never put Frances down as much of a seamstress. Before I had had time to decline the offer, she had seized the back of my skirt and pulled the seam apart with a horrible rending sound.

'There you are,' she said, pleased to be of help.

'Oh my God,' I wailed, craning round to inspect the damage. 'What have you done? You can almost see my knickers.'

'Not if you don't lean forward too much.' She had already moved on and was rummaging in a shoebox full of Lexi's discarded make-up. I watched her apply scarlet polish to her bitten nails. 'I don't know why I'm making so much effort,' she said, waving one hand in the air to dry, 'there won't be anyone decent there anyway.' By which she meant Nicky.

'No,' I agreed. The party was being given by a girl at school, and in recognition of the shortage of available males we had all been instructed to 'bring a boy'. (When my mother first saw the invitation she thought it said 'bring and buy' and offered me some home-made marmalade to take.) Naturally we were unable to oblige as we didn't know any co-operative boys. There was no possibility of asking Rad along. He was now in the sixth form and would have considered the event 'girlie' and quite beneath him. He was also too busy rehearsing a school production of *Much Ado About Nothing*, in which he was taking the part of Benedick. Only that day I had tested him on his lines and experienced the thrill of hearing him say to me without any embarrassment that he would live in my heart, die in my lap and be buried in my eyes. I had read *Twelfth Night* at school and was familiar with Shakespearean innuendo. It was only after some circumlocution and careful questioning that I learnt to my great relief that Beatrice was to be played by a reedy fourth year called Toby Arlington.

The party invitation had also required us to bring a bottle. Just before we left, Frances remembered this detail and went to check the fridge. 'We're in luck,' she cried, emerging from the kitchen holding a bottle of slimline tonic, two-thirds full. 'I didn't think there'd be anything.'

'You're not going out without coats, are you?' Lexi said, emerging from the sitting room to make her farewells. 'It's not all that warm, you know.'

We shook our heads in horror. 'Oh no, Mum, a coat wouldn't go with this at all,' said Frances. 'We'll be fine. It's bus most of the way.' I nodded my agreement. In truth I was already a little chilly, especially around the neck as Frances had put my hair up, but my navy school coat was unthinkable; I'd have been a laughing stock.

'And how are you getting home?'

'Oh, we'll get a lift off someone.' This seemed to satisfy Lexi. There was never any question of her or Mr Radley turning out to fetch Frances. My father, had he known what we were up to, would have insisted on taking and collecting us, door to door. As we were leaving, Rad came down the stairs three at a time, carrying the remains of his supper – a variation on that old favourite, the Greasy Dog – on a tray. He was wearing frayed, very faded jeans and a fisherman's jumper with paint on and great unravelling holes in the elbows.

'What do you think, Rad?' said Frances, striking a pose.

He looked us over for a second or two, taking in our underdressed state and painted faces. 'I think you look like a couple of tarts,' he said indifferently, and clumped off to the kitchen. I was ready to wash my face there and then but Frances was impatient to set off, so we let ourselves out and tottered up to the bus stop. Lexi was right about the weather: my arms had broken out in goosepimples long before the bus came. I must have spent most of my teens being the wrong temperature. Fashion was so insanely perverse: chunky jumpers tucked into tight jeans in midsummer, bare legs and no jacket in winter.

The house which was our destination was a short walk from the common, and the last part of the journey was made on foot over the grass. As we minced along on tiptoes trying not to let our heels sink up to the hilt with every step, I noticed a familiar car crawl down the road bisecting the common and pull over into a parking space.

'Isn't that your dad?' asked Frances, squinting, as I ducked behind a tree, dragging her with me.

'Yes, I think so,' I said, embarrassed and fearful that I had caught him out in some appalling deception.

'What's he doing?'

'I don't know. Keep still. What if he sees us?'

'He won't recognise you anyway,' said Frances, reasonably. 'Let's just hang around here and see what happens.' To my intense agitation she kept bobbing back and forth from behind the tree to give me progress reports. 'I think he's reading a book,' she said, baffled. 'He must be meeting someone.'

After half an hour or so of this, with nothing incriminating having come to light, Frances' enthusiasm for detective work began to wane. The cold evening air was turning our legs a blotchy purple, and I felt some stirrings of remorse about my navy school overcoat.

'He doesn't seem to be waiting for anyone,' Frances finally admitted. 'He's not looking up and down the road or anything. He's just reading.' As she said this there was the cough of a car starting and the Vauxhall Viva edged out and was soon lost in the traffic. Frances was flummoxed, but I thought I understood. When father vanished it was not because he had somewhere to go or someone to see. He just had to get away – from the house, from mother, perhaps even from me – and to sit alone and read his book in the privacy of his car was the finest freedom he could achieve.

18

Rad's performance as Benedick was treated as an event of some importance in the Radley household. A whole row of seats was booked to accommodate a growing party of friends and relations, including myself, Lawrence, Clarissa, Bill and Daphne and Lexi's widowed mother, Cecile, who brought along a sort of inflatable cushion. Even Mr Radley had taken a night off from guarding the nation's biscuits to attend, but in the event his seat, like Banquo's, remained empty.

'Where's your dad?' I whispered to Frances as we waited for the curtain to rise. All around us parents and friends of the actors were fidgeting expectantly, discharging their last coughs, and rustling programmes. I had turned to the cast list in mine straight away. *Benedick – Marcus Radley.* Strange to think that there might be people here who knew him as Marcus. I would keep the programme in a shoebox of other important mementoes under my bed – even his printed name was precious.

'He didn't feel too well at the last minute,' she said. 'He's in bed at home.'

I knew she was lying, not just from the lack of conviction with which she offered the explanation, but from the demeanour of the whole Radley party. Lexi, flanked by Lawrence and Clarissa, was sitting rigidly in her seat with the expression of someone determined to enjoy herself in the teeth of a thoroughly bad temper. Every so often Lawrence would reach over and squeeze her hand encouragingly and she would reward him with a twitch of a smile. Before I could challenge Frances further the house lights dimmed and she turned away from me.

I suffered a moment's anxiety before Rad's first entrance. Would he be any good? Would my infatuation withstand a public display of mediocrity? Fortunately my loyalty was not put to the test: from his opening lines it was clear that he was a natural. The most ornate lines of poetry were delivered as if they had just that moment occurred to him; it didn't seem like a feat of memory. All around me I could sense people sitting up, alert, attentive, relieved whenever he came on. His accomplishment had the regrettable side-effect of making the rest of the cast look rather workmanlike in comparison. He showed them up for what they were – schoolboy actors, diligently playing their parts, while he was just Benedick, being himself. It was curious to witness the transformation of the reclusive and monosyllabic Rad into this confident and swaggering character. Surely, I reasoned, if he could act the lovestruck hero so convincingly on stage, he must feel some sympathy with the type in real life?

During the interval we were funnelled out into the school foyer for refreshments: bitter coffee and knobbly home-made biscuits which Frances pounced on as though they were a delicacy. From all sides I could overhear snatches of conversation: '. . . that leading boy . . .', '. . . stage presence . . .', '. . . marvellous . . .', '. . . maturity . . .', '. . . drama school, surely? . . .' and felt myself glowing with the pride of association. The director of the production, Rad's drama teacher, a short, youngish man in a black leather jacket, pushed his way through the crowd, fielding words of congratulation, to where we were standing. He introduced himself to Lexi, whom he said Rad had pointed out from the wings, and then had to be introduced to us, which took rather longer. He was evidently somewhat in awe of Lexi, who had a significant advantage in height, for a faint blush rose up his neck as they shook hands and failed to recede all the time they were talking.

'I'm enjoying the production very much,' said Lexi, giving him her finest smile. She had managed to quell her bad mood.

'It's all down to your son – he's exceptionally talented. I was hoping to see you this evening because I've been trying to talk Rad into applying for drama school, but he seems a bit dubious. I wondered if you might be able to persuade him.'

'Oh, I would never persuade my children to do anything they felt dubious about,' said Lexi firmly, but still smiling. 'I respect their judgement too much for that.'

'Yes, of course.' The blush deepened a shade. 'I just don't want him to waste his talent – he is really exceptional.'

'But he's exceptional at so many things,' interrupted Cecile, rattling her bracelets which kept snagging on her lacy cuffs. She had a strong German accent, even though Frances said she had lived in England for over fifty years. But then I wouldn't have expected Lexi's mother to have adapted her behaviour just to blend in with the surroundings: it wasn't a family trait. 'English, French, History, Mathematics, Rugby, Swimming, Chess, Acting, Singing . . .' She was getting carried away. Rad couldn't sing a note. I glanced sideways at Frances to see how she was taking all this public adulation of Rad. That sort of thing could erode your confidence. She looked unperturbed: she was accustomed to hearing his many talents expounded. Her concentration, besides, was taken up with looking around for Nicky. She spotted him at last, standing with his parents, *Obs and Solic*, and stared at him with great intensity as though the force of her will could make him turn his head. Which it did eventually. He raised his coffee cup in greeting and she blew him a kiss which made him duck, embarrassed.

A bell rang for the end of the interval and the crowd began to shuffle back into the auditorium. Lawrence and Clarissa had slipped out for a cigarette. I could see them through the glass in the darkness beyond, robed in their private fog. As an entr'acte, a group of musicians in the orchestra pit was playing 'Greensleeves' on traditional Elizabethan instruments.

'What's that funny-looking thing?' whispered Frances, pointing to a sort of etiolated trombone.

'That's called a *shagboot*,' said Lawrence gravely, which sent the three of us into peals of laughter which were only stifled by the sudden blackout and the creak of the curtain opening.

I leaned against the unforgiving back of my wooden chair, felt every vertebra making contact, and began to wish I had Cecile's inflatable cushion. I concentrated on the luxury of being able to stare at Rad without constraint – something not permissible in everyday life – and enjoying that particular warmth that comes from watching someone you love excel themselves. This intensity of contemplation was hard to maintain as every so often Frances would jab me in the ribs with her elbow and whisper 'shagboot', and start shaking and snorting all over again.

There was a momentary frisson of excitement towards the end when on the line 'Peace I will stop thy mouth', Rad leaned forward and kissed Arlington on the lips. A tremor rippled through the audience and was instantly subdued as the dialogue rolled on, inexorable and reassuring.

After the final curtain Rad took his applause, which had grown from a patter to a roar as each successive rank of the cast came forward, with the faintest of smiles. Frances had to be restrained from putting two fingers in her mouth and whistling. 'Damn Michael,' I heard Lexi mutter to Lawrence through the clapping. 'He should have been here. Damn him.'

We loitered in the foyer waiting for our hero to emerge from the changing rooms, while Lawrence went off to find a seat for Cecile. He ended up commandeering a swivel chair from the secretary's office, on which Cecile perched like a little bejewelled gnome on a toadstool. The crowd had thinned out considerably by the time Rad appeared, clad in his familiar tatty jumper and jeans. Traces of black were still visible between his eyelashes and there was a smear of tan make-up under his chin from ear to ear. He was at once set upon by the family, kissed by the women and slapped between the shoulder blades by the men. Cecile's lipstick left two cyclamen crescents on his cheek.

'Well done, young man. I suppose it will be the West End next,' said Uncle Bill, who had, if truth be told, found three hours of Shakespeare an experience not to be repeated.

'Excellent performance,' said Lawrence.

'Well done, Marcus,' said Cecile. (He didn't hit *her*, I noticed.) 'You take after your mother in the acting.'

'Rubbish. He's far better than I was,' said Lexi. 'I'm proud of you,' she added.

Nicky wandered over. 'Congratulations,' he said, pretending to fawn over Rad's hand.

'You were the best,' I said.

'What was it like kissing that boy?' Frances wanted to know.

'Where's Dad?' said Rad, and then seeing Lexi hesitate, his eyes narrowed and he snapped, 'Oh let me guess,' and strode out to the car.

19

My mother left the piece of paper propped on the mantelpiece like a suicide note. It was an advertisement torn from the *Times Educational Supplement* for a Head of Classics job at my father's old school in Bristol.

'You'd stand a good chance, wouldn't you, as an old boy – a scholarship boy, too?'

It was a Sunday morning; mother had come back from church and put the lunch on and the three of us were in the sitting room reading the papers. It was my first weekend at home in months; Frances was in bed with flu.

'Oh no,' said father from behind the Arts section. 'I haven't got the right pedigree at all – especially not now that we've gone Comprehensive.'

'*Not the right pedigree?*' mother echoed. 'But you're one of them.'

'Would you like me to apply for it, dear?' my father said wearily, laying down his paper and staring at her through the top of his bifocals.

'Well, of course. Wouldn't you like to move back to Bristol? Get away from here and all its . . .' Even without looking up I could sense her glancing at me before she petered out. I had only been half listening to the exchange which had just taken place, but at the mention of 'Bristol' I was all attention.

'What do you mean move to Bristol?' I said stupidly. 'You mean *leave here?*'

'Yes, of course. Your father couldn't very well commute. It's a beautiful city – there are some lovely shops in Clifton. Good schools for you too.'

'But we wouldn't know anyone,' I said, panic rising in me like bile.

'Oh, you soon make friends,' said mother dismissively,

forgetting that it had taken me a full eleven years to meet the one friend I had.

'What about my cello lessons?' I knew this would carry more weight with mother than trivial concepts like friendship. I had just passed my seventh grade with distinction; my teacher was pleased with me, and had gone to some trouble to find me a place with a local youth orchestra that met every Monday evening. It was the moment when you either gave up or started to take it all seriously.

Mother hesitated. This was a tricky one, but there was no weakening now. 'There will be other good teachers in Bristol. There are probably schools which specialise in music. We wouldn't let the move jeopardise your cello-playing. Don't worry about that.' Opposing one of mother's sudden enthusiasms was rather like trying to escape the jaws of a shark: the more you struggled, the deeper the bite.

'But I don't want to move. I like it here.'

'We couldn't very well go without you,' said mother.

'You could – I could stay with Frances.'

This made her flare up. 'Don't be ridiculous. I dare say it's not as exciting here, but we happen to be your parents, and I don't suppose it's ever occurred to you that everything that goes on here is for your benefit. I couldn't even begin to explain what sacrifices have been made for your happiness.' Mother's cheeks were crimson and her eyes as close to tears as they ever got. She would have a migraine tomorrow and it would be all my fault.

Father intervened. 'The argument is academic. I haven't even applied for the job and if I did I wouldn't get it. Can we consider the subject closed?'

That night I lay awake for some time worrying. I knew my parents: if mother was determined that father apply then he would. As for his not succeeding, I couldn't entertain that hope. He was my father – how could any other candidate possibly be preferred? Some time after eleven I heard voices from their bedroom. My mother always kept the door ajar so that she would hear the phone if my granny should be the subject of some medical emergency overnight. I crept on to the landing.

'. . . hadn't brought up all that business about sacrifices in front of Abigail. What was she supposed to make of that little outburst? It was very unfair.'

'All right, all right. I regret it now. It just came out: I thought *she* was being unfair to us.'

'But could you really face the upheaval of moving?' This was father.

'Yes. This place has associations. It would be nice to go somewhere completely new.'

'Happy associations, too?'

'Oh, yes, Abigail and so on.'

'The thing is, Monica, I don't know if I could cope with a new job. I'm not very good at change.'

'But don't you have any ambition?'

'You talk as if it's a virtue.'

'It is, isn't it, in a man? Aren't you frustrated stuck where you are with all those youngsters getting promoted over you?'

'Mildly, I suppose, but . . .'

'Well then.'

'If you really want me to apply for it, dear, I will.'

'*I* don't want you to apply for it. I want *you* to want to.'

'I shall try my best to want to.'

As predicted mother had a migraine the next day. I knew this the moment I turned into The Close on my way home from school. Her bedroom curtains were closed – a signal as unmistakable as a quarantine flag on a ship. As I dropped my bag in the hallway she called down the stairs. 'Abigail, can you bring me some more frozen veg?'

I climbed the stairs, ice-pack in hand. Mother was lying in the gloom with a wet flannel on her forehead and a bucket by the side of the bed. This was a bad one, then. Her skin had a familiar grey tinge. She unpinched her eyes a fraction as I approached and reached out for the peas. The room smelled musty and stale as if all the air had been recently exhaled. I propped the door open, admitting a wedge of light from which mother shrank back fearfully like Count Dracula.

'Here, before Dad comes in,' she rasped. Her migraines

were often accompanied by a semi-paralysis of the vocal chords. I was never entirely sure whether this was a genuine symptom or whether, feeling rotten, she couldn't help assuming the cracked tones of an invalid. 'I just wanted a word about this Bristol business. I know how strongly you feel about moving, but I want you to promise not to put any pressure on Daddy. He wants this job so badly. Success is very important to a man, you see. Sometimes it's hard for us women to understand things like ambition . . .'

I nodded dully. It was a shock to have caught my mother out in a piece of vicious dishonesty, but I couldn't very well challenge her on the basis of my shabbily acquired knowledge. Liar and eavesdropper, we faced each other across the bed.

'I don't see why you couldn't stay the odd weekend with Frances if it came to it. Or have her to stay with us. And there's always the telephone . . .' She reconsidered quickly, remembering my frequent hour-long calls to Frances, '. . . or rather the post. You wouldn't have to lose touch.'

Lose touch. She had no idea. Didn't she realise that our friendship was proof against separation, conflict, change? I wasn't afraid of losing touch. I was just miserable at the thought of not seeing Frances every day, of missing her and Rad and Lexi and even Mr Radley; of no longer being part of their everyday lives.

'You do promise, don't you?'

'All right,' I said ungraciously.

And so father spent the next couple of evenings composing a letter of application. He would emerge occasionally and read out a paragraph or so for mother's approval and comment; if she ventured to suggest an improvement he would defend the original at some length and then retire to his study with a martyred air to make the alteration.

A week later he reported that references had been taken up. His headmaster had passed him in the corridor and said he had recommended father in the most extravagant terms. 'He's desperate to get rid of me,' was father's interpretation. The letter inviting him for interview arrived while he was at work. Mother, seeing the school's crest on the envelope, felt it, shook it and held it up to the light to try and divine its contents. 'It feels too short to be a simple rejection,' she said, weighing it in the palm of one hand. She pressed it against the glass of the front door. '"Dear Mr Onions, Thank you for your letter of application for the post of –" Oh bother! There's a sort of fold.' She would not have dreamed of opening the envelope: that would have been altogether too crude.

But her intuition proved correct, and so began the preparations for father's Great Test. Mother cut his hair with more than usual care, so that his fringe when combed actually lay straight rather than raked. His one suit, which had gone in and out of fashion all over again since its original purchase many years before, and which served at all official functions, including his last unsuccessful interview, was retrieved from the back of the wardrobe and inspected for blobs, moth-holes and signs of wear.

I had kept my promise, up to a point. I didn't mention my despair at the prospect of moving, and tried not to sigh and groan when the subject arose, and considered myself quite a pillar of neutrality. It didn't occur to me that my silence was itself exerting a form of pressure. In the few days before the interview father had the air of a man forced to choose the method of his own execution: upset me or disappoint mother – he couldn't win.

On the eve of the great day I had gone up to my room early to avoid the Poetry Circle who were meeting below to 'do' Tennyson. I had begun to nurture a vague contempt for this cabal, ever since we had started to study poetry at school and I had formed the idea, along with most of the class, that I alone understood it properly; that it had been written with me in mind. It irritated me that my mother's enthusiasm for her Wednesday night hobby didn't spill over into the rest of the week – I never saw her so much as glance at a poem at any other time. This struck me as the mark of a phoney. Father had been twitchy and nervous all through supper. I could see him drifting off every now and then into imaginary debates with the interviewer. Even when he was composing the questions himself he would come back to earth looking thoroughly worsted.

I was in bed reading *Mansfield Park* when I heard the study door open and then father's slow tread on the stairs. He hesitated outside my door before tapping lightly with one fingernail, a diffident pattering which lasted through several calls of 'Come in'. This was very different from mother's technique which was to knock once loudly and walk straight in.

'Oh good,' he said, hovering in the doorway. 'I thought you might be downstairs with the ladies.' He looked at my book. 'But I see you're in a more prosaic mood.' I nodded. 'Who's under the scalpel tonight?'

'Tennyson,' I said.

'Ah. *Into the jaws of Death, Into the mouth of hell*. Abigail will you be terribly unhappy if I get this job? You can say Yes.'

I wavered for a moment, and then said, 'I'll be happy for you, but unhappy for me.'

'Hmm,' he said. 'Good answer. Thank you.' And he kissed me on the top of the head and left.

The next morning all his anxiety seemed to have evaporated, and he looked almost cheerful as he ate his breakfast, his suit swathed in tea-towels to protect it from milk splashes and deposits of marmalade.

'I'm glad you're not too nervous,' said mother, observing him with some surprise. 'I thought you'd be in an awful state.'

It was then that I realised why father had questioned me the evening before. Overnight he had made his decision, and I was sure that when he came home from Bristol he would not have got the job, and we would not be moving. And so it proved. I never knew whether he had performed badly on purpose, was not good enough anyway, had been offered the post and declined it, or had simply not turned up to the interview. But I did know that this was another of those sacrifices made in my name to which mother had alluded.

For mother, of course, who was ignorant of our conversation, his failure was a sign of two things: the indifference of

Fate to her needs and desires, and an insufficiency in father himself. In future she would stop petitioning him to try for promotion, not because she had given up wanting the extra money and prestige, but because she could no longer envisage him as a success. In the past she had blamed the interviewers for their poor taste; now she blamed father for lacking whatever mysterious quality it was that they sought.

Since then I have often wondered how different things might have been if I hadn't chosen selfishness. We might have moved to Bristol; Father would have re-invented himself as a successful man; mother would have been proud or at least grateful, possibly happy; I would have moved out of the Radleys' immediate orbit; I would have missed Anne Trevillion's party; I wouldn't have gone back to the house alone on that terrible afternoon; I wouldn't have lost what I had so recently found.

20

Revenge, like mother's migraine remedy, is a dish best served cold.

'I'm going to ask Mum to move in with us.' Mother lobbed this into the breakfast-table silence like a grenade a few weeks later.

'You are *going to* ask her?' said father, a teacup arrested half-way to his lips.

'Well, I have asked her, in fact.'

'And what did she say?'

'She said "Yes".'

'Oh. So it's all settled then.'

'Only with your approval.' She looked at both of us. 'She knows I have to consult you first.'

There was a pause while we savoured the impressive dishonesty of the word 'first'. 'Isn't consultation more properly so called when it occurs *before* a decision has been taken?' Father's tone was as mild as possible – a dangerous sign.

Sensing irony, mother began to defend herself. 'What could I do? She's not safe on her own any more. She's half blind and she keeps leaving things on the stove. You know I can't go down there at the drop of a hat when I can't drive.' In an obscure way she blamed father for this problem of mobility, as if he had willed her to fail. 'One of these days she'll burn the house down. It's such a responsibility. You don't know how lucky you are not having parents to worry about.'

Amen to that, I thought.

There was some substance to her anxieties. Granny was indeed going blind. All that Thackeray under the bedclothes had finally caught up with her, and she could now no longer read at all. Large-print books and a magnifying glass had given way to audio-tapes to which she listened day and night at full volume, for her deafness had also seen no improvement with the years. She was gradually accumulating a houseful of gadgets and appurtenances to assist her in her independent life: an amplified telephone with huge numerals, Braille clocks, a hearing aid which she refused to wear because it whistled, an emergency buzzer which she was supposed to hang around her neck but which she inevitably left lying around and then lost, but none of them could withstand the vagaries of her memory or temper. Home helps were regularly accused of the theft of some item of mislaid jewellery which would later turn up in a new and bizarre hiding place – the tea caddy perhaps, or the fridge. Even the meals-on-wheels lady had been sent packing for calling out the social services when there was no reply to the doorbell. Granny had awoken from a midday nap to find a teenage policeman with one leg over the window sill. She now existed on a diet only slightly more varied than Auntie Mim's: toast and marmalade for breakfast, a tin of something heated up for lunch (as she couldn't see the labels she was never sure whether it would be pilchards or pear halves that ended up on the plate), and cheese biscuits for supper. All of this was supplemented by frequent snacks of sweets. Mother had been spending more and more weekends there, stocking up the larder, clearing packets of rancid butter and green cheese from the fridge, scrubbing away at marmalade spills which, left untreated, would get trodden right through the house on the sole of Granny's slippers, and listening more or less patiently to endless complaints about loneliness and debility.

Granny would not be an easy house-guest, that was certain. But however much aggravation mother was inflicting on herself by inviting her to stay, father would suffer more. The silence and privacy he so revered would be gone. He would become an unpaid and unthanked chauffeur, a fixer of broken gadgets, an untangler of bank statements and share dividends and income bonds and pension books and run-ins with the DSS, and all without the bonds of love and duty and shared memories which for mother would make it – just – bearable. I could see the dread on his face as we sat there, taking in the news, but he would not quarrel.

'I've told her she wouldn't be able to bring much clobber – only what will fit in the spare room. And there's room in the loft for a few boxes, isn't there?'

Father confirmed that there was.

'And I've said she can't expect us to entertain her – we won't have time to read the newspaper to her every morning the way we do when we're down there. It won't be a holiday, she understands that.'

'Mmm. When would you like me to fetch her?'

Unnerved at meeting so little resistance, mother faltered. She had not expected anything like this level of co-operation, and having prepared various arguments in her defence did not want them to go to waste. 'I know it will be difficult at first until we all get used to each other, but we couldn't possibly afford a decent nursing home, and one of those state ones is out of the question – you know how rude she is to anyone who doesn't speak the Queen's English.'

'Oh I don't think she'd last long in a home,' agreed father.

'Yes, you're always hearing of people going ga-ga after a week in one of those places. I couldn't have that on my conscience.'

'I meant no one would put up with her – she'd be expelled, rusticated, or whatever they do.'

'Oh I see. Well, I can't think what alternative I've got – every day I expect to get a phone call from the police saying she's drowned in the bath or burnt the place down. She's a danger to other people, not just herself.'

'Mmm.'

'And she'll contribute towards bills and food and so on here. You must admit the extra money would be useful.' Since you have failed to gain a salary increase, ran the unspoken sentence. I couldn't share mother's optimism about having tapped a new source of income. Granny was used to being able to save out of her state pension; her idea of a reasonable donation would be unlikely to cover the cost of keeping the bar heater in her room running. We would be worse not better off.

'Oh I don't know what to do,' mother finished, as if she had met nothing but opposition.

'Do?' said father. 'Our duty of course.'

Mother was wrong about it being difficult at first. *At first* it was just like having a visitor to stay: courtesies were observed and allowances made. When the World Service issued quite audibly from Granny's room at three in the morning we pulled the blankets over our ears. When she talked through a television programme that we were trying to watch, we made polite responses or switched the set off. When she walked in on father, asleep in his study on Sunday afternoon, with the words, 'Can somebody fix my torch/radio/hearing aid?' he would spring up to do her bidding. When she insisted on carrying plates through from dining room to kitchen and then dropped one, mother clenched her teeth and said, 'Doesn't matter'.

It was only after a few weeks that it began to register that this was how it would always be: the armchair which Granny had taken to occupying would become without any discussion hers and would be left free by the rest of us. We would grow accustomed to finding empty milk bottles inverted in a cup overnight so that the last few drops might not be wasted, and clotted balls of multicoloured soap made from those tiny fragments left over at the end of a bar. I knew thrift was one of her particular vices: when helping her to pack up her possessions in the Bognor house I had come across a cardboard shoebox labelled PENS THAT NO LONGER WORK; she still saved and ironed old wrapping paper even though she had not bought, much less *wrapped* a present for years; and she kept all her old calendars and only ever wrote on them in pencil because she had worked out that every fourteen years the days and dates would be back in sync again. When I was younger I used to be sent up into the higher branches of her apple tree to pick the out-of-reach fruit. A morning's prickly labour – scratched knees, near falls, and encounters with giant bees – would be rewarded with a bag of bruised and maggoty windfalls. The decent apples would be laid out in trays in the front garden and sold to holiday-makers.

21

In the summer of 1982 I achieved one of the great ambitions of my childhood: I was invited to join Lexi and Frances on their annual holiday. This was something I had secretly craved since that first letter arrived from Paris with tales of topless dancers and beggars on the Metro and single red roses.

My mother could not very well object: we would not be going away as a family at all, since my granny's potential as an arsonist was firmly established in my parents' minds. Leaving her behind was out of the question, but taking her with them would negate any benefits the holiday might bring. It was a holiday from her they needed. Lexi had taken the precaution of petitioning my mother and father first rather than leaving it up to me. A postcard of Burne-Jones's *Ophelia* – not the most reassuring image – arrived one morning with the message:

Dear Mr and Mrs Onions
 Frances and I would very much like Abigail to come on holiday to France with us this year. I hope you can spare your delightful daughter for a couple of weeks in August. We will take great care of her.
 Yours truly
  Alexandra Radley

Mother sniffed. 'She writes with red pen,' she said, as if this was a further sign of Lexi's moral turpitude. 'Doesn't her husband ever go with them?' she went on. 'It seems such a peculiar arrangement.' This year as other years father and son were going off together to The Trenches. The ritualistic significance of this was heightened as it was assumed that it would be their last trip. In September Rad was off to university; future holidays would doubtless be spent working to pay off debts. Though it was hard to picture Rad even managing to spend his grant. He didn't drink much or smoke at all, and only bought new clothes with the greatest reluctance and wore them until they disintegrated. Dependent upon his A-level results he had a place at Durham to read Philosophy. The idea of acting as a career had not in the end appealed. He could always get involved in drama on the side, went his reasoning, but when would he ever have another chance to spend three years just thinking?

'This is very kind of them,' said father, picking up the postcard. 'Your first trip abroad, Abigail.'

'I wonder how much it will cost?' said mother. 'You'll have to pay your way, you know, Abigail, petrol and so on.' But when the subject was finally broached over the telephone by father, at mother's prompting, Lexi dismissed the idea instantly.

'Oh no – there won't be any expenses. We'll all share a room anyway. She'll only need a little pocket money for ice creams and so on.'

In the event father gave me a thousand francs to take – a fortune, which I strapped to me in a money-belt like a holster under my clothes, and fretted over and checked twenty times a day.

Both my parents came with me to the Radleys' to see me off. Typically the annual argument about which party needed which car was in progress as we arrived. Husband and wife were standing either side of the disputed vehicles, Lexi still dressed in her housecoat and turban. Mr Radley was adamant that he needed the Estate. He and Rad were not leaving for another week and he was apparently intending to spend the time hawking his paintings round various galleries and shops. 'I can't very well fit them in the Triumph, can I?'

'But there are three of us,' Lexi was saying in her schoolmistressy voice. 'You can't expect one of the girls to sit on the bench seat all the way to Menton.'

'Why not? Blush is as skinny as a rake – she could fit in there quite easily.'

'Abigail is not "skinny"; she is beautifully slim,' said Lexi, who tended to bridle at any slur on the female form.

'Skinny, slim, what's the difference?' Mr Radley smote his forehead in frustration. 'The point is, she can fit in the back of a Spitfire more easily than a six by four canvas.'

'She is actually perfectly proportioned. Hello Abigail's parents,' Lexi said without pausing. 'We're just having a row.' And she took my small suitcase – locked and strapped against the rapacity of foreign chambermaids – and put it defiantly in the back of the Renault. Mr Radley promptly took it out and dumped it in the drive.

'Well . . .' said mother uneasily. This was her first encounter with the Radleys. Through the back gate I could see Frances taking washing off the line while Growth leapt up, snapping at the trailing garments. At the sight of me he came tearing up the drive, a pair of Lexi's lacy knickers between his teeth, two ribbons of saliva swinging from his jowls. Mother recoiled like someone walking into a cobweb as the apparition flung himself at us, barking and drooling and trying to keep hold of the knickers.

'We'd better say goodbye, Abigail,' she said at last. 'Have you got everything?' I nodded briskly to be rid of them. 'Passport, money, calamine lotion, diarrhoea tablets,' she went on, determined not to spare me. Mr Radley's lips twitched.

'Yes, yes,' I said, fairly bundling mother and father back up the drive. We exchanged hugs and kisses. 'Phone us some time to let us know you're safe,' said mother. She looked quite tearful.

'Cheer up,' I heard father whisper to her as they got in the car. 'She's not off to boarding school.'

'No, far from it,' came back the reply, before the car door slammed.

Rad had meanwhile appeared in the doorway. He had obviously been listening from the hall. 'If we take the roof off we can prop the canvases in the back of the Spitfire and you can hold on to them to stop them banging about while I drive.' Rad was now a legitimate licence-holder.

'Oh very dignified,' said Mr Radley, striding off indoors.

'Here, Rad, load these up,' Lexi ordered, considering the argument well won. She pointed to her own large cases and Frances' and my smaller ones. 'I've got to go and change.'

By this time Frances had finished with the laundry and had joined Rad and me in the drive. 'I suppose I'll have to spend next week driving Dad all over the south-east with his paintings,' said Rad gloomily, slinging the bags into the boot. 'What a waste of time. He hasn't flogged a single one in five years.'

'Don't worry,' said Frances. 'Rain's forecast all next week.'

'Ssh,' said Rad, at the sound of approaching footsteps. But it was only Lexi, dressed for the journey in white jeans, red boots and a poncho which looked as though it might have been made from Growth's least favourite car rug. Her hair was pinned up in a French pleat and a large pair of red-rimmed sunglasses covered half her face. The car keys dangled from her middle finger.

'We're off,' she called back into the house. 'See you in Arras. Look after him,' she said to Rad.

Mr Radley had the good grace to appear in the doorway, waving, as we reversed out of the drive. 'Behave yourself,' was his final injunction. Frances was already rummaging through a box of cassettes looking for some suitable music. Between us on the back seat was a plastic sack full of sweets which Cecile had given Frances for the journey – lollipops and sherbet fountains and liquorice pipes – as if we were eight-year-olds.

'Well, girls, I hope I can leave all the French speaking to you,' Lexi said, glancing in the mirror. I wasn't worried. There was no chance of Lexi fading into the background in any dialogue with officialdom, and her combination of polite and well-projected English and ferocious smiling would bring far quicker results than our bumbling O-level French. The journey to Folkestone was largely taken up with her delivering one of her lectures or exhortations. This one was on the preferability of the Many as opposed to the One, in the matter of boyfriends. 'When I was your age my friends and I all went around together in a gang – it never occurred to us what sex we were. If one of the boys wanted to see a film he might issue a general invitation, and any one of the girls might go with him. There was never any pairing off. Much better that way.'

Frances and I would have been happy to number half a dozen boys amongst our acquaintance. Apart from Rad and Nicky there was only the bus-stop brigade – the lads from the Boys' High with whom Frances enjoyed an on-going flirtation, and to whom I was about as interesting as her hockey stick. Less interesting, in fact, since the hockey stick could be seized and used for lifting skirts and making lewd gestures.

We were also instructed not to marry before the age of thirty. It was something to be contemplated only when all other areas of experience had been exhausted. This was puzzling. Lexi had married at twenty-three and didn't have the air of a woman plagued by missed opportunity. Another of Lexi's great precepts was that a girl should have no secrets from her mother. It was, of course, perfectly permissible for Frances to have secrets for recreational purposes, as it were, but she should never feel there was any subject that could not be broached.

'All right. What's oral sex?' asked Frances.

Lexi blenched slightly, before offering an explanation in measured terms. Frances feigned retching.

'Anything else you want to ask?' said Lexi, confident that the worst was over.

'Have you ever read my diary?'

'No, never,' said Lexi without a moment's hesitation. 'Mum read my diary when I was about your age because she thought I was seeing an unsuitable boy. There wasn't anything the least bit incriminating in it, but it was *years* before I forgave her. She should have known that the mere fact that I kept a diary was proof of my innocence. As soon as I started doing the things she disapproved of I abandoned the diary altogether. So you see I don't need to read yours – all the time you're writing it I know you're behaving yourself.'

Frances was flabbergasted.

'Anything else?'

'Why did you marry Dad?'

Lexi seemed more taxed by this question than by the earlier ones. I was shocked by it too, since it seemed to imply that Frances considered it an odd match, and although I had often privately wondered how two such divergent characters came together it felt like the sort of question which should never even occur to the product of the union.

'I loved him,' Lexi said finally. 'I mean I still do,' she added as an afterthought.

Once on the ferry we put our watches forward an hour, which made it lunchtime, so we ate our sandwiches, and then Lexi spread out her poncho on one of the long seats on deck and fell asleep in the sun. Frances and I roamed the corridors of the boat, losing the last of our English change on the slot machines, sniggering at our fellow passengers and gazing in the windows of the duty-free shops. Just outside Boulogne Lexi woke up, looking slightly crumpled, imprints of poncho tassels marking her cheeks, and disappeared to the Ladies to repair herself. She returned carrying a plastic bag containing two bottles of perfume – Chanel No. 5 for Frances and No. 19 for me. I was speechless with gratitude and delight. I had never been given such a lavish and frivolous gift before, had never in fact had any perfume of my own. An occasional squirt of my mother's Tweed and a forbidden dab of her ancient and acidulated bottle of Joy was the limit of my experience. I could hardly bear to disturb the packaging, whereas Frances immediately tore into hers and began spraying herself with a vigour which put me in mind of mother taking on the aphids.

'Steady,' Lexi reproved mildly. 'The effect you are after is one of subtlety.'

As the car rolled on to French tarmac I gave Frances a significant look, though the moment could not be expected to impress her so forcefully, seasoned traveller as she was. I scanned the scenery for signs of foreignness as Lexi, map open on the seat beside her, guided us along the right-hand side of the road towards Paris, our first stop. TOUTES DIRECTIONS/AUTRES DIRECTIONS offered one road sign. Frances and I devised a game which involved guessing the meaning of the advertising slogans on the hoardings by the side of the road: sometimes even identifying the product was hard enough.

Lexi, following established practice, was avoiding the motorway on account of the tolls, and, she said, to give us a better view of the countryside. Occasionally she would turn our music down to point out some church or monument, and we would be obliged to nod and enthuse. 'I'm only doing this so you have something interesting to write in your diaries,' she said.

Frances, sated by a big lunch and our earlier gorging on sweets, and half hypnotised by the chequered sunlight flashing through the windows, had soon dozed off and, fearful of being drawn into a conversation with Lexi in case it took a confessional turn, I closed my eyes too, mindful that I was missing my first experience of Abroad, and was pretty soon asleep.

We awoke to find that the fields and poplars and dusty linear villages had given way to the outskirts of Paris. The air was hazy with petrol fumes, and to either side of the road were grey factories, demolition yards full of wrecked cars, and grim, pastel-coloured apartment blocks with porthole windows, like giant cheese graters against the sky. Hoardings flashed past, streaked with grime. Much of the graffiti was in English, evidently the international language of hooliganism.

'Yuk,' said Frances, rubbing her eyes. 'What a dump.'

But there in the distance was the gleaming eggshell white of Sacré Coeur and the blurred silhouette of the Eiffel Tower, remembered from a thousand books and postcards. Our hotel was in Montmartre, not quite in view of Sacré Coeur itself, but on a pavement clogged with parked cars and pigeon droppings. On the pavement opposite a woman in a leather jacket and leopard print miniskirt was standing in the doorway of a sex cinema, scratching mosquito bites on her thigh and wearily exhorting passing men to step inside.

PERVERSIONS
COCHONNERIES

a faded poster in the window promised.

'Piggy perversions!' said Frances delightedly. Lexi pulled a face.

The doorway of the hotel was guarded, indeed blocked, by a sleeping Alsatian, who staggered to his feet and limped off to a distant corner of the lobby after we had all stepped carefully over him. The proprietress, Madame Orselly, a small dumpy woman with dyed red hair, greeted Lexi and Frances with rapture, kissing them twice on each cheek. 'And this is Abigail, our girlfriend.' Lexi introduced me, and more bonjours were exchanged before Madame Orselly summoned a spotty youth from the back room to take our bags upstairs. Even in the early evening of a bright sunny day the staircases and corridors were in darkness and our porter and guide would periodically slap switches indicated by a glowing orange bulb which would give us a few seconds' murky light before clicking off. I couldn't help noticing that the walls seemed to tremble as we trooped past, and on reaching out to touch the wallpaper, I realised that they weren't solid at all, but made of a piece of floral fabric stretched between a frame, flimsy as a stage set.

Our room had a double bed and a single covered with blue candlewick bedspreads, balding in places, rose wallpaper bleached by the sun, and an ornately carved dark wood wardrobe, almost big enough to park a car in. A hardboard partition, faced in the same rose paper and not quite reaching the ceiling, divided the ensuite facilities from the rest of the room. These consisted of a chipped sink, a squat, square bath with ledge for sitting on, and a bidet on wheels. After dismissing the porter untipped, Lexi stripped down to her knickers and, tossing the bolster aside, lay stretched out on the single bed with a flannel over her eyes.

'I'm going to recover for an hour or so before dinner,' she said, blindly. 'You girls can explore if you like.'

Our explorations took us no further than the bar downstairs, where we sat and drank lemonade and made a fuss of the dog, who was called Boubous, and passed critical comment on the arriving and departing clientele. Madame Orselly brought us a glass of pastis each and a carafe of water, setting them down on the table with a wink, and a burst of French of which we understood not a word, and we responded with nods and smiles and *merci*s until she retreated, satisfied.

When Lexi came down an hour later we were both slightly giggly. Not from the pastis, which both of us had found undrinkable – Frances anyway having a puritanical disapproval of alcohol – but from our attempts to dispose of it discreetly without hurting Madame Orselly's feelings. Tipping it into the carafe had to our surprise and mirth made the water turn cloudy, and we had resorted to slopping a little of the mixture into a vase of plastic chrysanthemums in an alcove behind us each time the proprietress's back was turned.

We dined in the hotel from the sixty-franc menu. *Assorted Pork-Butcher's Meat* offered the translation of *Charcuterie*. Frances and I stuck with pâté and steak, items which were at once familiar and foreign – the pâté served with mashed potato and gherkins and the steak, despite being *bien cuit*, still leaking blood into the chips. Lexi had quails, pathetic, wizened creatures with barely a mouthful of meat on them, and *haricots verts* thin as bootlaces.

For pudding Lexi insisted we all had crêpes flambéed at the table, even though Frances and I had been coveting the chocolate mousse we had seen being ferried to other diners.

'I don't want any alcohol with mine,' said Frances primly, as the chef sloshed amaretto into the pan and ignited it with a pop.

'Don't be ridiculous,' said Lexi. 'You can't *flamber* in Coca-Cola. Alcohol won't hurt you in these quantities.' She had had a modest half-bottle of red wine with her dinner.

'Delicious,' she said, spearing a dripping corner of pancake.

'It's poison,' said Frances vehemently, trying to squeeze as much of the liquid out of hers as she could with her knife and fork. It was only over the course of this holiday that Frances' aversion – which I had previously thought a pointless affectation – along with much else which puzzled me about the Radleys, began to make sense.

22

Early the following morning we settled down to planning our brief visit to Paris. Frances and Lexi had done the sights before, but I hadn't and time was short. I was invited to nominate two places of interest. My choice of the Eiffel Tower was vetoed by Lexi. It was boring, overrated and best viewed from afar. Notre-Dame, my second choice, was acceptable, but no one could visit Paris without seeing the Louvre. In the end we found ourselves deposited at the Louvre by Lexi to look around while she went shopping. She left us instructions to meet her at a particular café in the Champs Elysées at one. When we arrived, footsore from pounding through the galleries, we found her ensconced at a table with Lawrence, an empty bottle of champagne between them. Frances later explained that Lawrence attended an architects' conference in Paris every year at this time and regularly met up with them, although Lexi seemed to present his arrival as a fortuitous coincidence. 'Look who's here!' she exclaimed as we threaded our way between the tables towards them. 'Surprise surprise!' said Lawrence, raising his glass. He was wearing city clothes – a blue and white striped shirt with a dark suit, the jacket of which was slung over his chair. It occurred to me that he wasn't bad looking – for a man of forty-something, anyway. His face was tanned; when he stopped smiling small white creases showed at the corners of his eyes and mouth as if he even sunbathed with a smile on his face.

'Shall we find somewhere cheaper to eat?' said Lexi, gathering up her bags, but Lawrence waved her down, and, summoning one of the roving waiters, ordered four bowls of mussels, some wine and two Cokes for us. I was beginning to get used to having decisions made for me. It was what happened when someone else was paying the bill.

'How do you like Paris, Abigail?' Lawrence asked.

I replied that I'd been here less than a day but so far liked it very much.

'I've been coming here for thirty years,' he said . 'It's my favourite place.' The mussels arrived just as he was in the middle of an extended account of his first trip to Paris at the age of sixteen. 'It was an exchange visit organised by school – considered quite adventurous in those days. My opposite number was a lad called Alain who was as hopeless at English as I was at French. We spent the entire two weeks grinning at each other and shrugging. The father was a dour little civil servant who was out at work all day and couldn't take us anywhere interesting, and Madame didn't speak a word of English – well, she didn't seem to speak at all as far as I could see, she just produced this endless, alien food at every meal. It was absolutely miserable. But he had this cousin called Delphine who *did* know a little English, so they dragged her over from Versailles to talk to me and show me Paris – I think they were feeling bad that I was obviously not enjoying myself – and of course I fell madly in love with her and the whole visit was suddenly transformed. And then the fortnight was up and I had to come home and that was that.'

'Didn't you keep in touch?' demanded Frances, letter-writer of distinction.

'We did write for a couple of years, and then the letters stopped, so I finally wrote to Alain and asked after her, just in passing, and I got a letter back saying they were all devastated because she had drowned in the Seine – trying to rescue a dog apparently.'

'Oh!' said Frances. Neither of us had expected the story to take so tragic a turn. If it had been Mr Radley telling it we would have suspected fabrication.

Our bowls of mussel debris were carried off and replaced by four trays of snails in garlic butter, and four crochet hooks. I closed my eyes. I had already filled up on the bread.

'No way,' said Frances. (It was she after all who had to be given a vegetarian option during the dissection class in Biology.)

'Oh for heaven's sake,' said Lexi, selecting a shell and

starting to gouge. 'You'll eat a steak but you won't eat a snail. What's the difference?'

'I've trodden on snails,' said Frances. 'I've seen the stuff that oozes out of them. But if my inconsistency bothers you I'll give up steak as well.'

'All right, all right,' said Lexi, outmanoeuvred. They were all looking at me to see what I would do. I picked up my crochet hook. Loyalty was all very well, but I couldn't be expected to take up all of Frances' battles, and it would have looked a bit ungracious after Lawrence's hospitality. When next a tureen of casseroled guinea-fowl arrived at the table I could feel the sweat begin to break out on my brow. I eased the button of my skirt undone and the zip burst open like an overripe fruit.

The afternoon wore on. It looked as though Notre-Dame would go unvisited. Still, I had my catalogue of the Louvre as a souvenir of Paris to take home. I had wanted an ice cream and felt obliged to break into one of my hundred-franc notes by buying some item of cultural relevance of which father would approve.

Frances' obstreperous mood seemed to have set in for the day. Apart from her abhorrence of the snails she made no comment about the food, which was delicious, even to my untested palate. When Lawrence lit up a cigarette between courses, she flapped the smoke away irritably, and when Lexi reached for a second glass of wine she let out a great hiss of disapproval. And then just as the dessert trolley approached – usually the highlight of the meal for Frances – she suddenly jumped up and said, 'Look, there's a phone here – I could call home and check everything's okay.' And she started rooting for her purse.

'Not just at this minute surely?' said Lexi.

'Why not?' said Frances. 'I want to see if Growth's all right. And find out if Dad's sold any paintings. I won't be long.' And she strode off in the direction of the booth. Lexi shrugged, and then pushed her own chair back. 'I suppose I'd better go and have a word, too,' she said. 'Or they'll feel neglected.'

'Do you mind if I seize the moment?' Lawrence asked when they'd gone, indicating his cigarettes. He offered me one, which I turned down, before lighting up and leaning back in his seat and beaming at me as if we were confederates, old buddies. We did have something in common of course – we weren't Radleys.

'She's a funny girl, Frances,' he said.

'In what way?' I asked guardedly.

'She's an odd combination – wayward and yet judgemental. You wouldn't think the two would go together. She was completely out of control as a child – always running off and spending the night on Highbury Fields. Lexi was convinced she was going to go right off the rails. But now the judgemental side seems to be taking over. I'm willing to bet she'll end up a pillar of the community – a district nurse or a magistrate or something. You wait and see.'

I wasn't sure if I should defend Frances from the charge of impending respectability. It was hard to tell with Lawrence whether or not an insult was intended. 'She wants to be a film star,' I said. 'Or a dog-handler.'

'Mind you,' Lawrence went on, 'between ourselves the whole family isn't exactly what you'd call normal. Apart from Lexi. Rad's an odd bloke – intelligent all right, but there's a sort of coldness there, don't you think?'

'I don't know.' It felt scandalously disloyal to be discussing the Radleys while their backs were turned, but at the same time I riveted. I never normally had the chance to see them through someone else's eyes. And although I had been ready to leap to Rad's defence the moment his name was mentioned, Lawrence's comment wasn't easy to dismiss. There *was* something a little chilly about Rad. I had noticed it when he was acting, and had wished he was more like the character he was playing.

'I can't imagine how he and Mr Radley get along on holiday together. They're so different.'

'Oh, *Michael*,' said Lawrence, as if this was a whole new subject which would need lengthy consideration. 'There's certainly rivalry there – all on Michael's side of course. His trouble is he hates the fact that he's no longer twenty. He likes hanging around with young people, but at the same time he's madly jealous. He did have a decent job once, did you know that? At the Department of the Environment. But now, what is it? School caretaker? Bell-boy? Night-watchman? I forget.'

'Pizza delivery,' I said.

'Christ,' said Lawrence, shaking his head.

'But it's painting he's really interested in, isn't it?' I don't know why I felt obliged to stick up for him.

'Have you seen his paintings?' said Lawrence.

I nodded. 'Some.'

He tutted sadly. 'I've told him they're absolutely putrid, and he agrees, but he will keep on. He thinks it's solely a matter of persistence: if he splashes enough paint on to enough canvases eventually he'll produce something decent. But you don't want to take too much notice of his helplessness. I'm convinced it's an act. Left to himself he'd be as competent as anybody. It's all designed to . . .'

I never did find out what it was designed to do, as Lexi and Frances reappeared and Lawrence changed tack smartly. 'I didn't order pudding as Abigail was already bursting out of her skirt and you two weren't here, so I've just asked for coffee,' he said. 'Everything all right at home?'

'It's been raining all the time, so Dad hasn't been able to take any of his paintings around in the Spitfire,' said Frances, 'but he's entered one of his pictures of Mum in a national portrait competition.'

'He says he's submitted it in the name of Lazarus Ohene because it sounds more convincing than Michael Radley,' said Lexi.

'Doesn't it make you feel creepy – all those judges and people seeing what you look like with no clothes on?' asked Frances.

'Not particularly,' said Lexi. 'It's not an especially good likeness, if you remember. It's the "blue and bloated" one.'

'Oh.'

'Goodness, is that the time?' said Lexi, glancing at the

waiter's watch as he poured the coffee. 'I'm afraid Notre-Dame has had it for today. Will Sacré Coeur do instead? We can walk there from the hotel this evening.'

Next to us a group of French teenagers had just finished eating and was about to disperse. The departees were orbiting the table giving and receiving two kisses on each cheek.

'These continental farewells can take all day,' said Lawrence as we stood up to go. 'Consider yourselves kissed.' And he waved us off before sitting back down again and taking out his newspaper. We were on the Metro, heading back to Montmartre, when Lexi realised she had left her sunglasses behind.

'Oh damn,' she said, taking off her red straw hat and tipping the contents of her handbag into it. 'They were my best ones.' As she rifled through lipsticks, powder compacts, wallets, combs and pieces of paper, we offered to go back to the café but she shook her head.

'Perhaps Lawrence will notice and pick them up,' suggested Frances.

Back at the hotel Lexi lay on the bed with her hands across her chest like a knight on a tomb; Frances wrote up her journal and I settled down to read my Louvre catalogue to discover that I had picked up the Dutch language version by mistake.

I was woken in the early hours by the sound of two men brawling outside the window. Clientele from the cinema opposite, inflamed by the piggy perversions, no doubt. Frances remained comatose beside me. I dragged myself over the lip of the bed, suddenly desperate for the loo. As my eyes grew accustomed to the dark I could see that Lexi's bed was empty. I lay awake for some time after that, listening and waiting, but my eyes soon felt heavy and I let myself slip off. When I woke finally at seven Lexi was already up and packing, the lost sunglasses perched on the crown of her head.

23

Dear Mum, Dad and Granny

I hope you are all well and that everything is okay at home. I'm having a lovely time and Mrs Radley is looking after me very well.

Paris was great – we went to the Louvre and had lunch on the Champs Elysées with a friend of Mrs Radley. He paid. I am learning lots of new French words. The drive down to Menton was very long and hot. We stopped off for one night in a place called Beaune. The hotel room was so tiny and hot that we had to have all the windows open and I got badly bitten by mosquitoes. They seemed to leave Frances and her mum alone – I'm obviously tastier. I've eaten lots of interesting food – mussels, snails, quails and a steak which Frances said was cheval, *but I think she was joking. Menton is very pretty. There are 324 steps up to our villa and we always seem to be going either up or down them at midday when the sun is just about overpowering. The calamine lotion is coming in useful. You can't get a car through the village. Everyone seems to ride these little scooters – sometimes with whole families on the back. From the balcony of the villa we can just see Monte Carlo in the distance. Last night there were fireworks over the bay. The sea is amazingly blue. Nothing like Bognor. In the evenings we sit on the balcony and read or play cards or go for a walk down into the village. Tomorrow we are starting the drive back. We're meeting Mr Radley and Rad in Arras. That should be fun. I've only spent 125 francs of the money you gave me – mostly on ice cream. You'd think with all this food I'd have put on weight, but I still look like a twig – a red twig.*

lots of love,
Abigail.

Dear Beatrice

We spent last night in a place called something like Bone. The hotel room was minute and boiling hot – I spent most of the night sitting in the bath letting cold water in and out. Blush kept leaping up to swat mosquitoes. In the morning she had thirty-five bites on her legs and was feeling mightily sorry for herself.

I don't know, but there seem to be more steps this year. Perhaps they've raised the villa or lowered the beach or something. It's a bit too hot to sunbathe (not for Mum, of course, whose bikini top hasn't made an appearance yet). By the time you've got yourself oiled and in position you're in such a lather you have to go and swim to cool off. Blush's back and shoulders are bright red. We dabbed calamine all over her last night and now she looks like a bit of salami. There's a sort of raft about thirty metres out in the bay for diving off and there are always several bronzed frogs posing on it. I went out to it a few times on my own today – Blush can't swim and won't go out of her depth. I tried to teach her but every time she took her feet off the bottom she panicked and went under.

After supper, which was just the rest of the baguette and brie from lunch and a peach, Blush and I walked down into the village to the bar for a Coke. It wasn't long before a couple of French guys who I recognised from the raft this morning started leering at us across the tables. We ignored them, but a few minutes later they'd moved to a closer table and whenever I had to walk past them to go to the loo or get a drink they would make some comment in creaky English. Anyway they eventually came over and we did our best to communicate with a common vocabulary of about fifty words. The better looking of the two, Georges, offered me a ride on his moped, so we went haring around the village on that, dodging the dog turds, while Blush and the other one, Max, who had a squiffy eye, sat on the wall outside the bar waiting for us. When we pulled up they were in exactly the same positions as when we'd left. Afterwards Blush said neither of them had been able to think of a thing to say – in any language – and it had been totally excruciating. *'You could have practised your subjunctive on him,' I said. When it was time to leave Georges sort of fell on me and tried to kiss me, but I mumbled something about having a boyfriend back home who would be jealous. It wasn't a complete lie as I regard myself as eternally wedded to Nicky even though he hasn't yet shown any sign of returning my passion. Max didn't try anything with Blush, which was as well, as from the looks she was giving him he'd probably have got a good slap. She didn't say much on the way back here. I think she's in a strop.*

Holiday diary. Day 10

Note: Don't go to any more bars with Frances: bad for morale.

Last night after supper we told Lexi we were going for a walk, and her last words were 'Don't go into that bar in the village – it's always full of rough-looking boys', at which Frances perked up visibly. Naturally we made straight for the bar and found ourselves a table and Frances began her usual routine, familiar from the school bus stop, of keeping up a conversation with me at what I call performance pitch, at the same time scanning the room to see what effect she was having. It didn't take her long to settle on two French blokes who were minding their own business over the other side of the bar. After several trips to the loo, which involved squeezing past their table and knocking one of their beers over, she managed to get talking to them. One of the two was quite attractive, in an unshaven sort of way. He fancied Frances. The other one wasn't – in fact he was rather alarming-looking, with a wandering eye that was forever glancing over my shoulder, as if in pursuit of a more interesting object. He fancied Frances too. She wasn't the least bit interested in either of them – only that afternoon she had been bewailing her failure to ensnare Nicky.

The following day, the last of our stay in Menton, Georges and Max, undeterred by our frigidity, turned up on the beach where Lexi and Frances were giving themselves a final grilling. Itching all over with prickly heat and sunburn, I had commandeered the only shade for miles and skulked like a lizard in a cleft in a rock. They hailed us cheerfully and began to pick their way towards us across the stones, at which point

Lexi, who was trying to tan those parts that seldom see sunlight and was lying on her back with her arms above her head and her bent legs turned outwards like a frog on a dissecting slab, rolled over and reached for her bikini top.

Georges was carrying nothing but a rolled towel and a Walkman which was clipped to the front of his trunks; Max had a children's plastic football which we started idly batting to one another until a strange, netless, teamless, *pointless* volleyball game developed amongst the four of us. As we stood there in the ferocious sunlight, virtually naked, hitting the ball back and forth, back and forth, I had a curious feeling of kinship with prehistoric man. Even in the most primitive and savage societies people must have felt a need to stand in circles and throw stones or even skulls to one another, just to pass the time.

'Frances, get out of my sun,' Lexi would complain if her daughter's shadow fell even momentarily across her, at the same time swatting her with a copy of *The Times* which she had driven almost to Monte Carlo to track down.

When the heat became unbearable and I could feel the rash across my shoulders beginning to tingle, we ran into the water, shrieking and gasping. Georges, Frances and Max immediately struck out for the raft, on which there were already several bodies, prone like seals on a rock, while I loitered in the shallows enjoying the feeling of wet hair on my sunburn. Frances won the race easily. I could see her hauling herself out on to the raft. She gave me a victorious wave, before a hand rose out of the sea and closed round her ankle and she was dragged in again. It seemed an age before her head bobbed up. I was already on my feet, ready to panic, but there she was, flicking diamonds from her wet hair and laughing.

On the way back to the villa Frances hung back, pretending to shake grit out of her sandals until Lexi was out of earshot. 'They want us to go for a midnight swim tonight,' she said. 'What do you reckon?' Her eyes were bright with excitement. I could tell she had already made her decision.

'I can't see your mum agreeing, somehow.'

'Oh God, I wasn't going to tell Mum,' replied Frances, shocked at the suggestion. 'We could just slip out. She's used to sleeping through Dad arriving home at all hours – she'll never wake up.'

'But we hardly know them – they might be weirdos.'

'They're weird all right, but I don't think they're dangerous.'

'Look, I don't think we should go. Supposing your mum does wake up – she'll be *furious*. She'll forgive you because you're her daughter, but she won't think very much of me.'

Frances conceded there was something in this argument. 'Besides,' I added, 'it's all very well for you – Georges is at least good-looking. But Max is a hideous cross-eyed dwarf. And even he doesn't fancy me.'

'That's not very kind,' said Frances. 'He might be a really nice person underneath.'

'Yes, but how are we ever going to find out, with his English and my French?'

'Oh, okay, we won't go,' she said sulkily, but a moment later she cheered up as if the whole subject was forgotten.

I started to have my suspicions over supper when she suggested a game of cards rather than a trip to the bar for our final evening's entertainment, but it was the extreme insouciance with which she proposed getting an early night, and the agitation with which she watched my protracted preparations for bed that clinched it. She was intending to go without me. Wounded by this betrayal I decided to thwart her by staying awake, but my exertions in the volleyball game must have sapped my strength as I fell asleep almost instantly and when I awoke Frances was snoring gently in the bed beside me.

I was beginning to think I had misjudged her, but the moment she showed her head above the sheet I burst out laughing: above one ear her hair stuck up in a great crest, giving her the appearance of a bedraggled cockatiel. She had obviously crept back into bed with damp, unbrushed hair which had dried as she lay on it.

'Where did you get to last night, then?' I asked.

She was a little surprised to be caught out, and was obviously considering a straight denial before the urge to brag took over, and a smug expression settled on her face. 'Italy,' she whispered.

'What?'

'It's only a few miles to the border – Georges and I went on his moped to Ventimiglia.'

'For God's sake, Frances,' I snapped. 'What if something had happened? He could have just dumped you there – I mean anything could have happened.'

She brushed this off. 'No, he's all right. We just went swimming.' She saw my sceptical expression. 'Honest. Nothing happened. He didn't try anything.' There was a pause. 'Well, he *tried*,' she conceded, 'but he didn't get anywhere.'

'I knew you were planning something,' I said with some bitterness.

'You could have come,' she said. 'Only you didn't seem that keen when I mentioned it yesterday.'

It was true that I hadn't shown any enthusiasm for midnight bathing, but *Italy*: that was something quite different. I was suddenly so jealous, so frustrated, that I could feel my eyes beginning to smart, and I had to put my head down and pretend to be rummaging for my washbag so that Frances wouldn't see me blinking back tears. In the shower I let the water burst over my head like a hail of arrows. How at the advanced age of fifteen could I be so upset about something so trivial? It wasn't even as though I liked Georges. It was irrational. It was petty. But our feelings often know truths which our reason can't see: I was crying because all my experience of happiness came through Frances, but the equivalent was not true for her. When the time came, sooner or later, she would do without me very well.

24

We had arranged to meet Rad and Mr Radley at their usual hotel in Arras. It looked on to the Grande Place, which on the night we arrived was the site of a travelling funfair. Half a dozen dodgem cars parked in a minute arena beneath a row of flashing lights, paint-peeled stalls selling doughnuts and *frites* cooked in the same fat, and a rifle range offering a selection of grubby cuddly toys as its star prizes were the foremost of its attractions.

'Oh hell,' said Lexi, as disco music began to thump from a set of speakers covered with a tarpaulin. 'We'll get no sleep tonight.'

I had been looking forward to seeing Rad for the entire holiday, an anticipated pleasure which had to be kept to myself. Although Frances was about as candid as a person could be, and kept me minutely informed of the progress of her infatuations, I had always guarded my secret closely. In spite of her assumption that Rad must be universally admired, she would, I was sure, view my rather more concentrated interest in him as intolerably presumptuous.

From my point of view there was an added poignancy to this meeting: it would be the last time I would see Rad before he went off to university. He would be gone for ten weeks at a time, returning only for vacations or the odd weekend, and in the meantime there would be girls there, girls who had Done It no doubt, and who would be living in the same hall, on the same landing, and dropping in for coffee at any hour of the day or night to discuss Nietzsche. Envisioning this always made me feel slightly giddy and breathless, but I comforted myself with the thought that he would not be there for ever, and that whatever these imagined rivals might enjoy by way of beauty or intelligence, they would not have my patience. It was just a matter of waiting for him to recognise me, and when he did I would be ready and it would all have been worthwhile.

The object of this meticulously planned passivity was sitting at the bar reading an Ordnance Survey map of the Somme when we walked in. He slid off his barstool as soon as he saw us and came to help with our cases. He kissed Lexi and Frances and then sort of twitched in my direction but obviously thought the better of it and just gave me a nod and a smile. Perhaps it was just as well – last time we had had skin to skin contact he had left a scorch mark on my forehead.

'Where's your dad?' said Lexi, looking round.

'Just getting changed. He tipped a whole plate of *oeufs à la neige* into his lap at supper.' He dragged more stools up to the bar.

'How's it been?' asked Lexi sympathetically. 'I bet you've been bearing up marvellously.'

'We haven't had any catastrophes,' Rad said, 'but he's been driving me nuts. I'm definitely inter-railing next year. I know he's a creature of habit, but I swear he's getting worse with age – he always wants to go to the same places. I tried to tell him that we were hardly any distance from Agincourt, and that the field of Waterloo was only about an hour's drive, but he flatly refused to go. So we've done the same old tour as every other year: Ypres, Beaumont Hamel, Delville Wood, Thiepval.' He tapped the map in front of him. 'He must have memorised every name on the Menin Gate by now. The only place we've missed out is Vimy Ridge.'

'Poor Rad,' said Lexi soothingly.

'But he's so obsessive,' Rad went on. He had one hand in his hair as if driven to tear clumps of it out. 'There's this chip van in the square at Cambrai that we always stop at on the way down. I don't know why; they're not particularly good chips. But we got held up and when we arrived lunch was over and it was all shut up. And Dad threw the most unbelievable tantrum. I thought he was going to burst into tears and stamp his foot.'

'At least you could drive this time, Rad,' said Frances. 'That must have made it easier.'

159

'We shared the driving,' he admitted. 'I couldn't insist on doing it all. I didn't want to emasculate him.'

Mr Radley appeared in the doorway of the bar still doing up his shirt. 'Ah, bonjour,' he cried, bearing down on us with arms flung out, cuffs flapping.

'Oh God, that's another thing,' Rad whispered to me and Frances as Lexi advanced to meet her husband and kisses were exchanged. 'He always wants to send me into bars and cafés ahead of him so he can come in a few minutes later and do all this "bonjour, bonjour" stuff and slap me on the back. I used to find it funny when I was about twelve, but it's just bloody embarrassing now.'

'Hello girls,' said Mr Radley. 'You look brown, Frances, and Blush you look, er, pink.'

'Rad says you've had a successful trip,' Lexi lied smoothly.

'Well, we've had one or two hitches. That damned chip van in Cambrai. And we haven't managed to get to Vimy yet – I thought we'd go tomorrow . . .'

When, some time later, Lexi announced she was ready for bed, Mr Radley slapped two sets of keys on the bar. 'Rad and I have been sharing, but I booked two rooms for tonight, so what do we want to do? Boys in one, girls in the other? Or are you in with me tonight, Lex?'

'Well, that depends on whether Abigail minds sleeping in the same room as Rad.'

'Oh, she won't mind,' said Mr Radley with great confidence. The two of them often discussed me, affectionately, as if I wasn't there.

'You can't just assume that,' said Lexi. 'Some girls might find it very intimidating.'

'I wouldn't call Rad intimidating – look at him,' said Mr Radley. Rad was almost asleep at the bar, his head resting on his folded arms.

'Who says I'm not intimidating?' Rad protested sleepily, without looking up.

'I didn't mean Rad,' said Lexi. 'I meant that some girls of Abigail's age might be uncomfortable at the thought of sharing with a boy.'

'Well, why don't you ask her?' said Frances, a trifle impatiently.

Mr Radley turned to me. 'Well, Blush?'

'Who me?' I said. 'I'd sort of forgotten I was here.' And they all laughed at that, even Rad, who had sat up. I was in a predicament now. To agree too hastily would be like a slight to Lexi's sensitivity on my behalf. 'I don't really mind,' I said. Mr Radley picked up one set of keys and slid the other across the table towards me.

'I notice no one's asked if *I* mind,' Rad called after his parents' departing backs.

'He's done nothing but moan all week,' said Mr Radley to Lexi loudly on their way out. 'I don't think I'll invite him next year.'

I didn't sleep well. To avoid undressing in front of Rad I had stayed behind in the bar alone for a few minutes on the pretext of writing a postcard home – a transparently trumped up excuse: we would be back within thirty-six hours. By the time I went up the other two were both apparently asleep; a tuft of hair on the pillow was all that was visible of Rad above the sheet. Frances, in the double bed, had managed to work herself across the diagonal, and gentle kicks from me failed to stir her, so I had to be content with curling up in the small triangle of unoccupied mattress. It was a hot night and the windows were closed against the pounding music from the square. Throwing off the covers I lay perspiring into the pillow. Frances, still unrousable, had not shifted over – she had, if anything, edged closer to me. I could feel the heat coming off her body against my back. At half-past one, when the noise from the funfair finally stopped, I slipped out of bed to open the window, setting floorboards, loose as piano keys, creaking and banging under my feet.

'Who's that?' whispered a voice from the corner bed.

'Abigail. I'm just letting some air in.' There was the crack of fused paintwork separating as the window shuddered open, and warm soupy air, faintly redolent of chip fat and cigarette smoke, wafted through the shutters.

'I can't seem to sleep,' said Rad.

'Neither can I.'

'It was that racket out there. And the heat.'

'This should be better.' I fanned the window back and forth a few times to cool my face before getting back into bed. 'We should be able to sleep now,' I said, but the thought of us both lying in the dark, awake, listening to each other's breathing, proved too great a distraction and I remained tired but sleepless until the early hours.

'I don't know what it is with you young girls nowadays,' said Mr Radley as we took our places at the breakfast table the following morning. 'Is the intention to look as ugly as possible? Or is the dowdiness of your clothes meant to be a foil to your beauty?'

Frances and I were at that time disciples of a fashion whose watchword was Sloppy. She was wearing a black T-shirt several sizes too big over a not very clean jersey skirt which reached to her ankles and bagged around the seat and knees when she sat down. I had on a long, shapeless denim tunic, faded almost white by repeated washing, and a green T-shirt which I had attempted to dye black but which had come out the colour of seaweed, and blotchy. Flat shoes and a slouching gait were the necessary accompaniment.

'It doesn't occur to you that you're not the sort of person they're hoping to attract?' suggested Lexi.

'They look all right to me,' said Rad.

'Perhaps we've just got more important things to worry about than our appearance,' said Frances indignantly.

'Such as?' said Mr Radley.

Furrows of concentration appeared on Frances' brow as

she delved in vain for an answer.

'I don't know,' sighed Mr Radley. 'It seems such a waste somehow. It won't be long before you're hideous old hags of forty and it won't matter a damn what you wear.'

'Thank you,' said Lexi.

Mr Radley drew me aside after breakfast as I waited on the landing for Frances to retrieve her camera from the bedroom. There was a flake of croissant on his chin which I longed to brush away, and a further flurry of crumbs down the front of his shirt. He was the messiest eater I had ever seen: the fallout from a single piece of baguette could reach all four corners of the table.

'I suppose you girls have spent all your money on knick-knacks, eh?' he said.

I shook my head – apart from my Dutch language Louvre catalogue I had only bought a T-shirt with the word NICE stamped ambiguously across the chest. (It was destined to have only one outing, when it would be deemed cheap and nasty by mother and thereafter consigned to a bottom drawer.) Lexi had refused any contributions towards food and petrol, so my sheaf of notes was still largely intact.

'Oh, well, in that case you couldn't lend me a hundred francs, could you? Yes? Oh, that's splendid. I've run out and it's not worth cashing another cheque for one day. Actually, better make it two hundred.'

As promised we spent the morning at Vimy Ridge. We had decided to squeeze into one car. Lexi, Frances and I were in the back; Rad was driving. Every few miles Mr Radley would point out another cemetery at the roadside – rows and rows of identical gravestones like so many white teeth rising from the turf.

'Just look, Blush,' Mr Radley said, turning round the

better to catch my expression. 'Thousands of them, just names on stones. And yet every one was once a living, breathing human being – probably just like Rad here – and most of them volunteers, fresh out of school with everything still to come, the brightest and best of their generation.' As the only newcomer to the experience I was singled out to be the recipient of Mr Radley's wisdom and opinions. My ignorance of even the baldest facts about the First World War appalled him. I could just about summon up the dates; Archduke Ferdinand, Haig, Sir John French, Kaiser Wilhelm were just names from the void. They could have been racehorses.

'You don't know when the Battle of the Somme was? Dear God in heaven, what do they teach you at that school? I suppose, living with Frances, I ought to be used to ignorance on that level but, honestly, I expected better of you, Abigail.' I was used to being hectored in this vein by Mr Radley. Anyone who hadn't managed to acquire precisely the same body of knowledge as himself was an object of pity and derision: to know any less was evidence of imbecility; to know more was pointless, sterile, academic.

'If they've never been taught it, how can they know it?' said Lexi reasonably.

'I know, I know, it's their education. If that's not too strong a word for it. Have you read *Goodbye to All That*? No, of course you haven't. It's a great book. I reread it every year. I'll lend you my copy.'

I apologised for my stupidity and said I would certainly read *Goodbye to All That*. 'But I won't borrow it. I'll buy my own copy. If I'm going to take the trouble to read a book, I like to be able to keep it.' I could well imagine what sort of condition Mr Radley's copy would be in. Only that morning at breakfast he had picked Lexi's new hardback biography of Jackie Onassis out of her bag, and finding several of the back pages still uncut had seized his buttery knife and tried to hack them apart.

'You don't want to take too much notice of Dad's version of the war,' said Rad, glancing at me in the driver's mirror.

'He likes to romanticise. He thinks everyone who died at the Front was a poet.'

'It was a romantic war. It was about innocence and sacrifice – concepts which I wouldn't expect your heartless generation to understand. Can you imagine any eighteen-year-olds today rushing off to enlist?'

'Well, that's an advance, surely?' said Rad.

'Look, there's Vimy,' said Mr Radley, glad to duck out of an argument in which he was in danger of being worsted. In the distance in a chiselled-out clearing on the wooded ridge stood a monument like a great white tuning fork against the sky.

The sun was just emerging from behind the only cloud in the sky as Rad pulled into the car-park. Behind barbed-wire fencing I could see shallow snaking trenches, eroded now and smothered in closely cropped grass. Slender fir trees striped the sky. *Entrée interdite: munitions non éclatées*, read the signs.

'They're still finding unexploded shells even now,' said Mr Radley. 'It happens all over here – every year you hear that some poor kid has wandered into the woods and got himself blown up.' He appointed himself my personal tour guide and led me down into the Canadian trenches, preserved with concrete sandbags and duckboards, and made me stand at one of the machine-gun turrets and peer through the hole in the rusty metal at the giant craters which divided us from the German front line not forty yards away.

'Why did they make the trenches zigzag like this?' I asked.

'To stop the Germans firing along the length of the trench if it was captured. Of course it also made carrying stretchers rather difficult.'

It didn't seem possible that we were standing on the site of such carnage. The sun was warm; a gentle breeze was stirring the leaves; the trenches, clean and dry and empty, looked almost cosy; a golden cloud of midges shimmered above our heads; two young boys were rolling down the steep sides of the largest crater shrieking with laughter.

'There can hardly be anyone left alive who remembers all this,' said Mr Radley, pressing himself against the side of the trench to avoid being stampeded by giggling, panting children. 'And when my generation is dead there won't be anyone left who cares.'

'There'll be me,' said Rad, who had caught us up. 'I care. I'm just not morbidly sentimental like you.' By now I was thoroughly used to the adversarial style with which Mr Radley was often addressed by his wife and children and it no longer took me by surprise. I wouldn't be trying it out at home, though.

Frances and Lexi had walked ahead towards the memorial. Frances was cooing and clicking her fingers at a group of skinny sheep which were cropping the hummocks of grass on the ridge. One stopped chewing for a moment and fixed us with a blank stare as we approached.

'Ah, sheep!' cried Mr Radley warmly. 'Symbol of innocence.'

'And stupidity,' said Rad.

The wind was stronger on the ridge, snapping at the French and Canadian flags which stood at the approach to the monument, and whipping my hair into my watering eyes.

'You can see why this was such an important strategic gain,' said Mr Radley, gesturing with his arm. Below and beyond us the plain stretched away, strings of tiny houses dwarfed by volcanic-looking slag heaps. Plumes of white smoke rose from chimney stacks thin as pencils.

'Did any of our family fight in the war?' asked Frances, who had been inspecting the carved names of the dead around the base of the monument.

'No, my dear, you come from a long line of cowards,' said Mr Radley, patting her on the shoulder.

'I can't believe so many people died,' I said, indicating the lists of names that Frances was scrutinising for fallen Radleys.

'That's nothing,' said Rad. 'You should see the Menin Gate. Vimy doesn't really give you any idea of what it would have been like – it's all been smartened up. It looks more like a crazy-golf course than a battlefield. If you want to see some real trenches you should go to Hill 62. There's a fantastic old museum there too.'

'Is it near?' I asked.

'It's in Belgium. Ypres. Do you want to see it? We could get there and back in an afternoon on the motorway.' He seemed suddenly excited at the prospect.

'Well, I don't want to sit in the car for hours just to see another lot of graves and stuff,' said Frances.

'I bet Abigail has had to fit in with what you want to do all holiday,' said Rad. Before I could protest that I wasn't bothered one way or another, Rad was herding everyone back to the car-park, issuing orders. It was all arranged: Frances and Lexi would be dropped back in Arras and the two men and I would drive to Ypres. The fact that they had already visited the place once this week was no deterrent, apparently. Afterwards I would remember this incident as being the first time Rad had ever shown me special consideration that went beyond mere politeness.

Some ten miles the wrong side of Ypres, Mr Radley, who was driving, suddenly leaned across Rad and started rummaging in the glove compartment, sending an avalanche of sweet wrappers on to the floor. 'God, don't you girls ever throw anything in the bin?' he demanded, as the car swerved towards the central reservation. Rad grabbed the wheel. 'That's right – you steer for a minute.' At last he found what he was looking for – a cassette, which he flipped out of its box with one hand while retaking the wheel with the other. 'I thought we'd have some appropriate music – I got Bill to tape this on his fancy machine. Do you know Britten's *War Requiem*? No, of course you don't.' He snapped it into the tape machine and turned the volume up high. After a few minutes of punishing noise, Rad ventured to turn the sound down a fraction.

'What's wrong?' asked Mr Radley. 'Don't you like it?'

'No,' said Rad.

'It sounds a bit slow and dirge-like,' I said.

'Well of course it is, it's a bloody requiem. You don't expect the dance of the sugar-plum fairy. You are a pair of philistines, really. I admit Britten's an acquired taste,' he went on. 'Takes a lot of listening to.'

167

We endured the booming without further comment until the entrance of the tenor singing 'Anthem for Doomed Youth' made it apparent even to Mr Radley that Bill's fancy machine had been taping at half speed. He jabbed the eject button smartly. 'Hmm, seems to be something wrong with the tape,' he muttered, pocketing it. 'I thought it sounded funny.'

We stopped briefly to have a look at Ypres itself. In the cathedral a couple of elderly nuns were having trouble rigging up a new public address system. A length of electric flex was caught on the ledge at the top of a pillar and no amount of twitching would free it. I could see them eyeing their ladder with misgivings. It was propped unsteadily against the pillar, and wobbled when given an experimental push. I suddenly had an image of one of the nuns on top of the ladder like a pirate in a crow's nest, and gave Rad a nudge to share the joke. 'Look,' I said, pointing in their direction. He must have mistaken my motive because he said 'Oh,' and immediately hurried over to help. A moment later he was scrambling up the ladder while the two nuns stood holding the base and looking up fearfully. I felt slightly humbled by this incident, though I wasn't quite sure why.

On the way out I stopped beneath the marble-white figure of Christ with his golden halo of thorns and lit a candle.

'I didn't know you were religious,' said Rad, as I impaled the candle on one of the few unoccupied spikes on the rack which was spattered with molten wax like bird droppings.

'Well, I believe in the crucifixion,' I said.

Rad looked thoughtful. 'Yes, it's just what would happen.'

'You're an atheist, aren't you?' I said – a daring word to utter given the surroundings.

'No, I wouldn't say that,' he replied, holding the door open for me. 'I'm just a Nice Person. Non-practising.'

As we drove through the Menin Gate Mr Radley slowed down to point out the names carved over every surface. 'See all those, Blush. Those are just the ones they couldn't find to bury.'

'Why couldn't they find them? How could so many

people go missing?' I asked, bewildered.

'Well, for instance, if you were hit by a shell the . . . er . . . pieces might not be all that large,' he said.

The museum at Hill 62 turned out to be a couple of damp and draughty rooms at the back of a bar. Glass cabinets containing German helmets, guns, swords, badges, and pocket watches, none of them labelled, ran along one wall. On the floor beneath were heaped rusty shell cases, field glasses, fragments of barbed wire, bottles and a collection of single boots, crushed, rotten and still caked in dried mud. A dressmaker's dummy with a mannequin's head on top stood in the middle of the room dressed in a green overcoat and gas mask and chipped helmet. On a trestle table was arranged a collection of wooden contraptions containing sepia transparencies. Rad immediately sat down at one of the boxes and started to crank the handle round. He beckoned me over and I took his place, peering through the lens and watching the pictures rise into focus and then into 3D. There was a group of soldiers leaning against the side of a trench, holding tin mugs and staring out at me with unsmiling faces and glazed, bulbous eyes; a partly decomposed corpse sitting propped in a dugout as if having a rest. The next picture was of a dead horse in a tree.

Rad had wandered into the back room which contained still more unclassified militaria: guns, shell casings and more single boots. In the passage connecting the two rooms was, of all things, a plastic bubble-gum machine. Mr Radley appeared at my elbow, waiting until Rad was out of earshot before saying, 'I might as well wait for you in the bar. No hurry – take your time.'

In the woods just outside was an area of preserved trenches. These looked altogether less cosy than the grass and concrete recreations at Vimy. The soil was clay here, and was sticky and wet, even on a warm summer's day. Sheets of rusty corrugated iron were propped against the walls, and there was a smell of damp earth and rotting vegetation in the air. Rad was walking along the trench, biting his nails with an air of concentration. He and Frances were inveterate nail-biters; Frances sometimes bit hers so severely that they bled and then she would appear at school with plasters on each stump like a victim of frostbite.

At my feet was a perfect circle of large coffee-coloured mushrooms with skin like suede. I knelt down to feel one, and as I stroked the surface a tiny puff of spores exploded from the gills.

'Abigail,' said an urgent voice and as I looked up sharply there was a click and Rad lowered his camera, smiling. 'Thank you,' he said.

'I had my mouth open,' I protested, flattered and pleased even so.

'Ah, but you looked so natural. And the light was falling really nicely on those toadstools.'

'Oh, well, I'm glad the fungus was showing its best side,' I said, standing up and brushing mud from the hem of my dress.

Rad wound the film back and flipped the roll out of the back of the camera. 'It was the last shot anyway,' he said. 'It probably won't come out.'

So he had just taken it to use up the last exposure; not as a memento to take up to Durham and pine over: well, that would teach me to be vain. 'Are you looking forward to university?' I said, idly decapitating one of the mushrooms with the toe of one shoe.

'Yes and no. The course looks good, and the hall of residence is a sort of castle, but it's the thought of Fresher's Week and having to be sociable that's a bit intimidating.' He paused. 'And there's things about home I'll miss. I mean people, not things. In a way I wish I'd chosen London, like Nicky. But I suppose it will be good to get away from Mum and Dad. Dad especially.' He looked around in some alarm. 'That's a point – where *is* Dad?' I pointed towards the bar and was surprised to see his face fall. 'Oh God. How long has he been in there?' he asked.

'Since we arrived,' I said. Through the doorway I could see Mr Radley sitting at one of the furthermost tables, three empty beer bottles in front of him, in an attitude of deep contentment. He caught my eye and beckoned us over.

'Oh shit,' I heard Rad say under his breath. He looked furious.

'What's the matter?' I asked, but he just shook his head.

'Hello, all finished in there? Have a drink – I'm paying,' said Mr Radley waving my two-hundred franc note.

'I'll just have a coffee as I'll be driving back,' said Rad venomously.

'Oh, yes, good idea. That means I can have another beer. This Belgian stuff's marvellous,' his father said, summoning the waiter.

When the bill arrived and Mr Radley settled up there was only a couple of francs change which he left on the table. 'Terrible exchange rate,' he said, catching Rad's expression. 'They've got you over a barrel.'

'Inside a barrel in your case,' said Rad, and stalked out to the car.

Mr Radley smiled at me sheepishly. 'I think I'll stretch out in the back on the way home if that's all right with you. All this bright sunlight makes me drowsy.'

So Rad and I sat in the front, and he drove and I read the map and got us lost at a diversion near Armentières, and Rad got impatient – just like a proper married couple. Finally, when gentle snores from the back seat indicated that Mr Radley was asleep, Rad said, 'Sorry I got annoyed back there. It wasn't you. I'm all wound up because of Dad. I promised Mum I wouldn't let him drink, and the minute my back's turned . . .'

My God, I thought. So that's it. He's an alcoholic.

'He's not an alcoholic,' said Rad, and I blushed to have such a legible mind. 'He doesn't often drink, but when he starts he just keeps on until . . .' he trailed off. 'Mum's going to be furious. The thing is, I don't know where he got the money: I've been looking after all the cash.' I blushed again and looked down at my knees.

'He borrowed it from me,' I confessed. 'I didn't know . . .'

'Oh, he's such a furtive little bastard,' said Rad, a trifle loudly, for the figure in the back grunted and stirred in his sleep. 'Here,' he continued in a lower voice, easing his wallet from the pocket of his jeans and tossing it across to me. 'You'd better take it out of there. He'll never remember to pay you back, and I know you'll be too polite to remind him.'

Mr Radley woke up just outside Béthune, greatly refreshed and thoroughly pleased with our afternoon's jaunt. Once awake, though, he found he didn't like sitting in the back as it made him feel excluded, but insisted on leaning as far forward as possible, with his arms draped around the backs of our seats and his head jammed between us.

'Have I missed anything while I've been asleep?' he asked. 'What have you been talking about?'

'You,' said Rad.

Mr Radley gave me a beery smile. 'You don't want to take too much notice of Rad,' he said in a confidential tone. 'He's all right at abstract things, like trigonometry, but when it comes to finer feelings he's a bit deficient.'

'You sad old man,' said Rad mildly.

Lexi and Frances were already dressed for dinner, painted and scented and sitting in the bar when we arrived back at the hotel. Frances was writing her journal and Lexi was reading her buttered biography of Jackie Onassis. They had been shopping for shoes but had returned disappointed. Determined not to come back empty-handed Lexi had bought Rad a shirt.

'You didn't need to buy me any clothes, Mum. I've got plenty,' he said, looking at the new acquisition with dismay. It was orange.

'Yes, and look at the state of them,' she said, pointing to his leached grey T-shirt which had been washed so often it was now impossible to guess what colour it might once have been.

'There's nothing wrong with this. I can't just chuck things out because they're old.'

'Don't try and make a virtue of your slovenliness,' said his father. 'Your lack of vanity is a form of vanity. We're not fooled.'

While I was changing for dinner there was a knock at the door and Mr Radley walked in. 'Sorry,' he said, putting one hand over his eyes as I dived for a towel. 'Here's that book I promised to lend you,' and he slung an old Penguin copy of *Goodbye to All That* on the bed. Closer inspection confirmed my misgivings – an elastic band held it together, and when I tried to open it the pages sprang out and the whole thing collapsed like a deck of cards.

The atmosphere at dinner was strained. Lexi shot her husband a surprised look as he beckoned the wine waiter over, then raised her eyebrows to Rad, who shrugged back. Frances broke the silence as two bottles of red wine were brought to the table, the waiter uncorking them briskly as though wringing chickens' necks.

'Who are these for?' she demanded, glaring at her father.

'Last night of the holiday. I thought we should celebrate,' he wheedled, splashing wine into Lexi's glass before turning the bottle on me like a loaded gun. I wavered. Rad and Frances both had their hands palms down over their glasses. 'Don't take any notice of those two wowsers,' he said. After what Rad had told me I didn't want to give Mr Radley any encouragement, but then I reasoned that if I said yes there would be less left for him. So I let him pour me a glassful, but resolved not to drink it.

Lexi was dithering over the menu. During the holiday I had noticed that she was incapable of ordering a meal without interrogating the waiter as to its likely condition. 'Does that come with a sauce? Is it a *coarse* pâté? Is it very rich/ sweet/salty?' Likewise hardly a dish was ordered that was not sent back to the kitchen for some emendation: it was too rare, or overdone; too cold, or not cold enough. It wasn't that Lexi was a fussy eater: it was simply a demonstration of self-confidence – a refusal to be meek and accommodating and British. My upbringing had taught me to view this behaviour as anti-social: on the rare occasions my parents went out for a meal they would sooner choke back raw liver than resort to such an extremity. Finally her decision was made. She had opted for the cheapest menu, perhaps as a rebuke to her husband who had not only chosen the *menu gastronomique*, but had selected only those dishes which carried supplements.

Mr Radley was a great believer in shared eating and would shamelessly lean over and spear interesting morsels from everyone else's plates, and force us in turn to sample his own dinner.

'Get off,' said Frances irritably, flicking a snail back on to his plate with a clatter. 'Lawrence has already tried to make me eat those disgusting things once this holiday.' There was a moment's pause.

'Oh, he turned up again, did he?' said Mr Radley. He laughed indulgently. 'Faithful old Lawrence.' For a minute or two there was nothing but the sound of cutlery on china. Oh ho, I thought. Tension. Eventually Mr Radley broke the silence.

'And how did you like Paris, Blush? Your first time, wasn't it?' And before I had a chance to reply he had already started telling me how he liked it instead. 'It's a wonderful city. Second only to Rome, in my view. I'll show you Rome one day,' he promised. 'How old are you?'

'Fifteen.'

'It's taken you fifteen years to get to Paris. Let's say it takes another fifteen to get to Rome.' He looked at his watch. 'I'll meet you at eight o'clock on 23 August 1996 on the Spanish Steps, under Keats's window.'

This seemed unlikely. 'All right,' I said.

'She doesn't believe me!' he exclaimed to the rest of the table.

'Well, she's not stupid,' said Lexi.

As Mr Radley was having more courses than the rest of us we had to sit and watch him tackling his *moules*, which he did noisily and with great enthusiasm, as though he would have liked to cram in the whole lot, shells and all.

Frances started to explain to Rad the rules of a game called Ten Questions which we had devised on the journey down, to which he kept throwing up objections, while Mr Radley was swabbing out the bottom of his bowl with a piece of baguette. He made such a mess that the waiter, with his hand-held table sweeper, proved quite unequal to the task of clearing up and had to retire, defeated. Mr Radley thanked him effusively for his efforts. He always grovelled to waiters, perhaps in the hope of bigger portions or better treatment. Lexi, on the other hand, treated functionaries of all kinds as though invisible – unless she was complaining about something, when she would become overpoweringly civil.

'So you have to think of ten questions you would ask which would help you decide who to marry,' Frances was saying. 'My first one would be "Do you like dogs?" Blush's was "Who is the greatest composer?" and yours might be something like "Who is the greatest philosopher?"'

'But I don't want to get married,' Rad objected.

'No,' said Frances patiently, 'you just have to imagine the sort of questions which might be helpful in discovering your ideal partner.'

'I don't believe in the concept of an ideal partner. It's just a romantic myth.'

'It's just a game, Rad,' said Frances. 'Can't you play along?'

'You mean suspend my intelligence?' asked Rad.

Mr Radley choked on his wine. 'So *pompous!*' he spluttered, wiping his eyes. 'Do you think that's a Radley trait, or is that down to your side?' he asked Lexi. 'Anyway,' he went on, wagging a finger at Rad, 'I don't see why you should be so cynical about marriage with our example before you.' And he put an arm around Lexi's shoulder and gave her a blokeish squeeze which she shrugged away irritably.

'If Nicky doesn't notice me soon,' said Frances, oblivious to the deteriorating atmosphere at the table, 'I'm going to give up and marry for money.'

'You could do worse,' said Lexi. 'After all, one in three couples who marry for love discover their mistake.'

'You make yourself too available, Frances,' said her father. 'Everyone likes the taste of chocolate, but you wouldn't want to be force-fed boxes of the stuff.'

'I would,' said Frances. 'I sometimes dream about it.'

'That's another thing – you eat too much chocolate. Nicky might prefer skinny girls like Blush – have you thought of that?'

Frances and I were indignant and mortified in our turn. Lexi, champion of the female form in all its varieties, pitched in: 'That sort of remark is extremely offensive,' she said as if ticking off a naughty schoolboy.

'I didn't mean to be offensive,' said Mr Radley in an injured tone. 'A lot of men like a girl with a bit of meat on her. I was just saying Nicky might not.'

The meal proceeded in uneasy silence, punctuated by the occasional breezy remark from Mr Radley. These attempts to restart conversation were met by a deathly hush from the rest of the table. I kept my head down and concentrated on the food, as far as my diminished appetite would allow: my parents did not do this sort of thing. Politeness was everything to them.

When the dessert trolley rolled up Frances chose the richest, creamiest pudding available, a gesture whose defiance was easy to miss. Lexi and I followed suit with proper disregard for our figures. Mr Radley was languishing over his supplementary cheese course. He drained the dregs of the last wine bottle and then, seeing my still full glass, seized it and said, 'You're not going to drink this, are you?' and tipped it into his own.

'I think we should get an early night as we've a long journey tomorrow,' said Lexi firmly, as the last plates were cleared away to reveal a stencilled pattern of crumbs and debris around Mr Radley's plate.

'Good idea,' he said. 'You go on up to bed. I think I'll have a quick *dégustif* in one of those bars in the square.' And, to Lexi's fury, he sauntered out into the darkness, humming cheerfully.

At midnight I was woken by a tap on the door. It opened a

chink, sending a wand of light across my face, and Lexi's voice whispered, 'Rad, can you come here? I need help.' I waited until he had slipped out before creeping after him. At the end of the passage he and Lexi were trying to push open the loo door far enough for Rad to be able to squeeze himself through the gap. Mr Radley had fallen off the seat and was now either asleep or unconscious, wedged between the pedestal and the door. After a few minutes Rad reappeared half supporting, half dragging his father. I shrank back into the doorway as they passed and found Frances at my shoulder. 'Go back to bed,' she said coldly. 'They don't need you.' And I realised that what I had witnessed that evening was not an isolated incident, but had happened before, was perhaps as much a part of family ritual as the visit to the trenches.

I returned to an enthusiastic welcome from my parents: my presence would serve as a welcome diversion from my grand-mother's attentions. Both of them sought me out separately to tell me how much I'd been missed. I suppose my holiday had given them a foretaste of what life would be like when I left home in a few years' time. Endless days of unrewarded servitude beckoned. Since her arrival Granny had applied herself to becoming as helpless and dependent as possible in case the arrangement should prove only temporary.

The morning after my return I was in the front room searching through the bureau for her missing address book. It contained barely half a dozen names that were not scored through and annotated with a chilling 'D', and she could not read it anyway, but her agitation on mislaying it was such that the house was in the process of being ransacked, room by room, in order to find it. I had just turned up an old Post Office account book in my name which still had two pounds in and was practising my seven-year-old signature, in the hope of cashing it in one day, when I heard the jaws of the letter box clang shut and a parcel fall on to the mat. The parcel was addressed to me and contained a new paperback

Goodbye to All That, inscribed with admirable economy: *To Abigail from Rad.* I had not even attempted to read Mr Radley's tatty copy, but I began this immediately and within a couple of paragraphs had decided it was the best book ever written.

I never got round to thanking Rad for this present: the next time I went round to the Radleys' he had gone up to Durham. Mr Radley had insisted on driving him up there, even though Rad had tried to dissuade him, and the issue had threatened to become grounds for disinheritance. Privately, I couldn't help thinking it was a matter of bloody-mindedness rather than paternal pride on Mr Radley's part. As a self-taught man his attitude to universities had always been ambivalent: a combination of envy and disdain. Finally, it was the question of how many more books Rad would be able to take by car than by train that swung things in his father's favour. I later heard that Mr Radley had shown a rather cavalier disregard for the petrol warning light on the last leg of the journey and that the car had ground to a halt just short of their destination. They had been forced to push it the last two hundred yards to Rad's hall of residence, a humiliation which it would take him all term to live down.

25

A couple of months after our return from the holiday Frances came to school with the exciting news that *Nude on a sun-lounger with fresh figs* by Lazarus Ohene had come third in its category in the national portrait competition and that the Radley family fortune had increased by £500 at a stroke.

Petitioners immediately began to present themselves.

'We need a new hoover,' said Lexi. 'That one doesn't suck up the dirt any more, it just pushes it around. Oh, and my subscription for the golf club's coming up. Better forget the hoover.'

'I need a leather biker's jacket,' said Frances.

'You haven't got a bike,' protested Mr Radley. He turned to his wife. 'I'm not spending my winnings on anything prosaic like a hoover, thank you very much.' A thought occurred to him. 'It's not as if I even use it.'

'As the subject of the painting, I think I have some rights,' Lexi said.

'I should be entitled to a proportion of the money,' said Rad, who was home for the weekend. 'I cycled half-way across London trying to track down those figs. And it's not even as if it was a good likeness: any old fruit would have done.'

It had been agreed that Mr Radley would go to the presentation alone. With the exception of Frances, no one relished the prospect of reinforcing the Lazarus Ohene deception, and she could not be relied upon not to embellish the fiction still further, given a chance. For years I kept the cutting from the *Evening Standard* which showed Mr Radley, his face a rictus of embarrassment, clutching his cheque, flanked by the other prizewinners and the chairman of judges. Underneath was the caption: *Winners of the 1982 Sampson & Gould Portrait Competition (l to r) Judy Quaid, Louise*

Barrack and Lazarus Ohene receive their awards from Sir Gerald Sampson.

More important to the artist than the prize-money was the fact that the winning paintings would be exhibited in a private gallery in Bloomsbury and, with the artists' consent, offered for sale. Much energy was devoted to deciding the value of the painting; once Mr Radley had been allowed to rant and storm for a few minutes about Lexi's portrait having a value beyond all price, a figure of £300 was settled upon.

'It still seems rather dear to me,' said Lexi.

'It's a six by four. A hell of a lot of paint went on that canvas,' said her husband, for whom material concerns began to assume their proper significance once more. 'Not to mention the hours it took. And if the price deters the buyers, so much the better. I don't want to sell it anyway.'

Frances and I went up to the exhibition one evening after school. I had missed the opening which clashed with an orchestra rehearsal. It had been arranged that Lawrence would meet us up there and bring us home afterwards.

The proprietor of the gallery wasn't used to schoolgirl clients, and kept looking at us suspiciously, as if we might suddenly pocket an eight-foot canvas and run. Mr Radley's painting suddenly seemed so much more authentic framed and lit and hanging on a clean white wall than when I had seen it last, stacked like a giant slice of toast up against half a dozen other attempts in the attic. In fact it looked thoroughly at home among the other exhibits: Lexi's distorted and scowling face was merely one of many. When we arrived Lawrence was already standing in front of it, stroking his chin and looking thoughtful. 'Well, it's hideous all right,' he said to me, when Frances had moved off. 'But is it Art?'

The winning exhibit was a portrait of what I took to be an elderly victim of a mugging or other violent assault. One side of his face was the colour of raw liver, the eye reduced to a thin seam in the puffy flesh. The undamaged side was hardly more appealing, every wart, pock mark and nasal hair reproduced in fine detail. Purplish wattles of skin hung from jaw to collarbone and a fleck of spit foamed in the corner of the mouth. Lawrence grimaced and moved on to confront an image of a young girl with a shaven head and a cobweb tattooed on her forehead, snarling at him from the canvas.

'Do you think we can deduce from these that flattery is no longer the duty of the artist?' he whispered.

Some of the paintings, I noticed, had small orange stickers beside the title. 'What are they for?' I asked Frances as we caught her up.

'The stickers mean the painting's sold.' We turned back to the Radley entry with one movement. 'Dad's in a real lather about it. He's already spent the money.'

Apparently, having originally scorned the idea of selling the painting Mr Radley was now in a state of anxiety that it would suffer the humiliation of being the only one still unsold at the end of the fortnight. Between shifts at the pizza parlour he would scoot up to town on the delivery bike to check whether an orange sticker had appeared, returning home a little more dejected each time.

'It's not that I mind it sitting there like the only spinster at a wedding,' he said, a couple of days before the exhibition closed. 'It's just that it feels like an insult to Lexi.'

His model and muse blinked in surprise. 'You can rest easy on that account, I assure you,' she said.

'Perhaps it's too expensive – you could knock it down by a few quid,' Frances suggested.

Mr Radley bridled. 'It's not a punnet of soggy raspberries, for God's sake.'

His dignity was restored the following day by a phone call from the gallery to say the painting was sold. 'I had a feeling it would go for that price,' he said, flushed with jubilation. 'I wonder if they've got the name of the buyer. I could see whether he wants some of my other stuff.'

'Oh no,' said Lexi quickly. 'I think these transactions are usually anonymous.'

26

It was about this time that Frances' obstinate devotion to Nicky finally paid off. Whether Rad's departure to university had removed an awkward obstacle, or whether years of admiration had finally worn Nicky down, I never knew. But even after Rad had packed up his philosophy books and his holey jumpers and headed north, Nicky continued to be a regular visitor at the Radleys': he was studying dentistry at King's, and so didn't have far to come. This coincided with my spending rather less time there. My Saturday mornings were taken up with playing cello in the local youth orchestra, and it was usually mid-afternoon before I could catch up with Frances and the weekend could really begin.

One freezing Saturday in November I arrived with my usual overnight bag to find no one in. Fish was raking dead leaves into piles in the next-door garden, and then battening them down with black polythene and bricks. 'I think they're all out,' he said cheerfully. I rang and knocked several times and peered through the front room window but roused nobody except Growth, who had been asleep on the chaise longue. Auntie Mim was almost certainly in as a light was on in her bedroom but she never answered the door on principle. While I stood shivering and wondering what to do, the tinny rattle of rake on grass stopped and Fish appeared at the dividing hedge, which was clipped square on his side to exactly half-way across the top, and ballooned on the Radleys' side like the back end of a toy poodle. 'Do you want to come in to the warm for a cup of tea while you wait?' he asked, his head on one side in a pretence of shyness. 'They could be ages.'

I cast about for an excuse. Although he had stopped offering to turn the hose on Frances and give her 'a good spraying' whenever the sun shone, somehow the image had stayed with me, and I found the prospect of being alone with him particularly uninviting. I had in fact been prepared to let myself into the back garden and wait in the shed until someone showed up, but could hardly offer that to Fish as my chosen alternative. I was saved by the arrival of Lawrence in his Jaguar. 'Ah, there you are,' said Fish, failing to keep the disappointment out of his voice, and he turned his back and went on pawing away at the lawn with his rake.

Lawrence let us in with his key and went about switching on lights and turning radiators up as if he lived there. 'Make yourself at home,' he said, sweeping newspapers and dog toys off the couch, and settling down with his feet on the coffee table to watch the Grand Prix. I wandered out into the kitchen and started to tidy up. In the sink a tower of saucepans and crockery stood in six inches of greasy water. Fat had congealed at the edges of the bowl and potato peelings floated on the surface. The oven door stood open to reveal the curling remains of a lasagne in a foil dish. Every worktop seemed to be covered with lidless jars: marmalade, piccalilli, peanut butter, stuffed olives. God knows what they'd had for lunch. The swing bin was full and, rather than empty it, someone had started another rubbish bag which now hung, half full from the back-door handle. A note in Frances' handwriting was propped amid the debris. DAD IT'S YOUR TURN.

A protracted search turned up one punctured rubber glove. I gritted my teeth and plunged my hands into the sink, my fingers contacting a plug of lard which had to be excavated before the water could drain away. After twenty minutes my enthusiasm for the task was abating, and I left the washing up to drip dry – there was no tea-towel to be found – and dried my hands on an oven glove before creeping upstairs. I could still hear the whine of racing cars, and gabbled commentary coming from the television. I paused on the first landing and double-checked that there was no one in any of the bedrooms before continuing up to Rad's room. It would have been stripped of the essentials for a term's survival, but would still yield up clues. I don't know what I was hoping to find – a lock of my hair perhaps, pressed between the pages of Byron. I pushed open the door and felt a rush of cold air. The radiator had been switched off and the room already smelled damp and abandoned. I clicked on the overhead light and dust particles swarmed in its glare. The wardrobe door had been left open to reveal half a dozen empty hangers, Rad's old school uniform and three odd shoes. He owned so few clothes that he could hardly have afforded to leave behind anything serviceable.

On the desk was a letter rack containing a postcard from Nicky, certificates of proficiency in diving and life-saving, and a review, cut from the local paper, of his school's *Much Ado About Nothing*. One sentence from it – *Marcus Radley as Benedick was the undoubted star of this uneven production* – had been highlighted with yellow pen: an allowable piece of vanity, I decided. The walls were unadorned apart from a dartboard with all three darts in the bull's-eye and a peppering of holes in the surrounding plaster, and a collection of postcard-sized prints: Cézanne's *Baigneuses*, Botticelli's *Birth of Venus*, some severe-looking 1950s bathing beauties, David Hockney's swimming pools. What was that all about? Water. Wasn't swimming one of his many super-abilities? I vaguely remembered Frances telling me he had once saved a drowning girl.

I hesitated in front of the desk drawer. It was all right, I reasoned, to look at things that had been left out – that's what they were there for. But opening drawers was another matter. All the same. I would just look, I decided, but I wouldn't rummage. Rummaging would be shabby. The drawer turned out to be empty, leaving me with all the discomfort of a bad conscience without the gratification of discovery. I didn't snoop any further: Rad was not to be found amongst his things. As I emerged from his room I almost fell over Auntie Mim, who was carrying a jangling tray across the landing. A plate of violent green sprouts and pallid potatoes steamed beside a cup of grey tea, most of which was washing around in the saucer. A guilty blush surged over my cheeks. 'Hello,' I stammered. She would probably think I had been trying to steal something. Maybe she thought I'd been in her room. 'Do you want a hand?' I took the tray from her while there was still some tea left to save, and she pushed her door open and waved me in.

Auntie Mim's diet had led me to expect a certain austerity in her surroundings, but there was nothing monastic about this room. Every surface was covered with knick-knacks – china figurines and thimble collections, pill boxes, framed embroideries, entire tribes of peg dolls in frilly dresses. I hovered, still holding the tray while Auntie Mim picked the bedside cabinet clean, slotting the ornaments meticulously into new positions on the dressing table. The last item to be removed was an old black and white photo in a round silver frame about the size of a powder compact. It was of a young woman with an intelligent, determined face, dark eyes and a squarish jaw. Auntie Mim noticed me staring at the picture as she picked it up, so I said, 'Is that you?' It was impossible to tell what Auntie Mim might have looked like as a twenty-year-old, shrunken and lined as she was, but the girl in the photo was attractive enough for it to be a flattering observation, even if wrong.

And then she did the most surprising thing. She tapped the picture against her heart and said, 'The great love of my life,' before setting it down next to her bedside lamp. I was so astounded I almost dropped the tray, and managed to say nothing more than 'Oh!' before she had reclaimed her supper and was tipping the saucerful of tea back into the cup, and the moment for further confidences was past. I reeled down the stairs, angry with myself for remaining speechless at such a confession. My lack of interest must have looked positively rude, but it was only amazement that had paralysed me. Somehow Auntie Mim and forbidden passion seemed incompatible.

Downstairs I found Frances had arrived home with Nicky. They were sitting on the couch a little closer together than necessary and looking exceedingly pleased with themselves. Lawrence was still engrossed in the motor-racing.

'Oh hello, what are you doing here?' said Frances in a

voice that wasn't altogether welcoming. As I had been spending almost every weekend there for the past four years I didn't bother to answer this, but said, 'What were you doing *not* here?'

'Nicky came over this morning and said he'd got tickets to see *Les Enfants du Paradis*,' said Frances, with great authority, as though her acquaintance with the film hadn't begun and ended that very day.

'What did you think?' Lawrence asked, roused to interest all of a sudden.

'Amazing,' said Frances. 'Classic.'

'You fell asleep!' Nicky remonstrated, cuffing her.

'So did you.'

'I was up half the night, writing up an experiment.'

'Well, it was harder for me to concentrate with that huge bloke's head right in front of the subtitles.'

'It sounds riveting,' I said frostily, rattled by my ignorance of the film and by the unusual intimacy between Frances and Nicky. There was something going on. Neither of them would quite meet my eye, and my attempts to start up a normal conversation – one in which I could at least participate – foundered. Any subject that arose would be hijacked by Frances and Nicky and turned into an opportunity for an exchange of banter and mock insults, accompanied by playful shoving and jostling. Frances seemed to be experimenting with a new laugh to replace her regular cackle. Every feeble witticism from Nicky would prompt a flutey giggle, which he would then imitate, setting her off afresh. For this I had almost succumbed to the vile Fish! I thought. After half an hour or so of this I was about to demand whether they were feeling quite all right, when Lawrence, who had grown tired of the sports results, looked at his watch and said, 'It doesn't look as though Lexi's coming back. I've got a table for two booked at that Chinese place. Do you want to come, Abigail?' Nobody raised any objection to this scheme so I accepted and wished Nicky and Frances a curt goodbye.

'Oh, bye, have a lovely time. Lucky you,' said Frances,

beaming at this turn of events. But as Lawrence was helping me on with my coat she followed me into the hallway and said in a more contrite tone, 'I'll give you a ring tomorrow, yes?' and seemed relieved when I nodded.

'I'm afraid I made all that up about the Chinese restaurant,' said Lawrence as we reversed up the drive. 'I just got the impression that those two wanted to be alone, so I thought we'd better push off.'

'But Frances has been chasing Nicky for ages and he's never shown the slightest interest,' I protested, mortified at having my status as gooseberry articulated so baldly.

'Well, he's interested now, take my word for it,' said Lawrence. 'Now do you want me to drive you home or shall we get a takeaway and eat it at my place?'

'Don't feel you have to entertain me,' I said, failing to keep the martyred tone out of my voice. 'Home will be fine.'

Lawrence gave me a pitying look and made straight for the Chinese restaurant.

❦

'If Frances and Nicky do start going out,' Lawrence said later, forking noodles on to my plate, 'you and Rad could make up a foursome.' I looked up warily and caught the sly expression on his face.

'I don't think that's very likely,' I said, as neutrally as possible. We were kneeling either side of the coffee table in his house in Dulwich. The sitting room was on the first floor – an arrangement which struck me as highly sophisticated. The table was strewn with steaming foil containers and discarded lids. Lawrence had ordered far too much; his generosity would give us both indigestion before the evening was out. 'Rad's not really interested in girls – or boys,' I added, my jaws working mechanically at a piece of battered pork. I had long since stopped feeling hungry but didn't dare admit it in the presence of such prodigious leftovers.

'It certainly seems that way,' agreed Lawrence, inverting a dish of king prawns on to his plate.

'I don't honestly think Rad's noticed I exist,' I said.

'Ah, well. Patience.' He speared a prawn. 'That's something I know all about.' Then seeing my uncomprehending smile he changed the subject swiftly and started grilling me about my cello-playing – what grade had I reached; how often did I practice; who were my favourite composers, until the phone rang in the study next door and he left me alone.

'Hello . . . Sorry. . . There was no sign of you, and Abigail needed rescuing . . . No, we've already eaten . . . All right. I'll have to drop Abigail home on the way . . .' I could hear Lawrence's conversation through the wall and, feeling uncomfortable at overhearing myself discussed, I took the opportunity to go to the loo. 'Downstairs on the right,' Lawrence called, with his hand over the receiver, as I passed the study door.

The first on the right proved to be the dining room; the second door looked more promising, but as I groped for the light switch I lost my balance and stumbled into a large flat box propped against one wall. It came crashing on to my shin and I let out a yell which brought Lawrence leaping down the stairs. He switched on the light and I found myself in a generous-sized broom cupboard. My leg had a deep inch-long graze which would take about two hours to start bleeding. On the floor at my feet was a plywood packing crate of the sort used to protect paintings. It was about six by four and bore a label from the Bloomsbury gallery where Lazarus Ohene had enjoyed his recent triumph. Lawrence picked it up and, seeing my expression, gave a sheepish smile. 'I'd be grateful if you wouldn't mention this to anyone,' he said.

'Doesn't anyone know it was you?'

'Lexi does of course. It was her idea – to boost Michael's morale. And make sure the painting didn't come back and end up on the wall. So he absolutely mustn't find out. I keep meaning to get rid of the damn thing – give it away to someone, but I can't think of anyone I dislike that much. I'll probably end up giving it to a junk shop, or doing a Clementine Churchill. Anyway, don't let on.'

All of a sudden I was the keeper of secrets. Having extorted a promise from me Lawrence offered to drive me home. I felt a little cheated at the prospect of observing confidentiality. I had after all come upon the subterfuge through my own efforts – and had a wound to show for it – and if he hadn't happened to hear the crash the discovery would have been mine to do with as I chose. There was no fun in a secret that could never be told: the enjoyment came from stashing it away and watching it appreciate until it could be cashed in.

'Home on a Saturday night. We are privileged,' my mother said sarcastically as I limped into the hall. Lawrence's Jaguar had pulled up outside to be greeted by a hail of security lights from the front of the house.

'Like a Nuremberg rally,' he muttered, shielding his eyes.

Security was mother's latest craze. I had been issued with a bunch of keys no pocket could hold and made to memorise the number for a burglar alarm that would in all probability never be set as my grandmother was always in the house. Father was sceptical about these measures. 'If there's a fire we'll all be roasted alive,' he would say. 'But still, better dead than burgled, isn't that right, dear?' The nightly sound of rattling chains and deadbolts scraping home which accompanied mother's locking-up routine set his teeth on edge. 'I feel like old Mr Dorrit in the Marshalsea,' he once said.

'Hmm. What's that smell?' mother asked as she leaned towards me to kiss my cheek.

'Er . . . sweet and sour pork? Peking duck?'

She pulled a face. We never ate Chinese food. It was one of the things that triggered mother's migraines. 'No. Cigarette smoke. You haven't been to the pub, have you?'

'No. Lawrence smokes.'

'Oh. Well, I'll hang your coat in the porch overnight if you don't mind, so it doesn't fumigate the cloakroom. You're not going up to your room, are you?' she said as my foot touched the bottom stair. 'I'm sure your dad and Granny would be pleased to see you. It's not often we have you here at the weekend.'

In the sitting room father was taking Granny through her accounts. On the table in front of them was a drift of share dividends, tax receipts and bank statements. Granny was not well off but, in terms of administration, she made her poverty go a long way.

'Now where's that cheque from Cable and Wireless?' she said, riffling through the heap, scattering papers, until my father pushed it into her hand. 'I can't read. I'm blind. How much is it for?'

'Three pounds seventy-one,' said father. He tapped the ledger. 'We've already done that one.' His glasses were not quite horizontal – a sign of tension. They were evidently on their second or third run-through.

Mother was right. 'Abigail,' he said, pouncing on the diversion joyfully, 'let me get you a cup of coffee.'

'Nice to see you, Abigail,' said Granny, as he escaped into the kitchen. 'Not that I can,' she added.

27

Lawrence's prophecy came true, but not in quite the way he had envisaged. Frances and Nicky did indeed become a couple, and when Rad came down for the Christmas holidays we would go out, or stay in, depending on whether we had any money, in a foursome. This was not, however, the fulfilment of all my hopes, as Rad appeared to be quite unmoved by the spectacle of grand romance enacted daily by Frances and Nicky, and showed no sign of following suit. He simply tagged along as Nicky's friend and Frances' brother and was not about to be pressurised by the demands of mere symmetry. This arrangement at least legitimised my presence. Without Rad we had made an uncomfortable threesome: I didn't have the dignity to retire, and Nicky and Frances hadn't the heart to tell me to clear off. We settled into a new routine. I would spend Friday night at the Radleys' and leave on Saturday morning in time for orchestra. Frances would see Nicky on Saturdays and both of us were invited for Sunday lunch. This meant that all my Saturday evenings were now spent at home: I had no other friends. I had never needed to make the effort – there had always been Frances. My mother was soon as dismayed to have me slouching around the house as she had ever been at my readiness to be gone. She took my predicament as a personal slight, and began to entertain uncharitable thoughts about Frances.

'It's not natural for a girl of your age to be in every Saturday night. Don't you have some other friends you could ring up? You could invite someone to stay here – that would show Frances. What about the people at orchestra? Surely after all this time you must have got to know someone?' It was pointless trying to explain that my aloofness was made of sterner stuff. I didn't mind staying in for the evening. It was only a matter of getting through it, and then it would be Sunday and off I'd go again.

I watched a lot of television at that time. I was abetted in this by father, who had recently acquired a remote control set and took such joy in his new gadget that it was possible to acquire a working knowledge of the material on all three sides at once. His continual grazing between channels exasperated my mother, who could often be caught out and find herself transported in and out of several programmes before realising what was happening. Any display of interest in what was on the screen would instantly provoke a burst of channel-switching from father. The only way to ensure your programme stayed put was to affect complete indifference – pick up a magazine for example. But mother would never learn. She would sit forward, or say, 'Ooh good,' as *Gardeners' World* appeared, and *click*, we'd be in the middle of *Coronation Street* or *Dad's Army*. He seemed to regard it all as a great game. 'I've got the conch,' he used to say, settling down in an armchair with one finger poised on the button like a contestant in a quiz show.

Even this sacrifice on my part was not enough for Nicky. Having come to ardour rather late in his acquaintance with Frances he was now making up for lost time, and begrudged her every minute she spent away from him. Sometimes he would come down from college in the middle of the week and stay overnight. Rad's room became his official second residence. They obviously sat up late on these occasions as the next day Frances would come to school wilting with tiredness. Her academic standing had never been lower. Her work was regularly returned with comments like *3/20 – Frankly, pathetic*, or *U – Is this a joke?* The only subject at which she exerted herself was English, where she would produce pages of breathless scribble about *Jane Eyre* or *The Eve of Saint Agnes* with the maximum recourse to personal opinion and experience, and the minimum of textual analysis. These offerings were welcomed by the teacher as a sign of interest and her enthusiasm, however incoherent, was given every encouragement.

'I wish Nicky was a bit more romantic,' was Frances' only criticism.

'Romantic like what?' I asked. 'Do you want him to serenade you under your window by the light of the 194 bus?'

'Yes,' she said, jumping at the idea. 'Yes. Oh, you know, I thought he might write me poems and stuff.'

'That's a bit much to expect, isn't it? He's a trainee dentist not a poet. I bet you couldn't even write a poem yourself.' I knew she would take up the challenge, but by the end of double biology she had only produced one feeble couplet: 'Nicky Rupp you make me frantic / Is your soul so unromantic?' The following day, however, she slid a piece of folded paper into my lap during assembly. We were sitting in the front row of seats — those more junior had to sit cross-legged in the dust at our feet — and I was feeling rather exposed. I eased the note open under cover of my hymnbook as the headmistress and deputies processed down the aisle, and read:

> *Nicky Rupp you make me frantic;*
> *Is your soul so unromantic*
> *That you couldn't write a line*
> *Of verse to let me know you're mine?*
> *Could you not describe a rose*
> *In something more intense than prose?*
> *Consider as you pull a tooth*
> *That Truth is Beauty; Beauty Truth;*
> *Ever let the fancy roam*
> *Far from halitosis' home.*
> *Your gentle hand would suit a quill*
> *Much better than a dentist's drill,*
> *For there must beat a heart beneath*
> *That thrills to something more than teeth.*

I glanced sideways at Frances and she bared her teeth at me. I looked away hurriedly and dug my fingernails into my palm as my eyes started to water. I could sense twitching next to me but didn't dare look up again. Laughing in prayers was regarded as an insult to God.

'Frances Radley and the girl next to you, get out,' hissed the headmistress as soon as she gained the platform. 'We take our worship seriously here!' she added in a menacing tone.

'You never wrote that,' I said when we had slunk out of the hall.

'No,' she admitted. 'I got stuck after two lines so Dad finished it off. I'm going to send it to Nicky anonymously.'

Nicky was given the opportunity to prove himself a man of grand gestures before long. Rad was down for the weekend and the four of us were planning to spend the day in London. Nicky, who was coming straight from his hall of residence, was to meet us at the bus stop at Waterloo station and we would walk over to King's to have lunch in the canteen before going to see a film at the Empire. I had only realised that morning that it was Valentine's Day because an unsigned card had arrived for me – as it had every year since I had been a visitor at the Radleys'. I knew it was from Mr Radley as Frances also received one addressed in the same handwriting, which he had made no attempt to disguise. These cards were intended to console us in the face of being otherwise unloved: at sixteen I took this as an impertinence.

We were a little late arriving as I had been obliged to set off from home with my cello as if on the way to orchestra, and then double back to Frances' place. I didn't want my parents to know I was playing truant: they had just spent £500 on a new bow for me after the old one started to moult, and it might have looked ungrateful. Rad, typically, was critical of these measures.

'Are your parents very fierce? Do they beat you?' he asked, watching me stow the cello in the cupboard under the stairs next to Lexi's golf clubs. 'Or do you just like complications?'

Nicky was nowhere in sight when we got off the bus so we started walking and met up with him about half-way across the bridge. He was wearing an expensive-looking jacket of distressed leather and carrying a large irregular-shaped parcel, about the size of a fat pillow, wrapped in red foil.

'Hello pooch,' he said, closing on Frances. Rad and I gazed out over the Thames as they kissed passionately. The water was dark grey and rippled like beaten metal. A pleasure cruiser, half-empty, passed underneath us on its way to Greenwich. It wasn't a good day for sightseeing: there was a stinging wind and a few raindrops were starting to fall. My hair was whipping itself into a tangle, so I twisted it into a coil and stuffed it down the back of my coat. The kiss continued. Rad tutted to himself. Passers-by were beginning to stare. The rain started to come down harder and all around us umbrellas burst into bloom. Frances and Nicky broke apart. 'Is that new?' she asked, emerging from within his jacket. Nicky's expenditure on clothes was the subject of much leg-pulling in the Radley household. Only Lexi bought as many new clothes as him – and she invariably took them back after one wearing.

Nicky fingered the lapel. 'Yes. Do you like it?'

'Is it meant to look like that?'

'It's the fashion, Frances. I know that's an unfamiliar word to you people.'

'You mean scruffy is In? Hey, Rad, you'd better watch out or someone might mistake you for a follower of fashion.'

'I knew my time would come,' he said.

'What's that, anyway?' Frances pointed to the parcel, her curiosity getting the better of her.

'Oh, sorry,' said Nicky, collecting himself. He thrust it at her. 'Happy Valentine's Day.'

Frances tore off the paper, which the wind promptly snapped out of her hand. We watched it cartwheel into the middle of the road where it was run over by a succession of cars. The contents of the parcel were revealed as a large fluffy white teddy bear holding a red satin heart. Her face fell.

'Thank you,' she said, a second too late.

'Don't you like it?' Nicky asked.

'Ye-e-es,' said Frances, without much conviction.

Nicky looked crushed. 'I thought girls were supposed to like that sort of thing. Cute cuddly toys. The shops are absolutely full of them.'

'That's the whole point,' said Frances. 'Anyway, I haven't said I don't like it. I'd like anything that was from you.' And then the death-blow: 'Did you keep the receipt?'

'What's wrong with it?' He appealed to me and Rad.

We all stood around the bear, surveying it critically.

'Well . . .' Rad began, struggling to unite honesty with tact. 'It's a bit lacking in the good taste department.'

'Oh God, I've really screwed up, haven't I?' said Nicky. 'I knew I should have got flowers.'

'Oh, it's not *that* bad,' said Frances, giving the bear a forgiving squeeze which must have activated a switch somewhere deep in the fur, as it gave an electronic squeak indicative of a creature in great pain.

'No, you're right, it's total crap,' said Nicky decisively, and before any of us could respond he snatched the bear and tossed it over the parapet.

'Oh *Nicky*!' Frances let out a shriek worthy of a mother whose baby has just fallen into the Thames, as we watched it spin through the air. 'What did you do that for? I didn't hate it that much. Poor little thing.' And she burst into tears. Indeed it did look rather forlorn, bowling along on its back in the oily river.

'I'll get it back for you if you want it,' Nicky said heroically, struggling out of his jacket. 'Look after that,' he added, spoiling the effect somewhat.

'Don't be . . .'

'You're not . . .' Rad and I said simultaneously.

'I'll be all right.' And he swung his legs over the parapet.

'For Christ's sake,' said Rad.

'Frances, stop him,' I said. But she hesitated, and in that second's pause Nicky jumped.

The three of us watched in horror as he plummeted towards the water, his legs kicking slightly, as if he was already regretting it. He disappeared beneath the surface as if sucked under, and everything seemed to stop – the traffic on the bridge, the boats on the river, the people on the embankment below, as if time itself was holding its breath, and then, perhaps four seconds later, Nicky popped up like a cork some twenty yards from his point of entry, struggling vainly against the incoming tide that was pulling him upstream and out into the middle of the river. The teddy bear was well on its way to Westminster Bridge by now, and quite unreachable.

'Oh God, he's going to drown. Rad, you'll have to go in after him,' said Frances hysterically. Rad didn't move.

'No don't,' I said. 'Look.' Below us a police launch was chugging into view. It swung round towards Nicky, its wake tracing a milky circle around his thrashing figure. The current was so strong that each time the boat attempted to come alongside him Nicky would be swept further out of reach. By this time we had been joined on the bridge by a small group of spectators, hopeful of witnessing a successful suicide attempt. A murmur of anxiety, or was it excitement?, ran through the crowd each time the launch failed to pick him up. It took several circuits before one of the boatmen could get close enough to fling out a lifebelt on a line, and Nicky was hauled in. He stood, round shouldered and dripping, in the bow of the boat as it disappeared under Westminster Bridge.

'If he'd drowned that would have been your fault, Frances,' Rad said severely.

'What do you mean?' she said, red-faced with guilt and anger.

'You could have stopped him but you didn't.'

'You could have jumped in after him but you didn't.' They faced each other, glaring. It was the first time I'd ever seen them in a confrontation. The few bystanders, cheated of tragedy by the efficiency of the river police, turned towards Frances in anticipation of fresh drama.

'All right, calm down,' Rad muttered. 'There's no point in standing here in the rain arguing.'

'Where do you think they'll take Nicky?' I asked. 'To Saint Thomas's? He'll probably need his stomach pumped if he's swallowed any of that water.'

'They're more likely to have taken him down to the cells for making a nuisance of himself.'

'They wouldn't be able to charge him with anything, would they?' asked Frances.

'Dunno,' said Rad. 'Breach of the peace?'

'Dropping litter?' I suggested. Frances started to giggle, her familiar madwoman's cackle, which set us off, and I don't know whether it was just a release of tension, but the three of us were soon crying with laughter. We were still gasping when we reached the underpass, where we stopped on the kerb to cross just as a black taxi hit the only pot-hole on the bridge, sending up a filthy sheet of water which left an arc of oily spray on Nicky's new jacket.

It emerged later that Nicky had been taken to the police station – 'for a change of clothes and a bollocking' as he reported it. His rescuers had gone on to pick up the bear as well, not as a favour to Nicky, but in a spirit of tidiness, and he was able to present it to Frances when he finally caught up with us back at his halls.

'Sponge clean only,' said Frances, reading the label, as she squeezed the waterlogged teddy over the sink. 'Do not soak.' Now violently attached to it, she took it home in a plastic bag and sat it on her radiator, where it took two days to dry out, lost its shine and its squeak, and gave off a powerful smell of drains.

28

Frances' way of atoning for the reckless endangerment of Nicky was to visit a seedy parlour in a side-street in Streatham which specialised in tattoos, body-piercing and other forms of mutilation, and to return indelibly marked behind one shoulder with a green letter N entwined with a bunch of grapes.

She showed this off to me while it was still fresh – raised, puffy and sore-looking – but kept it hidden under a plaster when changing for netball or hockey at school. She had known better than to take me with her on this mission.

'I thought you had to be over eighteen to have a tattoo,' I said, trying to disguise my revulsion – after all she was stuck with it now.

'The guy did ask, and I said, "Why, don't I look eighteen?" and he just laughed. I didn't even have to lie.'

'That must have been a great comfort to you,' I said, and she pulled a face. 'What does Nicky think of it?'

'Well, he was pretty shocked at first, but now he's flattered.' The truth was his principal feeling was one of dread that he might be expected to reciprocate, and then relief when it became clear that this wouldn't be necessary. 'Have you shown your mum and dad.'

She shook her head. 'They're broadminded,' she said, bravely. 'They won't mind.' All the same, I noticed she didn't make a point of displaying her bare shoulders. She was finally caught out one afternoon when Lexi came into the bathroom while I was helping Frances wash henna wax out of her hair. The henna hadn't made much impression on her black curls, but the bath was running with red as though she'd slit her throat.

'Oh my God,' said Lexi, looking at the bloody splashes across the tiles. 'I thought you'd injured yourself.'

I couldn't keep my eyes off the tattoo, right there next to Frances' bra strap. How could Lexi miss it? Before I could throw a towel round Frances' shoulders, Lexi had pounced. 'Oh, that's not a . . . Oh, you haven't . . . Oh, you stupid girl.'

Frances, somewhat disabled by having her head upside down in the bath, struggled to her feet, flicking her wet hair back, spraying us and the wall with orange droplets. 'What's wrong?' she said, then realised. 'Oh.' Her fingers strayed to her shoulder. 'Don't you like it?' she asked, fatally misjudging the mood of the moment.

'Like it? Are you mad?'

Mr Radley, hearing the commotion, poked his head around the bathroom door. 'Who's mad?'

'Look what she's done. Turn round, Frances.'

Mr Radley laughed – his usual response to any sign of delinquency on Frances' part – not out of tolerance or good humour, but because there is a certain melancholy pleasure in having one's low expectations confirmed.

'Do you realise what that lovely plump bunch of grapes will look like in fifty years' time? A pile of raisins. Very alluring,' he said.

'Honestly Frances, I think I'd have preferred it if you'd gone off and married him. At least that's reversible,' said Lexi.

'It won't last for ever,' said Frances. 'The guy in the shop said it was only semi-permanent.'

'*Semi*-permanent,' said Mr Radley. 'Now that's an interesting expression.'

'A semi-permanent tattoo!' said Lexi. 'He said that, did he?'

'Well, not in so many words,' Frances conceded. 'I said, "This is for ever, isn't it?" and he said, "Nothing lasts for ever, darling."'

I caught Mr Radley's eye at this point and the two of us burst out laughing, taking some of the heat out of the confrontation. This set Frances off, too. Only Lexi remained straight-faced. I'd noticed before that she didn't have much of a sense of humour: if someone made a witty remark she would wait for it to pass, like a fit of sneezing, before resuming whatever it was she had been trying to say. This was one of the few things she had in common with my mother.

'I suppose you'll be wanting a ring through the nose next,' said Lexi, recognising that the argument had run its course.

'They did nipples for five pounds each if you're interested,' said Frances, a wicked look in her eye. 'A tenner for three.'

'Three?' echoed Lexi, as our laughter rang round the tiled walls.

29

In his first long summer vacation Rad took a job in a bakery, hefting red-hot trays of loaves in and out of ovens. He would return home at nine in the morning, exhausted, with flour in his hair and eyebrows and weals on his hands. He didn't need the money – in fact he had already saved enough from his grant to buy a second-hand car – but he had some odd notion, inherited from his father perhaps, about the nobility of manual labour. His knack of living on almost nothing was a source of concern to family and friends.

'I'm worried about Rad,' I heard Lexi telling Clarissa over the phone. 'He seems to be saving out of his grant. What can he be doing up there?' This was unusual because Lexi never worried, on principle.

Nicky, who managed to be in debt almost before term started, and who had to be bailed out regularly by Obs and Solic, was disgusted. 'It's people like you who give students a bad name. The government will never put grants up if it gets out that someone can actually manage.'

'There's nothing I need to buy,' Rad protested. He was wearing ripped jeans which he had attempted to patch up with black insulating tape, and Frances' old P.E. shirt which had 'Greenhurst School for Girls' embroidered across the chest and her netball, tennis and swimming colours down one sleeve.

Only Mr Radley appeared to welcome this state of affairs. 'I think it's very encouraging that he has a responsible attitude towards money. Er, Rad, you don't happen to have any on you, do you?'

'I must be the only student who comes home for the weekend and ends up giving his father money,' Rad grumbled, reaching for his wallet.

In Rad's defence it must be said that he hadn't saved quite

enough to buy a *good* car. It was a tinny Citroën 2CV, reliable only in the respect that its unreliability could be depended upon, and therefore precautions were taken. Nevertheless it was treated by Nicky, Frances and myself as an object of veneration since it offered us the prospect of day trips to the coast, picnics in the country and broadened horizons. In truth we spent as much time sitting in the car awaiting the RAC recovery vehicle as enlarging our horizons, and still more time dithering over where to go. Our deliberations were marked by a lack of leadership: no one wanted to be held responsible for nominating a venue which would turn out to be a dud. Invariably by the time a decision was made half the day would have elapsed.

One Sunday in July Nicky, Frances and I were lying on the living-room floor looking at an Ordnance Survey map of Surrey, hoping to have fixed on a destination by the time Rad came in from work. Although it was early it was already hot, and Growth kept sidling over to find a cooler spot and flopping on his stomach, panting, in the middle of the North Downs. Lexi's recommendation of Kew Gardens had already met with derision.

'What is Kew Gardens exactly?' Frances had wanted to know.

'It's a botanical gardens.'

'What is there to do there?'

'It's a botanical gardens,' said Lexi patiently. 'You go there to look at the plants. There's an Azalea garden and a tropical palm house and a lovely rose pergola . . .' Frances gave an exaggerated yawn. 'Hmm, you're probably too young to appreciate it,' Lexi acknowledged, knowing this would rile Frances.

'What about Shere?' suggested Nicky, pushing Growth, who gave a growl.

'Been there,' said Frances, heaving herself up to open the windows. I watched her move a dead cactus out of the way so she could kneel on the sill, and then carefully replace it.

'What about the sea – Hastings or somewhere?'

'Too far.'

'Box Hill?'

'It's just a hill,' said Frances. 'Oh, look, that's a nice name. Half Moon Street.' She planted a stubby finger on the map.

'I know that place. I've been there,' I said. Suddenly it was before me as clearly as a remembered dream: that day out with father, the pub, the lake, turquoise sky, apple-green leaves, the cottage, mud, my ruined sandals. 'It's lovely.'

'Well, let's go there, then,' said Nicky, after I had described it to them. 'It wouldn't take more than an hour.'

'Settled,' said Frances.

When Rad came back and was happy to fall in with the plan I rang father to check that the Half Moon Street on the map was the same place I had in mind.

He had been in the garden installing Granny in a deck-chair under the magnolia and was puffing slightly as he picked up the phone. I could picture him, hot and flustered, in his jacket and tie. My question took him by surprise and it was a while before he answered. 'Did I take you there? . . . Good heavens, fancy your remembering a thing like that . . . Yes, it's not far from Dorking.'

'Was there a pub near by?'

'That's right. Half a mile back down the lane, where you leave the car.'

'It's probably not even there any more.'

'Well, you should never revisit childhood haunts – they always disappoint.' He wished us a happy day and then excused himself. He was not keen on the telephone and I could always sense his agitation to cut things short. 'I'd better go and check your grandmother. I left her in that deck-chair that snaps shut like a clam.'

'Where's Mum?'

'Church. Cleaning the brasses. Do you think it's too late for me to take up religion?'

'Yes.'

My memories hadn't let me down. The pub was still there

and Rad, flush with a week's bread money, treated us to lunch. We sat in the garden eating peanuts and dodging wasps while a girl in a greasy apron turned our steaks on a spitting barbecue. Afterwards I led them down the sunken lane to the lake with a proprietorial air. Within the tunnel of trees it was cool, dark and silent, like the interior of a cathedral. An occasional spear of light shot through a chink in the leaves, and as we turned the corner the sunlight burst off the surface of the water, making us cover our eyes.

The cottage was still there, though uninhabited and boarded up, and the garden overgrown with dandelions and nettles. At the water's edge a warped and flaking boat drifted back and forth on its leash, causing only the faintest tremor in the reflection of the treetops and sky. The NO BOATING NO FISHING NO SWIMMING sign was still tacked to a stake in the water.

'I told you,' I said, nudging Frances. She had been keen to swim and insisted on bringing swimsuits and towels in spite of my warning. Rad had been obliged to dig out a spare pair of trunks for Nicky, while Frances offered me her second best bikini.

'I hope these aren't held together with insulating tape,' was Nicky's comment.

On the opposite shore a couple were walking hand in hand. The man was wearing a backpack in which a baby perched, swaying, a knotted hanky on its head. Every few seconds its little hand would reach up and drag the hanky down over its face and it would cry until the woman straightened it up again, and the whole performance would be repeated. Someone was taking a setter for a walk in the woods just beyond them. The dog kept bounding out between the trees and shivering to a halt at the water's edge before tearing back again. On our side two girls were lying on their stomachs on the grass asleep, or just sunbathing. The walk had been enough to deter other visitors.

'I thought you said it was a lake,' said Frances, when we had arranged ourselves on a dry patch of grass. 'This is more like a pond.'

'I was only six when I was last here,' I said. 'Everything looked bigger then.'

Rad had brought a book – *Narziss and Goldmund* – and was lying on his back reading. Frances and Nicky were playing poker. I didn't know the rules and couldn't be bothered to learn, so I made daisy chains for a while and then lay down with my eyes shut and watched the red and yellow lights swim beneath my eyelids.

'Typical bloody Rad,' I heard Frances say a moment later. Rad carried on reading. 'You're so anti-social.'

'What's anti-social about reading?' he said, without looking up from the page. 'What would you like me to do? Morris dancing?'

'You could talk to Abigail. She brought us here, and she's bored.'

Rad sighed and put down his book. 'What do you want to talk about, Abigail?'

'I don't,' I said. 'It's Frances who finds silence unnerving, not me.' This was quite true. During our O-level exams the previous year I used to call round at the Radleys' house to be told that Frances was upstairs revising, and find her lying amongst her books, singing along to the radio. 'I can only work with music on,' was her excuse. 'Silence distracts me.'

'Thank you,' said Rad, rolling on to his front and finding his place again. Watching him covertly I could see that he was not reading properly – the pages were not turning fast enough – and when Nicky brought up the subject of their forthcoming holiday he was happy to be distracted. They were intending to travel around Europe at the beginning of September, 'when the kids are back at school.'

'I wish you'd go earlier,' grumbled Frances. 'Then this kid could go with you.'

'You can't come,' said Nicky, ruffling her hair in a patronising manner. 'We're going to be sleeping on stations, scavenging for food, living on our wits.'

'That wouldn't bother me. Do I look like someone who needs pampering?' Nicky had to concede that she could probably scavenge with the best of them.

'Your mum and dad wouldn't let you come anyway,' he said.

'Mum wouldn't mind – she thinks you and Rad would look after me.'

'Don't know why she thinks that,' said Rad.

'It's Dad who's being difficult.'

The itinerary was still in dispute. Nicky favoured the Greek islands; Rad wanted to go to Berlin.

'We've got to spend a few days crashing out on a beach somewhere hot.'

'We've got to get behind the Iron Curtain.'

'We don't want to spend the whole holiday on trains.'

'We want to cover as much ground as possible.'

The only point on which they seemed to be in agreement was a determination to avoid Switzerland at all costs. 'Too expensive,' said Nicky.

'Too clean,' said Rad.

'What's your dad doing this year?' I asked Rad.

'He keeps whinging about having no one to go with – Mum's going to a health farm with Clarissa. I suggested one of those activity holidays for the lonely – you know, sketching in the Trossachs or something. He didn't think it was very funny.'

'*That* explains why he won't let me go with you,' said Frances. 'He's jealous that you're going off without him, so he wants to make sure someone else has a rotten summer.'

'What are you doing, Blush?' asked Nicky.

'Granny-sitting in suburbia.'

Rad was just about to turn back to *Narziss and Goldmund* when Frances, anticipating him by a second, snatched it up and with a triumphant cry slung it over his head to Nicky. Rad lunged, a moment too late, and then, recovering his dignity, sat back resignedly as the two of them chucked it back and forth. 'Children, children,' he said in a nanny-ish tone. 'Don't scrunch the cover up,' he added, more seriously. He was fanatical about the condition of his books. I had often observed him trying to read a fat paperback without breaking the spine by holding the book open a fraction and squinting between the pages.

Nicky and Frances, provoked by his failure to rise, were getting closer to the water's edge. I could see what was going to happen. Sure enough, Frances next throw was a high lob; Nicky leapt, too early, and the book went winging over his head and hit the water, where it floated for a few seconds before sinking gracefully.

Rad looked at the empty ripples in disbelief. 'You complete bastards,' he said. 'I'd throw you in after it, but you'd only make my car seats wet.'

'I'll buy you a new copy on the way home,' said Frances. 'If you lend me the money.'

'What about my annotations?' he demanded, and when we burst out laughing even he had the grace to laugh at himself.

By mid-afternoon the sun was getting too much for us: our patch of shade had shifted and the air was like hot treacle. Frances suggested a walk in the woods to cool off, but once we'd packed up and brushed the grass out of our clothes and hair it seemed pointless to prolong our departure.

'Good choice, Blush, well done,' said Rad as we made our way back up the lane between the walls of exposed tree roots, and I felt as pleased with myself as if I'd invented the place.

'You'll know not to bring a book next time,' said Frances.

'I'll know not to bring you two jerks next time,' he corrected her.

We drove home with the roof peeled back and the car radio on – a piece of extreme frivolity for Rad, indicative of unusual good humour. Frances flagged down an ice-cream van just outside Redhill and bought four unnaturally white whippy ices which melted and ran down our arms faster than we could eat them.

'De Is–r–ael–ite,' sang Desmond Dekker and the Aces on the radio.

'The ears are alight?' said Rad.

On the way back we stopped at the local pool as Frances was adamant that the swimming costumes and towels she had packed shouldn't go to waste. Mine was the only dissenting voice. I used the excuse of my fear of water, but privately what put me off was the fear that Frances' 36D bikini top wouldn't do me any favours. I was overruled of course.

'You can't swim?' said Rad in amazement, as if I'd just admitted that I couldn't do joined-up writing. He and Frances, who had been tossed into a pool as babies by Mr Radley and could swim like dolphins before they could walk, tended to assume the ability was inborn. 'What if you fell in a river or something?'

'I'd drown. Unless someone rescued me.'

'Didn't you have lessons at school?' asked Nicky.

'My mother had a morbid fear of verrucas,' I said. 'She made me wear white rubber sockettes which filled up with water and dragged me under.'

'I remember that,' Frances said. 'The rest of us would be up at the deep end in our pyjamas diving for bunches of keys and Abigail would be sitting on the side of the kiddies' pool trying to shake the water out of her surgical socks.'

'I never quite understood what emergency diving for keys while wearing pyjamas was supposed to prepare us for,' she said later as we stood elbow to elbow in the crowded changing rooms. 'A flooded bedroom?' She was struggling into a tight black one-piece designed to flatten the female form into a torpedo shape for Olympic competition. The white bikini she had lent me gaped in every direction. Even if I had been able to swim only the sedatest of movements would have been safe. If I jumped in the top would be over my ears; if I dived in the bottoms would be round my ankles.

Rad and Nicky were already in the water by the time we waded through the freezing antiseptic footbath to the pool. Nicky was doing lengths, ploughing up and down the fast lane, head down, scattering children. Rad was diving off the high board, as graceful as a seabird. Frances went to join him while I dawdled in the shallow end, lying on my back with one hand on the rail, and letting my hair fan out behind me like a peacock's tail. All around me small, fearless children were leaping off the side, shrieking and bombing each other. On the wall a sign illustrated with cartoons said NO RUNNING NO SPITTING NO SPLASHING NO

DUCKING NO BOMBING NO SMOKING NO PETTING. Every so often the pool attendant, a small man in very tight white shorts, would blow his whistle and point at someone or summon them to the edge for a telling off. I put my head back and my ears filled with water, muffling the sound of splashing and squealing which echoed off the tiles, and I watched the light playing on the ceiling. When I stood up Rad was next to me.

'Your hair looks amazing from above,' he said.

'Thank you.'

'Like seaweed,' he added as he swam off, which qualified the compliment rather. Even so I allowed myself to feel flattered, and put my head back again until my hair spread out and the attendant gave a blast on his whistle and told me to go and tie it up or wear a swimming cap because it was unhygienic.

30

Dear Mrs Gledloe

My son, who is an undergraduate at Durham University, is planning a sightseeing tour of Europe in September and has agreed to act as chaperone for Frances. In view of the enormous cultural and educational value of such a visit I am entirely in its favour and hope therefore you will excuse Frances from school for the first three weeks of next term.

Yours truly
Alexandra Radley

Dear Mrs Radley

Thank you for your letter of July 12. I'm afraid we would be extremely unhappy for Frances to absent herself from school for the first three weeks of the autumn term. The Upper Sixth year is a crucial one for students and attendance at lessons is taken very seriously. Even if Frances were assured of good grades next June I would be against the idea of her missing so much work, but in view of her uneven performance in this summer's exams I have no hesitation in withholding permission. I hope on reflection you will accept that we have Frances' best interests at heart.

Yours sincerely
J. A. Gledloe

Lexi was on the phone straight away. It was a Saturday but this didn't deter her. 'There can't be that many Gledloes in the book,' she said, finding the page in the directory and forcing it flat with her fist until the spine broke. 'Glebe, Gledhill, here we are.'

'You can't call her at home,' Frances protested as Lexi shut the hall door on her. 'Dad, stop her.'

'Yes, I would certainly be prepared to come into school to

discuss it,' Lexi could be heard saying in her most unctuous voice.

'As if I could,' said Mr Radley, twitching the letter open. 'Narrow-minded old trout,' he snorted. '"Uneven performance"! Bloody cheek – when you've gone to the trouble of being a dismal failure in *all* your subjects.'

Frances pulled a face at him as Lexi came back into the room. 'I'm going to see her on Monday,' she said, in a tone which suggested the battle was as good as won.

'I'll come with you,' said her husband. 'I'd like to ask her what they teach at that place which compares so favourably with the Uffizi or the Sistine Chapel.' He still hadn't forgiven the school for failing to pass on the dates of the Battle of the Somme.

'I don't want you there,' said Lexi.

'Why not?' he said. 'I always enjoy witnessing a clash between two determined women.'

In the event Lexi went alone. Exactly what passed at the interview is not recorded, but Mrs Gledloe wasn't the push-over Lexi had predicted. 'I'm afraid my charms were wasted on her,' she reported. 'The woman is so utterly charmless herself, she would be incapable of recognising the quality in anyone else.' After half an hour of discussion stalemate had been reached. Mrs Gledloe was unmoved by the vision of Frances drinking from the fountain of European culture while the rest of us had our heads down over the Past Historic; Lexi was not persuaded of the relative value of three weeks of classes. Mr Radley, having been violently opposed to the idea of Frances accompanying Rad, was now, at the first hint of institutional resistance, violently in favour.

'Perhaps she'd be happier if a parent went with them?' he said, hopefully.

'No way,' said Frances.

'I've already told you, you have to be under twenty-six for a railcard,' said Rad. 'Why don't you go to the health farm with Mum? You know you're overweight.'

'I'm *underheight*,' Mr Radley corrected him.

'I'm not having him,' said Lexi in horror. 'It's supposed to be a holiday.'

'I thought we'd agreed we'd go away somewhere together this year,' he said.

'We did,' said Lexi, 'but I changed our mind.'

The final communication on the subject was a curt note from the headmistress at the end of term.

We look forward to seeing Frances back at school on 6 September. Failure to attend will be taken most seriously and lead to a review of Frances' continuation as a pupil at Greenhurst.

That settled it.

The only other issue left in dispute was the sleeping arrangements. Rad and Nicky had been intending to share a two-man tent, but Lexi was keen for Frances to have separate quarters.

'It's not as if we'd exactly get up to anything with Rad there,' grumbled Frances.

'I could lie between them like a sword,' Rad offered, but this wasn't good enough for his parents. I was interested to see what would happen here, as I had been wondering for some time whether Nicky and Frances were sleeping together. The way they handled each other in public suggested even greater liberties in private, but I didn't dare ask. The answer would either be an indignant 'Of course we haven't!' or an indignant 'Of course we have!' When we were twelve or so Frances had intimated that she was never going to let any boy 'muck about' with her, but her opinions had obviously undergone some revision over the course of time.

A couple of days before the travellers were leaving I casually asked Frances if she was packing her diary and she had admitted that she no longer wrote one. Oh ho, I thought, they've Done It all right. Didn't Lexi say virginity and diary-keeping were related?

Lexi's solution to the accommodation problem was to present Frances with a brand-new tent of her own. 'This is for you, and the boys can share the other one,' she said, fixing Nicky with a meaningful stare.

When they returned from the holiday Frances told me they had unpacked the new tent on the first night for Rad to sleep in and found that Lexi had accidentally bought an upright cubicle tent for enclosing a portaloo. 'I'll have to pretend I slept standing up,' she laughed.

⁂

They were away for the whole of September. I had never realised a month could last so long. There had been no question of my accompanying them. My mother would never have allowed me to miss even a day of school and was scandalised by the Radleys' encouragement of their daughter's truancy. I had, anyway, offered to look after my granny for the last week of the holidays to give my parents a break. This piece of selflessness on my part had presented them with a dilemma: anxiety at leaving me behind un-guarded, against desperation to escape.

The situation at home was becoming intolerable as my grandmother's demands grew more exacting. She expected everything and was grateful for nothing. It was impossible to perform a one-off act of kindness like reading to her, taking her out, setting her hair or bringing her breakfast in bed without her interpreting it in the most malevolent light. 'It's about time someone read to me. Do you know, I sat here yesterday from seven o'clock in the morning until suppertime without seeing a soul? Talk about bored: I'll be glad when I'm dead. So will you, I dare say.' What might begin as a favour soon became a duty. A treat was in no time considered a Right. And, such is human nature, though the performance of this duty would appear to bring no pleasure, its neglect would occasion the most bitter complaint.

Not content with being a most ungracious invalid by day, Granny had developed acute insomnia and would while away the hours before dawn listening to the radio at full blast. Fortunately my bedroom was at the far end of the landing, but my parents, whose room adjoined Granny's, had to suffer this nightly bombardment. They had tried various dodges to reduce the noise. Father bought an adaptor with its own ear-piece which Granny was supposed to wear like a hearing aid, but she would fidget in bed and get tangled up in the wire and finally rip it out of its socket in frustration. He then bought a special speaker attachment slim enough to fit under a pillow, but Granny, who seemed to have developed the sensitivity of the heroine in *The Princess and the Pea*, claimed that it was like lying on a brick.

My parents had looked into the possibility of putting my grandmother into a home for a week so that the three of us could go away together, but a very brief look indeed sufficed to persuade them that this wouldn't be a successful arrangement.

'It wouldn't be fair on the staff, or the other inmates. Residents, I mean,' mother said to us one evening on her return from an inspection of some of the local establishments. 'There seemed to be a sing-along in progress at the last one. I can't see her co-operating with that somehow.'

The cheaper places were too depressing, had shared bedrooms, ITV on all day, bingo, and catatonic occupants, and reeked of urine. The expensive ones smelled better and had nicer wallpaper but were, well, expensive.

'A pity,' said father, scanning a glossy brochure with pictures of well-groomed, smiling elderly women and well-groomed, smiling nurses sitting in what looked like the gardens of a stately home. 'You obviously get a better class of dementia at these places.'

'I'm not going to be dumped in the kennels,' grandmother retorted when the subject was broached. 'I'm perfectly capable of taking care of myself. For a week,' she added, in case they got the wrong idea.

'We're not leaving you on your own. Suppose you had a fall?' said mother.

'I've said I'll stay. I'm quite happy to look after Granny,' I said. 'For a week.'

Accepting this as the best solution, mother and father went off for their walking holiday in Snowdonia. With the guilt at leaving Granny and the worry over leaving me they were guaranteed to have a rotten time.

'Here's our phone number for the first night,' said mother, handing me a full A4 sheet giving minute details of their itinerary, from which it would be possible to track them, hour by hour. 'The cottage hasn't got a phone, but you can leave a message at the Post Office during the day. And if you need to get hold of us in the evening there's a pub opposite, and you ring this number and ask for Mr Pollitt and he'll come and get us.'

I nodded, not really listening. Over her shoulder I could see father staggering out to the car with a box of provisions. They always did this: bought everything beforehand, leaving nothing to chance, in case muesli or Earl Grey might be hard to come by in Wales. 'I'll ring you from the callbox every night at five past six if you can be in. If there's no reply I'll try again at ten.' Mother's voice droned on. '. . .There's some money in the bureau for emergencies. Don't forget to water the roses if it's dry – don't use the sprinkler because it will make the petals go brown. The hanging baskets need doing every day. Oh, and there's some mince in the fridge which is nearly off, so it'll need eating. Have a good time.'

The week was enlivened only by a crackly phone call from Frances. She barely had time to impart the information that they were in Rome, having a brilliant time, it was baking hot and she had just been thrown out of St Peter's for wearing shorts, before the line went dead. This was my only communication from the European travellers apart from a postcard which arrived the day they were due back. Each of them had scribbled a line.

Although my sainted namesake was supposed to be an animal lover, there are No Dogs Allowed in the basilica. Growth wouldn't approve. Frances. XXX

We have paid our respects to the ossified remains of Saints Clare and Francis. Very keen on bones these Catholics. Growth would approve. Rad.

We are writing this in the local ristorante. Veal excellent. Nicky.

On Frances' return her reception at school was no warmer than it had been at the Vatican. Mrs Gledloe's threat had not been an idle one, and the Radleys were invited to withdraw Frances from Greenhurst so that she might avoid the distinction of being the first girl in the school's history to be expelled. She was duly transferred to the local sixth form college – a sixties glass and concrete block in the centre of town – where she was allowed to wear jeans, smoke in the canteen, and attend classes if and when the fancy took her. The second of these liberties was of no interest to her, but of the first and third she took every advantage, and her jeans-clad figure was only the most occasional presence in those graffiti'd halls.

31

Anne Trevillion's party was the party I had been preparing for all my life, and yet I didn't know her before it and have never seen her since.

It was the end of my final year at school, a year in which my star had risen as swiftly as Frances' had declined, to the extent that the headmistress now knew my name and could write me a favourable report. My mother attributed this state of affairs to my deliverance from Frances' malign influence and, indirectly, I suppose, she was right. I had worked harder than ever before, in class and at my cello, because there was nothing else to do. My audition had gone well: a place at the Royal College of Music was contingent upon easily manageable grades; my exams had not thrown up any horrors; all I had to do was wait.

My invitation to the party came through Rad and Nicky. It was Wimbledon fortnight, and the two of them were on their way back from a day at the tournament when, passing some public courts on which a game was in progress, Nicky was struck and almost felled by a tennis ball which came sailing over the fence and hit him full on the back of the head. His assailant was a teenage girl. She must have been unable to believe her luck at having bagged two respectable blokes so effortlessly. In the course of the long conversation that followed her effusive apology it emerged that it was her eighteenth birthday the following weekend and she was having a little party. Would they like to come? If they gave her their addresses she'd send them a proper invitation.

'How nauseating,' said Frances, when Nicky related the incident. A practitioner of the Stand and Deliver school of flirtation, she was thoroughly contemptuous of feminine wiles of a more subtle shade. 'And what did you say?'

'I asked if we could bring anyone with us, and she said,

"Fine – bring loads".'

'She was probably hoping you meant the rest of the rugby team. God, you're dim sometimes, Nicky.'

'I don't suppose we'll even hear from her,' said Rad, who was stretched out on the couch reading *Private Eye*.

'Pity,' said Nicky, to needle Frances. 'She was well sexy. Wasn't she, Rad?'

'Not bad,' he admitted. 'Nice teeth.'

'*Teeth*,' said Nicky scornfully.

The invitations arrived the very next day. 'She's keen,' said Frances. 'She must have rushed out and posted them the minute you said goodbye.' She looked from Nicky to Rad with narrowed eyes. 'The question is, which one of you is she keen on?'

Nicky pointed at Rad. 'She was all over him. You needn't worry about me anyway,' he said. 'She's totally out of my league.'

Frances grunted. She wasn't sure the implication that she herself *was* in Nicky's league was such a compliment.

Rad was looking at the invitation. 'That's the road on the edge of Wimbledon Common,' he said, pointing to the address.

'They must be loaded,' said Nicky. 'Those houses are massive. You could tell she was rich just by looking at her.'

'She won't even remember a couple of proles like you,' said Frances, who had conceived an earnest dislike of the girl for being rich and good-looking and beyond the reach of rational criticism. 'She'll probably set the dogs on us.'

'You're not actually going, are you?' I said. 'You won't know anybody.'

'Just the sort of party I like,' said Frances. 'At least there's a chance something interesting might happen.'

We weren't seen off the premises by dogs, although two Irish wolfhounds did come shivering out of the garden door as we walked up the driveway, circled us twice and slunk back the way they'd come. Frances and Nicky had spent most of the journey quarrelling. Nicky had thought it would be bad form to arrive late; Frances insisted that no one turned up at parties until the pubs shut whatever it said on the invitation. Rad and I favoured a discreet entrance in the middle of the evening, and this compromise had been settled upon, though the argument about who was the more conversant with party protocol continued.

I had the feeling Rad was annoyed with me because earlier that evening he had asked me to cut his hair and I had professed an expertise I didn't possess, and then lost my nerve half-way through the job, so he'd had to finish it off himself.

We were sitting in Frances' room eating doughnuts when he walked in, a towel round his bare shoulders, wet hair flopping into his eyes. 'Can you cut hair?' he asked, pointing the handle of a pair of scissors at me.

'I can,' said Frances with unnerving enthusiasm, wiping sugary fingers on her pillow and holding her hand out.

'I don't trust you – you'll probably hack off an ear. Can you do it, Blush?'

'Yes,' I said, with great confidence, though the extent of my experience was snipping half an inch off my fringe every couple of months. 'Where shall we do it?'

'I don't want whiskers all over my room, thank you,' said Frances, as if the room didn't already resemble a jumble sale after the good stuff has gone.

'The kitchen's the best place,' said Rad. 'You can sweep that floor afterwards. One can. I will,' he corrected himself, seeing my expression.

Downstairs Rad tugged the comb through his hair a few times, breaking several teeth in the process, before handing it and the scissors over and settling down in a hard-backed wooden chair. Frances perched on the kitchen table, swinging her legs and leafing through Lexi's *Vogue*.

'What sort of look are we after?' I said in a simpering voice.

'Er, I'd like to be able to see. But I don't want to look like a squaddie. If you can manage that.'

'No problem,' I said, wondering where to start. I made a

few experimental snips round the back before catching his eye in the reflection in the oven door. I gave a nervous smile. He didn't smile back. Growth wandered in, did a few circuits of our ankles in the hope of titbits and finally came to rest between my feet. I snipped on with greater resolve. A little drift of black curls formed at my feet, turning to fluff as they dried. It was wavy, I reasoned. Slight imperfections wouldn't show. There wasn't much room to manoeuvre in the kitchen between the table, the chair, the units and the dog, and I found myself apologising again and again for squeezing past or catching Rad on the back of the head with my elbow. Frances was entertaining us by reading out beauty tips. 'Avoid the formation of unsightly frown lines by putting a piece of sticky tape between your eyebrows overnight.'

'Or try not frowning,' I said.

'Sticky tape can also be used to construct a cleavage.'

'Christ almighty. Women are so trivial,' said Rad.

'I couldn't agree more,' said Mr Radley, appearing in the doorway. 'I'd advise you to have nothing to do with them.'

'Careful what you say,' said Frances to Rad. 'Abigail once cut off a girl's pigtail because she got on her nerves.'

Rad glanced at the scissors.

'Really?' said Mr Radley, looking at me with new respect. 'I'd like to have seen that.'

'I was only nine,' I said.

'And look at you now. What happened to that fighting spirit?'

'It was crushed out of me by my suburban upbringing,' I replied, knowing that this would delight him.

'Well, that's probably true,' he said, easing past me to get to the fridge. 'Empty as usual,' he said in disgust. 'Oh no, wait – what the hell's this doing in here?' He retrieved a bottle of blood-red nail varnish from the egg tray.

'It stops it going sticky in the heat,' explained Frances.

'Typical. Nail varnish in the fridge, but no food. Is anyone planning to do any shopping in the near future? Are we actually going to eat tonight?'

'Well, *we* are,' said Frances. 'We're going to a party.'

'Oh, fine, as long as you're all right,' said her father. 'It looks as though I'll be dining at my club tonight.' This was how he always referred to the Greek restaurant in the high street. He produced a ten-pound note from his back pocket. 'This is the money I owe you,' he said to Rad.

'Oh, thanks,' said Rad, holding out his hand.

'Only I'm going to have to borrow it back again to get a kebab,' he said, replacing it. 'Enjoy your party,' he added. And he left, humming.

I was still combing and chopping, but with less and less conviction. Every few minutes I had to wet the comb – Rad's hair was drying faster than I could cut it.

'Are you sure you know what you're doing?' he ventured to enquire, as the sides got shorter and shorter in my quest for evenness. I stood in front of him, wedged against the oven, biting my lip with concentration.

'Of course I do,' I said faintly, tugging at the clump of hair over one ear as if attempting to straighten a wig that had slipped.

'Ow. Pulling isn't going to make it longer.'

I put the scissors down. I felt like a mountaineer seized with vertigo half-way up a rock face. Can't go on. Can't go back. 'I'm stuck,' I said.

Rad opened his mouth to say something, then thought better of it and instead gave a sigh expressive of patience tested to the infinite before picking up the scissors and going off in search of a mirror.

'I won't charge you for the bit I've already done,' I called after him.

'You know something,' Frances said to me as we were getting changed. 'I think Rad's got his eye on this Anne Trevillion. Why else would he be so keen to go tonight? Normally he hates parties. He's even washed his hair.'

'I can see what's going to happen,' I said, rummaging in her dressing-table drawer for the mascara, though there hardly seemed any point in making an effort now. 'Rad will disappear off with the lovely Anne, you and Nicky will be nose to nose all evening, and I'll be left in the kitchen eating

Twiglets.' From the bottom of the drawer a pair of eyelash curlers glinted back at me like instruments of torture. I wasn't about to waste my time with anything *trivial*. I had been intimidated by Nicky's predictions about the grandness of the event into wearing my one smart dress – a short black thing with thin straps and tiny jet beading which made a crunching noise when I sat down. Now standing in Frances' bedroom, looking at myself in her streaky mirror, I suddenly felt overdressed. The only appropriate shoes I had were a pair of uncomfortable black slingbacks with pointed toes and a spike for a heel. I would be freezing cold and crippled by the end of the evening – that much was certain.

'Why do women wear such stupid things on their feet?' Rad said, as he watched me hobble out to the car.

'Now, we're going to find Abigail a man tonight,' Frances announced when we were finally on our way. 'Red light!' she shrieked, as Rad hit the brake.

'You needn't make it sound such a challenge,' I grumbled.

'I'm glad we parked the rollerskate round the corner,' Nicky said as we walked down the drive, which resembled the forecourt of a luxury car showroom. The house, overlooking Wimbledon Common, was a three-storey mansion protected by heavy iron security gates such as my mother might dream of, and a high brick wall over which wisteria and honeysuckle swarmed.

We were headed off at the front door by a man in black tie who directed us around the side of the house into the garden. It was hard to tell whether he was a party-goer or a professional usher. I couldn't help feeling like an impostor, on the verge of being publicly unmasked. Nervousness was forcing the muscles of my face into a fixed smile.

'Stop looking so shifty,' Frances hissed in my ear. 'We've got a perfectly sound invitation.'

Earlier there had been some uncertainty about what we should bring. 'It's not going to be the sort of party where you take a six-pack,' said Nicky.

'We ought to take her a present as it's her eighteenth,' said Frances. 'But how are we supposed to know what she's already got?'

'Get something cheap,' Lexi suggested. 'It's bound to be way off the mark whatever you choose. But wrap it lavishly.'

In accordance with this advice Frances was now carrying a Basil Brush finger puppet, boxed, wrapped and trailing ribbons and bows. She would forget to hand it over on our first introduction to our hostess and would still be holding it at the end of the evening.

In the garden the party was well under way. Tiny fairy lights twinkled in the trees, and on the croquet lawn an old-fashioned wind-up gramophone was playing some crackly Viennese waltzes while a few couples – mostly of my parents' age – spun each other expertly around. In the middle of the lawn was a marquee from which people kept emerging carrying plates of food. Waitresses in uniform were circling with champagne and canapes. Most of the younger people were very dressed-up. Several of the girls were in full-length ballgowns and their partners were in dinner suits. Suddenly my black dress didn't feel quite so smart.

'I knew I should have worn black tie,' Nicky grumbled.

'I don't think I've got a tie,' mused Rad. 'Not since Mum flogged off my old school uniform.'

'Which one is she then?' asked Frances.

Rad and Nicky scanned the groups below us on the lawn. 'She's tallish, blonde, and quite good-looking,' said Nicky. This didn't help much.

'They all look the same to me with their hair up,' said Rad, shaking his head.

'I was concussed, remember,' said Nicky.

We hadn't advanced far before a girl in a green taffeta dress broke away from her group and came rustling over the grass towards us. Her blonde hair was swept up into a savagely lacquered pleat.

'You're here!' she said with evident surprise and pleasure, showing very white, even teeth. 'I'm so pleased. Let me get you a drink' – she broke off to summon one of the tray-bearers with the merest tilt of her chin – 'and then I'll take you to meet some people. I'm Anne, by the way,' she said to me and Frances in the face of Rad and Nicky's failure to introduce us. 'I'm a bit pissed actually,' she confided, 'so I'd better do this bit while I can still remember everyone's names.' Thoroughly disarmed, we allowed ourselves to be hawked from group to group until our assimilation was finally achieved. This was a slow and laborious process: conversations would be cut off mid-flow as introductions were made, and then after an awkward silence resume again as if nothing had happened. But our hostess was indefatigable and wouldn't falter until she had parked Nicky and Frances with some of her schoolfriends, Rad with a few of her brother's rowing eight, and me with her parents.

Mr Trevillion was tall with grey hair and a pair of dramatic black eyebrows which looked as though they might once have formed part of a false-nose-and-glasses kit, but were in fact real. He seemed somewhat bewildered to find so many strange people enjoying themselves in his garden.

'You're a tennis-playing pal of Anne's?' he said, tugging my hand. He hadn't really been concentrating during his daughter's gabbled account of the slender chain of circumstance which bound us together. I didn't fancy running through the story again: he was already looking over my shoulder in search of more promising company.

'Sort of,' I said.

'Jolly good. Let me get you another drink.' And he seized my empty glass and made his escape. That was the last I saw of him until the party's unfortunate termination a couple of hours later.

'You're not one of Anne's schoolfriends, then? No, no,' said Mrs Trevillion, who had an unnerving habit of asking a question and then anticipating my answer and supplying it a fraction of a second before I could get there. 'Have you had far to come? Not too far, no, good.' Out of the corner of my eye I could see Nicky enacting the moment of impact of the fateful tennis ball.

'We've been terribly lucky with the weather,' Anne's mother was saying, glancing at my bare shoulders. 'I don't know what we'd have done if it had rained.' This was followed by a pause as we both gazed at the cloudless sky. My cheeks were beginning to ache with smiling. Think, oh think of something to say, I urged myself. The art of framing simple sentences, taken for granted since early infancy, seemed to have eluded me. It wouldn't do to compliment her on her outfit, elegant as it was.

'It's a beautiful garden,' I finally managed, and was rewarded for this banality with a delighted smile.

'Do you like it? Oh good. It's my absolute passion. I've got a marvellous chap who does all the heavy stuff and leaves me to do the fun bits. Would you like a tour?' My heart sank – my shoes were already pinching. I followed her around the marquee, aerating the lawn with my heels, while she pointed out the espaliered pear trees and the quince hedge, tolling the names of the shrubs as we passed, like a Latin mass. At the bottom of the garden was a large shed with a padlock on the door. 'That's my son's workshop,' she explained. 'He tinkers around with these old bikes.' Through the dusty windows I could make out the shapes of half a dozen vintage motorbikes in different stages of assembly. The one completed model was a masterpiece of restoration, every inch of chrome as bright as diamond. Clearly what went on in here was tinkering of an expert nature.

'Anne used to sleep in the summer-house when she was a little girl.' Mrs Trevillion pointed out an octagonal clapboard pavilion beside a row of poplars which marked the edge of the territory. 'You couldn't do that now, of course. It never even crossed our minds that anyone might get in.'

There was still more garden on the far side of the house, less cultivated, with longer grass and wild flowers and apple trees just starting to fruit. It didn't seem possible that someone living in London could have so much space. At the end of the orchard were three beehives. Leaning against one of them was a boy in a black T-shirt and jeans, smoking a roll-up. He ducked as we passed, and as Anne's mother hadn't noticed him I made no comment. As we left I looked back and saw him sitting in one of the trees swinging his legs. He made a lewd gesture with his tongue, and I turned away again, pretending not to have seen.

'Do you do much gardening?' asked Anne's mother, pausing to dead-head a fat rose. 'I don't suppose you do. You're too young. It's an extremely middle-aged sort of thing.'

I thought of our garden at home with the grass shorn into stripes and mother's pom-pom marigolds and dahlias like poodles' tails, and the bedding plants parked in great dollops of colour from June to September then ripped out again. Could you be *extremely* middle-aged? I wondered. Could you be extremely in the middle of anything? Probably not. In moments of self-doubt pedantry could be such a relief.

'Remind me to give you some honey to take home with you,' my hostess said as we returned to the fray. 'Do you like honey? Of course you do.' On our way we passed Rad and Anne's brother, Neil, heading in the opposite direction. I caught Rad's eye and he winked at me – an utterly uncharacteristic gesture which made me blush to my shoulders. Mrs Trevillion deposited me at the marquee before making her excuses and hailing a new arrival. 'You've just rescued me from a peculiar friend of Anne's,' I heard her whisper. I plucked a glass of champagne from one of the circling waitresses and drained it, feeling the bubbles bursting in my nose. I couldn't see any of the others so I picked up a plate and joined the queue for the buffet, putting on the nonchalant expression of someone who has been only momentarily separated from her partner. I drank another glass of champagne while I was waiting, and then another. There was an intimidating amount of food on offer. The servers seemed to be competing with one another to clear their dishes: my plate was full before I was even half-way round. There would be no room in the Trevillion fridge for nail varnish.

I couldn't see a spare seat under cover, so I made my way back outside and found a niche on a wall between two pots of white geraniums. I looked at my watch. It was only a quarter to ten. I was just wondering how I was going to fill the rest of the evening when Frances arrived with a brimming plate and squeezed in beside me.

'*Twiglets,*' she said scornfully.

'Where's Nicky?'

'Probably getting drunk somewhere. He's found his own stash of champagne. Where's Rad?'

'Don't know.'

'Oh ho.' Frances gave me a significant look. 'I bet I know who he's with.' Her confidence was dented a moment later as the subject of her suspicions emerged, Radless, from the house and made her way towards us. The hem of her dress was down at the front and every few seconds she would catch her foot in it and stumble. Stiff strands of hair were beginning to escape from her french pleat.

'Sorry to interrupt,' she said, slipping a chilly arm through mine and pulling me off the wall, 'but I want you to meet someone. One of Neil's rowing friends keeps asking me who the girl with long hair is, so I promised I'd introduce you. He's a really nice person,' she added, which didn't give me great hopes as to his appearance.

'Is he very tall?' I asked.

'No, about average,' she replied puzzled.

'Oh, good, then I can take these off,' I said, removing my shoes and allowing my poor, crushed toes to uncurl in the cool grass. I left the shoes on the wall beside Frances, who was busy clearing my plate.

'I hope you don't mind my asking, but are you and Rad a couple?' said Anne, as we passed the marquee. 'I did ask Frances, but she just sort of laughed hysterically.'

For a moment I contemplated a blatant lie: if she knew Rad was available she'd be after him like a greyhound with an electric rabbit. But then again any prior claim of mine might not be a great deterrent. She owed me no loyalty, and had the air of someone used to getting her own way. Still, there was no point in making it easy for her.

'It's complicated,' I said, with a meaningful look and she gave me a sympathetic, knowing, woman-to-woman smile.

'What's complicated?' said a voice directly behind me, and I almost fainted with embarrassment as Rad poked his head around the tent flap, an amused expression on his face.

'Nothing. Everything. I can't stop,' I stuttered, pointing after Anne who was striding on ahead. That would teach me to be devious. 'I'm going to meet an oarsman.'

'A Norseman?' said Rad as I fled.

'I hope he didn't hear all that,' I said.

'Yes. That would really complicate the complications,' said Anne innocently. I had a feeling she'd rumbled me. 'That's Frank,' she added, pointing to one of the dinner-jacketed types I'd seen earlier having trouble with the waltz. 'He's at Cambridge.' She'd just caught his attention and was waving him over when she stopped suddenly, her grip on my arm tightening. 'Oh *shit*. What's he doing here?' I followed her gaze and saw the boy in jeans who'd been sitting in the apple tree. He was loitering at the edge of a group, half-smiling and bobbing up and down as though he was part of the conversation, which he patently wasn't. He didn't look altogether sane.

'I saw him earlier by the hives,' I said.

'I wish they were killer bees.'

'Who is he?'

'My ex-boyfriend, Grant. I told them to put someone on the gate to keep him out. Shit shit shit. Frank, this is Abigail. Can you look after her?' she said to my appointed guardian, who had advanced, champagne bottle in hand. She turned on her heel. 'I've got to go and find Dad and Neil. Sorry.' And she picked up the dangerous hem of her dress and walked briskly back the way we had come.

'Hello Abigail,' said Frank, filling my glass.

'Hello.' He had a big freckled face and an accent, a friendly one. What was it? Canadian?

'You look a bit cold.' Irish. It was a warm, reassuring sort of voice and, besides, I didn't fancy him, so I could relax.

'I am,' I said. 'Evening wear for men and women seems to have been designed for two different climates. Have you noticed that?'

'You need thermal undies,' he said. 'Or terminal undies, as my granny calls them.' He tested the temperature of my goosepimpled arms with the back of his hand. 'You can have my jacket,' he said gallantly. 'Though it's a shame to cover up your pretty dress.' He helped me into it, and I stood there with the tips of my fingers protruding from the cuffs, like a ten-year-old in a school blazer that will have to last the next five summers. With my shoes off and a jacket on it was the first time I'd felt comfortable all evening.

'You're at Cambridge,' I said. 'What do you do?'

'Rowing mostly. Drinking. Cricket in the summer.' He looked me up and down. 'You should do some coxing, you know. You've just the build for it.'

'Thanks. I think.' I wasn't used to having my body described in terms of 'build'. It made me think of a chimney stack, or a silo. 'I can't swim anyway.'

'That's all right. You don't get thrown in the river every day.' He refilled my glass which seemed to be empty again. I decided I rather liked him.

'I meant what subject are you doing?'

'Oh, I do a little history between hangovers. They keep threatening to kick me out, but I'll keep my head down next year and claw my way up to a two-two, you'll see.'

'Claw your way up to a tutu?'

He laughed. 'Now what about you? You don't row. I don't suppose you play cricket. What do you find to do all day?'

'I've just left school. I'm waiting for my results – I'm going to the Royal College of Music in September.' It would be a while before I started to define myself as a cellist or a musician.

'I don't know a bloody thing about music,' Frank said cheerfully, and then out of the corner of his mouth, 'Is that your boyfriend over there staring at us?' I turned round to see Rad leaning against the wall and looking over Frances' shoulder towards us with a sour expression on his face. He'd walked off before I could wave. 'No,' I said. 'He's my friend's brother. I think it's Anne he's after, actually.'

'Really? He'd be well advised to keep clear Her last boyfriend ended up as mad as a hatter.'

The crackle of a loudspeaker and the sudden boom of music from the marquee warned us that the disco had started.

'Do you want to dance?' asked Frank. 'Or not?' He inverted the bottle and the last trickle of champagne foamed in the bottom of my glass.

'Why not?' I said, feeling suddenly happy. I was eighteen, barefoot, slightly drunk and without a worry in the world.

We followed the general drift towards the tent and peered inside. I was almost as unsteady without my shoes now as I had been earlier wearing them. The chairs and tables had been cleared to the perimeter and a few people were already jigging around on the dancefloor. Stacks of flashing lights pulsed in the corners, throwing distorted shadows on to the canvas walls. As my eyes grew accustomed to the flickering I spotted Nicky, his arms and legs moving rhythmically, though not alas to the rhythm suggested by the music.

'I quite like dancing,' Frank was saying in my ear. 'But I always have the feeling that if a load of Martians landed and saw this weird and totally pointless activity they'd think we were a pretty primitive species.'

'I feel much the same way about cricket,' I said.

He looked genuinely shocked. 'And I was just thinking what a nice girl you are.'

Anne's brother, Neil, came up looking agitated. 'Where's Matt?' he demanded.

'Dunno. Why?' said Frank.

'I want him to keep a lookout near the back gate. I've just chucked Anne's ex out and if the wanker tries to get in again I'm going to smack him one.' He marched off, fists clenched. Frank sighed.

'The mad boyfriend I was telling you about. I suppose I'd better try and prevent bloodshed,' he said. 'It's been nice talking to you.' He gave me a kiss on the cheek and headed after Neil. 'Don't go home with my jacket,' he called over his shoulder. 'It's hired.'

Nicky caught my eye and danced over. 'Come on Eileen,'

thumped the music. 'Come on Abigail,' said Nicky, grabbing my hand and pulling me on to the floor.

'Where's Frances?' I bellowed in his ear. He gave a careless shrug, palms up. Oh ho, I thought. A row. My bare toes felt rather vulnerable in such close proximity to the dancers' clodhopping feet, but I couldn't now remember what I'd done with my shoes. Nicky's erratic movements were in any case proving effective at clearing a space: anyone who strayed too near was likely to be accidentally clouted.

Dexy's Midnight Runners had given way to Madonna. 'Like a vir-ir-gin,' Nicky sang at me with an infuriating smirk. I turned my back on him and he gave my head a condescending pat. 'Only joking,' he wheedled, and then dug me in the ribs and pointed through the throng towards one of the tables, at which Rad was sitting alone, arms folded, a bored expression on his face. 'Look at the miserable old git,' he laughed, wiping a sweaty fringe from his eyes. The heat was starting to build up. 'Come on,' he yelled, when after some arm-waving he had finally secured Rad's attention. 'Come and dance.'

Rad curled his lip in disdain. Mr Darcy, I thought. Wasn't he brought to his knees for just such a slight? Emboldened by this precedent I approached the table. The sneer modulated into Rad's usual look of disapproval. There was a momentary lull between records as the DJ fumbled the changeover.

'Nice shoes,' he said, sarcastically.

'Nice haircut.'

We glared at each other. 'You didn't waste much time,' he said, nodding at Frank's jacket.

'What do you mean?' The music erupted again, drowning his reply.

After a few bellowed exchanges of 'What?' 'Speak up', Rad stood up. 'Let's go,' I lipread, and he propelled me back out into the garden where it was now cold and dark. Little galaxies of fairy lights glittered in the branches and a yellowish glow spilled from the house as far as the croquet lawn. A strong breeze was tugging at the women's dresses and snapping the loose flaps of the marquee.

'What were you saying in there?'

'I was saying it didn't take you and that Irishman long to get into each other's clothes.'

'*That Irishman!*'

'Whatever his name is.' There was a pause. 'Frank,' he capitulated.

'We didn't exactly get into each other's clothes. He only lent me his jacket because I was cold. You wouldn't have offered.'

'I'm not wearing a jacket,' he protested. 'You want me to take off my shirt?'

'It's Nicky's shirt anyway.'

'Oh-oh,' said Rad, seizing my elbow. On the steps below the french windows Anne was standing peering into the gloom, evidently trying to locate someone. 'Have you seen Rad?' we heard her ask Neil, who was trying to light a cigarette into the wind.

'Quick,' said Rad, pulling me into the summer-house and closing the door. It was warm and dry inside, with a musty smell of sunbaked wood. I brushed one of the bench seats that ran around the walls and great flakes of white paint chipped off in my hand.

'Here.' Rad passed me a faded cushion and we sat down, a few inches apart, listening to the muffled sounds of the party.

'Don't you like her?' I asked. 'Frances thinks you do.'

'Frances doesn't know anything. What do you think?'

'It's none of my business.'

'She's a bit too blatant,' he said. 'She keeps sending her friends over to interrogate me. They seem to think I'm going out with you.'

'I don't know where they got that idea from.'

'No. Ridiculous, isn't it?' We laughed and shook our heads over this example of human folly, and then silence descended like a thick fog.

'It's quarter to eleven,' I said, finally, looking at my watch. 'It feels as though it ought to be later. Or earlier.' *Moron*, I thought. Fortunately I appeared to have got away with it.

'I'm probably going to regret this,' said Rad.

'Well, don't do it then.'

'But I might regret it if I don't. Do you mind?' And before I had a chance to reply he leaned forward and kissed me.

This is Rad, was my only thought.

'There. I've been meaning to do that for ages,' he said, as if kissing me was another tiresome chore, like getting his shoes reheeled, which could be ticked off the list. 'Now you're probably going to slap me round the face or say something completely crushing.'

'No I'm not,' I said, still too stunned to come back with anything clever.

'Well, that's a relief.' He kissed me again, more confidently this time, and even as it was happening I was already memorising every detail of the moment so that I would be able to relive it a thousand times in my imagination. As he pressed against me his shirt buttons must have got caught up in the threads on the front of my dress because when we pulled apart there was the popping sound of breaking cotton and hundreds of tiny jet beads clattered to the floor. Rad started trying to retrieve them, and then gave up. Every time I moved more would shake loose. 'You seem to be disintegrating, Abigail,' he said, smiling at me from the floor. And then he looked puzzled and said 'Abigail' again in an abstracted sort of voice, as if trying to refamiliarise himself with a word which suddenly sounds strange. When he stood up there were two round patches of dirt on his trousers where he had been kneeling. He took a step towards me and then stopped. 'I can smell burning.'

At first I thought he was joking, and I was about to come out with some resounding cliché about it being my heart, but he wasn't listening.

'The shed's on fire,' he said, plunging through the door. I followed him, scattering beads. Flames were snaking around the base of the shed, and an orange glow from inside showed that they had already taken hold.

'Hey!' Rad yelled up the garden, over the pounding music. 'The shed's on fire!' A few people who were just emerging from the orchard saw the flames and came running across the lawn towards us, then thought better of it and went haring back up to the house to raise the alarm. Within seconds there was pandemonium: screaming, running feet, and a crowd of people hovering helplessly. The music had cut out abruptly and everyone came spilling out of the marquee to watch the drama. 'Haven't they got a garden hose?' someone was saying, but any reply was drowned by the explosion as the petrol in the bikes caught, the shed windows imploded, and great sheets of flame unrolled over the roof. The crowd shrank back. In a matter of seconds the shed was engulfed.

Neil pushed his way to the front. 'My bikes,' he shouted, distraught, pitching himself towards the burning building. He was restrained from this suicidal rescue-mission by a couple of his friends who dragged him clear.

'It's that fucking wanker Grant's done this,' he ranted, to anyone who would listen. 'Grant,' he yelled into the darkness as though the arsonist might still be hanging around. 'You're dead!'

The wind was blowing the flames dangerously close to the marquee, and sparks were showering down on the canvas. 'That'll go up in a minute,' Rad said. This observation was heard by Mr Trevillion, who was standing near us, comforting a sobbing Anne. He took command.

'Get this thing down,' he ordered, upon which a dozen or so of us, glad to have something useful to do at last, set about dismantling the marquee with more haste than method. Guy ropes were ripped up and stakes wrenched out, and after a minute or two the whole structure swayed and sank forward like a woman in a crinoline falling down drunk. There had been no time to take up the floor or even remove the tables and chairs. It later emerged that Nicky had been stretched out asleep on a row of chairs at the time. He had woken to find himself almost smothered and in total darkness, and had been forced to crawl around the perimeter underneath the tables, like a rat, in search of the exit. Mr Trevillion, Frank, and some helpers were busy tearing down a panel of fencing at the side of the garden to give the fire engine closer access than was available from the front of the house. The fire brigade arrived with a scream of sirens just as this was completed. Ribbon hoses were unfurled like party banners and within five minutes the shed was reduced to a blackened, steaming skeleton.

'Let's go,' said Rad. 'They won't want people hanging around now.'

'What about Nicky and Frances?'

'I told Nicky ages ago that they'd better be back at the car at midnight if they wanted a lift, but he was probably too pissed to understand. To be honest I couldn't care less if he has to walk home. He's such a liability when he's had a few.'

I recovered my shoes by the wall. Someone had planted them, toes down, in one of the pots of geraniums. For some reason they didn't feel nearly so uncomfortable now. Half-way down the drive I remembered I was still wearing Frank's jacket. There was no sign of him near the house, so I went round the back again and hung it from the branch of a cherry tree.

The scene in the garden was one of devastation. The marquee, still not fully dismantled, sat on the lawn like a great sunken soufflé. All around it on the grass lay discarded plates and empty champagne and beer bottles. People who had earlier been dancing were standing about, aimless and embarrassed, waiting to be turfed out. Some of the rowers were planning to form a posse to trawl the streets for Grant. Anne was still crying inconsolably, her mascara leaving inky trails over her cheeks. And at the end of the garden the burnt-out shed still dripped and smoked, and Neil crouched among the ruins picking over the remains of his charred motorbikes.

The police were just pulling up as we left.

'Where are we going?' I said, as Rad set off in the opposite direction from his car.

'I don't know,' he said. 'Let's just walk.'

So we did, side by side, a foot apart, in silence, along the edge of the common past the grand houses with their eight-foot walls and gates like drawbridges against the world, until I was beginning to wonder if I hadn't imagined the whole episode in the summer-house. But there was the bald patch on the front of my dress to prove it. I plucked idly at a stray thread and another strip of beads unravelled in my hand and cascaded to the floor.

'Weird evening,' said Rad, shaking his head.

You can say that again, I thought, but before I could say anything Rad caught hold of my hand and pulled me off the path into the trees, setting my heart thumping with excitement and fear. 'Look,' he said, pointing upwards. 'Bats.' I peered between the branches and saw a couple of black shapes, like burnt flakes of paper, fluttering and wheeling. And then, because we were under a tree and it was a shame to waste it, Rad pressed me back against the trunk and kissed me, rather fiercely.

'I don't know,' he said afterwards, which struck me as the nicest thing he'd ever said, and the only time I ever heard him express uncertainty. He ran one hand down the length of my hair. 'I love your hair. Don't ever cut it.'

'Haircutting isn't really my thing. As you know.'

He returned to the path and I followed, shedding more beads, and this time he put his arm around my shoulders and I put mine around his waist and we walked along, clashing hip-bones awkwardly, because it isn't really a very comfortable way of getting around, but neither of us would admit defeat. Besides it was a relief to be walking so closely alongside him that he couldn't see my burning face. Even at such an extremity, at this moment of openness, I couldn't help feeling that we were treading a tightrope: the wrong word, the wrong gesture and we would be plunged into an abyss of embarrassment from which there would be no rescue.

'Did you really mean that about having wanted to do this for ages?' I asked, as we turned down a side-street of tall redbrick Victorian terraces. It would be nice to think it wasn't just a whim of the moment.

Rad nodded.

'How long?'

'Oh, I don't know. Since France, I suppose.'

'*France?* What took you so long?'

'You never gave me any encouragement.'

'You never encouraged me to.' We stared at each other, almost crossly, as if we felt ourselves victims of some time-wasting practical joke.

'You were always so aloof.'

'But you were supposed to be able to interpret that. Anyway, a minute ago you said you didn't like blatant women.'

'A glimmer of interest is all that's required. Even when you were cutting my hair tonight you were standing about half a mile away, doing it all at arms' length. No wonder it's such a botched job.'

'I didn't want to crowd you.'

'And come to think of it I did give you encouragement. I drove you to Ypres that time on holiday. And then I bought you *Goodbye to All That*. For which, incidentally, you never thanked me.'

'I would have done, but you'd gone off to Durham. I couldn't very well ask Frances for your address – she'd have been suspicious.'

'I almost made a move that afternoon at Hill 62 – do you remember those trenches in the woods outside the museum?'

I nodded. 'So why didn't you?'

'Well, we had the old man with us for one thing. And we'd just been looking at all those pictures of corpses and bits of horses in trees, and it didn't seem quite the right moment.'

'I didn't realise you were so particular.'

'I almost didn't pluck up courage tonight, but then I saw Frank chatting you up and I sort of panicked.'

'He was nice,' I said.

Rad pulled a face. 'I suppose I should be grateful to him for getting you drunk.'

'I'm not drunk,' I lied. The pavement was flowing beneath my feet like an airport walkway. The stars looked brighter and more numerous than ever before, and above us shone the thinnest fingernail of moon, like a rip in the backcloth of the sky. At the end of the road we stopped.

'Which way?' Rad said. On the corner opposite stood a large, ugly house at the end of a curved drive. It had turret rooms on either side, and asymmetrical windows on the upper storey, giving it a skewed look, like someone whose glasses have been knocked off one ear. The house was guarded by a pair of gateposts surmounted by the head of a lion in mid-roar, and a vicious-looking eagle.

'I've been here before,' I said.

'I often have that feeling,' said Rad. 'Even without the drink. I was reading somewhere quite recently that *déjà vu* is caused by a kind of short circuit in the brain,' he rattled on.

'No. I mean I've actually been here before. Years ago. My dad stopped here on the way to Half Moon Street to deliver a parcel. I remember being frightened by those carvings.' I started to walk up the driveway.

'What are you doing?' Rad said.

'I'm going to ring the bell.'

'It's nearly midnight. Are you mad?'

'There's a light on downstairs.'

'What are you going to say?'

'Hello.' I don't know where this surge of irrationality came from; maybe it was the champagne making me show off, or the euphoria at being with Rad, or something altogether weirder. But I only started to lose my nerve when I reached the front door, and by then the sound of my heels on the path must have been audible through the open window, as a face appeared briefly at a gap in the curtains, the hall lights were thrown on and before I could retreat the door was snapped open a few inches, and then closed again as the unseen occupant grappled with the chain. I was suddenly sober, embarrassed, and would have fled back down the path if I'd thought I could get away with it. Rad was still hanging about in the shadows at the bottom of the drive, ready to rescue me or run if necessary. Oh God, what have I done now? I thought. Perhaps I'll just pretend to be lost and needing directions.

'Sorry,' we both said, as the door opened.

Standing opposite me was a girl, perhaps two years younger than me. She had long fair hair, my eyes, my nose, poor thing, and when she gave a little laugh of surprise, I

239

could see she had my crooked tooth. We stared at each other for a moment or two.

'Hello,' I said finally. 'I'm Abigail Onions.'

'I know,' she said, making a sudden, unsuccessful movement with her foot to detain a skinny cat, which shot past us into the rhododendrons. Even her voice sounded like mine.

'Who are you then?' I must have been experiencing one of Rad's short circuits, because I seemed to hear the words before she had even spoken them.

She put a hand out for me to shake. 'I'm Birdie,' she said.

IV

32

The fuse that had been burning for sixteen years had reached the charge at last and my family was blown apart.

It was my father who left home, although mother would have preferred to make that gesture: fill a suitcase, bang the front door, there, do your own ironing, I'm not spending another night under the same roof. But she couldn't very well leave my grandmother behind in the enemy camp. So it was up to my father – somewhat belatedly – to do the decent thing. He didn't want to go: he had abased himself thoroughly and done his penance many years ago now, or so he thought, but my mother's forgiveness turned out to have been a loan, rather than a gift, and she was now calling it in.

He hardly took anything with him, and chose the most wretched accommodation that could be imagined, as if he couldn't really believe what was happening, and wouldn't admit that it could last. I went to visit him there after a couple of weeks: he was renting a bedsit in a large Victorian house about three miles away. There was a strip of carpet on the stairs so worn that on every tread you could see the wood beneath. In the hallway was a dead weeping fig in a wicker stand and a pile of unsorted post on the doormat. The tenants would obviously rifle through the mail, take out what was theirs, and chuck the rest back on the floor.

Father's room was on the second storey. It had brown paintwork and porridge-coloured walls pockmarked with drawing-pin holes and tiny blobs of blu-tack. Some of the pins still had fragments of paper attached, from posters torn down in a hurry. It was the sort of place you would be quick to leave. There was a single bed over which was spread a knitted blanket from home, a table with his school work and typewriter on, a chipboard wardrobe which was standing at a diagonal in one corner to hide a boiler, and a hand basin with a seaweed green streak from tap to plughole. Under the basin was a Baby Belling, the oven part of which father was using as a filing cabinet. He didn't seem to be intending to cook. From the smell of the room and the wrappers in the bin I deduced he must be living on kebabs and curries.

I made a move to the large sash window overlooking the dustbins and whirligigs of the neighbouring gardens.

'Can we open this a bit?' I said. The heat was stifling, and added to the kebab smell was one of unwashed laundry and pipe smoke.

'It's nailed shut,' said father. 'Presumably to prevent any occupants hurling themselves out in despair.'

'Don't say that.'

'Sorry. How's your mother?'

'All right.'

'Good, good. And your granny?'

'I'm still not living there,' I admitted. I hadn't stayed overnight at home since I had made my discovery. Unable to confront my parents to their faces I had left a cowardly note which gave me an opportunity to vent some of my anger without fear of an open confrontation.

Last night I met, by accident, my half-sister. I am still in a state of shock – not so much at her existence, but at the fact that you kept it a secret from me for so long. In particular I can't forgive Granny for the lie she told me about my having had a sister who died. This was cruel and unnecessary. I'd prefer to stay at Frances' house until I have sorted my feelings out.

   love

     Abigail.

This note had been through many versions – some long and histrionic, some cold and terse. The 'love' was a great concession. It hadn't occurred to me that my parents might separate over it. Mine! Who hardly ever even argued, and who never raised their voices. I was thinking only of myself and the apologies I was owed.

The Radleys accepted my arrival without a murmur, and treated me with the respect due to someone who has, against all expectations, brought drama into their household. That my family should have risen up and proved itself tragic and interesting seemed like an affront to nature. The strangeness of things was underlined that Sunday by all the Radleys, plus Auntie Mim, Nicky and myself, sitting down to a lunch of roast beef, cooked by Lexi, during which conversation was co-operative and civil, while a few miles away my parents were tearing their marriage apart.

Within twenty-four hours of my father's expulsion, mother was on Frances' doorstep begging me to come home. Rad answered the door.

'Hello, R . . . er, is Abigail there?' Mother had always had an aversion to nicknames: she simply couldn't bring herself to articulate something that wasn't actually on a birth certificate. I couldn't very well invite her in to the Radleys' for a heart-to-heart, so we walked down to the high street looking for somewhere to sit. She suggested the Wimpy Bar – my first indication that she was in a desperate mood.

'Please come back,' she said, trying not to cry. 'There's no need for you to go too.' We stirred our tea with plastic rods. Neither of us felt much inclined to drink it.

'Why has Dad left now? I don't understand. If you've always known about Birdie, what difference does it make that I know?' *I'm the injured party now*, I wanted to shout.

'It makes all the difference. It's easier to forgive something in private. Soon everybody will know.' A young woman manoeuvred past us with three toddlers on reins like a pack of dogs, and mother lowered her voice – as if they might be interested in eavesdropping on our family secrets! 'Everybody at church, and the surgery, and my Wednesday group.' Her chin gave a tremble.

'How will they find out? I won't tell anyone.'

'You've already told Frances, haven't you?' she said. 'And the whole family now knows, I suppose.'

'I had to. Rad was with me at the time. I've got to talk to someone, anyway. If you hadn't lied to me in the first place –'

'We never lied!' She was unswervable on this point. 'We just decided it was something you never needed to know. I didn't know Granny had made up that awful story. That day when you said you'd found a photo in Dad's wallet, she just told us she'd calmed you down and made you promise not to mention it ever again. I'm furious with her.' Her mouth collapsed. 'Nobody's talking to anybody now.' I held her hand across the table as she reached for a tissue. I could sense us being observed with interest by the two girls behind the counter. A brown skin had formed on the top of my tea. I scored a cross in it with my stirrer.

'It was all done for you. We've tried to give you a happy childhood.'

'I know, I know. I am happy,' I quavered. 'I just wish you'd told me before I found out like that.'

'We weren't to know you'd ever run into her. It seemed so remote.' There was a pause while she exchanged her wet tissue for a dry one.

'Did you ever meet the woman?' I asked, in some trepidation in case this provoked more tears.

'No. Never,' she said. 'She was a student teacher at the school. Your father was supposed to be looking after her because she was finding things difficult. It was just a one-off thing. It wasn't an affair. And he confessed immediately. And we were all right. But then she told him she was, you know, going to have a baby.' Her voice became watery again. 'And it was just awful.'

I could hear her talking as if from a great distance. We were sitting in the Wimpy Bar, my mother and I, talking about my father, who wore a tie every day, even on holiday, who wouldn't park on a yellow line, *getting someone pregnant*. I suddenly felt overwhelmed with pity for her. It seemed so obvious now that my parents' marriage hadn't been conventionally happy – had in fact been cold and empty. And it was plain that years of acting out a forgiveness she didn't feel, for my sake only, had diminished her, and made her thin and sharp and bitter.

'You were only one and a half. I made him choose. Us or

246

Them.' I watched the skin on my tea re-form itself. She squeezed my hand. 'And he chose you.'

❧

Father offered me a cup of tea. He had bought a tiny travel-kettle from Boots, which he filled at the handbasin. He hadn't brought anything useful with him from home, and wouldn't buy anything that smacked of long-term independence. This was an acceptable compromise: the sort of purchase you might make with the next fortnight in mind, but no longer.

'These things are rather handy,' he said, indicating the tea-bags as he dropped them into mugs. He was pleased with this discovery. We always had leaf tea at home, warmed pot, tea-cosy, china cups. Frances wouldn't even have recognised loose leaf – she'd looked in the caddy at our place once, and said, 'What's that? Snuff?'

Dad fetched the milk from the window sill where it had been standing in full sunlight. He sniffed it and pulled a face. When he shook the carton I could hear the slip-slop of jelly against cardboard and the bile rose in my throat. 'Black's fine,' I said.

'Isn't it time you moved back home?' He carried the wet tea-bags over to the bin in a spoon, leaving a trail of drops. 'Your mum must be missing you. And you shouldn't be taking all this out on her.'

'I will if you will.'

'She doesn't want me back yet. It's too soon. I'm better off here for the moment so she can have some time to herself. Anyway, the Radleys can't put you up all summer.'

'They don't mind. I'm like a daughter to them,' I said without thinking, and could have bitten my tongue off when I saw the hurt expression come and go on his face in a fraction of a second.

'I'm so sorry about all of this,' he said, lifting his shoulders in a gesture of helplessness. 'Whatever you think of me, you know how much I . . . care about you. I didn't want to lie to you, but telling you seemed even worse.'

247

'Birdie knew all about me.'

'Well, naturally, her predicament was rather different. You've spoken to her at some length, I gather.'

'Yes.'

'How is she? Is she well?'

'Yes. She looks just like me. And you.'

'Ah.'

'Why did you stop going to visit her?'

'I saw her when she was a baby, and I used to take presents over at Christmas, and Easter eggs and so on.'

Easter eggs, I thought, a memory struggling to be born.

'But of course it used to make your mother unhappy, and when Birdie was old enough to ask questions she started to find my visits confusing and upsetting, so Val, her mother, told me to stop. I still sent money for a few years after that, but then that was returned, so I assumed she had got married.' He raised an enquiring eyebrow.

'Yes,' I said. 'But they got divorced a couple of years ago.'

'Ah, well, it's the national sport.' And he gave a ghostly smile.

'So all those times when you go off in the car, you're not going to see them.'

He seemed astounded by this suggestion. 'No, of course not. I haven't seen either of them for at least twelve years. When I go out, I just . . . go out.'

How could you have done it? I wanted to say, but I could see what agony this conversation was for him, and I didn't have the will to probe any deeper. As I left he scribbled down the number of the pay-phone in the hallway on the back of an envelope and gave it to me. 'You can call me at any time,' he said. 'If it's not me who answers, just ask for room five and one of my fellow prisoners will come and knock on the door.'

'Do you know any of them?'

'We nod on the stairs. Some people leave angry messages on the bathroom door about the cleaning rota. It's rather like being in university digs again. Only without the fun.'

33

Birdie was welcomed into the Radley household with their usual unstudied hospitality. That strange night when I had rung her doorbell she had invited us in and we had sat up talking until three, when Rad finally fell asleep with his head on the kitchen table, and I had had to shake him awake and ply him with coffee so that he could drive us home. Since then I had only met Birdie on neutral territory – in a park, or café, or at Frances'. She had introduced me to her mother on that first occasion, but I sensed it wouldn't be appropriate for me to make a habit of dropping in. Valerie Cromer was working at a desk in a sort of windowless broom cupboard, and swung round on her swivel chair as we knocked. Her hair was brown with streaks of grey and was scraped up into an untidy ponytail, and the skin on her face was starting to sag into the hollows, though she can't have been more than forty.

'Well, well,' she said, when Birdie told her who I was. She looked at me over a pair of large red-rimmed glasses and nodded slowly. 'You do look like sisters.' And then she turned back to the pile of papers and that was it.

'She's busy,' Birdie had explained. 'Marking exam papers. Forty-eight pence a script – can you believe that?' She saw injustices everywhere.

I could tell straight away that we were going to be friends, that we wouldn't simply meet and part and carry on our separate lives. You get a sense within minutes of meeting someone whether or not anything further can develop, and with Birdie the feeling of recognition went deeper than our appearance. She looked up to me in the same way that I used to with Frances; as someone who might prove a gateway to a more interesting existence. It was strange and pleasant to be on the receiving end of this sort of unearned admiration for once. It can't just have been my seniority that impressed her.

Although she was two years younger than me she had the confidence of someone older. Being socially disadvantaged had given her some advantages after all. She loved it at the Radleys' because it was like home – casual, messy and informal – but with more company. And they liked her, too, because her origins were romantic, and because she had fiercely held opinions which they could mock. She had obviously been brought up in a household where political debate was common. She knew all the lingo: things were either 'sound' or 'unsound'; there were lefties, but not righties, wets but not dries, scabs, trots, fascists – words which meant nothing to me but which she pronounced with great authority. My mother had always insisted it was bad manners to talk about politics – unless you were a politician, and even then she didn't much like it. Opinions were not things to be aired, shared or modified, but things to be kept hidden away like a piece of expensive jewellery which is always shut up in a box and never worn in case it gets damaged.

Within two weeks Birdie had converted Frances to vegetarianism, to Lexi's great dismay. This meant Frances could no longer be made to prepare any of the family's meals which contained meat. Mr Radley loved to argue with Birdie: nobody else would give his views the dignity of a dispute. They disagreed about practically everything.

'We're carnivores, look, look,' he would say, baring his fangs at her. Or 'Equality? You women can have it as far as I'm concerned. If you want to spend your lives in a pin-striped office until you're old and exhausted and think that's freedom, be my guest.' Or 'Do you honestly think it's going to make the *slightest difference* to your daily life which party is in power? I've never voted in an election in my life.'

'When's your sister coming back?' he asked me the day after Birdie's first visit. 'It's not often I get a chance to argue with a real feminist.'

'She said she couldn't bear to waste another breath on such a hopeless old bigot,' Frances improvised. 'We're feminists anyway,' she added indignantly. Mr Radley roared with laughter.

It was some days before Rad and I found a moment to be alone for more than a few seconds. During the drive home from Birdie's that night we had hardly spoken.

'Never a dull moment with you, Abigail,' Rad had said, faintly, as we had set off, and I had laughed, but couldn't find the right words to pick up the conversation. My brain felt scrambled. It was as if these two great events – Rad's discovering me and my discovering Birdie – to which it now seemed my whole life had been leading, had by the cruel coincidence of their timing cancelled each other out. An equation – never properly understood – from school physics lessons kept replaying itself in my head: light plus light equals darkness. How could I think about my relationship with Rad when my mind was full of Birdie? What was a whole tribe of sisters to me compared with him?

By the time we had reached my house, where I had asked to be dropped off so that I might compose my martyr's farewell note and collect a few belongings, I had convinced myself that Rad would in any case have written off the entire episode at the party. But as we pulled up outside, just as a blue dawn was breaking, he said, without looking at me, 'I know you've got more important things on your mind now, and I know you were drunk earlier, but I wasn't, and I did mean it all,' and I knew we would be all right.

Relaunching our relationship under the high wattage scrutiny of the rest of the Radleys wasn't easy, however. Flirting didn't come naturally to Rad, and the reassuring nods and smiles we gave each other in company could have gone undetected for months. I decided that telling Frances straight away was the quickest method of spreading the news.

Even though I had always suspected that she would disapprove, her lack of enthusiasm still took me by surprise.

'You're having me on,' she had said, when I broached the subject.

'I'm not.'

'But you're totally unsuited.'

'Why?'

She gave up this line of argument. 'What if something happens – if you split up? It will be really hard for us to be friends.'

I laughed uneasily. 'That's taking family loyalty a bit far, isn't it?'

'Not really,' she said. 'I mean if you and Rad had a big bust-up I'd have to choose, wouldn't I? And I'd have to choose Rad.'

'The same applies to you and Nicky, then?' I said.

'I know,' she said. 'I worry about that, too.'

Lexi was more encouraging. 'Oh *are* they? What a good idea,' she said, when Frances passed on the information, as if convenience had been our driving motivation.

Rad was back at the bakery again for the summer, so one morning the following week when Lexi was at the office and Mr Radley was off delivering sanitary bins to all the pubs on his round (his latest descent down the employment ladder), I turned down Frances' suggestion of a shopping spree, and encouraged her to go without me.

'Are you waiting for Rad?' she asked. 'Because he'll probably be late back. Mum gave him a whole list of errands to do.'

'It's all right,' I said. 'I'm used to waiting.'

I prowled around the house, moving from room to room in search of diversion. I took out my cello – one of the only things I had imported from home – and played a few easy pieces in the dining room where the bare floorboards set up a nice resonance. Then I remembered Auntie Mim upstairs and put it away. I've never liked playing unaccompanied to an audience: the anonymity of the orchestra suits me fine. Growth was loitering at my heels, wanting to play. I took pity on him and threw his rubber bone around the sitting room while he tore back and forth to retrieve it, his eyes rolling with joy. I idly traced my name in the dust on the television screen, then realised this might look as if I was trying to make a point, so I cleaned the glass with a tea-towel. This made the rest of the room look even dirtier, but I was damned if I was going to spend all morning washing and wiping. You'd never finish a job like that – you'd go under.

Rad was back before lunch. I watched him staggering down the road with two carrier bags of groceries in each hand and half a dozen of Lexi's newly dry-cleaned dresses over his shoulder. I waved as he came down the path, but before he saw me he was waylaid by Fish, who was digging up his driveway, and it was ten minutes before he could extricate himself.

'Moron,' he said, kicking the front door shut behind him, a remark I took to refer to Fish, not me. 'Oh, hello.' He brushed his lips against mine as he passed me on the way to the kitchen with the shopping, which he started to unpack. After emptying one bag he stopped, taking in the unusual quietness of the house. 'Are we the only ones in?' he asked, tossing boxes of set meals into the freezer.

'Apart from Auntie Mim.'

His pace increased fractionally. 'Right, that's done. I'm going to get changed.' He patted his T-shirt, sending up a puff of flour. 'Are you coming up?' he added, a shade too nonchalantly.

'Erm . . . okay,' I said, aware of the significance of breaching the threshold of his bedroom, and followed him upstairs with a sense of impending calamity.

Rad had already dragged the old T-shirt over his head by the time he reached the top landing. It was dropped on a pile of laundry just inside his doorway. The room's only chair was occupied by a stack of open books and pages of handwritten notes – an essay in progress – so I perched upright on the edge of the bed while Rad stood in front of his wardrobe contemplating his three shirts as though overwhelmed by the breadth of the choice before him.

What if he takes his trousers off? was my main thought. Am I supposed to watch or not?

But he just pulled one of the shirts from a hanger and sat down next to me on the bed, buttoning it up.

'Are you all right?' he said at last, taking my hand.

'Yes, of course,' I said.

'You haven't been avoiding me, have you?'

'No. It's just there's never a moment . . .'

'I know,' he said. 'There's no privacy in this place.'

There was a silence. In all my daydreams and fantasies about Rad, rehearsed and refined over many years, things had never progressed beyond that initial moment of admission, that first kiss, and now I had the strange and unnerving feeling of being on stage with no script. What was supposed to happen next? How were we meant to negotiate that tricky terrain between drunken euphoria and normal, unthinking, devoted coupledom?

'If this was a film it would be over by now,' I said. 'It would have ended in the summer-house with the flames going up in the background.'

'What are you talking about?'

Sometimes when I was following a line of thought in my head I wasn't sure which bits I'd actually said out loud. 'Sorry. I was just thinking I wish we were back at the party. It was easier to talk there, for some reason. Perhaps it was because it was dark.'

'Well, we can close the curtains if you like,' said Rad, mistaking my meaning. He didn't wait for a reply but drew them anyway. When he sat down again he was that much closer to me. In the gloom I could see specks of flour, white on his black eyelashes.

Just how deaf was Auntie Mim? I wondered, thinking of the party wall.

There was a rattle from the letter-box. 'Coo-ee,' called a voice. 'Anyone in?'

Growth, roused from sleep, started barking irritably. Rad put a finger over my lips. 'We're not here,' he whispered, peering through a chink in the curtain. 'It's Clarissa.'

A key grated in the lock, and then we heard the front door opening. 'Helloo! Lexi!'

'Oh, typical Mum. Half of London must have a key to this bloody house.' He stood up, admitting defeat. 'Hello,' he called over the banisters.

Clarissa was standing in the hallway scribbling a message on the telephone pad. She jumped at his voice. 'Oh, Rad, you startled me. I thought there was no one in. Hello Abigail, are you here too?' she added, as I appeared at Rad's elbow. 'You weren't in bed, were you?'

'No, we were on it,' said Rad. We made our way downstairs.

'Where's your mum?'

'At work, isn't she?'

'She's supposed to be having the day off so we can go to the Flower Show. She was meant to be picking me up an hour ago.'

'She must have forgotten.'

'Has she got something on her mind?' asked Clarissa. 'This is the second time she's stood me up in a fortnight.'

'Perhaps she's worried about Frances' A-level results?' I suggested. Rad and Clarissa seemed to find this idea highly diverting.

'I was going to borrow some of her clothes anyway, so I might as well take them while I'm here.' She thumbed through the dry-cleaning which was hanging from the picture rail. 'These will do,' she said. 'Carry on,' were her last words as she strode down the drive, trailing yards of ballooning polythene.

Within minutes of her departure Frances was back from the shops with a new pair of jeans and a bag of apple doughnuts, and the moment for carrying on with anything was, to my great disappointment and relief, past.

'Perhaps she's going through the change of life,' said Birdie, putting down her copy of *To the Lighthouse*. She was sitting in the Radleys' front room, sideways across an armchair, legs dangling.

Her habit of coming to visit us and spending the entire time buried in a book struck Frances as bizarre and troubling. 'Why bother to trek all the way over from Wimbledon just to sit and read? She could do that at home.' But Birdie seemed content merely to be with us and had no need for any additional entertainment. I found this reassuring. It was natural, unforced; it was what a sister would do. (It only occurred to me later that it might not have been us she came to see.) I was cross-legged on the floor in front of her chair, restringing a set of Lexi's amber beads. Frances was customising her new jeans by cutting slits in the knees and seat and lining the holes with flesh-coloured material. Rad was asleep on the couch.

'Does it make you forgetful then?' asked Frances. 'I thought you just got hot and sweaty.'

'No. Some women go totally barking.'

The object of their concern was Lexi. She had just poked her head around the door to tell us she was off to play golf with Clarissa, and we had heard her clattering around in the cupboard under the stairs where she kept her clubs. A moment later she had emerged with the hoover over her shoulder, and before any of us could intercept her, had slung it in the boot of the car and driven off.

'She might be worried about Auntie Mim.' It was generally agreed that Auntie Mim was ailing: the range of her appetite had contracted still further; she had had nothing but weak tea and aspirin for days now.

'Mum doesn't believe in worrying.'

'Neither do I,' said Birdie. 'If you've got a problem, do

something about it. If there's nothing you can do, worrying won't help.'

Here at last was evidence of some genetic variation: I worried about things like an outbreak of Legionnaire's disease in a country I had never visited. If there was a report on the television about a small asteroid on a collision course for Earth, my mind would immediately turn on the likelihood of it landing on me. When it came to disasters I always felt like an actuarial phenomenon waiting to happen; if I read a newspaper I tended to identify only with the very unlucky – the person who choked to death on a peanut rather than the pools winner.

'It must be overwork,' said Frances.

'Who's overworked?' asked Mr Radley, strolling in. 'I certainly am.' He flung himself down on the chaise longue and began clicking through the TV channels. Rad stirred as the sound erupted from the set, but his eyes remained closed. 'This picture seems bright,' he said. 'Have you been fiddling with the controls, Frances?' She said she hadn't. I kept my head down. 'Funny,' he mused. 'Must be a power surge.' He watched Frances attacking her new jeans with the kitchen scissors. 'You know in more primitive times, Frances, women used to sit around *mending* old clothes, rather than vandalising new ones.' Frances stuck two fingers through the rip in the seat of her jeans and waggled them at him.

'Now you two,' he went on, ignoring her, 'make such a marvellous picture, I'm inclined to ask you to sit for me.' We were flattered in spite of ourselves.

'What, right here?' said Birdie.

'No, no, upstairs, where the light's better. You wouldn't mind just sitting still for an hour or so every afternoon? You've nothing better to do, have you?'

'Suits me,' said Birdie. 'I can get some reading done.'

'Can't I read as well?' I protested.

'No – I want you holding those beads,' said Mr Radley.

'Can I wear a Walkman?'

He raised his eyes to heaven. 'I might let you read once I've done your hands,' he conceded.

'Can I buy the painting when it's finished?' Birdie pleaded. She wasn't yet familiar with his work. 'Unless Abigail wants it too.'

'You'll have to toss for it,' said Frances. 'Loser gets to keep the painting.'

A thought struck Birdie. 'Do we have to take our clothes off?'

'No, no.' Mr Radley laughed indulgently. 'Not unless you want to.'

'We don't,' I said.

'It wouldn't bother me, actually,' said Birdie. 'There's nothing shameful about nudity.'

'Have you been talking to Mum?' asked Frances.

'Artists are just like doctors,' Birdie went on. 'I mean, you wouldn't think twice about stripping off in front of your GP.'

'You might if he had no qualifications and no talent,' said Rad from the couch, without otherwise moving.

Mr Radley affected to be convulsed with mirth. 'I knew he wasn't really asleep,' he said. 'My son is easily provoked,' he explained to Birdie in a loud whisper.

'I *was* asleep until you thoughtfully put the TV on.'

Mr Radley ignored this. 'Anyway, Rad, though I admit you might have certain territorial rights over Abigail, I don't see why you should extend the franchise to her sister.'

Rad's response to this sort of joke, which he hated, tended to be a sudden attack of pomposity. 'I don't claim any *rights* over Abigail,' he said. 'Or anyone else. It was just friendly advice.'

His father gave an infuriating smirk, glad to have succeeded in winding Rad up.

Birdie, who was somewhat in awe of Rad, decided that, on reflection, Art would be just as well served by her remaining clothed.

Mr Radley was an exacting portraitist. He seemed very rapidly to forget that it was at his request that we were there in his studio at all, and came instead to view the enterprise as a huge and tiresome favour on his part. Birdie was all right – she was rattling through Virginia Woolf. I was stuck on the floorboards with those damn beads. When I requested music to relieve the tedium Mr Radley offered me Gregorian Chant or nothing, and he tutted when I got cramp and had to hobble around the room.

At first Birdie and I couldn't chat without turning round or making each other laugh and twitch out of position, but gradually we got used to talking without being allowed to move or make eye contact, and after a while we were able to ignore Mr Radley's sighs and groans and the squeak of charcoal on canvas, and carry on as if there was no one else there. Our conversation always had a way of returning to the same subject – Us.

'Birdie isn't your real name, is it?'

'No. It's Elizabeth. Elizabeth Katherine Cromer. But when I was born I was premature, and Mum said I had this thin dark hair on my head like wet feathers, and tiny chicken legs, and I just looked like a baby bird that's been pushed out of its nest. No one's ever called me anything but Birdie.'

'If you'd always known about me, didn't you ever feel like tracking me down and confronting me?' I asked her one afternoon.

'I wasn't allowed,' she said. 'Mum told me you didn't know anything about us. Anyway when I was younger I used to really hate you.'

'Oh.' I didn't like the idea of being hated, even in absentia and at a distance of several years.

'For some reason I imagined you were really rich and living in some flash house, with a pony and everything, while Mum and I were stuck in a flat, without any central heating, being poor.'

'We haven't got central heating either,' I said, suddenly proud of a fact that had annoyed me for years.

'I did come to your house once – about three years ago. I knew Mum would have your address somewhere, and I got the train and the bus and got totally lost and walked miles, but

I found it eventually. I spied on the house from the end of the road for about ten minutes. Then I started to get a bit brave and I came right up to the house. I saw your dad' ('your dad', I noticed, not 'Dad') 'through the window, and then you came out the front door and I ran for it. There's nowhere to hide in your road. I was quite relieved to find that you weren't rich or anything. Actually I remember you were wearing a really bad ra-ra skirt.' (Mr Radley gave a snort of laughter at this point.) 'It made me feel a lot better.'

'I've still got it somewhere,' I said, vowing then and there to chuck it out at the first opportunity.

❧

It was during one of these conversations that various odd coincidences came to light. Like me, Birdie had been bullied at school; she had never had her hair cut short; she couldn't swim, and she played a musical instrument – the violin. When we compared notes it emerged that our respective orchestras had attended the same music festival the previous summer. We had perhaps come within a bow's length of discovering each other then.

On the strength of this shared interest Birdie suggested we went busking. 'Have you ever done that?' she asked.

I said I hadn't. Somehow the cello didn't strike me as having the sort of sound that lent itself to tube stations or sub-ways. A concert hall, or the garden of an Oxford college, yes.

'Let's do it. You can make good money,' she insisted. 'I could round up another violinist and a viola player, no trouble, and we could do some chamber music one day.'

'Chamber music?' said Frances, a little dejectedly, when told of the plan. 'That means no vocals, I suppose.' She quite fancied herself as a gravel-voiced club singer, and would have liked nothing better than to belt out 'Hey Big Spender' at embarrassed commuters.

'Where are you going to do it?' Rad wanted to know. 'You'll have to be careful you don't trespass on someone else's patch.'

'There's that blind accordionist who does the stretch by the shopping centre car-park,' Frances agreed. 'He looks like he could turn nasty.' I had a sudden image of running battles between rival gangs of musicians.

'Don't let them put you off,' said Birdie. 'It'll be fun. We'll treat you to a pizza with our earnings,' she promised them.

Brother and sister looked at each other. 'We'll eat beforehand just in case,' said Frances.

In the event Frances couldn't resist coming along. We had selected a pitch in a complex of subways in the town centre where they converged at an open-air intersection whose chief feature was an octagonal patch of dead grass. The chosen site had the benefit of interesting acoustics without being too oppressively subterranean. It smelled like a urinal nevertheless. We installed ourselves – instruments, music stands, a chair for me – rather self consciously between two daubs of graffiti: FREE NELSON MANDELA and, further along, TRACIE IS A FAT SLAG.

Birdie had brought along some string duet arrangements – nothing too technically demanding: we were there to beguile pedestrians, not to extend ourselves, after all. The other half of the promised quartet had, predictably, cried off at the last minute. I wondered whether Birdie had invented them. As she propped her empty violin case at our feet and dropped in some loose change a few passers-by, seeing our preparations, quickened their pace.

Frances, finding herself under-employed, left us to play our first pieces and made a quick tour of the other tunnels and stairways to check how far the music carried. 'It sounds lovely,' she said when she reappeared, adding tactlessly, 'It must be the echo.'

After a while Birdie and I began to relax. We started concentrating less on our playing and more on trying to guess which of the people who passed would be likely contributors to our pizza fund. A few general principles soon emerged. People who speeded up, kept their eyes fixed straight ahead or stared down at their feet were no-hopers, as were other teenagers, old ladies with shopping-bags-on-wheels and young mothers with pushchairs. Perhaps it was something to do with having their hands full. The softest targets were men in suits, particularly those travelling in packs: if one gave they all bowed to the pressure.

'Do you think men are more generous than women?' I asked Birdie, when our statistical sample seemed to have reached significant proportions.

'No. They just have more money,' was her reply.

Bored with her passive role, Frances had taken to performing circuits of the subway system in the guise of a passer-by, ostentatiously tossing coins into the violin case as an encouragement to others, and then retrieving the money when no one was around. 'Beautiful isn't it?' we could hear her saying to someone as they made their way down the steps towards us.

'Very,' said her companion, an expensively dressed woman, about my mother's age, keeping a firm grip on her handbag.

'Tightwad,' muttered Frances, as the woman tacked off smartly across the dead grass before she came within range of our begging bowl. 'I'm going to the café to get a drink; I'm parched,' she added, helping herself to a handful of change. 'Do you want anything?' Birdie asked for a Coke.

On Frances' return, some while later, traces of crumbs down the front of her top confirmed that she had been gorging on chocolate cake. She had forgotten the Coke of course. She looked approvingly at the layer of silver in the bottom of the violin case. 'We're doing well,' she said.

'We?' said Birdie and I, simultaneously laying down our bows in protest. The subway was momentarily deserted so we allowed ourselves a break.

'I'm keeping your spirits up, aren't I?' said Frances. There was a sound of footsteps in the distance. 'Quick, get playing,' she commanded. I was hoping it might be Rad, who had promised to come along and spectate if he finished his essay in time. But the figure who came round the corner was a rather less agreeable proposition. He was about Rad's age, possibly older, with a thin white face topped by a small woolly hat. His T-shirt and jeans looked as though they hadn't parted company from his body in several months, and he was swaying slightly and muttering, slapping the subway wall occasionally with one hand, to steady himself perhaps, or because there was nothing else available to hit.

He slowed down when he saw us – unlike most people – and gave a sort of lurch in our direction. I must confess that my bowing action became less than fluid at this point, but beside me Birdie played on without wavering. As he drew level he stopped, and for an insane moment I thought he was going to give us some money, but instead he gave a horrible leering smile and then leaned forwards and spat a gobbet of bilious green slime on to ground about two inches from Birdie's right shoe. Our music came to a skidding halt, and the three of us stared in amazement at his departing back.

'Another satisfied customer,' said Birdie, and began to giggle. We were still breaking into laughter over it five minutes later as we packed up, when Rad arrived.

'Oh no,' he said, as I flipped home the catches on my cello case. 'I'm not too late, am I?'

I could tell Birdie would have been prepared to unload everything again just to oblige him, but Frances had been bored for some time by now, and I had had my fill of the subway. 'Twelve pounds,' said Birdie, jangling a plastic bag of the afternoon's takings in his face.

'Not bad,' he admitted. 'But at least in the bakery you get free bread – and all the flour you can inhale.'

'Ah, but you don't have the fun of being spat at by mad dossers,' said Birdie, and related the incident, with many interruptions and embellishments from Frances.

The plan was to go back to Balmoral Road to drop off our instruments and wait for Nicky, and then send out for a pizza – perhaps two, depending how far the funds stretched. I had skipped lunch and was beginning to feel slightly giddy with pleasure at the thought of food. When we reached the railway station Rad was in the middle of explaining the breakthrough he had just had in his essay on Kant, and I was trying to remember the four toppings on a Quattro Stagioni and only half-listening, when Frances suddenly dug me in the ribs and said 'Aha, there's Gobber.' Sitting against the wall near the taxi rank on a greyish sleeping bag was our erstwhile critic, in his filthy jeans and woolly cap. It was still a rare sight to see a young person begging openly – especially in the suburbs – and I was shocked at the abject way he kept his head down and his hand out, all the while muttering the refrain 'Spare some change please'. Nevertheless revenge is a primitive need, and the moment I saw him I could feel my mouth start to fill with saliva.

'That's the bloke who spat at us,' said Frances to Rad. 'Go and belt him.'

'Do you mind if I don't?' said Rad.

Birdie, who hadn't given any sign of recognition so far, indeed seemed to have drifted off into a reverie of her own, all of a sudden came to and said, 'Allow me. You don't mind, do you?' she added, as the three of us hung back wondering with some unease what form this confrontation was going to take, and before any of us could stop her she had crossed the road and dropped the plastic bag containing our entire afternoon's earnings at his feet.

It would be pleasing to relate that the recipient of this majestic act of charity showed some degree of gratitude or mortification, but he merely gave Birdie a blank stare and pulled the bag a little closer towards him.

'Do you think I did the right thing?' said Birdie, taking in our dismayed expressions.

'Oh brilliant,' said Frances bitterly. 'There goes our dinner.'

'I wasn't that hungry anyway,' said Rad, seeing Birdie blush at the rebuke.

Artichokes. That was the fourth thing, I remembered.

With the continual traffic of visitors at the Radleys – Birdie, Lawrence, Clarissa, Nicky – my elevation to artist's model, and Rad's anti-social working hours, the opportunities for

Rad and me to be together were scarce. He started his shift at the bakery at 3 a.m. so late nights were out of the question. He resented wasting daylight hours on sleep, and came to bemoan the amount of time I spent stringing beads on the studio floor. 'Dad gets to see more of you than I do,' he complained one afternoon when Mr Radley had extended one of our sessions because things were going well. 'I think he's doing it on purpose.' I laughed, faintly. I knew what his impatience was all about.

35

On the day Auntie Mim was finally admitted to hospital, Rad and I made a return visit to Half Moon Street, alone. Mr Radley had cancelled our sitting in order to take her in himself and see her safely installed. He had packed her bag with clean night-clothes and her ivory-backed hairbrush and the Agatha Christie Omnibus which was the only book I'd ever seen her reading.

Rad and I, meanwhile, had packed his car with the dog-blanket from the chaise longue, and a picnic consisting of sandwiches made with the end of a jar of peanut butter, a couple of softish apples, and the remains of the day before's treacle tart. Rad didn't take a book – a fact which struck me as significant. As I was washing the apples – one of which had an ominous curve of puncture marks, as though a small dog had picked it up in his teeth and dropped it – Rad came into the kitchen carrying two towels. 'Shall we take swimming gear?'

'It says No Swimming,' I reminded him.

'If there's no one there . . .'

'There are always people there.'

'There might not be. It's not that sunny.'

'If it's cold enough to put people off going, it'll be too cold to swim,' I pointed out.

'Shall we take them just in case?'

'Rad, you know I can't swim.'

'I'll teach you.'

'I don't want to learn.'

'You must do.'

'I don't.'

Rad sighed, and returned the towels to the airing cupboard. We didn't speak much on the journey. There was an awkwardness between us that was something to do with my refusal to swim, and was about something different too. The last time we had been to Half Moon Street had been a year ago, with Frances and Nicky. Rad had bought us all lunch, we had sat on the grass, *Narziss and Goldmund* had ended up in the water, we had eaten ice cream on the way home, Rad and I were just friends: we were all happy. Today I was nervous. If I said or did the wrong thing, would I be cast off?

Rad was fiddling with the radio, which seemed to offer nothing but hiss and crackle and the odd burst of German. Occasionally when he spun the tuning dial it would let out a high-pitched whistle and cut out altogether. I was then called upon to smack the top of the dashboard with the A–Z to try and revive it.

'I hope Auntie Mim gets better quickly,' I said at one point. 'She needs feeding up – but I don't suppose they have potatoes and sprouts on the menu every day.' She had looked terrible being helped into the car by Mr Radley. I'd hardly ever seen her on the move before – she had always been sitting in her armchair – and it struck me how tiny she was, and how brittle. If she had fallen on the driveway she would surely have broken into a thousand pieces. My granny's bones were like steel: she could crack a paving stone with one blow from her hip. Auntie Mim had given us a little wave from the front seat, tiny clawed fingers trembling at the window.

'*Feeding up?*' Rad laughed at me. 'You're such an optimist. 'She'll never come out of hospital.'

'What do you mean?'

'They don't try and *cure* people her age.'

'But they have to try and preserve life, don't they?'

'Oh, they'll stick her on a drip and do "tests", but . . . She knows she's not coming back. I went into her room to see if she wanted anything carrying down, and she'd packed all her stuff up in boxes, ready for Mum to take to Oxfam.'

'No.'

'It's true.'

She put her affairs in order, I thought with a shudder. We hit a pot-hole in the road and the radio came back on suddenly and loudly. 'Our lips shouldn't touch, move over darling,' sang Doris Day. The sun was shining, love songs were playing on the radio, children were out on their bikes, and Auntie Mim was packing up and moving into Death's waiting room. I thought of that bony hand at the window.

'She's a lesbian. Did you know that?' I said.

'Doris Day?'

'Auntie Mim.'

'Never. That must be one of Dad's tall stories.'

'Honest. She sort of confided in me one day. She showed me this photo of a woman – a black and white, really ancient-looking, must've been taken in the 1920s or something, and said it was the love of her life.'

'What did you say to that?'

'I don't think I said anything. I just gaped.'

'I won't be able to look at her in the same way now you've told me that,' said Rad.

'You won't get the chance to look at her at all if your prognosis is correct.'

Rad pulled a face. 'That's going to be one quiet funeral.'

'I've never been to a funeral,' I said.

The cottage at Half Moon Street was still abandoned and boarded up, though one of the upstairs boards had fallen off, giving the place a one-eyed look. There were plenty of other people about, walking by the water or sitting on the grass. It wasn't sunbathing weather, or swimming weather – the clouds had started to roll in as we walked down, hand in hand, from the pub car-park. We made our way automatically to the spot we'd occupied last time, and sat eating our sandwiches and treacle tart. I offered Rad the two apples to choose from and he obligingly took the mauled one, waited until I'd finished mine and then lobbed his into the undergrowth. We hadn't thought to bring any drinks with us, and the combination of peanut butter, treacle and yesterday's pastry left us gasping with thirst.

'Shall I go back to the pub and get something?' Rad offered, clambering to his feet and brushing the crumbs off his jeans.

'It's too far,' I protested half-heartedly: it was over half a mile to the pub, but I was ready to plunge my head in the lake if I didn't get a drink soon. 'Shall I come too?'

'No, I'll run.' And he set off, self-consciously, knowing he was being watched.

I threw the soggy pastry crust we'd rejected to a flotilla of ducks at the water's edge. They were soon joined by some Canada geese. Peeved at arriving too late, they waded out on to the grass and bore down on me, honking, until I was forced to beat a retreat.

By the time Rad came jogging down the path with two well-shaken Coke bottles the geese had given up and flopped back into the water, and the first fat drops of rain were starting to fall. Although there was blue sky at the horizon, above us it was black. 'It's just a shower,' he said, as the clouds opened and the rain came down like spears. The few other people still at the lakeside were dashing for the cover of the trees. There would be no chance of making it to the car. We would be drenched in seconds. 'Come on,' Rad ordered, flinging the rug over his shoulder and wading through the knee-high grass and poppies to the cottage. He peered through a chink in the boards. 'It's all right,' he said. 'There's even some furniture.' The front door was locked, but the back door, itself rotten and crumbling, was secured by a rusty padlock which fell apart in Rad's hand. Rad leaned gently on the door which shuddered open, scratching an arc on the flagstones.

Inside it was dark and cool and smelled of soot. Thin wands of light from holes and cracks in the boarding striped the walls and floor. The 'furniture' consisted of a cast-iron range and a couch whose seats had been ripped out to reveal the springs and webbing. Through an archway a further room, apparently empty, was visible. Rad dropped the rug on to the stone floor in front of the range and sat down. He passed me one of the bottles. 'Don't . . .' was all he managed to say before I had twisted the lid off and showered us with a foaming fountain of Coke. 'I suppose you'll want to drink mine now,' he said, when we'd wiped our faces.

'No,' I said bravely. 'There's a full inch and a half left in here.' He opened his a degree at a time until it had stopped hissing and then handed it to me.

'Go on.'

When we had shared the drink I stood by the window and listened to the rain drumming on the plywood. Rad by now was lying on the rug, propped up on one elbow, idly spinning the empty bottle, waiting for me. I could feel embarrassment welling up inside me like hot lava. In these situations I am either struck dumb or I start to jabber. On this occasion silence prevailed. I don't know why I was so hesitant. I'm not such a hopeless romantic that I'd imagined I would lose my virginity between white satin sheets in a four-poster on my wedding night, but somehow I'd never envisaged it happening on Growth's blanket. I suppose it was fear – of giving too much away and having nothing left in reserve for emergencies.

'Well, are you going to spend all afternoon gazing out of a boarded-up window, or are you going to come here?' Rad asked finally, and I spun round guiltily, like someone tapped on the shoulder by a store detective. My heart was thumping wildly – you couldn't have beaten time to a rhythm like that; it was all over the place. Perhaps I'll have a heart attack, I thought as I lay down beside him, then I won't have to Do It. A few seconds later we were kissing and for a while it was like it had been in the summer-house – a sense of discovery and relief – and I relaxed and thought, it's all right, nothing's going to happen. The back of my head was pivoting around a piece of grit under the blanket, so I reached back with one hand to dislodge it. Rad must have interpreted my sudden squirming as a sign of encouragement, as he began to undo first my jeans then his own.

'What are you doing?' I said, breaking away.

He shrank back as though I'd thrown cold water in his face. 'What do you think?' he said, looking rattled. 'It's all right, isn't it?'

'I don't think we should?' I said, unable to meet his eye.

'Why not?'

'I . . . I don't know you well enough.'

'You've known me for six years.' We were sitting up by this point, cross-legged, not facing each other but at right angles, like two sides of a triangle.

'No. I mean properly. Like this. We've hardly even talked about things.'

'What do you want to talk about?'

'Nothing specific. I just . . . you've done this before, haven't you?'

'Abigail. I've been at university for two years. I'm not a monk.'

'Well I haven't, so it's a bigger deal for me.'

'Are you worried about getting pregnant?'

'No,' I said, a trifle shrilly. It was at this point that I did my trousers up. 'I mean, yes, that would worry me too, but that's not it.'

'It must be me,' he said. 'You've gone off me.'

'I haven't,' I insisted. 'I just need to feel sure of you. I could only Do It with someone I love, who loves me.'

'Oh, I see,' said Rad in a disappointed tone. 'You want me to tell you I love you, is that it?' And I felt myself shrivel under his gaze.

'Only if it's true.'

'I can't do that,' he said after a moment's reflection. 'No. It would be a bit like paying for sex.'

If I hadn't already been so reduced, so mortified by this exchange I would have gasped. Instead I said, 'You must hate me to say something like that.' We were on our feet now, tucking our shirts in, trying to preserve what remained of our mortally wounded dignity.

'Love. Hate. Nothing in between will do for you.'

'I don't understand what you're talking about,' I said. Any second now I'd be in tears and there would be nothing for it but to chuck myself in the lake, or emigrate.

'You know me,' said Rad. 'In spite of what you say, you know what I'm like. I don't know about "love", and I won't

271

say something that isn't true, even if that's what it takes to get your knickers off.'

'I'm just frightened that you're going to screw me and then dump me.'

'Why would I do that?'

'Because you can.'

'So could you.'

'Oh no. It won't be me that splits us up. It'll be you. You're the one who isn't sure of your feelings.'

'I'm sure that I prefer you to anyone else I know, and that I'm not looking over your shoulder for someone else, and that I wouldn't intentionally do anything to hurt you. But that's not enough for you, is it?'

I opened my mouth to retaliate and then shut it again. I was suddenly overwhelmed with misery and weariness. I slumped down on the arm of the broken couch. 'I've really messed everything up,' I said. What I really wanted to say was 'Am I still your girlfriend?' but I knew this would be received with even greater derision.

Rad softened a little. 'Come on, let's go home and forget all this. It doesn't matter.' He pulled the door open, flooding the room with watery sunlight. 'When you're ready,' he said, and I wasn't sure whether he was urging me to get a move on or referring to the larger issue, but from that time onwards there was a sort of restraint in the way he kissed me, and he was careful not to touch me in any way that might cause a repeat of that day's unpleasantness.

36

'I'm going to see your father today,' Birdie said one morning as we stood in the launderette loading the driers with Radley bedding. It was an indication of her thorough assimilation into the household that she was now a full part of the chore rota. I was slightly taken aback by her news. Birdie had been dropping hints in that direction for some time, and I had vaguely envisaged arranging a meeting, but had done nothing about it. I hadn't even broached the subject with father. I suppose I was nervous on his behalf in case they didn't hit it off or, as was more likely to be the case, had nothing to say to each other. But there must have been an element of jealousy, too, because my protective feelings towards Birdie started to diminish almost from the moment she said she was going to see him. I felt outmanoeuvred.

'How did you arrange that?' *Without me*, I asked.

'I wrote him a note, and he wrote back and told me to ring at a certain time, and we talked on the phone for a bit and he said he'd meet me in the Central Library this afternoon.'

Typical father. Only he could arrange such a potentially hazardous reunion in a library, where it would be impossible to talk comfortably. Birdie must have read my mind as she went on, 'We're only meeting there, because it's somewhere we both know. We'll find a café or something. He obviously couldn't come to my house, and he said his wasn't fit for visitors.'

'You'll recognise him because he looks like us,' I said. 'And he'll be wearing a tweed hat, whatever the weather.'

I had half a mind to skulk around the library steps and watch this bizarre encounter, but didn't of course. What was particularly galling was that all my information about the occasion would have to come from Birdie. I didn't feel able to call father and casually ask how things had gone. He was hopeless at recounting detail anyway; all I would get would be monosyllables.

Instead Rad and I paid a visit to Auntie Mim in hospital. Mr Radley, who to my surprise went to see her every day, had warned us that she wouldn't be looking well. She had been refusing food and was now being fed through a tube which she kept trying to yank out. 'It'll take her back to her youth,' said Mr Radley. 'She used to be a suffragette.'

We bought some flowers in the foyer shop and I picked up a copy of *Country Living*. It was what mother always took to people in hospital, with the idea that pictures of beautiful furniture and landscaped gardens might transport them from their gloomy surroundings. Or perhaps that envy might be a spur to recovery, I don't know.

'We can't even take her grapes,' said Rad.

We made our way through the labyrinthine corridors, our shoes squeaking on the vinyl. In Feltham ward where we had expected to find her the bed was empty and stripped. We exchanged a look of alarm before approaching the desk, behind which a nurse was sitting, filling in a time-sheet.

'She's been moved to Fairfax 2,' she said, jerking her Biro in the direction we had just come from. Another half-mile of corridors took us out of the modern block through a covered walkway into the Old Buildings which had been condemned to demolition and reprieved several times. The floors dipped up and down like a switchback, doors were no more than thick polythene flaps, dusty pipes swarmed over the walls like vines, and the whole place had such an air of dilapidation and neglect that the prospect of successful recuperation there seemed remote.

Fairfax 2 was a female geriatric ward with six beds. Rad nodded at the nurse on duty, and twitched the bunch of flowers to indicate that we were visitors. 'There she is,' he said, approaching a bed in which a tiny, shrunken old woman was sitting propped up, asleep, mouth open. I noticed a basket of fruit on the bedside cabinet, and an open packet of biscuits.

'I don't think it is her,' I said.

'Isn't it?'

We peered at the occupants of the other beds. In hospital night-gowns, with no make-up, white, once-permed hair now limp and straight, and papery skin sagging from cheekbone to jaw, *they all looked the same.* Any or none of them could have been Auntie Mim. We retreated to the desk, unnerved.

'We're looking for Mrs Smith,' said Rad.

The nurse showed us to a smaller side ward with only three beds. Our relief at recognising Auntie Mim at last was somewhat tempered by dismay at her surroundings and condition. Even basic standards of cleanliness and hygiene seemed to have been abandoned: there were balls of dust and fluff and dried drops of God knows what on the floor. The windows were streaked with smears, and some of the curtains had great frayed rents in them. On Auntie Mim's chair was a pile of dirty tissues, and a soiled bedpan had been left on the trolley at the foot of her bed. The patient herself looked extremely poorly. There was a tube up her nose, taped to her top lip, and a drip in her hand, which was bruised from wrist to knuckles. From beneath the bedclothes another tube emerged, leading to a plastic bag which was half full of clear, reddish liquid. My stomach heaved, and I buried my head in the glossy, scented pages of *Country Living.* Box hedges, yellow wallpaper, Toiles de Jouy, I turned the pages feverishly, Gieves & Hawkes, William Morris, Sissinghurst, quilts, that's better.

'She's asleep,' said Rad helpfully. 'We'd better hang about for a bit to see if she wakes up. Are you any good at flower arranging?' he asked, handing me the carnations. On the bedside cabinet was a slim vase containing a wilting posy of bluebells and daisy marigolds and other varieties of flower to be found in the front gardens of the houses adjoining the hospital: a gift from Mr Radley. I removed them and thrust our own offering into the murky water. We had obviously been sold a rogue bunch as most of them had broken stems and flopped down over the edge of the vase, leaving the remaining few standing up like fence posts.

'Very nice,' said Rad.

We hovered around the bed for a quarter of an hour or so before giving up. I sensed that Rad was as relieved as I was that she hadn't woken while we were there. The only sounds in the room were faint snores and the scratch of a pen as the nurse laboured at her paperwork. And somewhere in the distance the hum of a floor polisher.

'Do you think they ever go round and check who's still alive?' I said.

As we were leaving the woman in the opposite bed, who like all the other patients we had seen had been apparently comatose, started to groan as if in agony. The nurse glanced up briefly then carried on writing. On the way out Rad deposited the used bedpan on the desk and was rewarded with a cold stare and a bitten-off 'thank you'.

'We'll come back another day,' Rad said to me without much enthusiasm when at last we stepped through the automatic doors and breathed fresh air.

'Oh yes,' I said, colluding.

'How did you get on then?' I asked Birdie that evening.

'Good. We recognised each other straight away. I'd have known him even if you hadn't told me about the hat.'

'What did you talk about?'

'Oh, you know, he asked me what I'm studying and what I want to do at university. We didn't talk about the past at all. He didn't even really acknowledge that he's my dad: it was a bit like meeting some long-lost godfather. At one point he said he was really pleased to have met me at last and that he was glad I'd turned out so well. But I could tell it was going to get emotional, so I headed him off. He asked how Mum was and I just said, "Fine", and he said, "Good, good", and that was the end of that subject.'

'So what else did you talk about?'

'Books mostly. He wanted to know what I was reading and I said Virginia Woolf and he pulled a face and we had a bit of a dispute about whether she was a genius and then he told me to read Gibbon. Whoever he is.'

'That's his answer to everything,' I said.

'I just can't work out how he and my mum ever got together. They're so different. I mean he's so sweet and old-fashioned.' I was about to agree – indeed to chip in with a few anecdotes of my own – when she added, 'like you.'

'Do you think you'll see him again?' I said as if we were picking over last night's date. I found myself unwilling to examine my feeling of relief when she said, 'We didn't arrange anything. I'm still wondering how or whether to tell Mum. She'll find out sooner or later; I'm bound to let it slip.'

'Will she mind?'

'I'm not sure. She won't like being deceived.'

'I know the feeling,' I said.

As a quid pro quo I told her about our afternoon in the hospital. She grew quite pale. 'I'm not going to get old,' she said, shuddering. 'I'm just not.'

37

We would have been the last members of the family to see her, though she, of course, had not seen us.

The hospital telephoned early the next morning to say she had died during the night. Mr Radley seemed to take the news worst of all: for the rest of that day he sat in the armchair, staring out of the sitting-room window and biting his lip, absorbed in his own thoughts. When I brought him a sandwich at lunchtime he looked at me as if I was a total stranger, before saying, 'Thanks, Birdie, leave it on the table,' where it stayed untouched until I cleared it away in the evening. This surprised me. I'd never put him down as a man of deep feeling where other people – real people – were concerned. He could work himself up into a lather of sentimentality over long-dead strangers – names on the Vimy memorial, for example – but he tended to step over beggars in the street.

Lexi, meanwhile, was in organisational overdrive: hospital, registrar, undertaker, solicitor, crematorium, all were being treated to her curious blend of tyranny and charm.

The funeral would only be a couple of days away. There was no need to delay: there were no distant friends or relatives to be rounded up, and the crematorium was very accommodating. Apparently death has its favoured seasons, and business was slack in August.

'Well, people are off on their holidays,' was my mother's interpretation of this statistical quirk.

My granny took a great interest in the details of Auntie Mim's death. 'I'll be next,' she said, 'thank God.' Ever since I had known her she had been predicting her imminent demise with complacency. She was only seventy-eight, but her blindness had limited her activities cruelly and she was as bored with life as any ninety-year-old. 'Did she leave anything?'

I said I didn't think so. Legacies were another of Granny's

long-standing obsessions. She used the necessity for scraping together an inheritance for my mother as an excuse for a miserliness which was becoming ever more ambitious and eccentric. Lately she had taken to saving and washing out the flimsy plastic bags in which the butcher wrapped raw meat. She had rigged up a piece of string in the kitchen on which to dry them, and they would hang there like damp little ghosts. When dry they were consigned to a drawer until the day dawned that a purpose could be divined for them. Even when her eyesight had failed she insisted on darning laddered tights. My mother had to supply her with a threaded needle, and she would sit at the kitchen table, a grapefruit forced into the toe of the holey stocking, creating a very tangly piece of mending indeed, cursing and yelping as she jabbed herself, but inwardly delighted to be saving forty pence.

By some unfathomable method she had calculated the cost of her share of the food mother served her each week to be £2.67. There was no quarrelling with such a precise figure. Every Sunday, just as mother was dishing up the roast she would stump into the kitchen and decant just this amount, coin by coin, from her purse to the table, while mother would sigh and tutt and pound the potatoes to a mush.

I was wrong about Auntie Mim. She had left her jewellery – none of it especially valuable – to Frances, £1,000 to Clarissa and the rest, which would be about £90,000, to Lexi.

'Did you know she had any savings?' I asked Frances on the way to the crematorium. Rad was driving us: Nicky and Frances were in the back. The adults – Mr and Mrs Radley, Uncle Bill and Auntie Daphne were in the Renault. Clarissa and her mother, Cecile, and, separately, Lawrence, were coming by taxi. There were no limousines.

'She sold her cottage before she came to live with us, so I suppose I knew she must have something. I never really thought about it. She always looked so poor.'

'It's the looking rich that costs the money,' Nicky pointed

out. The atmosphere in the car was cheerful: it was ridiculous to mourn the death of a ninety-three-year-old, Rad said. We should be happy she lived so long. This was the best sort of funeral, Nicky agreed, as if he was a connoisseur: one where you could give someone a good send-off without feeling too upset. Frances leaned between the front seats and switched the radio on. We were all under twenty-one. By the time our turn came someone would have discovered a cure.

Inside the chapel the eleven of us managed to fill the first two rows by spreading out a little. Lexi was in any case taking up as much space as two normal people on account of her outfit – a black jacket with huge shoulder pads, a peplum, a tight black skirt and a wide-brimmed hat smothered with quivering ostrich feathers. Frances herself had had to be restrained from wearing the bequeathed pearls. She made Nicky sit next to Cecile who was wearing a fox fur. 'I don't want to brush up against that dead thing,' she said loudly.

The service was over in a quarter of an hour. Lexi had instructed the chaplain not to go on too long. 'She was ninety-three, so for heaven's sake let's keep it brief and jolly.' There was no music – there weren't enough of us to carry a hymn, and the Radleys weren't keen singers. The chaplain rattled through the order of service at a jaunty pace. It's not easy to say 'We come into the world bringing nothing, and we take nothing with us when we go,' in an optimistic voice, but he managed it. He gave the eulogy, using the biographical details furnished by Lexi, with such conviction that by the end of it I was almost ready to believe that he would miss Auntie Mim as much as those of us who had actually met her.

Outside the chapel our few floral tributes had been placed on the grass for our inspection. The lady funeral director had told us we could take them home with us if we liked. 'If I'd known that, I wouldn't have ordered a wreath,' Cecile complained. 'I'd have got something that would have done as a table decoration.'

Clarissa was admiring Lexi's outfit. 'I like the peplum. Very skittish.'

'Oh do you?' Lexi smoothed it down over her hips. 'I don't know if it's me. I'll probably take it back – unless someone dies in the next day or two, of course.' And she gave a throaty laugh. It was the only time I ever heard her attempt a joke.

There were drinks and snacks back at the house. Cecile, on account of her seniority perhaps, was allowed a glass of sherry. Everyone else was on orange juice. Lexi had bought some boxes of ready-made cocktail snacks which were tipped on to plates and handed round.

I noticed that the miniature photograph of Auntie Mim's One Great Love was now on top of the bureau with the other family pictures. I decided to test Lexi out. 'Who's this?' I asked, as she passed me holding aloft a plate of cheese straws.

'Marigold Bray,' she said, without hesitation. 'She was Auntie Mim's girlfriend. Lovely, isn't she?' And she whisked off again. Cecile, a more enthusiastic purveyor of tittle-tattle, had been listening to this exchange and swiftly moved into the space vacated by Lexi.

'She was a lesbian, you know, when she was younger,' said Cecile, as if it was a hobby one grew out of. 'She had a sort of *relationship* with another teacher at the school where she worked. She was only in her twenties then. Did you know she used to teach? Yes, cookery. Impossible to believe, really, considering.'

'So what happened then?'

'Her parents found out and had her put in an institution. She was in there for six months and when she came out she was completely cured. Mind you, she never married. And do you know, it was from that time on that she ate nothing but potatoes and sprouts. Isn't that curious?'

'She was not "cured", she was completely crushed.' Lexi had re-entered the room and overheard the last part of our conversation. 'I shudder to think what they did to her in that place. She never worked again for the rest of her life.' The room had fallen silent during this exchange. Everyone was listening.

'What did she live on for the next seventy years?' I asked.

'She went back to live with her parents and they kept her until they got too old, and then she looked after them. Her older sister – Mum's mum – had already married and moved to Belgium, and Mim was condemned to be a maiden aunt from the age of about twenty-five. They never had any visitors, and never went anywhere, so she had no chance of meeting anyone.'

'Why did she only eat sprouts and potatoes?' asked Frances, who had caught up by now. 'Is that all they fed her in the loony bin?'

Lexi tutted. 'I don't really know. Before she was put away she'd been a teacher, and a really beautiful cook, apparently. I think it was her way of showing her parents that they'd damaged her.'

'Why didn't she and Marigold tell them to sod off?' said Frances.

'Children respected their parents in those barbaric times,' said Mr Radley.

'She didn't have it in her to rebel,' said Lexi. 'And her teaching career was over – it was much harder for women to be independent.'

'I wish I'd known all this while she was alive,' said Frances with indignation. 'I'd have made more effort to take her out and show her a good time.'

'You mean down at the tattoo parlour, or trying on the make-up in Miss Selfridge?' said Rad.

Frances ignored him. 'Why didn't she get out and do something when her parents had died?'

'She was about fifty by that time.'

'That's only the same age as you, and you're not too old to go out and have fun.'

'She'd probably lost the knack by then. Self-denial can become a habit like anything else.'

'My wife is an expert on self-denial, as you all know,' said Mr Radley.

'Now I think about it,' Lexi went on, talking over him, 'she once told me that after her mother had died she did try to trace Marigold, and eventually found that she'd gone to live in Kenya. That would have been thirty years after they'd lost contact, and Auntie still hadn't got over her.'

'Well, I've always said that love lasts longer if it's frustrated,' said Clarissa.

I glanced automatically at Rad, and was treated to one of his sardonic looks. Beyond him, unnoticed by anyone else, Lawrence was staring straight at Lexi.

38

The portrait of Birdie and me is nearly finished. The background is looking good; our faces are still blank. We creep up and inspect it from time to time – just to check that Mr Radley is genuinely working on it. Sometimes I am struck with the mad idea that he isn't painting us at all, but just pretending, and it's all a joke, keeping us prisoner in the attic each day. I can't think why he would do this, but then it wouldn't altogether surprise me.

Mr Radley is dithering at the easel. He always has a problem starting the figures, he says. A sort of painter's block. Birdie says why doesn't he do Still Lifes then. Or landscapes. He says when he wants her opinion he'll give it to her. We are the only ones in the house apart from Clarissa, who is on the scrounge again. This time it's Lexi's golf clubs she's after. She has a new boyfriend and is keen to introduce him to the game. Lexi went to the hairdresser's early and is still not back. Mr Radley keeps looking at his watch. Nicky, Frances and Rad have gone wind-surfing with a friend of Nicky's from King's. As a non-swimmer and coward my role will be restricted to sitting on the edge of the reservoir watching the others have fun, so I decide to stay behind. In the evening we are all going out for a meal – this part I can manage. I am no closer to understanding my relationship with Rad. He seems to treat me in some ways as his girlfriend, but ever since that day at Half Moon Street he is careful not to touch me when we're alone. Now I want him to; now he won't. I'm not sure what is going on. He won't tell me and I won't ask.

There is a terrific clatter from below and some choice language from Clarissa audible up two flights of stairs. I can guess the cause: retrieving the golf bag from the hall cupboard will have brought down an avalanche of mops, brooms, buckets, ironing board, hoover and flex. It happens every time. Mr Radley ventures to investigate. Birdie and I relax and stretch. The phone rings and is picked up. 'Oh,' he says. 'Oh, all right . . .' he sounds disappointed. 'What about food? You don't want me to save you anything? Okay, fine. Where are you anyway? . . . Oh really?' His voice hardens. 'Can you put her on? . . . No, I didn't think you would, because in fact Clarissa happens to be here.' And the phone is slammed down.

Birdie and I look at each other nervously. 'What was that about?' she whispers.

I shake my head. I'm just worried that any minute now Mr Radley is going to come back up here in a rage and take it out on us. But he doesn't. We hear the click of the front door, and Clarissa's car starting up. After five minutes or so we creep downstairs. The sitting-room curtains are still drawn although it's late afternoon and Mr Radley is sitting in there in the gloom. I'm not sure what to do. If we withdraw without a word he'll know we overheard. If we bounce in pretending to wonder where he is he might growl at us.

'Let's go,' says Birdie. That settles it for me, and we make our separate ways home.

At about six I make my way back. I don't want to miss the meal. The others will probably be back by now, wondering where I am. When I arrive, though, the house is quiet. The sitting-room curtains are still closed but Mr Radley isn't there. I decide to have a bath before the others come in and hog all the hot water. Although I have 'officially' moved back home with mother, I still often stay the night in Frances' room, and keep most of my favourite clothes there. Mother and I are thoroughly reconciled, but I still find it hard to be in my granny's company for long. She hasn't apologised, or acknowledged any part in the crisis.

While I am in the bath I can hear someone moving about. I emerge, dizzy and puffy from the over-hot water, wrapped in a king-size towel, and bump into Lexi, dragging two huge suitcases across the landing. She looks slightly dishevelled, and not altogether pleased to see me.

'Hello,' I say. 'Are you going on holiday?'

'In a manner of speaking. Give me a hand with this one, will you?' It doesn't seem to occur to her that I'm only wearing a towel. Clutching it and the suitcase I hobble down the stairs after her.

'I've lost a gold and pearl earring,' she says on the doorstep, pulling at her earlobe. 'If you come across it put it aside for me.' These are her last words to me.

I am standing by Frances' wardrobe wearing my bra and knickers when Mr Radley walks in. He doesn't seem to care about or even notice my state of undress, but walks straight over to the window and watches the space where until a few moments ago Lexi's car was parked. Then he sits on the bed and puts his head in his hands.

'She's gone,' he says. 'What am I going to do?'

'What do you mean?' I say, although I know. I'm not sure how my experience of life so far has taught me that it would be rude to carry on dressing while someone is trying to tell me that his wife has left him, but I stand there in my underwear and wait for him to say it.

'She wants to marry Lawrence.'

'Oh dear. I'm so sorry.' My vocabulary is wide, but this is the best I can do. There is a long pause. I find I am staring at the thinning patch on the back of his head: beneath it his scalp is tanned and shiny.

'I said, "What do you want to marry him for? You see him every day as it is." But that's not enough.'

'She'll come back,' I say. 'She's probably under a lot of pressure at work, and she's just flipped.'

He looks up. 'That's just it. She says she's had enough of working her arse off so I can sit around. She says Lawrence is going to support her properly. Do you know what she said? "I'm going to stay at home. I might even take up painting."'

'You poor thing.' I am in agonies of embarrassment and can see no way out. My torment is taken to new heights when he gives a sort of sob, reaches out blindly and pulls me on to his knee. I sit rigidly, like a garden gnome. In any other context than this I would leap away and run for it – perhaps even slap him – but I can't do that now. In any case his arms are tightly round me, as if he's trying to uproot a tree. It's not a terribly threatening embrace, but even so. He must sense me flinch, as he says, in a tone that manages to combine pleading with impatience, 'Oh, don't pull away. I'm not going to rape you. I just want to hold someone. If you're that bothered I'll go and hug the bloody dog instead.' I have to laugh at this. His grip relaxes. 'What am I going to do? Do you think I'm a selfish bastard? Perhaps I am. I thought we were happy. Of course I knew she'd always fancied Lawrence – he's a good-looking man. Do you think he's good-looking? I never stopped her going out with him.' He rambles on, not appearing to expect an answer, for which I am grateful, because I haven't got one. 'She doesn't even want anything. She said I can have the house – that's how desperate she is to get away.' He strokes my hair absent-mindedly: perhaps he thinks he's holding the dog after all. I decide to risk hinting that I'm getting cold as soon as he comes to a pause, but the words keep on coming. 'She's been waiting all this time – God knows how long she's been planning this – for Mim to die. Not for the money, but because she couldn't leave her behind. And now she's dead – boom, that's it, she's packed her bags and left. Even Frances will be off to some poly or other in a month's time, and I'll be on my own, and Rad will go back up to Durham . . .' He doesn't get any further because at that moment the door opens and Rad himself appears, saying in a cheerful voice, 'We're back – oh!'

And I do the stupidest thing. I leap away from Mr Radley as if I have something to be guilty about. As if there's something going on. I am pulled up short as the buckle of Mr Radley's watchstrap becomes entangled in my hair, and I have to stand there in my underwear, half bent over, with my neck cricked, while he releases me in an unhurried manner, and Rad looks on in disbelief.

'What's going on?' he says.

'Nothing,' I say, grabbing my dress and struggling into it, my face burning with shame. Well go on, tell him, I silently urge Mr Radley. I can't tell him his mother's just left home. But Mr Radley, a few moments ago so weak and vulnerable, doesn't say anything. And in the second or so that it takes Rad's expression to change from confusion to anger I realise that he has no intention of coming to my rescue; that he *wants* Rad to think something has been going on, and he doesn't care if I go under as a result.

Rad interprets the silence in the worst possible light. 'Get out,' he says, suddenly seizing my wrist and dragging me towards the door. I start to scream. 'StopitstopitIhaven't doneanythingit'snotwhatyouthinkaskhimaskhim.'

'You won't let me touch you, but you'll sit there and let him grope you.'

'I didn't!'

'*He'd* tell you he loved you. He'd say anything.'

'It wasn't my fault.'

'Don't worry, I hate him too.' He bundles me down the stairs, past an astonished Nicky and Frances. Growth, roused by the commotion and assuming Rad is being attacked, launches himself at me, barking and snapping. He catches the hem of my dress in his teeth and swings there, legs whirling. The backs of my calves are being lacerated by his claws.

Mr Radley calls in a half-hearted tone, 'Oh do calm down, Rad,' which doesn't help. Nicky and Frances still haven't moved: they've never seen Rad in a rage before. Neither have I. I'm so shocked and humiliated, and so frightened of further savagery from Growth, that it's almost a relief a second later to find myself out on the doorstep, alone. Pulling the dog away from my dress with a rending sound, Rad's last words are 'Just fuck off and don't ever come back here', before he slams the door on me.

I haven't got anything with me, my purse, shoes, nothing, but I'm not about to tap on the door and ask for them. I walk all the way home on hot, gritty pavements. Other pedestrians give me a very wide berth indeed: I must look like an escaped lunatic. My dress is torn, I'm barefoot, my legs look as if they've been beaten with brambles and my face is awash with tears and snot. I pray that there will be no one in, but mother is out in the front garden with a soap spray, on aphid patrol.

'Abigail, what's the matter? Where are your shoes?' she

says, betraying her priorities. I've just mastered my tears but the sound of concern in her voice sets me off again. I can't tell her what has happened. It will confirm all her long-simmering prejudices about the Radleys: that they are unreliable, probably unhinged, definitely not respectable. She will be scathing about Lexi's desertion. After all, she and my father have separated over a moral problem, not because they want to increase their chances of happiness. Even at this extremity I feel bound to defend the Radleys – to be loyal to my image of them.

Mother abandons the aphids and steers me indoors. 'What's happened?'

'R–r–rad doesn't like me any more,' I say, pathetically, through my sobs. I must have used just the same words about my old friend and enemy Sandra when I was nine.

'Why?'

'I don't know. He doesn't want to see me ever again.' We sit on the stairs and she puts her arm around me. For a moment or two I feel comforted, but then reality crowds back again.

'Oh darling, I'm so sorry.' She is desperate to tell me I'm better off without him, that she's never liked his holey jumpers and his long hair and long words, but she restrains herself. And besides, she has another worry. She goes slightly pink and bites her lip before saying, very fast, 'Abigail, I know you won't have, but did you sleep with him?' I shake my head and she almost collapses with relief. 'Oh, thank God for that.' For mother this seems to make it all right. I haven't been used and cast off – just cast off, which is nothing. To me, though, not having slept with him is not the consolation it was meant to be. Now I wish I had. I wish I was *pregnant*. Anything to preserve the connection.

'He'll probably have changed his mind by tomorrow,' she says. Having satisfied herself that we haven't Done It she is prepared to concede that much. 'You know what a temperamental lot they all are.' She can't resist this little dig.

'What's the row?' My grandmother has been woken by our voices. I give mother a beseeching look and bound up the stairs to my room to avoid Granny's inquisitorial welcome.

She's right, I tell myself. In a minute he will phone and apologise. Mr Radley will have explained, exonerating me entirely. Rad will be feeling overpowered by remorse and guilt. I convince myself so thoroughly of all this that soon I am planning what line I am going to take when he rings. Magnanimous: we'll just forget it ever happened. A little aggrieved perhaps, or even deeply wounded. I may refer to my scourged legs. As the evening wears on, minute by minute, and the phone remains silent the response I have been rehearsing becomes more and more conciliatory. I begin to doubt that the phone is working, but when I pick it up the dialling tone is there, mocking me. As I replace the receiver it occurs to me that Rad may have chosen that very second to ring, and hearing nothing but the engaged signal will have given up or changed his mind. Oh please, please make him ring me, I plead to the God that Rad doesn't believe in. What can they be doing there? They can't surely have gone out for that meal, tonight of all nights, with Lexi gone and me exiled and suffering. Perhaps he was beginning to hate me anyway and was just waiting for an opportunity to throw me off. I pace my room, anxiously trying to calculate what time they would be likely to return from the restaurant. I compute the length of time it will take them to drive, park, order, eat, pay and drive again. As the appointed moment approaches and passes, time, which has dragged all evening, begins to gallop, and it is midnight and all hope is extinguished.

Mother comes up and brings me a cup of hot chocolate – I have refused supper – and persuades me to go to bed. Her patience with Rad is wearing thin: if she gets to him before I do she is quite likely to tell him what she thinks of him. Her loyalty to me is touching, but burdensome all the same. I am exhausted with crying anyway, as if all my energy has leaked out in the salt water. I'm like a spent battery. My night's sleep comprises a series of pleasant dreams from which I wake with a momentary sensation of deliverance, which gives way to crushing disappointment as I remember.

In the morning I find on the doorstep a cardboard box containing my shoes, purse, and the rest of the clothes I'd been keeping in Frances' wardrobe. Rad must have brought them over in the middle of the night to avoid seeing me. I scrabble through the contents frantically, hoping to find a note, a line of his writing, something, but there's nothing of course. He hasn't even written my name on the box. The clothes have been neatly folded. I can't decide if this is a good or a bad sign, but a sign it surely is. I see portents everywhere: the blue sky means hope; the single magpie, disaster. If I get back upstairs before mother calls me he'll phone; if I don't, he won't. She asks me if I want any breakfast when I'm still half-way up and I almost bite her head off.

At nine o'clock I cave in and dial the Radleys' number. It's the only one apart from my own that I know by heart. I can hardly hold the receiver still, my palms are so sweaty. I haven't planned what I'm going to say and by the time the phone has rung ten times my mouth has dried up anyway. I pray it won't be Mr Radley who picks up the phone. I don't feel equal to confronting him yet. Eventually there is a click and a terse 'Yes?' from Rad, and I manage no more than a 'Hello' before he cuts me off. I ring straight back. My dignity has been fatally compromised by now, and I am too distraught to care about anything but getting a hearing. There is no reply.

'I'm going round there,' I tell mother. She looks alarmed at this: she is still suspicious about the provenance of the scratches on my legs, and, besides, has thoroughly embraced the idea that I am the injured party and should therefore await the apology that is due to me. Her vote for passivity having been rejected, she recommends that I powder my nose, as if this might be the clincher. Looking in the mirror I can see her point, but my attempts at restoration are doomed. My skin is so taut and shiny from crying that the powder glides straight off, and applying mascara to wet lashes leaves a crescent of smudged lines and blobs beneath my eyes like so many exclamation marks.

I am not going to turn up empty-handed. As revenge for the anonymous parcel on the doorstep I will return the copy of *Goodbye to All That* which Rad gave me two summers ago. It seems appropriate. Even as I am making my preparations I can't quite believe that I've got the courage to go. I'm not altogether sure that I won't just hang around, staking out the house and then slink home again. The bus is full, and I have to stand, lurching and swaying every time we take a corner. I feel like Marie-Antoinette in her tumbrel – and with as much confidence in the outcome of my journey. I look at the blank faces of the other passengers: they have all fallen into that stupor that afflicts people being transported to work en masse. They probably think I'm one of them, a fellow drone. They can have no idea of the urgency of my predicament; that I'm on my way to a meeting which may decide the course of my life for years to come.

It's Frances who opens the door. 'Oh,' she says, 'it's you.' She doesn't invite me in. If anything she edges the door shut by a degree or two. 'What do you want?' Her voice is dull – not hostile, exactly, but not warm.

'Rad won't answer the phone,' I say, feeling the tears rise again. There is a swelling, like a fist in my throat.

'That's because he doesn't want to talk to you.'

'I've got to explain it wasn't what he thinks.'

'He knows you weren't getting off with Dad,' she says, impatiently. It sounds so strange to hear her say those words. 'He knows Dad came in and grabbed you, because of Mum and all that. But you didn't exactly resist. You must have known that was the one thing that Rad would really hate.'

'I was too embarrassed. He'd just told me about your mum going off with Lawrence. He was nearly crying.'

'How would you feel if you'd found me in my knickers on your dad's knee?' The image conjured up by this is so bizarre, so incongruous, that I can almost see her point of view. It's him they're angry with, I think. But they're stuck with him, so it's me who's got to go.

'Can I just talk to Rad?'

She shrugs and shuts the door on me, as if I'm some

unsavoury caller selling double glazing or religion. A moment later she's back. 'He doesn't want to see you.' She sounds faintly apologetic. I take comfort from the fact that she doesn't personally hate me. She glances at the book I'm holding. 'Do you want me to give that to Rad?'

'Yes. I'm returning it.'

'Fair enough.' She takes it.

'You're weak, Frances,' I say with a sudden burst of courage and indignation. 'You know I'm not to blame. You should have stuck up for me. All this is between Rad and your dad. It's nothing to do with us.'

'Our family's in pieces,' she says. 'You're the least of my worries.' And with another shrug she closes the door.

39

I spend the next few days sitting in my room like a zombie, staring out of the window at a world that is newly grey. Occasionally I go for a walk to the children's playground where I sit on the swings and cry. My presence there drives away the usual clientele, though once a group of seven- or eight-year-old boys kicks a ball around me as though I'm invisible, which I am to them. When I look into the future I can see nothing to entice me: from now on every day will be identical to the last. I will withdraw from the world and eat nothing but sprouts and potatoes. I bitterly regret giving up *Goodbye to All That.* Now I have nothing of Rad's left. On Day Three (I am chalking them up in my head like a hostage) I remember Birdie. I still have Birdie; she has access to them. She will intercede for me. Forgetting that she doesn't come to my mother's house, I ring and beg her to come over. She knows something has happened; she has had a version of it from Frances, and is eager for details.

Mother is magnificent. I suspect that privately she is glad to have her curiosity satisfied at last. She welcomes Birdie warmly, like a special friend. 'It's so nice of you to come and cheer Abigail up.' Their common knowledge of each other goes unremarked. Birdie, who is expecting to have to be smuggled in through a hatch, is completely disarmed. Mother makes a Victoria sponge for us, something she hasn't done for months. I abandon my hunger strike: perhaps I will go the other way instead and eat myself to death. I give Birdie my account of events and she listens, brows furrowed. She takes my side as I knew she would.

'Because he's Frances and Rad's father he's in a parental relationship to you, so it's tantamount to incest for him to touch you like that. Besides which he's a man, he's older, it's his house – the power is all on his side.' Her mother is a

Samaritan and Birdie has absorbed much of the literature of counselling – on their shelves are books with titles like *Leaving Violent Men* and *Diary of an Abuse Survivor*. Within the space of twenty minutes she has half-convinced me that Mr Radley is an incipient rapist, and that my predicament is a paradigm of women's suffering through the centuries. 'He was totally out of order,' is her summary, which puts me in mind of a broken toilet or vandalised phonebox. I am uneasy about this. Since calling on Frances I have begun to wonder whether I wasn't partly to blame: behaviour ought to be dictated by more rigorous criteria than mere embarrassment after all. But it is still a relief to have my feelings of victimisation so soundly endorsed. In spite of Birdie's grim interpretation of the incident she is happy enough to enter the rapist's den. In fact she agrees with alacrity. 'I'll talk to Rad,' she promises. 'See if I can persuade him to ring you.' Part of me is reluctant to let her go as it means I'll be alone again. Her company has distracted me from my current misery, though we have talked of nothing else. She has even made me laugh. But her intervention is my last hope. It is at least a way of keeping my presence before them so they can't erase me completely, and so I send her on her way, with the faintest of misgivings, to plead my cause.

She doesn't contact me until the following day. She has not met with success but is evasive about the details. I sense that she is trying to spare me bad news.

'He's very stubborn,' she says.

'What did he say, exactly?'

'That he doesn't want to talk about it. So he didn't.'

'Did he seem upset, or different, or anything?'

'Ye-e-es, he's more withdrawn. But they're all in a bit of a state because of Lexi going. He's not talking to his dad. Frances is trying to hold things together. She's the only one who is still talking to everybody.'

'So if Rad wouldn't discuss me, what did you do for the rest of the time?'

'Oh, we talked about other things.'

Somehow time passes. The sun rises and sets on my misery with majestic indifference. The days are long and hot. It would have been a good summer. One afternoon I catch the bus over to Balmoral Road and spy on the house. I skulk in the oblong of shade offered by the bus shelter. By way of disguise I have a pair of sunglasses and a thirty-year-old cricket cap of my father's which would fool no one. The only moment of excitement comes when the front door opens and Frances, still in her pyjamas, brings in the two bottles of warm sour milk from the doorstep, and disappears inside.

A fortnight of solicitude has exhausted mother. She has tried various strategies to bring me to order and has now lost all patience with me. The first of these is to occupy my time with numerous household chores, so that I won't have time to brood. But I am too versatile for her: I can iron handkerchiefs and brood at the same time. The second is to set herself up as an example of someone who has proved resilient in the face of adversity. She has survived the break-up of a twenty-four-year marriage. There are times, she tells me, when she would have liked to go to pieces, but she Pulled Herself Together. The third and most useless of all is to hint at the greater suffering of vast portions of humanity.

At some point in August the exam results arrive. I have done well. My place at the Royal College is assured, but I can't stir myself to celebrate. I wonder how Frances will have done, and where she will be going. She has applied without any consistency to polytechnics across the land for courses as various as Media Studies and Nursing. In the evening I find my mother at the kitchen table drinking the half-bottle of Moët & Chandon she has been keeping in the fridge in anticipation of my success. Guilt rises up in me like nausea, and I fetch myself a glass.

'You'll get a headache,' I tell her.

'I haven't had one for ten weeks. Hadn't you noticed?' This is how long father has been gone. 'It's a miracle.'

'Cheers,' I say.

'I thought I might try coffee next. See how that affects me.'

'We could have a Chinese take-away one night.'

'I don't know. I think I'll take things slowly. Don't want to go mad.'

The last time I drank champagne was at Anne Trevillion's party. At my first taste the memory unspools in my mind.

Mother pushes the rest of the bottle towards me. 'It's horrible stuff, champagne, isn't it? Thank goodness we don't often have anything to celebrate.'

I am sitting alone at my dressing table looking at my reflection and rehearsing chronologically in my mind every word Rad has ever spoken to me. The mirror has two ear flaps which can be adjusted so that you can see yourself in profile, or, with some fine tuning, from behind. Sometimes as I waggle the flaps I catch whole avenues of myself with the same bleak expression.

This exercise in remembering is not taking long. I have done the early stuff and am up to the party – my favourite bit. There can't have been many couples for whom the word 'Bats' was a prelude to a kiss. 'Don't ever cut your hair,' he had said. My hand automatically pulls open the dressing-table drawer, and there, amongst the brushes and bottles and tubes is a pair of scissors. Their presence is entirely providential: on one handle is a loop of ribbon with the word KITCHEN written in permanent marker. Mother uses them for cutting coupons out of magazines. Starting just below my left ear I chop roughly towards the nape of my neck and watch the swathes of hair drop to the floor. After the first cut I have a sudden attack of vertigo, but it's too late now, so I keep going. It's harder than you'd think to cut thick, dry hair: it slides away from the blades as they close and makes a nasty grating sound. When I have finished my head feels light and free, like a balloon whose guy-ropes have been cut. Unfortunately I look like an inmate of a Victorian orphanage or madhouse. I have been left with a lop-sided Joan of Arc cut with chewed edges and doorsteps. I shall have to start washing my neck.

On the carpet at my feet the fallen hair seems darker and duller: I gather it up and it forms a soft, jumbled nest in my lap. It would have been better, I now realise, if I had plaited it first and cut it off as one long serpent, but that would have required assistance, and self-mutilation is essentially a private business. I ransack the study for a padded envelope big enough to hold all the hair and tough enough to defeat Growth. I don't need to disguise the writing as my hands are shaking anyway with the sheer nerve of it. Imagine the shock when he puts his hand inside and contacts all that dead stuff. I could get addicted to melodrama, I think, as I venture out, hatless and brazen, to the post-box, though this particular gesture will have to be a one-off. It would take another eighteen years to get a harvest like that.

Creeping back into the house I bump into mother in the hallway. She gives a shriek and covers her mouth with her hand. For a minute she just stands like that, staring at me, round-eyed with horror. Here is confirmation at last of my unbalanced state.

'Your beautiful hair,' she says through the hand. 'What have you done?'

'Er, yes,' I mumble, ruffling the chewed edges of my hair. 'I've cut it off.'

'What's your father going to say? He would never let me cut your hair when you were little. This will break his heart.'

What do you care about his broken heart? Or mine, for that matter, I think. She walks round me, taking in the catastrophe from all angles. 'Whatever possessed you?'

I shrug. 'I wanted to get rid of it.'

'Oh, well,' she says, adding without any attempt at irony, 'on your head be it.'

Mother has given me twenty pounds to get my hair sorted

out. I have never been to a hairdresser's in my life and I don't know the drill. There are two local salons: one is neon-lit, white-tiled and staffed by people with leather trousers and platinum-blond mohicans or shaven heads. The other is decorated in tones of beige and has a row of hood dryers in the window, beneath which old ladies sit waiting for their perms to cook, like seedlings under cloches. I choose the beige one. Inside a woman in a flowery apron is sweeping up clippings. She steers the growing pile of grey fluff towards a door, which she opens, and then pushes the whole lot inside, broom and all, and slams the door smartly.

When I am directed to the basin, which has a curious bite taken out of the rim, I go to kneel on the chair the way I do at home over the sink, and the astonished hairdresser has to tap me on the shoulder and turn me round. She brings me a cup of coffee and a copy of *Cosmopolitan* to read while the conditioner soaks in. The coffee is placed just out of reach, but I peel across the pages of the magazine until the following line in bold type catches my eye. **The cure for heartbreak: a haircut! 75% of women who have split from a partner change their hairstyle.** *'It's a control thing,' says Amanda, 22, whose relationship broke up last year. 'It's about taking command of one area of your life.'*

I close my eyes and put my head back on the block. A drop of well-conditioned water trickles down my neck and between my shoulders to my bra-strap. It will take me a while to come to terms with the banality of my suffering.

40

It is early September. Nothing has happened to me. Birdie
has called a couple of times, but is frequently unavailable. I
suppose it is only to be expected. She has other friends, and
her loyalty to me is only half-strength. I have been to visit
father. He is dreading the approaching school term, but is
otherwise cheerful. Mother has summoned him for a meeting
tomorrow, which he takes as a good sign. They need to
discuss money, apparently. He is sorry to hear about Rad and
can be relied upon to say the right thing. 'I rather liked him.
Perhaps he'll come to his senses.' As I leave, it occurs to me
that he hasn't even noticed my haircut. Perhaps his eyes look
straight at the soul; or perhaps he's got other things on his
mind.

On the day normal life stops I am sitting in my bedroom
gazing out of the window into the middle distance – a recent
hobby of mine – when I see the familiar green Citroën pull
up, and Rad limps down the driveway. My heart lurches: it's
here, the moment I've waited for, he's back. I take the stairs
in three bounds and open the door as the bell rings. He looks
terrible – pale, greasy-haired and unshaven. I haven't
anticipated quite this degree of contrition.

'Can I come in?'

'Of course.' We go into the sitting room. He waits until I
have sat down before sitting on the couch opposite. 'What
have you done to your foot?' I can't help asking. It is fatly
bandaged and he is wearing a pair of old-man's slippers.

'What? Oh, cut it. It doesn't matter.' There is a silence. 'I
don't know how to say this.' He is avoiding eye contact. I
don't care how he says it. I only know that there will never
have been such a grateful recipient of an apology, and that I
will make it as easy for him as I can. Any minute now I am
going to be happy again; I can sense myself preparing for it.

He stands up as if to give himself courage, but it doesn't work so he sits down again, abruptly.

'You don't have to say anything if you don't want. I understand.'

He looks at me at last with the faintest expression of hope. 'You've heard already? Who from?' The air between us is thick: his words seem to take a long time to reach me.

'Heard what?' I am starting to grasp that what is coming is not an apology – nothing like it.

'About the accident?'

'What accident?'

The glimmer of hope has gone. 'Oh, I thought you meant you knew.'

'No. I don't know anything. What's happened?'

'Birdie's–' his voice goes high and he stops for a second and swallows. 'Drowned.'

'Drowned?' For a second I can't remember what the word drowned means. It sounds so strange. 'You don't mean she's dead?'

He nods. 'Yesterday night. I didn't want you to hear it from anyone else.'

'How drowned?'

'We took a boat out on the lake at Half Moon Street, and it capsized. I tried to save her, but I couldn't even find her.'

As with hurricanes and tornadoes, in the midst of calamity there is a terrible calm. And so in spite of what I am hearing, I don't burst into tears or collapse. Instead I say something so despicable that it will haunt me for years to come: 'Why were you at Half Moon Street with Birdie?'

Rad peers at me as though he can't quite understand what I've just said. 'What does it matter why we were there?'

'I meant, what happened? How did it happen? Are you sure she's dead?' I babble. 'Can't they do something? Doctors.' There is such a pounding in my ears that I don't take in a quarter of what he says. It is only much later that I am able to piece together the events. One image gets through, though. Rad, soaking wet, running the half-mile back up the lane to the pub, now dark and shuttered, and beating on the door screaming, 'My girlfriend's in the lake. My girlfriend's in the lake.'

'Will you be all right?' He is getting up to go. 'I've got to go and see her mother. She knows, but only from the police.' He is keeping the muscles in his face tense to stop himself collapsing into tears. We could comfort each other, I think. But we don't.

'I'll be okay. My mother will be back in a minute. I'll sit and wait for her. I can't believe she's dead. I can't think properly. I can't . . .' My mind is so leaden that I can't even say what it is I can't do.

Rad doesn't even say goodbye, he just sort of shakes his head and then he's gone and I'm alone. I lie back on the couch and look at the ceiling through a kaleidoscope of floaters. I can hear Granny moving about upstairs. I think of Birdie, my sister, whom I have known for just three months and will never now know any better, and then of her mother, the Samaritan, whose years of counselling the bereaved and the desperate will now prove of so little help.

41

What happened was this: Rad had driven Birdie to the pub at Half Moon Street. They had a meal in the restaurant and then at closing time went for a walk around the lake. He was surprised to find that she knew the place already; her mother had brought her there as a little girl.

The cottage was still empty and boarded up, and they had gone inside for a while. It was a warm evening and there was a bright moon on the water and Rad had suggested they go skinny-dipping, but Birdie had refused. Like me she couldn't swim. The old boat was still tethered to the NO BOATING sign, so Rad had waded out and dragged it back to the jetty. It looked sound enough, and was dry inside, so Rad rowed Birdie out to the middle of the lake. He pulled the oars in and let the boat rotate slowly, and the two of them lay back and watched the stars and talked. The conversation had turned around to me and the two of them had started to quarrel, lazily. Rad, half-teasing, said he was going to swim back and leave her marooned in the boat. She said, fine, go ahead, I'll row myself back, but don't expect me to jump in and save you if you get stuck. Rad took off his jeans, shirt and shoes and dived off the boat, swimming down as deep and far as he could underwater, hoping to come up so far away that Birdie wouldn't see him. But when he broke through the surface and shook his wet hair out of his eyes he saw that his dive from the boat had capsized it – the oars were floating on the water and Birdie was nowhere to be seen. He had called her until he was hoarse, and then for the next fifteen minutes he dived under the boat, threshing the reeds at the bottom with his arms, coming up only for a gasped breath before plunging back down again, taking in wider and wider circles. The water was as black as hell and his frantic searching stirred up the mud from the lake floor so that he couldn't even see his hand in front of his face in the soupy darkness. After what felt like hours, but was in fact minutes, when he had found nothing but a single muddy deck shoe and was on the point of expiring himself, he struggled back to shore and ran, dripping wet and nearly naked, the half-mile to the pub. His cries for help roused the landlord who came to the door holding a snarling Dobermann, to find Rad slumped on the step with blood pouring from one foot. He had trodden on a piece of broken bottle in the lane without even noticing. The landlord wrapped him in a towel and left him sitting in the dark in the bar while he phoned the police. Rad was taken to hospital where he had his foot stitched and so was not there when police divers brought Birdie's body up at five minutes past one.

42

Until the funeral itself I find it impossible to absorb that Birdie is dead. I have cried, of course, often, and I have willed myself to understand, but there is a degree of detachment about my grief. I feel as though I'm somewhere deep inside my own body, awaiting excavation: nothing that this body does is real any more. It's too early to miss her, to realise at any but the most superficial level that I'll never see her again however much I want and need to, that I will grow old and die myself, and still won't have seen her, that everything else will carry on except Birdie.

I am not strong enough to break the news to father. He hears it first from mother, who has surprised me by crying great rending sobs herself and arranging for special prayers to be said at church. My father comes home to comfort me and be comforted. We sit on the bench together in the garden, surrounded by the scent of dying roses and the whirring of bees, and talk. He seems absolutely stricken by the mention of Half Moon Street. Mother hasn't passed on this detail in her account.

'You used to meet Val there, didn't you?' I say. We don't look at each other as we talk, but straight ahead across the lawn.

'Yes,' he says quietly. 'I wanted you to see the place because I knew you'd like it, not because it meant anything to me. It was wrong of me to take you there.'

Mother brings us tea but otherwise allows us our privacy. 'I must write to Valerie tonight,' father says, thinking aloud. Composing such a letter of condolence will almost break him, I know, but even this penance is preferable in his view to a personal visit.

When it is time for him to leave, mother comes out to say goodbye. 'Thank you for the money,' she says, referring to some transaction of the week before.

He waves away her gratitude. 'If you need any more . . .' They walk up the garden, slightly ahead of me. 'The roses must have been good this year.' He has missed the best of them.

'Yes. I've been ignoring the hose ban,' says mother. 'Unfortunately the lawn keeps growing.' She draws a parting in the long grass with the toe of one shoe.

'Would you like me to cut it while I'm here?' asks father, pleased to be useful, and even more pleased with himself for recognising the cue.

'Would you?' says mother. 'That would be wonderful.' And within seconds father is struggling out of his jacket and making for the shed, and mother is putting an extra chop in the casserole. I don't know whether it is grief or guilt or a need for comfort that effects this reconciliation, or what unwritten contract is drawn up in the privacy of their room, but father doesn't go home that night, and only returns to his grim little bedsit the following day to collect his belongings and take a last thankful look through that nailed-up window on to the eviscerated garbage bags and broken down bikes in the alley below.

43

The dead have many friends. Practically the whole of Birdie's school has turned out for the funeral. From the car-park where father and I sit, having arrived far too early and almost gatecrashed the wrong service, we can see armies of girls and boys converging on the chapel. Nearly all of them are in black in spite of Valerie's suggestion that people should wear normal, bright clothes. The older generation have complied, but the young are superstitious. Some of the boys don't have mourning wear and are in their school uniform instead. A few of the girls are wiping their eyes already. I look away hurriedly: I can't afford to cry now when there is so much worse to come. A ripple runs through the crowd as the hearse pulls up smothered with flowers like a carnival float, and when I see that box inside an icy drop of fear runs the length of my spine. To think of the lid just inches from her face. From the accompanying car Birdie's mother emerges, tottering, on the arm of a friend. I remember her as being strong, athletic-looking, but now she appears shrunken – her skin like cloth on a wire frame; a cough could blow her away. Even the largest of the three assembly rooms at the cemetery isn't big enough and it is standing room only at the back: father and I, the first to arrive, are the last to enter, and take our places by the doors which are then closed upon us. Even at a moment like this I catch myself looking out for Rad, and am filled with shame and self-loathing. But there he is, just a few rows in front of me, next to Frances and Mr Radley. He keeps his head down, as well he might.

Birdie's mother has chosen a secular version of the traditional service. If she ever was a believer she certainly isn't now. Meditations rather than prayers will be led by a man in grey trousers and a sports jacket with leather patches on the elbows, who looks like a schoolteacher. He gives himself away as a mere functionary as soon as he opens his mouth by welcoming us to what will be a time to recall and celebrate the life of Elizabeth Cromer. At the mention of the name Elizabeth the congregation stiffens as one. Birdie never, ever used her real name. Half the people present probably don't even know what it was, but no one has the courage or presence of mind to correct him and he is allowed to compound this terrible blunder by referring throughout to a total stranger. Elizabeth wanted to be a lawyer; Elizabeth loved to discuss politics; Elizabeth's friends are now going to read for us. All around I can sense people bracing themselves every time the name comes up. A schoolfriend of Birdie's takes over the lectern to read a poem by Christina Rossetti, and another reads 'Fear no more the heat of the sun' in a voice that never wavers. There is a constriction in my throat that swallowing cannot shift. The bravest performance of all comes from a girl of about fifteen who sings, unaccompanied, the aria 'Ach ich fühl's' from *The Magic Flute* in a creamy soprano that finally springs the lock. The tap tap of her shoes on the tiles as she returns to her seat is accompanied by muffled sobs and choking sounds from every corner of the room. I can feel my eyes starting to sting, and a prickling sensation in the top of my nose that gives me a few seconds' warning before the tears come, and once they've started nothing can stem the flow. In front of me Rad brushes his shirt cuff across his eyes and slumps even further forward; Frances' shoulders are heaving. The heat in the hall is intense: during the minute of silent reflection there is some scuffling from the group in the corner alongside us: someone has fainted and is carried outside to be revived. The sudden gust of cool air from the open door seems to turn the salt water on my cheeks to acid and my skin flares.

Though we are among the first out, father and I hang back before following the procession to the plot chosen for the burial. It is a long walk through the cemetery and the crowd has strung out in a straggling line by the time the coffin has reached the graveside. Father offers me a large, white handkerchief – one of the ones I have painstakingly ironed as part of mother's programme of occupational therapy. On the way I notice some of Birdie's friends giving me sidelong glances, nonplussed by this unexplained resemblance. I keep my head up, bearing my likeness proudly. Let them wonder.

The crowd around the grave is five deep, so I am spared the sight of the coffin being lowered down. Instead I look up at the sky and watch the few clouds blowing across the sun. *Where are you?* I think. There has been no talk of the hereafter at the service. Only Birdie's past is allowed to matter, which seems cruel to me. At a time like this surely even a non-believer can admit a whisper of hope? On the trimmed grass beside us are more flowers than I have ever seen: the individual wreaths and sprays have been packed close together to stop them overrunning the neighbouring plots; it looks as though the whole thing could be picked up by one corner and laid over the grave like a quilt.

I only realise it's all over when the crowd starts to break up. There are small clusters of girls leaning on one another for support; their heads together like conspirators. White hand-kerchiefs flutter in the wind like flags of surrender. Father gives a great sigh and pulls at his beard; he is thinking the thoughts that lie too deep for tears. I have no more crying left in me, for the moment at least. I feel wrung out, like a used floorcloth. On the way back to the car we pass Frances and Rad, who nod at me, as someone they used to know.

That night I wake at about four in the morning with a dry mouth and pounding heart, a great slab of grief pressing down on my chest. I haven't drawn the curtains properly and from my bed I can see the moon, a perfect semi-circle of brilliant white, and beyond it pinpricks of light from hundreds of stars that may no longer even exist. And for the briefest moment I experience with sudden clarity, *and with every fibre of my being*, the vastness of the universe and my own infinitesimal span on this tiny spinning ball of dirt and fire, and I under-stand at the profoundest level what it will mean not to exist throughout the rest of eternity. The vision, if that's what it is, lasts only a moment or two, and I am me again, lying in bed, drenched in sweat and worrying about death in the regular, abstract way that can be managed and keeps us all from madness.

I don't see the Radleys again. Lexi has gone, Rad goes back to Durham, presumably, and Frances to whatever institution has offered her a place, and the next time I pass the house there is a For Sale sign outside.

I start at the Royal College and move into an inter-collegiate hall of residence in Kensington. From my window I can see the Natural History Museum and the roofs of red routemasters. The rooms are box-shaped with brown nylon carpets that cause such a build up of static that every time I touch the door handle I get a shock. The bathroom is a windowless cell of streaming white tiles with blooms of black mould on the ceiling and growing up the shower curtain.

My cell-mate is a girl called Eva who is studying at the School of Hygiene and Tropical Medicine. She has a boyfriend in Saint Albans, and is almost never around. She has a coffee machine which she forgets to turn off and which hisses and gasps in the corner and emits acrid fumes. On the same corridor is a Welsh lichenologist and a hard-rock geologist who plays heavy metal so loudly that it makes the posters fall off my wall. He hosts Dungeons and Dragons parties to which I am invited, but never bother to go. The invitations soon dry up. These are supposed to be the best years of my life.

After a month or so mother forwards a letter from Frances. She is doing drama at a northern polytechnic and having a wild time. She and Nicky have split up and Frances has a new boyfriend. I can't help resenting the triumphal tone of her letter, which makes no allusion to or apology for the past. I take some trouble to compose a reply that doesn't reek of reproach and self-pity. A much shorter note arrives in due course, and then nothing.

I work hard for want of better things to do, and my tutors are pleased with me. They praise my technique for its control. Mrs Suszansky, my new teacher, says in her overblown way that I make the cello sing with a voice full of tears.

What of my much-prized virginity? I lost it to a fellow student called Dave Watkins in his bedsit in Dalston after a party on 28 January 1986. I remember the occasion particularly because it was the same day *Challenger* exploded and the spirit of mourning was already in the air.

It so happened that I was in Rome in August 1996 with the orchestra, and on the day appointed by Mr Radley all those years ago for our meeting, in a spirit of curiosity and nostalgia, I found myself drawn to the Spanish Steps and Keats's last lodgings. Mr Radley didn't show up, of course, but I saw Keats's writing desk, and his death mask, and the branch of McDonald's a few yards from his doorway, and I thought how much that would have infuriated Mr Radley, so I went there for lunch and drank his health in yellow milkshake.

V

44

One thing I've learnt: we never learn.

As the evening wore on I forced myself to mingle but my orbit didn't cross Rad's again, and he made no move to return. Every so often I would pick him out in the crowd – he was being passed around like a plate of sandwiches. All those girls with their swept up blonde hair and bootlace-strap dresses couldn't get enough of his drains evidently. I'm not going to manage it, I thought. I'm not going to dredge up enough courage to approach him again, even though I've got a thousand questions to ask. I will hover on the fringes and if he catches my eye I will look away casually so that he doesn't think I'm a sad, desperate, eaten-up old maid, and then with my dignity intact I will slink back home and churn with disappointment and probably give myself cancer.

I met Grace in the Ladies'. She was changing into a brown velvet dress. 'God, you look sour,' she said cheerfully. 'Are you off home?'

I nodded. 'Do you want to share a taxi?'

She produced a tub of loose powder and a huge, splayed brush, and dusted her face violently. 'No, I'm going to Ronnie Scott's with some people. Why don't you come?'

'I would if I wasn't got up like Mrs Danvers,' I said, flapping my long skirt. The fluorescent light above the mirrors gave my face a mottled, purplish tinge. 'I am definitely past my prime,' I said, grimacing at my reflection. 'Which implies I must once have been in it.'

Grace twisted up a chisel-shaped lipstick and began to paint her lips in firm sweeping strokes the way my mother used to, with no consideration at all for their natural shape. 'Oh go on,' she said, dropping it back into her make-up bag which she snapped shut, and giving me a significant look, 'I bet you're more attractive now than, say, thirteen years ago.'

There was half an inch of loose wet snow outside, and it was still coming down in fat flakes. A long queue had formed at the taxi rank, so I decided to walk up to the main road carrying the cello. My car could wait until tomorrow to be rescued. It would give me something to do. I was standing on the corner at Aldersgate when a motorbike rider pulled up next to me at the kerb and gesticulated with a gloved hand. Instinctively I took a few paces back and tightened my grip on my handbag. He was dressed in leathers, with a black crash helmet, which he started to remove. A taxi appeared in the distance, yellow light glowing, and I had just stuck my arm up when a familiar voice said, 'I thought it was you,' and Rad emerged from his carapace.

'Oh,' I said, with untrammelled relief. 'I thought you were a mugger.'

'Well, I'm not. Look, I'm sorry we didn't have much chance to talk.' The taxi drew up behind him, engine rattling, and the driver leaned across and slid the window down. 'Vassall Road, Vauxhall,' I said. 'Can you hang on a minute?' He glanced at his watch and nodded.

'I would have offered you a lift,' said Rad, 'but . . .' He looked from the bike to the cello. For a moment I pictured myself riding pillion, the cello bumping along at my side.

'I meant to ask how your parents are,' he said.

'They got back together – that same summer. They're fine. What about yours? How's Lexi?'

'She's still with Lawrence,' said Rad over the sound of the idling engines. 'They live in Chiswick. I've seen them quite a bit since I've been back. Dad's got a proper job – at the eleventh hour. One of his old colleagues from the Department of the Environment has wangled him something – it's pretty low key, but . . .'

'Has he remarried?' I asked, brushing snowflakes off my eyelashes.

'No. He was going out with a twenty-five-year-old quite recently, until she came to her senses. Mum takes him out to dinner every so often. Now that she's married to Lawrence it's Dad she goes out with.'

The taxi driver was tapping impatiently on the steering wheel. Presently he leaned towards the nearside window again. 'I won't be a second,' I said beseechingly, thinking, you bastard, you've blown your tip, mate.

'How's Frances?' I asked. 'What's she doing now?'

'She lives in Brisbane.'

'*Brisbane?*' I had never imagined her straying any distance from home, but then once the house in Balmoral Road had been sold she wouldn't have had a home.

'She's married to an Australian called Neville. They've got three kids and a couple of dogs.'

'Neville,' I said. 'That's fortunate.' Rad looked puzzled. 'I was thinking of her tattoo. Her semi-permanent tattoo.'

He laughed at the memory. 'It wouldn't be a problem. He's a plastic surgeon.'

'What does she do?'

'She's a kindergarten teacher.' It took me a few minutes to digest this information. Frances, a teacher. Dimly I recalled something Lawrence had once said: 'You wait, she'll be a pillar of the community.'

The snow was falling faster now. Rad's hair was speckled with grey flakes and the top of my cello was growing a lacy skullcap. 'You haven't got her address, have you? I'd love to write to her.'

His hand strayed to a zipped pocket in his jacket. 'I used to know it by heart, but they've just moved. Look, give me your address and I'll send it to you.' He handed me a two-inch stump of wax crayon. 'I'm not on the phone,' he added apologetically. Resisting the urge to upturn my handbag on the pavement, I picked decorously through the clutter until I found an old cash machine receipt on which I crayoned my address, wiping snowflakes off its dampening surface. I didn't put my phone number. I thought that might be pushing it.

'I don't suppose Growth is still around?' I said.

'No, he's dead. When Dad sold the house and moved into his flat he wasn't allowed pets so Growth had to go back to Bill and Daphne. But he escaped and tried to find his way back to Balmoral Road and was hit by a car.'

317

'Oh dear.' I wasn't sure how far you could sensibly go in condoling over the death of a dog thirteen years ago. Poor Growth, I thought. One of the innocent casualties of divorce. 'I'd better go,' I said, as he put the scrap of paper carefully in the zip-up pocket.

'Well . . .' we both said and then laughed awkwardly. Then he put his crash helmet back on, gave me a wave with his gloved hand and swung the bike out into the traffic, at which point the taxi driver, seeing his moment for revenge at hand, put his foot down and roared off, leaving me standing on the kerb alone with the blizzard blowing around me like confetti.

Two days later a card dropped on to my doorstep. It was postmarked Staines and showed a pen and ink drawing of a house. 'The lock-keeper's cottage, Penton Hook', said the caption. I noted the first-class stamp with relief. It would be hard to feel optimistic about someone who would be prepared to keep you waiting an extra couple of days for the sake of 6p. Along the top Rad had written an address of sorts: Wentworth, Riverside, Laleham, which made me think of a stately home with gardens dipping into the Thames, and the message itself was brief.

> *Dear Abigail,*
> *It was good to see you yesterday. Here it is as promised:* [followed by five lines of Frances' Brisbane address] *Do write.*
> *Yours Rad.*

I spent the next five minutes subjecting this bald little note to the most punishing analysis in an attempt to reinterpret it in an encouraging light. 'Do write' was ambiguous, wasn't it, given that he had supplied two addresses, and he hadn't attempted to rule a line under the past by using the name Marcus. I couldn't help feeling disappointed that there was no suggestion, however vague, of a future meeting. He hadn't even thrown in a question which would give me an excuse for replying. I would reply, though.

I fetched down a box of postcards which had my address and phone number printed across the top, and hunted down my fountain pen from a drawerful of red Biros and broken coloured pencils. I wrote the name Rad a few times on a piece of scrap paper, and then Marcus, to see which looked better. Oh dear, I thought, I really ought to have grown out of this by now. My reply went through several drafts and took up most of the morning.

> *Dear Marcus*
>   *Thank you for sending Frances' address so promptly. I will certainly write. I can't quite believe she's a teacher – and a mother of three. It was so strange to bump into you again after all this time. I hope you aren't too depressed to find yourself back in the middle of a British winter. If you're ever passing this way do call in. I'm often at home.*
>   *Best wishes*

No, too blatant.

> *Dear Rad*
>   *Thank you for your note. It was good to meet you again. I often think of the happy times I spent at Balmoral Road. Do you remember Nicky jumping in the Thames? And Lazarus Ohene?*

Ridiculous. Embarrassing. He'd think I was taking the piss.

> *Dear Marcus (if I may)*
>   *I'm sorry our interesting conversation of the other evening was cut short by a combination of foul weather and the uncouthness of London taxi drivers. If you would like to continue it I am available on the above number.*
>   *Yours very truly*

Absolute dead loss. Pathetic.

Dear Rad

Thanks for Frances' address. I'll certainly write. Sorry we didn't have a chance to talk properly the other evening. I was glad to hear that your parents are well. Remember me to them.

Abigail

I glanced over the four postcards before selecting the last one and chucking the rest into the bin. Even my handwriting wasn't consistent from one to another – a sure sign of a weak personality. I put on my overcoat and boots and walked out into the freezing December morning, the snow creaking beneath my feet. The council salt trucks had been out in the night and the gutters were banked with gritty brown slush. The postman was just emptying the pillar box as I arrived, so I dropped my card into his open sack. There, I thought, as I watched the red Royal Mail van pull away from the kerb, sludge churning under its wheels, the ball's in your court now.

The ball stayed there, and after a couple of weeks I stopped bothering to listen to the rattle of the letter box, and stopped being the first one into the hallway to sort through the daily drift of mail. For a while I regretted that I hadn't made my message a little warmer, but then as time wore on I grew relieved that I hadn't betrayed too much. Clearly that five-minute encounter had been enough for Rad. He'd come back to England to restart his life; the last thing he needed was some wraith from the past intent on dragging him down. I began to wish I'd never been to the bloody concert. Until then I'd been, if not exactly *happy*, at least normal and settled. Over the years I'd discovered that the key to contentment is low expectations. I wouldn't wake up in the morning expecting to be happy, but sometimes, without any deliberate effort from me, the day might turn out well and I'd find that I was. Now I was agitated, discontented and unable to concentrate. That brief meeting had succeeded in chipping away at the protective structure that time and all the comforting rituals of my existence had raised around me.

It was a month or so before I remembered that the ostensible point of the exchange of notes had been to secure Frances' address, and even longer before I got round to the job of writing. Where do you start when you haven't seen someone for thirteen years? You can either say everything or nothing. You can attempt to give a chronicle of your experiences and achievements from then until now, or just keep it light and ask a few questions in the hope that you'll get a reply.

Once I sat down to it, though, it wasn't as hard as I'd thought.

Dear Frances

I hope you don't mind me writing to you out of the blue, but I was at a charity concert the other night (playing the cello) when I bumped into Rad. We didn't have much opportunity to talk, but we exchanged a bit of news and he passed on your address. I was really amazed to hear that you've emigrated – and that you've got three Australian children. If you have time I'd love to hear what you're up to, and especially see some photos. I could only find one half-decent picture of me and it's not all that recent. It's a publicity shot for a recital I gave at the Wigmore Hall a few years ago, so naturally it doesn't look anything like me. That was about the high point of my career, but I didn't pull it off as a soloist and now I'm strictly orchestra material. I teach the cello too, which is unbelievably depressing as the children are mostly crap and completely unmotivated and the ones that are any good are good at everything else too and invariably give it up to concentrate on their exams. I'm living in a flat in Vauxhall at the moment – I don't know why I say 'at the moment' because there's no likelihood of this changing. My parents still live in our old house in The Close – they got back together round about the time of Birdie's death. My granny died about five years ago so they've got the place to themselves again and they seem happier now than they've ever been. They go off on these weekend breaks to cultural hotspots and visit art galleries and churches. Although these jaunts have been getting steadily less ambitious as my father can't walk far without getting breathless. He's given up smoking his disgusting old pipe, anyway, which is a good thing, though too late of course. They have abandoned all hope of grandparenthood as I've shown no sign of settling down. Perhaps I'll end up like Clarissa – you know, golf and gentleman friends in the afternoons – though realistically I would say the chances of this are slight. I'm more likely to turn into Auntie Mim.

I've often thought about you and wondered how you are – I've half expected to see you crop up on television. I always imagined you becoming an actress. I don't suppose with three small children that you ever manage to come back to England, but if you do I'd love to see you.

    With love
    Abigail

I posted this one, again, into the abyss, not knowing if it would ever be read.

45

On Mother's Day I went over to my parents' house to cook lunch. I first did it four or five years ago and in that short time the gesture has acquired the status of a cherished tradition. To try and dodge the ritual and just go back to daffodils would be a kick in the teeth now. I don't mind doing it – I quite enjoy the challenge of preparing a three-course meal in mother's kitchen without barking at her for tidying away the things I still need, and I like using all the old gadgets and pans that remind me of when I was a child. There can't be many people who feel nostalgic about kitchen utensils, but I'm one of them.

There were crocuses out on the green in front of the house. Next door's magnolia was already in bloom, waxy lightbulbs perched on every branch. Spring had come early. Mother was scarifying the lawn with a leaf rake when I arrived, ripping out chunks of moss and combing them into a heap.

'You shouldn't be doing that,' I said, brushing her cheek with my lips. 'It's your day.' She wears so much face powder nowadays it's a bit like kissing a bap.

'Someone has to,' she said, a touch resentfully.

Indoors father was sitting in his armchair with a wooden pocket chess set balanced on the arm. He was playing against himself. These games could drag on for days, only brought to an end when someone accidentally tipped the board over. He struggled to stand up as I came in, setting the chess pieces rattling in their peg-holes.

'I don't know why she bothers,' he said. 'Moss is green, and it doesn't need cutting as often as grass. What we want is more moss, not less.'

'Do you know who I met at a concert a few weeks ago?' I asked as we were eating.

'Simon Rattle?' Mum guessed, hopefully.

'No, no. I don't mean someone famous. I bumped into Rad. Do you remember Rad?'

'Oh,' said Mum, inevitably disappointed. It would have been impossible for me to trump Simon Rattle. 'I'm afraid I never liked that boy. I thought he treated you appallingly.' By this stage I couldn't remember what she knew about the true circumstances of our break-up so I couldn't contradict her with any assurance.

'What's he up to?' asked Dad, sensing that mother's display of grudge-harbouring wasn't the response I'd been seeking.

'He's been out in Senegal for the last five years, working for a charity setting up water-aid projects.'

At the word Senegal mother rolled her eyes in alarm. 'Well, for heaven's sake don't do anything silly. You know AIDS is absolutely rampant in Africa.'

'Mother!' I said, shocked by the speed with which her thoughts had turned to sex. 'I only exchanged a few words with him. He asked after you both, actually.'

'Oh really?' she said, somewhat mollified.

'Did you find out what Frances is doing now?' asked father. He had always liked her.

'She lives in Australia.'

'Senegal. Australia. They've got around, haven't they?' said mother.

Unlike me, I thought.

'She's married to a surgeon.'

Mother raised her eyebrows. 'She's done well for herself.' At the mention of Australia she had clearly imagined Frances shacked up with some sun-tanned jackeroo or surfing instructor. 'Her mother must miss her. I hope you don't get any ideas about emigrating.'

'I bet she goes out to visit them every year,' I said, ignoring her last remark. 'Especially since Frances has had kids. Mind you, I can't picture Lexi as a granny somehow.'

'One can't see her knitting matinée jackets,' father agreed.

'There's no justice,' said mother, a keen knitter.

When I left them, just before teatime, I drove to Balmoral

Road and parked outside the house – something I'd never done before. I have no reason to go in that direction nowadays; it's not on any of my routes. The house had been altered beyond recognition. The tobacco-coloured brickwork had been stone clad to match Fish and Chips' side, and aluminium windows with fake leaded lights replaced the old wooden sash-frames. The lead strips were not quite parallel, giving the glass the appearance of a bulging net. A dismantled car was jacked up on the driveway, its innards all over the crazy paving. At least the dead cactus had gone from the window sill.

A car horn tooted: I was blocking the neighbour's drive. I reversed out of the way, waving an apology, and as the car swung past me I saw Fish at the wheel, and a middle-aged woman – not Chips – beside him. He glanced at me and then looked again in recognition. I've passed the age of bad manners now, so I didn't roar off, but waited, smiling, until he approached my door as I knew he would. He didn't look that much older – he had less hair perhaps, but I would have changed more.

'Hello,' he said, as I wound the window down. 'It's thingummy, isn't it? Frances Radley's friend.'

'That's right. I was just passing, and I thought I'd look at the house, you know, nostalgia.'

'They moved years ago,' he said. 'Do you still see the family?'

'Not any more. We lost touch.'

'Funny lot,' he said, encouraged by this admission. 'I shall never forget that dog – bloody great lump on its side. I don't know why they didn't take it to the vet and get it sorted out.'

I just smiled. It wasn't my job to defend their standards of petcare. 'How's your mother?' I asked.

'She's been in a home since I got married. We've just come from visiting her, actually.'

His companion had got out of the car by now and was standing by the porch, arms folded impatiently. She was wearing shiny white knee-high boots of the sort that might have been acceptable on someone half her age in 1965, and a jacket of black bobbly wool which put me in mind of a poodle. The look on her face wasn't especially friendly. 'That's my wife, Pauline,' he said with some pride. She didn't return my smile but turned on her heel and let herself into the house, slamming the door behind her. A jealous woman, I thought, as Fish made his excuses and hurried down the drive after her.

That evening I tidied my flat. It was already tidy, but once you start looking there are always things to be done. Then I put on Britten's *War Requiem* – loud – and lay on the couch with tears sliding into my ears until the woman in the upstairs flat knocked on the door and asked me to turn the music down because she was trying to get her baby to sleep.

Three weeks after I'd posted my letter to Frances her reply arrived on a misty spring morning. Her chubby schoolgirl handwriting on the envelope was unmistakable. It was written on one of those flimsy aerogrammes that are impossible to open without demolishing half the text, and there was 50p excess to pay because she'd enclosed a set of photographs.

Dear Abigail

I was so pleased to get your letter and hear all your news, and I'm really glad you've made it as a cellist. Are you in fact more famous than you're letting on? Have you, for instance, made any recordings? Copies please, if so.

I've been here eight years now and feel totally Australian. The only thing I can't get used to is the midsummer Christmas. I get all sentimental about White Christmases (there's probably a word to describe that feeling of nostalgia for something you've never actually experienced). But apart from that, and family of course, I can't say I miss Britain at all. I applied for citizenship last year –

it seems crazy to be a different nationality from my own children (photos enclosed). We live about five minutes from the beach, so we're down there most afternoons: there's a whole group of mums and kids who meet up. I help out in a kindergarten in the mornings. The twins (Esme and Hera, 5) are at school now, and Tyler (3) comes to kindy with me. I'm not intending to continue with this domestic slavery indefinitely, in case you were wondering. As soon as Tyler's at school I'm going to university to do a psychology course, so that I can become a psychotherapist to this community's many nutters. Nev, my husband, is a plastic surgeon, and tends to run up against a fair few of them in his line of work, so he will be able to put some business my way. (Only joking.) He does a lot of work with burns patients and road crash victims as well as a bit of 'vanity' work, but he hasn't put me under the knife yet – as you can see from the photo I am entirely unenhanced. He says he'll give me a discount if I make a block booking – liposuction, tummy tuck, breast reduction, and he'll throw in a free nose job.

It's true I haven't been back to England since the children were born – a family visit is out of the question, but I haven't ruled out a solo trip. Mum and Lawrence have been out twice now: we all went up to Cairns for a fortnight and took a boat out on the reef. Can you imagine Mum in a snorkel? Dad was here last summer – he was really good with the children – very grandpaternal. Perhaps I'll try and persuade him to move out here. Nev's parents live right down in Melbourne so we're painfully short of relatives.

I couldn't work out from your letter whether you're still in contact with Rad; if you are you'll already know about his accident. He came off his motorbike in the snow in January and broke his arm, leg, collar bone and some ribs. He spent about six weeks in hospital but he's apparently out now. I had all this from Mum who's been nursing him. I haven't seen him since my wedding – nearly seven years, but he writes good letters. I suppose it's him I miss more than anyone. If you ever find yourself hankering to escape an English winter – or an English summer for that matter – we'd love to have you. I wish I could promise to keep in touch but I'm the world's slackest correspondent nowadays. Nev does a 'Dear friends' mailshot on the computer at Christmas

but, frankly, it's completely unreadable – so I'll spare you that. Nevertheless please write again anyway if you have time.
　Love
　Frances
P.S. Do go and visit Rad if you can as he is bored and lonely.

There were four pictures – a studio shot of the three children and others of Frances and Nev, the whole family, and the outside of the house – a large, white, single-storey building with a green tiled roof and a lemon tree on the front lawn. I didn't pay them the attention I might have because my mind was still racing from Frances' news about Rad. I reread the crucial paragraph. *He came off his motorbike in the snow.* That would have had to be during the three or four days following our meeting, as the snow had not lasted long and we'd had none since. Perhaps he'd never received my card – had been taken to hospital before I'd even posted it. I read on: *he's apparently out now.* The letter was dated a fortnight ago. The feeling of hope that had bloomed a moment earlier wilted as I realised he would have had plenty of time by now to respond to my card if he was the slightest bit interested. Maybe it was his writing arm that was broken? I thought, trying to picture him plastered from shoulder to fingertips, prone on a bed somewhere, fumbling helplessly with that two-inch piece of crayon, surrounded by the litter of a dozen illegible messages to me. This didn't seem terribly likely somehow; it would take more than a few broken bones to deter someone truly keen and resourceful. *Do go and visit Rad if you can as he is bored and lonely.* Well, that makes two of us, I thought, reaching for my road map.

Even my jumbo sized *A–Z* couldn't help me with the meagre information Rad had supplied by way of an address. There were roads called Riverside in Twickenham, Richmond and Woolwich, but not Laleham. I began to wonder whether my card could possibly have arrived at all. I toyed with the idea of driving over to The Close to borrow Dad's Ordnance Survey map of the relevant area but decided a trip into town to buy one would be quicker and less exasperating. It would take us hours to crack the arcane filing system that had come into play since the study had been redecorated, and of the whole set of maps, amassed over many years, it would inevitably be the one missing or out on loan that I required. I'd been caught that way too many times before.

I spent some time at the shops trying to find a suitable visiting gift. Was it okay to take flowers to a man? *Country Living* was obviously out in this instance. A book would be no good. He might already have it, or hate the author. If I chose one I hadn't read I couldn't vouch for its being any good, but to go for an old favourite of mine on the assumption that he hadn't read it seemed bossy somehow – like giving homework. Finally I settled for some expensive chocolates – I didn't want them to look like an afterthought, picked up at any old garage on the way – and a bunch of daffodils. You can't go wrong with daffodils: you can just ram them in a beer mug and they look fine.

The OS map wasn't any use as far as Riverside was concerned, of course, but it did offer some clues. At Laleham the river Thames had carved out a meander so deep that it had almost formed an ox-bow. Before that could happen a navigation had been dug through the short cut, and there was now a lock and a small island. The area was called Penton Hook: the place illustrated on Rad's postcard. It occurred to me that he might be living in the lock-keeper's cottage itself; if not, someone there might be able to point me in the right direction.

It took over two hours to reach Laleham. Even with the maps spread out all over the passenger seat I lost myself several times, got enmeshed in a one-way system in Kingston and ended up on the wrong side of the river. My attentiveness in Mrs Twigg's second-year mapwork lessons had been wasted apparently. Identifying escarpments and giving the co-ordinates for a youth hostel and a church without tower or spire had not proved adequate preparation for work in the field.

Eventually I found what I was looking for. An alleyway between two houses in a quiet residential street led past a building site to the river, and there it was: the lock and the white cottage from the picture that had been propped on my mantelpiece for the past two months. A man in overalls was sitting on the doorstep in the sunshine fitting a new tyre to a bicycle wheel using a couple of spoons. He squinted up at me as I approached. 'Do you know a place called Wentworth?' I asked, feeling suddenly foolish. He gave a little nod. 'I can give you directions, but if you're looking for the guy who lives there, he's out on the island, fishing.' He pointed across the weir.

I thanked him and waited impatiently by the lockside while the gates swung open to let a pleasure cruiser pass downstream. The mists had all dissolved now and a milky sun shimmered on the water as I crossed the weir to the island.

He was on the far side beyond the trees, sitting on the bank on one of those legless green canvas chairs with his back to me. There was a fishing rod propped in front of him, parallel with the river, and he had his head down as though reading, but as I came closer I saw that he was asleep, an open copy of *Huckleberry Finn* face down on his lap. A small silver bell hung from the tip of the fishing rod. The devil entered me and I reached down and gave the line a tug, setting the bell jangling. Rad started violently and lunged for the rod, sending *Huckleberry Finn* tumbling down the bank into the river. He gave a sort of splutter of annoyance, which turned to surprise as he saw me.

'Sorry,' I said, aghast, dropping the chocolates and daffodils and scrambling down the bank to retrieve the book which was now lying under about six inches of muddy Thames water. I wiped it on the grass and handed it, dripping and buckled, back up to him.

'Hello,' he said, giving me one of his sardonic looks. 'You're the first bite I've had all week.' He offered me his hand and pulled me up out of the mud on to the grass beside him.

'I shouldn't have done that,' I said. 'I just saw that little bell there and I couldn't resist it.'

'I thought you were a twenty-pound pike,' he said.

'Sorry to disappoint you.'

'Oh, I'm not disappointed.'

'Frances wrote and told me you'd had a bad motorbike accident and needed cheering up.'

'So you thought you'd come and knock my book into the river.'

'I hadn't planned that bit. I thought you might need things doing – shopping and stuff. Frances gave me the impression that you'd broken every bone in your body.'

'I'm afraid you've been dragged here under false pretences: one of my legs was fine.'

'I didn't mean to sound cheated. I'm glad to see you looking so well.'

'I looked more impressive a few weeks ago when I was still in plaster. I feel a bit of a fraud now, although I still can't walk far.'

'How did you do it?'

'I was riding back from work in the snow – I suppose it wouldn't have been long after I'd bumped into you at the Barbican – and this little kid came flying down his driveway on a sledge and straight out into the road. I swerved and went into a skid and got thrown against a parked car with the bike on top of me. It was my fault – I was going too fast.'

'God. You're lucky to be alive.'

'I suppose so. When I was lying in hospital all strapped up I honestly didn't know whether I felt lucky or unlucky.'

'What got broken?'

'My collar bone, three ribs, my right arm and my left leg. The worst of it is the bike's not even mine – I was borrowing it from the bloke who's taken over my job.'

'Are you having physiotherapy?' What did I care about someone or other's bike?

'Twice a week at the moment. This woman gets me moving my arm around and squeezing tennis balls and lifting incredibly light weights. But she seems to spend most of the time just massaging my shoulders, and chatting.'

I bet she does, I thought. I remembered the chocolates and daffodils – now somewhat battered – that I'd flung down earlier, and retrieved them. 'I wasn't sure what to bring,' I said. 'You probably hate flowers.'

'I don't actually,' he said in a matter-of-fact voice. 'When I was working in Senegal I went to dinner with one of the local dignitaries. He was quite well off by their standards and had some really beautiful furniture – ebony tables inlaid with brass, and fantastic carpets, and he insisted on showing me his prized possession, which turned out to be a vase of plastic daffodils. I've looked at daffodils through different eyes since then. I see you didn't think I was up to *Country Living*.'

'It was the other way round, I assure you.'

'I ought to put these in some water,' he said. 'I'm only a few minutes' walk away – would you like a cup of tea. Or a beer?'

'Tea would be nice,' I said, as he reeled in the fishing line and put the lids on his various containers of bait, hooks and lures, and stowed them along with his soggy paperback in a duffle-bag. I picked up the canvas chair and we walked back to the lock in silence.

'I was going to come to your house,' I said, finally, as we made our way along the lane to the street where I'd parked the car. 'But I couldn't find you on the A to Z.'

'Ah. No, you wouldn't. How did you know I was on the island?'

'The lock-keeper told me. I asked him for directions.'

He nodded. 'He's a good bloke – let's me use his phone, and he's been bringing me milk and bread over every so often. I've been living on sandwiches.'

Rad led the way between two large detached houses down to the river again where we picked up the towpath. 'I'm just along here. You'll have to excuse the state of the place. I don't get many visitors.' Ahead of us, moored to the bank by a fixed gangplank, was a small houseboat. Its white paint was chipped and peeling and the varnish on the woodwork was crazed and crystalline like shattered barleysugar. The name

Wentworth was stencilled on the hull in broken letters. On the deck section stood a folding picnic table and a faded sun-lounger.

'A houseboat,' I said, enviously. 'Lucky you.'

'It's not mine; I'm just renting it,' he said as he helped me across the gangplank. 'From the same person who lent me the bike.' He ducked down to unlock the door, fiddling with a selection of keys. 'I don't know why I bother – there's nothing worth pinching,' he said, sliding the door open and stepping aside to let me through.

I found myself standing in a long, narrow sitting-room and galley area. There was a two-ring gas burner and sink under the windows along one side, with a tiny fridge, some cupboards and open shelves on which were various unappetising tins: pilchards, rice pudding, processed peas and some frankfurters in brine, bearing a price tag for one and fourpence. Rad caught me staring. 'They came with the boat,' he assured me. On the draining board stood one cup, one bowl and one spoon. There was a dark wood table and a maroon vinyl banquette in one corner – rather like the seating arrangements in a steak house. The only other furniture was a bookcase, a single armchair, and a low coffee table, on which was one slate coaster, a pile of newspapers and a radio.

'It's a misanthropist's dream,' he said. 'There's only one of everything.'

'I like it,' I said, watching him unpack his fishing bag. He put the sodden paperback on the draining board and leaned out of the window to tip the maggots into the river. He collapsed the chair and the fishing rod and stowed them in one of the cupboards. 'I'd have thought it would move more,' I said, walking from one side of the room to the other in a couple of strides.

'It's got a fixed mooring. It only sways a bit when something big goes past. It's not like being in a boat.'

While he filled an old aluminium kettle with water and hunted for the matches to light the gas I picked up *Huckleberry Finn* and tried fanning the pages out so that it wouldn't dry in a solid block like a barbecue briquette.

'I do feel bad about this,' I said, then added innocently, 'I hope you haven't lost any valuable annotations.'

He looked at me through narrowed eyes for a second, then caught on. 'Did I really say that? Christ, I was pompous.' He added in a pompous tone: 'I would like to apologise formally for my pomposity.'

'In that case I accept, on behalf of everyone who knew you,' I said, and we both laughed.

'Now I come to think of it, Frances never did replace *Narziss and Goldmund*, and I never did finish it,' he said a moment later, from inside one of the cupboards from which he produced several crushed packets of tea. 'There's Earl Grey, Lapsang Souchong and something called Relaxing Tea, but I don't know how long they've been hanging around as I inherited them with the boat. Or there's the normal stuff, which is mine.'

'I'll have the normal stuff then.'

The kettle gave a whistle which turned to a scream while Rad dropped tea-bags into two Royal Wedding mugs. 'You must be the last person in England still using a whistling kettle,' I said. Through a half-open door at the far end of the cabin I could see a double bed heaped with clothes.

'Feel free to look around,' said Rad, following the direction of my gaze. Without waiting for a reply he walked over and pushed the bedroom door open to reveal a small wood-panelled cabin only just big enough to contain the bed and a trunk which functioned as a bedside table. From a pole suspended from hooks in the ceiling in front of the window hung half a dozen shirts and a jacket on wire hangers.

'Oh, I haven't drawn the curtains yet,' said Rad, sweeping the shirts apart to let in some daylight. I couldn't help laughing.

'Rad, it would be the work of five minutes for me to rig up some curtains if you want them.'

'It's okay. I quite like this arrangement. I'm always awake before it's light, anyway.'

'I'm serious,' I said. 'If there's anything practical I can do. I mean how do you get your food. And what about laundry?'

'Mum comes to visit every week and takes a bag of washing with her and brings everything back clean and ironed the next week.'

'Crikey – Lexi doing your washing! That's what I call role reversal.'

'I know men always say this about women, but she honestly seems to enjoy it.'

'She's probably glad to have one of her children living in the same country as her – at any price.'

'Is that it?' he said. 'You're probably right. I'll stop exploiting her. This is the bathroom – palatial, isn't it?' He slid back a door adjoining the sitting-room area on the smallest conceivable space in which a loo, shower and hand-basin could be accommodated. The basin was so tiny Rad would only have been able to wash one hand at a time. 'There's another bedroom at the other end; it's even smaller than mine and full of junk.' He walked over to the kitchen and opened a round-cornered door which I had assumed concealed a cupboard. Inside was a single bunk like a railway couchette, on which was a pile of clean ironing. On the floor were three cardboard boxes of books and papers.

'Is this everything you own?' I asked.

'Just about. I used to have furniture and stuff, but I sold it all or gave it away before I left England. Mum and Lawrence have got a couple of boxes in their attic. Once you start getting rid of your belongings, though, it gets addictive. You look at everything and think, Do I need it? Do I love it? and anything that doesn't pass the test ends up in the bin. Sometimes I come back and chuck out another pair of socks just for the hell of it.'

I burst out laughing. 'You're mad,' I said, at the same time making a mental note that my collection of pot-pourri baskets had to go.

'Well, there was no point in buying anything in Senegal – not that there was much to buy – because I wouldn't have been able to bring it home. I suppose I'll have to get back into the habit of acquiring things now I'm here.'

'Do you think you'll stay in this country?' I asked, trying

to sound casual. 'Buy a house?'

'I don't know. I've made Alan – my replacement – an offer for this houseboat. Here,' he handed me my tea. 'Do you take sugar?' I shook my head. 'That's good, because I haven't got any.'

Lady Diana Spencer smiled shyly up from the side of my mug. 'I cried when they got married,' I said. Rad raised his eyes to the ceiling. 'And when she died. I didn't cry when they got divorced, though. I wonder why.'

'I can't remember the last time I cried,' said Rad. He took a drink of tea. 'Oh yes I can,' he added quietly, and I knew the occasion he meant. There was a silence which seemed to set like glue, as we stood there at the table drinking our tea.

'Look–' we said, simultaneously, and I ploughed on: 'I really came here to be of some use, so are you sure there's nothing I can do?'

He thought for a moment. 'Actually there is something, if it's not too much trouble.'

'Come on then, spit it out.'

'I've been a bit cooped up – first in hospital and now here because I can't get about. Mum visits, and Dad comes and takes me to the physio, but what I'd really like is to go out somewhere. If you've got a car . . .'

'Of course. I can drive you somewhere if that's what you'd like. Where do you want to go?'

'I was thinking of Kew. Are you sure you don't mind?'

I shook my head. 'I'd be happy to go to Kew.'

'Will Mr Jex be able to spare you for a day?'

'Mr Jex?' I said.

'Your husband. I thought . . .'

'I'm not married: Jex is my professional name. I made it up.'

He looked genuinely uncomfortable. 'When you were introduced as Abigail Jex I just assumed you were married. I suppose I should have guessed you're not the sort of woman who'd take a man's name anyway.'

'I bloody would,' I said. 'If you're saddled with a name like Onions you'd take anything. Besides, I can't see the point of keeping your own name when you marry – I mean I wouldn't want to end up with a different surname from my own children.' I could have bitten my tongue off.

'You want children, do you?' he said.

'I suppose so, ultimately. But it's not desperately relevant given the life I lead now. Anyway,' I said, firmly. 'Kew.'

46

It had been agreed that I would pick Rad up on the next fine day that I was free. I couldn't reach him by phone; I would just have to turn up. 'How will you know I'm coming?' I asked. I tend to prefer more concrete arrangements.

'I won't. If it's fine and you don't turn up I'll know you were busy.'

'How will I know you're going to be in?'

'I'm bound to be in. Where am I going to go? I suppose I might be on the island, fishing, but I'll leave you a note on the door.'

That night I sent up a prayer for drought but for the next three days it rained and on the fourth the sun shone but I was teaching. I was uncharacteristically short with my students and sent one girl off in tears.

'Stop,' I commanded, half-way into the piece which I had set her the previous week and which she was evidently sight-reading, having set eyes on it for the first time that morning. I had half considered letting her saw and stumble her way to the bitter end as a punishment, but the sound was intolerable and I called a halt. The sawing stopped and the girl looked up, a combination of fear and relief on her face.

'Sarah,' I said, wearily. 'People always look at great classical musicians and say, "How do they play like that?" as if it's just a matter of luck. And the answer is that they've been practising for hours on end every day for ten, twenty, thirty years.'

Sarah smiled politely, uncomprehendingly.

'What I'm saying is if you don't practise – and I can tell you haven't practised this piece *at all*' – I waved away her half-hearted murmur of protest – 'these lessons are a complete waste of time. You'll never make any improvement in the half an hour a week we have together.' I was warming to my theme now. 'You'd be better off back in the physics lab or wherever it is you're supposed to be now. You might learn one interesting fact there, which is more than you're doing here. Do you actually enjoy playing the cello?'

'Sometimes . . .' Her foot traced a scratch in the polished floor. 'No,' she conceded. 'I enjoy talking to you, though. It's just the practising I hate.'

'Well, I think you should consider giving up.' I surprise myself sometimes. I don't normally recommend this course of action to a pupil with any ability – it's too much like making a case for my own redundancy – but I suddenly felt inspired to preach Rad's gospel of minimalism. 'When I'm having a clear-out at home,' I improvised, 'I look at things and think, "Do I need this? And if not, do I love it?" And if the answer is No, I bin it.' It's the same with this: you clearly don't *need* to play the cello, and you've admitted you don't love it. So . . .'

'. . . Her parents rang up the head the next day to complain that I'd told their daughter to throw her fifteen hundred pound cello in the bin.'

'And did she?'

'Er, metaphorically speaking, yes. She's given up. But the head asked me to be a little more restrained in my careers advice next time.'

Rad laughed. 'I didn't think you'd start holding me up as an example to your students.'

'Oh, but you've completely converted me. You won't believe how many pairs of shoes I've chucked out in the last few days.'

Rad glanced at my feet. We were walking along the broad path to the ornamental lake at Kew. He had been sitting on deck on the sun-lounger reading the paper when I arrived, his bad leg outstretched. He had dark glasses on so from a distance I couldn't tell the direction of his gaze and had to make a long, self-conscious walk along the towpath, wondering whether I was being watched. Just as I came within about twenty yards of the boat he had, without otherwise moving, raised one hand palm outwards, and I knew he'd seen me all along.

In my zeal for clearing out my flat I had of course forgotten the inside of the car which was full of old drink cartons, sweet wrappers, crisp crumbs and broken cassette cases.

'There was no need to go to the trouble of tidying up for me,' Rad said, absolutely deadpan, trying to find some footspace amidst the junk.

'I know,' I said. 'That's why I didn't.'

❧

'I feel rather a hypocrite now,' Rad said, peering into the lake, looking for chub. 'While you've been throwing things out I've just gone and bought something. Two things.'

'What?'

'The houseboat. And a chair. I decided having only one was a bit anti-social. And now I've got the new one I've realised how uncomfortable the old one is.'

'How on earth did you get a chair back there?'

'Dad and a roof-rack.'

'The first time I ever saw your dad he was shifting furniture,' I said, then shut up abruptly, realising that Rad might not particularly like to reminisce about his parents' move into single beds.

'He didn't actually do any of the lifting: he just bullied the two shop assistants. I made sure I was wearing my sling so I wouldn't be expected to help.' He raised his bad arm and tried to mime a tennis serve, a pinched expression on his face. 'I'll never win Wimbledon now,' he said, with a hint of self-pity.

'A distinct possibility, was it?'

'No. But I don't like anything to be ruled out. Do you?'

We made our way between flowerbeds laid out like mosaics of purple and pink. Symmetry was king here: tulips all grew to the same height and pansies bloomed simultaneously. Rebel, I urged them silently. Go on: wilt, keel over.

Although it was warm in the sun there was a cold breeze and the sudden blast of hot damp air that greeted us as we entered the Palm House took me by surprise. Condensation streamed down the windows, and high above our heads jets of fine mist bloomed on metal stems. Rad looked up at the balcony running around the inside of the roof. 'You go up if you like,' he said. 'I'm not sure I'll manage the spiral staircase.' By the time I'd climbed to the top, my shoes ringing on the treads and making the white iron banisters sing, I was dizzy and breathless. The heat and humidity were overpowering; moisture dropped from the ceiling on to my hair. Through the veils of water vapour below me I could see Rad moving amongst the plants, crouching to read their names. The only other person on the balcony was an old woman in a flowery dress, pop sox, walking boots, a horse-blanket overcoat and a bobble hat. She was making notes in a diary and muttering uninhibitedly. That'll be me one day, I thought, suddenly. A mad old crone in American Tan pop sox and comfy shoes, visiting botanical gardens and stately homes on my own. A fat drop of water hit my cheek, and as I pulled a tissue from my coat pocket one of my gloves – a frivolous pink leather thing – which was rolled up inside, sprang out and sailed between the bars of the parapet to land with a slap not a yard from where Rad was standing. He looked up as if expecting an avalanche, and when he saw me leaning over the railing, wagging the other glove in apology he pretended to tut impatiently and picked up its partner. A moment later there was the clang of feet on the stairs and he appeared on the balcony.

'I accept your challenge,' he said, handing back the glove, 'whatever it is.'

'I doubt it,' I said, facing him, and for a moment a little current of fake antagonism crackled between us.

'Excuse me, excuse me,' said a voice, and we pressed ourselves back against the warm water pipes running around the walls to let the woman in the bobble hat pass us, still muttering.

'I'm going to end up like her,' I whispered to Rad, once she was safely out of earshot. He looked critically at her departing figure, taking in the pop sox at half mast, and the moulting overcoat, and then looked back at me with an appraising glance.

'Ambition's a terrible thing,' he said, and strode off to the far staircase before I could think of a crushing reply.

Downstairs we made our way past tamarind and ebony trees, banyan and sugar cane and an oil palm with its hairy trunk like an ape's arm. In the basement were giant kelps, electric-blue and yellow fish and red algae like crushed velvet.

'Have you got a garden?' Rad asked, as we finally emerged from the tropical heat of the palm house to the chill of an English spring.

'No, I've got a window box full of dead things,' I said, pulling my coat collar over my ears.

'I can see that gardening might be quite fun,' he mused. 'I mean when all other possible sources of fun have been exhausted.'

I nodded. 'We're not quite at that stage yet, though.'

He shook his head. 'No, not quite.'

I could tell he was beginning to flag as we reached the Cherry Walk. His bad leg was obviously giving him trouble, and I noticed for the first time that he was walking with a limp. The sky was overcast by now. It was only a matter of time before we were rained on. We made it to King William's Temple, which had obscene graffiti scored into the stonework and stank of cigarettes like a bus shelter, just as the first shower came. *Tanya is a fridged cow*, read one of the messages. Rad pulled a face at the smell and the gougings in the wall. 'I hate this country,' he said in disgust. This was how he had been all day – joking one minute and then withdrawn or morose the next. Much of our circuit of the gardens had passed in silence. I stood near the doorway looking through the curtain of water at the steaming gardens beyond. I couldn't help remembering the last time we had taken refuge from the rain together, in the cottage at Half Moon Street, and didn't dare catch his eye in case he might have been thinking of it too. 'Come on, it's only rain,' I said, stepping out into the monsoon. I didn't want to hang around like someone waiting to be kissed.

'That was a good idea of yours,' he said a little later as we sat in the café, water trickling from the ends of our hair and rolling off the front of our coats. After only the first few seconds' dash from the temple we were so thoroughly soaked that further haste was pointless. 'We should have brought an umbrella,' Rad said, watching me unwind the scarf from around my neck and wring it out into the plant pot beside me.

'I've got a brand new one in the boot of the car,' I said, as if this was of any interest now. 'I've been saving it for a rainy day.'

He put down his coffee untasted. 'I was going to tell you you haven't changed,' he said. 'But I've just realised that you don't blush any more. Do you?'

I shook my head. 'I don't much nowadays. I must have got all my embarrassments out of the way early.'

This was his first hint, in all our conversations since I'd first found him fishing on the island, that such a thing as a shared past even existed.

'You seem to have more confidence.'

'That's funny,' I said, stirring brown sugar crystals into my coffee. 'Because you seem to have less. But then you had far too much before anyway.' I smiled to let him know I was joking, which I was, almost.

'I think when you're young you're an extreme version of yourself and as you get older your personality moves towards the norm. Then when you get really old it swings to the extreme again.'

'Is this a theory you've formulated over the years?'

'No, I just thought of it,' he admitted.

'I remember you used to be very tough on me and Frances. Trivial was a word that came up a lot.'

'Really? In what context?'

'Oh, you know, high heels, nail varnish, jewellery – all that girly stuff.'

'Did I? I quite like high-heeled shoes on women now.

343

Though they're obviously not for walking in, are they? Just for looking at.'

I raised my eyebrows. 'You *have* changed . . .'

'I'm all in favour of a bit of trivia now and then. Like your earrings, for instance. The fact that you've gone to the trouble of putting a little gold moon in one ear and a gold star in the other – that's nice.'

'. . . On the other hand,' I said, 'you can still be as *deliciously* patronising as ever.'

'Sorry,' he said, shrugging his shoulders. 'It's years of practice.'

On the way back to the car Rad offered to cook me dinner on the houseboat. I was pleased, of course, that he wanted to extend our day together, but an image of that shelf of tinned pilchards and rice pudding rose up unbidden. I could almost taste them on my mind's tongue, and a look of anxiety must have crossed my face because Rad said, hurriedly, 'No, of course, you've probably got other plans –' and his forehead puckered into a frown.

'I haven't,' I interrupted. 'Well, I've got to get back at some point to feed the cat, but not this minute. Shall I stop on the way to pick up some food?' I added casually. 'You didn't have much in when I was last there.'

'You're worried about my cooking, aren't you?' said Rad. 'You're thinking of that tin of frankfurters.' In the face of such percipience I could hardly deny it. 'I told you they weren't mine,' he said.

'I'm not a fussy eater,' I explained in mitigation. 'But my tastes have evolved a little since the days of the Greasy Dog.'

'So have mine,' said Rad. 'Unfortunately my abilities haven't. So it'll just be a packet of spaghetti and a jar of pesto sauce, if that's not too basic for your evolved taste.'

'That'll be fine.'

'It's Mum's sixtieth birthday party a week on Sunday,' said Rad suddenly as we were driving through Richmond Park on the way home. 'Will you come?' He was attempting to wipe the inside of the windscreen with a shred of tissue that I had unearthed from the glove compartment. Even the full might of the car heater was not equal to the clouds of vapour coming off our wet clothes, and the windows kept fogging up.

'I'd love to,' I said, peering at the road through a fist-sized patch of transparent glass.

'Everyone will be there – except Frances of course. I mean Dad will be there . . .' he trailed off.

'That's okay,' I said evenly. 'I'd like to see them all.'

'I know Mum would love to see you again. And Lawrence. He gave me such a hard time when we, you know, lost contact.'

I smiled at the notion of our 'losing contact', and even at a distance of thirteen years I was pleased to imagine Rad having a hard time. 'Not being Radleys was a strong bond between us,' I said, and then, 'Sixty. I can hardly believe it. Is she grey?'

'Underneath,' said Rad. He looked out of the window at the traffic crawling away through the park. 'Is it me, or are there more cars around nowadays? The rush hour seems to go on all day.'

'It's getting worse,' I agreed.

'Makes me proud that I haven't got a car.'

'Yes,' I replied. 'Much better idea to get a lift from someone who has – that way you can feel superior without having to get the bus.'

He gave me a look that said *smartarse*, and started to pick through my selection of classical cassettes that were jammed into the cubby hole in the dashboard.

'Who's the greatest composer?'

'Mozart,' I said, without a second's hesitation. 'Who's the greatest philosopher?'

'Hume,' he said. 'But then I never finished the course.'

I couldn't help laughing at this. 'What did you do when you left?'

'I can't remember. I think I had a bit of a breakdown. I just about got through that autumn term after Birdie's death, sort of sleepwalking, but then at Christmas I went slightly mad. I was so obsessed by the idea of death I couldn't see the point in anything – eating, working, getting out of bed, getting into bed. Mum sent me off to see this psychotherapist in Battersea. She just sat there with her hands folded and occasionally replied to one of my questions with another question, and after about three months of this twice a week I worked out what it had cost and thought, Christ, I could have gone round the world for that and got more answers, so I packed it in. Then once the idea of travel had occurred to me I started to think about VSO and within six months I was in India.'

'You'd have thought they would try to screen out people who are just running away.'

'I wasn't *just* running away. Anyway, I reckon about ninety per cent of the volunteers I met out there saw the whole thing as a sort of equivalent to joining the Foreign Legion.'

'How long were you there for?'

'Two years. Then I came back and got a job with this Arid Lands project and after a few years in the office the posting came up in Senegal.'

'And now here you are.'

'Yes. Here I am,' he said, not sounding terribly convinced.

On the houseboat Rad lit the Calor Gas stove and hung our coats in front of it over the back of a rickety drying frame. He looked at my jeans which, like his, were soaking from knee to ankle, and then vanished into the spare cabin and reappeared carrying a couple of towels. 'Do you want a shower while I slave over this jar of pesto? It's the only way to get warm in this place. You can borrow a pair of my trousers while these dry off if you like.' He pushed the cabin door open and pointed to the piles of clean laundry. 'Help yourself.'

This is a bit kinky, I thought, selecting a pair of brown corduroys, ironed by Lexi with a crease down the front, and a faded denim shirt. In the bathroom I inspected Rad's toiletries for any signs of female habitation: shampoo, soap, deodorant, toothpaste, shaving foam and a Bic razor. So far so good. Outside I could hear him clattering saucepans, and the whine of the tap running. The shower was so low on the wall only a dwarf could have washed his hair without stooping, and even infinitesimal adjustments to the dial could not deliver water at a temperature between freezing and boiling. I squealed as Rad turned off the kitchen tap and scalding water erupted from the shower head.

'Sorry,' he called. 'I forgot to mention that the dial is stuffed. You need the touch of a brain surgeon.'

There was no room in there to get dressed, and besides every surface was awash by the time I'd finished, so I was forced to emerge, wrapped in a towel, red-shouldered and flustered, and make my way to the spare cabin, dropping and retrieving items of clothing along the way. Rad, who was sitting on the bench seat with his leg up, reading and drinking red wine, watched my undignified progress with amusement. 'I'm afraid a bit of water went on the floor,' I said, underplaying the facts rather.

'Never mind,' he said. 'Help yourself to wine.' And then, 'Godalmighty, what were you doing in here?' as he stepped into the bathroom with a splash.

I poured wine into an empty glass – one of those indestructible types they give away in petrol promotions. I still had a few like that back home; they outlived all the decent ones – practically bounced when dropped. On the cooker the saucepan lid started to rattle, so I stood a sheaf of spaghetti in the bubbling water and watched it collapse against the side of the pan. On the dresser was a jar of green pesto and a hunk of parmesan which looked as though it might have spent a couple of weeks in a mousetrap. There was no cheese grater, of course, so I was reduced to hacking chunks off the block with a blunt fruit knife.

How can anyone live like this? I asked myself as I nearly

took off the end of my finger for the second time. Making do with stuff you'd find in a badly equipped caravan. All this ad hockery was perfectly acceptable for a fortnight's holiday, but Rad had been here over four months and now owned the place. You could have too much of this minimalism, I decided.

Once I'd disposed of the cheese and given the spaghetti a stir I removed my coat, now steaming, from the drying frame and replaced it with my wet jeans and jumper. Then I settled down on the bench with my wine and picked up Rad's book, an ancient Penguin edition of *Three Men in a Boat* priced three and six, and opened it at the first page. 'There were four of us – George, and William Samuel Harris, and myself, and Montmorency . . .' A bookmark fell out on to the table. It was my card: the one I had sent some three months ago now and which he had never followed up. *Sorry we didn't have a chance to talk properly the other evening.* As I went to slip it back between the pages, about half-way through, where I guessed it had been lying, I saw that on the back, all around the address, he had doodled the name Jex over and over again, dozens of times, in large and small handwriting. I felt my scalp prickle, and then the bathroom door opened and I dropped the book guiltily and stood up.

'It's nearly done,' I said, pointing at the pan. He burst out laughing when he saw my outfit. And I suppose in his over-sized shirt and trousers, with everything rolled up several times at ankles, cuffs and waistband, I did look rather like one of those home-made guys that you see slumped outside tube stations on Bonfire Night. While he was in his cabin changing I cast around to try and check my appearance, finally turning up a chipped mirror tile on the inside of a cupboard door at about chest height. Clearly the boat's last owner hadn't been one to preen.

The pasta was cooked by now so I hunted vainly for a colander, but found only a buckled tea strainer with a ten-pence-sized hole in the middle, and was forced to make do with the saucepan lid. Rad appeared in dry jeans and a white shirt, rubbing his wet hair with a towel, to find me picking strands of spaghetti out of the sink. We were so hungry by this time that if it had been faintly scented with Fairy Liquid we wouldn't have noticed. Rad sat on the bench seat with his bad leg up and I sat opposite on the new chair – a handsome but rather hard Victorian carver. Rad had found a night-light which he stood in a jam jar and placed on the table between us. 'There,' he said, 'I hope all this luxury isn't making you uncomfortable.'

'If I'd known I was going to have a candlelit supper I'd have worn my jewels,' I said, rolling up the trailing cuff of my borrowed shirt for the hundredth time.

Pudding consisted of an apple and a bar of fruit and nut which we shared with coffee. I was glad to see that the chocolates I'd bought him on my previous visit didn't put in an appearance. It would be hard to admire the sort of self-control which could make a box of truffles last nearly a week.

'They'll be wanting you back at work soon, won't they?' I asked as we washed up. 'You must have been off for a few months now.'

'They've been very good about it,' Rad said. 'They just want me fit and well.' From the clipped way he spoke I sensed that he didn't care to pursue this, though I couldn't for the life of me imagine why. 'What about your job?' he asked. 'You haven't told me anything about it.'

'There's not much to tell. I rehearse, I perform, I quite often travel. I teach, too, but not very well because I'm away so much. I have no social life whatsoever because my evenings are taken up with concerts. When I do get a morning or an afternoon free there's no one to share it with because all normal people are at work. Still, I'm not complaining. I know I'm lucky to make a living from my hobby.'

'It must be very important to you, your career – you've been playing since you were how old?'

'Nine. I suppose it is. I mean I'm not fit to do anything else.'

'Competition must be pretty fierce at the top.'

'I don't know. I'm not at the top – I'm B-list material through and through.'

'I'm sure you're not.'

'No, honestly. I thought I might make it as a soloist when I left the Royal College because I'd won a few competitions. But it just didn't happen. I was lucky to get a job with a provincial orchestra – and even luckier when this one in London came up. It's not like other careers where you work your way up slowly to a position of eminence. Here, if you miss the boat that's it.' Story of my life, really, I thought.

'How can you say you've missed the boat? You play with one of the best orchestras in the country. In the world for all I know.'

'I said I'm not complaining. I just don't want you to have the wrong idea about how famous or successful I am. Because I'm neither.'

'It's strange to think that all the years we knew you you were quietly working away at something which you turned out to be brilliant at. I don't think any of us ever even heard you play.'

'I remember Nicky was quite surprised to find out that I played the cello,' I said, looking up at Rad through my fringe. '"I can't imagine her getting anything between her legs," I think he said – to your great amusement.'

Rad, who had been washing up the pasta saucepan, stopped and then started again slightly faster. I couldn't quite see his face because he had his back to me and it had grown dark by now, the only light coming from the candle and the blue and orange glow of the gas stove.

'Don't tell me I've succeeded in embarrassing you?' I said.

He gave an awkward laugh. 'I don't remember that conversation, but I'll take your word for it because it sounds like vintage Nicky, and it's obviously seared itself on your memory.'

'Well, I'm afraid it reinforced that totally false impression you have in your teens that one way or another *everyone* has an opinion about you. It's such a relief when you get older and realise that no one has given the matter a moment's thought.'

'You exaggerate,' he said.

'Not at all. When I got to thirty I suddenly decided that I was never going to worry what people thought of me again. You'll have missed out on this peak experience because you never did care what anyone thought of you.'

He acknowledged the truth of this with a smile. 'I meant you exaggerate when you say no one has an opinion about you. I do for instance.'

'Oh yes?' I said in as neutral a tone as I could manage.

'But I wouldn't dream of telling you what it is because you've completely convinced me that you're not the least bit interested in other people's opinions.'

The wet tea-towel gave a crack as I flicked it at him, catching him just above the elbow. He laughed, infuriatingly, and took a step back. 'Yes, I can see indifference written all over your face.' *Crack.* He dodged and the draught extinguished the night-light, leaving us with only the glow from the heater to see by. 'You wouldn't use violence against a helpless cripple, would you?'

Crack. This time he caught the end and we stood there in the dark with the tea-towel taut between us. 'All I was going to say was that you've improved with age,' said Rad.

'Like a cheese?'

He ignored this. 'Although you're still very bad at taking compliments.' The tea-towel slackened and I took it back.

'Well, I don't get the practice,' I said, folding and refolding it. 'And if you don't mind my saying, I'm not sure you're so hot at giving them: "improved with age" sounds as though I was a bit defective when I was young.'

'That's because you take a masochist's pleasure in disparaging yourself.'

'You're very confident in your pronouncements on my character. After such a short re-acquaintance.'

'I haven't had much else to think about these last few days.'

'You want to get out more.'

'I intend to. That was what today was all about, if you remember.'

'Was the experiment a success?'

'So far. The day isn't over yet.'

I looked at my watch: 11 p.m. 'It nearly is,' I said.

'Then these last few minutes are going to be critical. It could still go either way.'

'We'd better tread carefully then.'

'No. Being careful would be disastrous. A careful person would pick up her coat and handbag and go home to her tidy little flat to water the pot plants and feed the cat. Recklessness is what's called for here.' He took a step towards me and I thought for a second he was going to kiss me, but instead he started to unbutton my shirt.

'What are you doing?'

'It's my shirt. I'm just taking what's mine.'

Later, as we lay in the tiny cabin, looking at the moon through a gap in Rad's shirts, I said, 'Did you sleep with Birdie?' and then immediately felt ashamed. Even at a distance of nearly fourteen years I could still feel jealous of someone as dead as Mozart and Hume.

He rolled on to his side and leaned up on one elbow to look at me. 'No, of course I didn't. She was your sister – I'm not completely depraved.' There was a pause, then he added, more quietly, 'I could have done, though,' and I loved that little flash of male vanity almost as much as the denial itself.

'I only asked because when you came that day to tell me what had happened, you said you'd banged on the pub door calling, "My girlfriend's in the lake."'

'Did I? God, it must be a curse having your memory,' said Rad, looking at me with a combination of bewilderment and pity. 'I was probably just trying to get someone's attention. It wasn't exactly the moment to start explaining the complicated nature of our relationship.'

'Sorry.'

'It's all right.'

'Do you remember what I said when you told me?'

'Abigail, I'm afraid I don't remember anything much of that conversation. It's nothing personal – it's just been erased.'

'Good.'

He kissed me on the forehead. 'Have you ever been to visit her grave?'

'Only two or three times. I was always afraid of bumping into Val. I'm a coward, you see. Someone visits though, because each time I went, there were already fresh flowers there.'

'Val doesn't bear a grudge. I met her again at the inquest when I was giving evidence. She said to me afterwards, "Don't let this ruin your life." That helped me more than all the counselling and therapy.'

'You also said that Birdie already knew Half Moon Street.'

'Yes, she'd been there with Val.'

'Dad and Val used to meet there. He took me there once when I was little, and he told me he had happy memories of the place, but we never went there with my mother.'

'Perhaps Birdie was, you know, conceived there,' said Rad, thinking aloud, then he shut up quickly, realising that he was implicating my father in an image I might prefer not to contemplate. 'Well, probably not,' he said, and put his arm around me. 'Will you be able to sleep like that?' he asked, as I fitted myself into the crook of his elbow.

It only seemed like seconds later that Rad was shaking me. I'd been deep in a dream about, of all things, the Last Night of the Proms, and it was a while before I could shake off the feeling that I was still swaying in the audience at the Royal Albert Hall.

'Can you smell anything?'

I sniffed. 'Smoke.'

He clambered over me to the door and opened it. In the fraction of a second before he slammed it again I could hear the low roar of fire.

'Oh shit, the boat's on fire,' he said, leaping to the end of the bed and sliding the window open. 'I forgot to turn off the gas heater and that bloody clothes drier must have fallen on top of it.' I was hardly listening: it had only just dawned on me that the windows opened out on to the river, not the bank. Stupefied, I watched him pull on a pair of boxer shorts and a T-shirt. 'Come on, we can't hang around. The gas canister might explode. It's only about a six-foot drop to the water. I'll go first and catch you.'

I shook my head. The rest of me was paralysed with fear. 'I can't jump into water,' I said. 'Can't do it. Can't we make a dash for it?'

'You must be joking. It's like a furnace out there.' I reached for the door handle but he seized my wrist. 'Don't touch that door!' he yelled, and I cringed back on the bed. 'Look it's only a few yards to the bank. I promise I won't let you drown.' A look passed between us that acknowledged more than we could ever have said about that terrible night at Half Moon Street. 'I don't want to leave you alone in here,' he said then, 'but I've got to go first so I'm there to catch you. Do you promise you'll follow?'

I nodded, and he pulled himself up to the window, which was only about eighteen inches square, and wriggled out, head first. I heard the splash, then silence for a moment and then Rad's voice, urgent outside the window: 'Abigail, where are you?' I dragged on the knickers and shirt I'd been wearing earlier, my fingers fumbling with the buttons. Even at such an extremity I couldn't face the thought of being dragged naked from the river, dead or alive. It hadn't occurred to me until I saw Rad dive out that there was no way I would be able to get my feet over the sill first and lower myself down. I climbed on to the end of the bed and peered through the window. Rad's pale face looked up at me from the inky water. 'Hurry up,' he called. I leaned out, balancing on my stomach on the metal lip of the window. As I hesitated I heard the crack of breaking glass from the main cabin, and out of the corner of my eye saw flames surging over the roof of the boat, and then I closed my eyes and launched myself into the darkness.

The shock of the cold water closing over my head drove all the breath from my lungs and my gorge rose and I tasted death at the back of my throat, and then I felt Rad's arms around me and cold air on my face.

'I've got you. Don't struggle or you'll pull me under,' he

said, and when I felt how firmly he was holding me, and saw how close we were to the bank I stopped thrashing and let myself be rescued.

When we were finally dripping and shivering on the grass Rad did the strangest thing. He put his arms round me and hugged me fiercely, and I realised he was crying. 'Thank you,' he kept saying, and for a moment I thought he was addressing the God he'd never believed in. But he wasn't; he was talking to me. As far as he was concerned, *I* had saved *him*.

47

Rad accepted my offer to put him up in my flat until the boat was repaired. He brought with him a few clothes, a toothbrush and a razor in one of those climbing-frame rucksacks that students take on their travels. In fact it *was* the rucksack Rad took on his trip to Rome with Nicky and Frances and the infamous portaloo tent. I hated seeing it propped by the front door, trailing its straps. 'It makes me think you're about to go off somewhere,' I said, and Rad laughed. Uneasily.

Three Men in a Boat had perished in the fire. 'You'll always be associated in my mind with unfinished books,' Rad said. '*Narziss and Goldmund*, *Huck Finn* and now this.' He had also lost his new chair, along with the rest of the contents of the main cabin. 'You see what happens when I start getting all greedy and acquisitive,' was his interpretation.

'It was putting that crappy old drier too close to the heater that caused the fire. Not greed.'

'Which wouldn't have happened if our clothes hadn't got wet. Which wouldn't have happened if you hadn't made us sprint half-way round Kew Gardens in the pissing rain.'

He affected to find the flat shockingly luxurious, but was in fact rather glad to be able to stand upright in the shower, and lie flat out on the couch watching television. And he nearly died laughing when he found my rowing machine in the spare room. 'The perfect sport for the non-swimmer,' he said. 'What are you practising for, exactly? Henley?'

Sometimes when I came home in the early evening after a rehearsal or a day's teaching I might find him in the kitchen concocting something disgusting for dinner – pork chops in mushroom soup, for example, or baked beans with mackerel – and we'd eat together at the kitchen table before I went off to my concert.

One morning after a week or so of this I woke up in the

early hours to find the bed beside me empty and Rad standing by the window looking out at the flats opposite. Before we'd fallen asleep we'd been talking about the circumstances of my expulsion from the Radley household, and we'd managed to laugh at the memory of Growth swinging by his teeth from the back of my dress while we'd ranted at one another.

'If you knew how bad I felt after you'd gone,' Rad had said. 'It wasn't you I was angry with, not really. It was Dad. But you can't finish with your dad.'

'You could have answered the phone or come to the door. I gave you so many chances.'

'I know, I know. But I'd dug myself such a hole, I just couldn't climb out. It was easier to stay there and suffer. I would have come round and apologised eventually, I know I would. I always meant to. But then after Birdie died it seemed unacceptable – well, wrong – even to consider my own happiness. I thought, I can't use this as an excuse to get back to you. It would be obscene to profit from her death in any way. I chose misery instead.'

When I woke up and saw him silhouetted against the curtains, there in my room, I had that same sense of dread that you get when the phone rings in the middle of the night: blood roaring in the ears, pulse racing. *I don't know you*, I thought.

'Are you all right?' I whispered. It occurred to me that he might be sleepwalking.

He started and then his shoulders slumped a little. 'Yes. Fine.' He came and sat back on the bed, not quite facing me. 'Oh God, look.' He risked a glance at me. 'I haven't been completely honest with you.' And at these words the temperature in the room dropped to zero. My mother had been right all along.

'You've got HIV,' I said, pulling the sheets up around me.

'No, no, it's nothing like that. Where did you get that idea?'

'What then?'

'I'm . . . I'm going back to Senegal.'

357

'When?'

'July. Sooner if I'm up to it.'

'For good?'

'No, no. Just a year. Eighteen months at the most. I've got to get a new water-aid project running. Then I'm out of there.'

'How long have you known?'

'A few weeks after the accident one of the directors came to visit me in hospital and practically begged me. That's why they've been so accommodating about my sick leave. I said okay the day I came out.'

'You could have told me.'

'I know. I should have, and I selfishly didn't. I'd ask you to come with me, but I know you've got your own career . . .'

'You could ask anyway.'

'Come with me?'

'I can't. I've got my own career. And my parents. And a cat.'

He gave me a crooked smile. 'There you are.'

'Can't they send someone else?'

He shook his head. 'I am the someone else. The first person they sent has cracked up. Don't try to talk me out of it. I'm definitely going.'

I nodded slowly, trying to work out what eighteen months felt like. What was I doing eighteen months ago? 'Why did you buy the houseboat if you knew you were leaving again?'

'I've got to have somewhere to live when I come back. And I wanted to prove to myself that I am going to come back.'

'Did you have to choose the middle of the night to tell me about this? I won't sleep now.'

'I'm sorry. I've been trying to pick my moment for days. I kept waiting until you were in a really good mood, but then I'd lose my nerve because I didn't want to spoil things. But time's running out now because someone's bound to mention it at Mum's party tomorrow.'

'And you didn't want me making a scene in front of the guests?'

'You're not a scene-maker.'

'You're right. I haven't got the energy,' I said, lying back on the pillow with my arms across my face.

'If it's any consolation I wouldn't have taken the job if I'd known you were going to reappear like this.'

'But you'd already met me once at the Barbican by then.'

'You were masquerading as a married woman. That didn't give me much grounds for optimism.'

'If you'd bothered to do the smallest bit of research . . .'

'Oh, forgive me for not applying myself better. Anyway,' he added, 'it seemed perfectly logical to me that you'd be married. I mean, who wouldn't want to marry you?'

'You, for a start,' I said, rolling over on to my stomach and pretending to try and sleep.

'Yes I would. I mean, I do.'

I lay very still with my face on the pillow waiting for the punchline, the pulled plug.

'We could get married before I go,' he said. 'If we get a move on.'

Not even vaguely funny, I thought. Very substandard. After a minute or two Rad tapped me on the shoulder. 'Are you awake?'

'Are you serious?'

'Are you interested?'

'You don't believe in marriage.'

'Okay, I admit that I've never seen the need for it. Living together would be enough for me. But if we can't actually live together – for a while at least – I can see that it might be reassuring to be married.'

'People will think we're mad. Getting married and then living in different countries.'

'But that's fine, because when you reached thirty you stopped worrying about other people's opinions, remember? And I never started, so –'

'This is going to offend my mother's sense of propriety.'

'Can I take that as a Yes?' said Rad.

48

'We won't mention anything about this today, will we?' I said to Rad as we pulled up outside Lawrence and Lexi's house in Chiswick. 'It's your mum's celebration – we can't hijack it.'

Rad looked uneasy. 'Actually I haven't even told them you're coming. In the excitement of nearly burning to death I forgot to mention it. In fact I don't think they know it's you I'm staying with. It'll be a nice surprise,' he said, squeezing my leg, ignoring my indignant gestures.

It was Clarissa who opened the door. She kissed Rad and had to look twice before she recognised me. 'Abigail!' She gave me a scented hug, crushing the flowers I'd brought for Lexi. 'Rad, you sly dog. Where did you find her after all this time?'

'On the end of my fishing line,' he said, leading me down the hallway.

'Everyone's out in the garden,' said Clarissa, throwing our jackets into an armchair in the study.

I dumped my bouquet of flowers on the kitchen table where half a dozen others, still with their wrappers and cards, were propped like tributes at the scene of an accident. Through the open window I could see Lexi, in a white trouser suit, a wide red scarf round her dark hair, holding court. I was disconcerted to see how few faces I recognised. There was Cecile, reclining on a planter's chair in the shade. Her hair was the same shade of strawberry blonde, with that permanent pencil line of grey at the parting, and was coiled into a bun and secured with diamante pins in the shape of lips. Uncle Bill, former owner of Growth, was shuttling between groups, a bottle of champagne in one hand and a jug of orange in the other. I couldn't see Lawrence or Mr Radley anywhere. 'Your dad's not here,' I said to Rad as he handed me a glass of wine.

'He'll be late,' said Rad. 'If he makes it at all.'

'Does he still drink?' I asked. I'm marrying into these genes, I thought. I'm entitled to ask.

'It's much like before, really. He's fine for months and then he'll go out somewhere – like this – and just keep drinking until he's made a complete fool of himself. Parties are his downfall.'

'And weddings?'

'I'm afraid so.'

Rad was mobbed before we'd taken two steps into the garden. A lot of the people there wouldn't have seen him since he came back from Senegal. Everyone knew about his motorbike accident, though his ordeal by fire and water was a new twist. I tried to shrink into the background, but Rad had me by the hand.

'Mum, I've brought someone to see you.'

Lexi gave a squeal of surprise and handed her glass of champagne to her neighbour the better to hug me. 'You look wonderful,' she said, shifting her sunglasses on to her forehead. There were deep lines around her eyes and mouth but the skin on her cheeks was smooth. 'Oh Rad, you are naughty,' she said, pulling the wrapping paper off our present – a new putter, which she would carry around with her for the rest of the afternoon like a fancy cane. 'I told you not to get me anything.' She gave a dandelion an experimental swipe. 'It is lovely though.' A thought struck her. 'So Abigail is the "friend" who's putting you up?'

'That's right,' said Rad. 'Remind me to give you our phone number.'

'Our?' said Lexi, raising her eyebrows, before turning back to me. 'I'm so glad you've turned up again,' she said, as if I had spent the intervening years at the back of a drawer, and then taking both my hands she looked me up and down. 'I've got a couple of dresses that would fit you perfectly. With a belt,' she conceded. 'Don't let me forget to give them to you. None of my other friends are slim enough.' I liked that 'other'. I had to smile: dressing up in Lexi's clothes had been an important initiation rite when I was eleven – for her, nothing had changed. For a second Lexi's eyes looked as though they might water. 'I can't see you standing there without thinking of my Frances,' she said. 'You know she's in Brisbane?'

'Rad gave me her address: we've written to each other, and she sent me some photos of herself and the children.'

'She's sent me a home video of the family for my birthday,' she said. 'I made Lawrence go out and buy a VCR yesterday. When I went to bed at midnight he was still trying to tune the damn thing in, so I don't know whether we'll ever get to see it.'

'Is she good at keeping in contact?'

'Not bad. Better at phoning than writing. We've been to see them twice now. When I'm really decrepit I shall go there every year to escape the winter. Imagine never having to endure an English February. You know Rad's leaving me again?'

'Yes. Not permanently though.'

'Well, that's what he said last time – and then he comes back for all of six months and spends half that time in plaster. What about you? You're not dashing off anywhere, are you? No, you wouldn't desert your parents.' She shot a reproachful glance across the garden at Rad who was talking to Uncle Bill.

'No. I'm staying put.'

'Good, then you must come and see us. Do you play bridge?'

I said I didn't.

'Lawrence will teach you. You'll enjoy it.'

I could feel it happening already, the assimilation. Within minutes Lexi would be lending me Lawrence's cottage in the Tarn, trying to put me up for membership of her health club, marking me down as a house-sitter, granny-sitter and fourth man at bridge if I didn't watch myself. She was amazed and impressed to discover that I still played the cello, and with an orchestra she had heard of, possibly even heard, though she wasn't a hundred per cent sure on that point. 'You must get me tickets,' was her parting instruction as she was summoned by Clarissa to greet more guests.

I joined Rad, now grazing at the food table, which was in the middle of the garden protected by a striped canopy. Every so often the whole structure would lurch as someone tripped, cursing, over one of the guy ropes.

'I'm back in the family,' I said, watching him steal the topmost of a pyramid of strawberries. 'After only fifteen minutes.'

'It's a good thing I'm going abroad,' he replied. 'Being Mum's daughter-in-law is going to take up all your time – I'd just be in the way.'

I began to protest that I'd envisaged being married rather than colonised, but Rad cut me short by popping a strawberry into my mouth.

'Don't do that,' I said, trying to sound cross. 'People will guess.'

'Let them.' He picked up a stack of meringues and a filament of smoked salmon. 'Come on, let's circulate. The quicker we get round everybody, the quicker we can go.'

I'm not sure whether on occasions like this people are simply glad to see a representative of the next generation or whether Rad was popular for being Lexi's son or on his own account, but within the confines of this garden he seemed to have achieved an enviable measure of celebrity. Even those friends of Lexi's he didn't know knew all about him. After hearing Rad answer the same questions about Senegal and his motorbike accident and the near incineration of *Wentworth* half a dozen times, it occurred to me that I hadn't yet set eyes on our host, so I slipped back to the food table and picked up a plate of coronation chicken and headed indoors.

In the kitchen Clarissa was arranging flowers in a selection of vases, buckets and beer mugs. The floor was strewn with discarded leaves.

'Is Lawrence around?'

She paused in the act of smashing the ends of some long-stemmed roses with a meat tenderiser. 'Probably still trying to plumb in the video.' She glanced at my plate. 'Oh, that's a good idea – take him something to eat. He'll miss the whole party at this rate.'

I found him crouched on the sitting-room floor, surrounded by polythene and cardboard and chunks of moulded polystyrene. In front of him sat the video machine, trailing wires, the word ERR flashing ominously in the display panel. He was studying an instruction booklet which had been ripped into pieces and then sellotaped back together.

'I just cannot . . . oh this *bloody* . . .' he was saying through clenched teeth, as I announced my presence with a cough. He swung round and for a moment a frown lingered on his face, and then turned to a look of recognition and delight. 'Abigail, what a lovely surprise.' He stood up and kissed me on both cheeks. His hair was quite white now, but there was plenty of it and his face was tanned. He was still handsome. He pointed an accusing finger at me. 'You've come with Rad, haven't you?'

I nodded. 'It's so nice to see everyone.' We glanced at the debris at our feet.

'You've just saved me a couple of hundred pounds,' he said.

'How?'

'Because when you came in I was on the point of picking this thing up and throwing it through the window.'

'I see the manual has already taken some punishment,' I said, smiling.

'That was at midnight last night, when Lexi accused me of not reading the instructions properly. You know I don't think people kill their wives over big things like adultery. I think it's little things – like this.'

I nodded. 'I was just reading in the paper the other day about a man who killed his lover during an argument about the best way to marinade a chicken.'

'Exactly,' said Lawrence. 'I hope the jury was lenient.'

'Would you like some chicken, by the way?' I said, offering him my untouched plate. 'You're going to miss out on the food if you're not careful.'

He accepted gratefully. 'You are kind. You'll come and see us again properly, won't you? Lexi will need consoling when Rad goes away.'

I promised I would. 'I don't play bridge, though,' I warned.

'Oh, that's all right. I'm sure Lexi will find other ways you can be useful,' and we both laughed disloyally.

Just before I left to rejoin the party Lawrence pointed out a painting on the wall. It was a watercolour of a stone cottage, delphiniums and geraniums in the foreground, fields and copses in the middle distance and a rocky plateau at the horizon. It was rather good.

'Lexi did it,' he said, gratified by my expression of surprise. 'It's our cottage in France. It turns out she's got some talent in that direction.'

In the garden Lexi, from the comfort of a deck-chair, was canvassing the guests for expertise in electrical gadgetry. Rad was sitting in the shade of the apple tree eating his fifth meringue and being lectured by Cecile on the decline of modern manners. She had observed that men of his generation no longer stood when a woman came into the room. Rad wanted to know whether the rule applied to gardens. 'I mean, there are people to-ing and fro-ing all the time here: I'd be bobbing up and down like a jack-in-a-box.' Nevertheless he offered me his deck-chair and was about to fetch me a bowl of strawberries when there was a muffled howl from inside the house. A moment later Lawrence appeared at the french windows waving a white handkerchief.

'Oh, leave the machine and come and join the party,' said Lexi. 'We'll have to get a man in.' I could imagine her later, going through her diary.

Soon afterwards, as the main detachment of guests began to depart, Rad signalled that he was ready to go.

'Don't get up,' he insisted, keeping one hand on Lexi's shoulder as he kissed her goodbye.

'Now ring me next week, Abigail, and we'll arrange a time for you to come over,' said Lexi from the deck-chair.

I said I would make a note of it, congratulating myself on having escaped without the dresses, and we waved a general goodbye to the remnant of visitors.

The front door had only just closed behind us and I was savouring that moment of pleasant introspection and relief which always makes leaving a party the most enjoyable bit, when there was a loud tooting from the kerb below and a man in a dirty white estate car gestured to us impatiently. He seemed to be restricted in his movements by a large, flat board the width of the car which extended from the back windscreen to the nape of his neck as he sat almost pinioned against the wheel.

'Oh blast!' said Rad. 'If we'd only left two minutes earlier.' He strode towards the car and pulled the passenger door open.

'Don't just stand there, get the boot open,' the man ordered, ripping the keys out of the ignition and flinging them at Rad. It was only when I heard his voice that I recognised Mr Radley. Between us Rad and I managed to remove the package, which was about six by four, wrapped in brown paper, and which proved surprisingly light, and stand it on the kerbside up against the wing, while Mr Radley climbed out of the driver's seat looking crumpled and harassed. He was fatter and balder, and to compensate for the diminishing hair on his head had grown a rather lush beard. 'I've driven all the way from Highbury like that,' he complained, still not acknowledging me. 'If anyone had hit me in the rear I'd have been decapitated.' He peered at me like someone who ought to wear glasses but doesn't. 'It's *Blush*. For a moment there I thought Rad had got a new girlfriend,' he said, reintroducing me in a few brief words to his peculiar brand of tactlessness. 'What have you been doing all these years then? Married? Children?'

'No, nothing like that.'

'Neither's Rad. Perhaps you could marry each other.' He turned to Rad. 'You could do a lot worse. Seriously.'

'Thank you,' said Rad. 'I'll bear it in mind.'

'Anyway, I can't stand here chatting,' said Mr Radley, as if we were the ones who had waylaid him, 'or I'll miss the party.'

'You already have missed it,' said Rad. 'You're three hours late.'

'Is your mother angry?' he asked.

'No. Somehow the other thirty guests managed to hold things together.'

'All right, all right, no need to be sarcastic. She'll forgive me everything when she sees my present anyway. Such an incredible stroke of luck.'

'What is it?' asked Rad, trying to peep through a flap in the brown paper.

'I always regretted selling it, because it was after all an act of homage. To your mother. And about six weeks ago I was browsing round this junk shop – well, antique shop, really – in Camden, and I found it again. My guess is the person who bought it must have died and house clearers took the lot. It still had a sticker on the back – Second prize: Lazarus Ohene. I can't wait to see her face.'

'What are you laughing at?' Rad asked as we drove back towards the city.

'It's a family secret,' I said. 'Listen . . .'

49

That was some months ago. I am happily married now, and alone. Rad has gone back to Senegal, which I look at on the *Times* Map of the World on my kitchen wall but can form no picture of. He writes often – unexpectedly funny, romantic letters without any hint of the *National Geographic* about them. Sometimes he phones, but the line is usually bad, we end up having to shout, and endearments lose something when bellowed. It makes him seem further away rather than nearer, so I prefer the letters. Restoration work on *Wentworth* is nearly complete. Sometimes on Sundays I go over there to check on its progress. Then I lie on the bed and look at the moon between the new curtains I have made and reflect on the fact that eighteen months is not long to wait to be happy, that time passes quickly even when we want it to, and that nothing – grief, ecstasy, even tattoos – can last for ever.

NIGHT SHALL OVERTAKE US

Kate Saunders

'If it is possible to imagine Jeffrey Archer and Jilly Cooper pooling their talents, *Night Shall Overtake Us* is exactly the sort of book they would produce' *Sunday Telegraph*

In Edwardian England a vow of friendship is a thing of innocence. Even when tested by the passionate militancy of the suffragette movement or the rigorous demands of the Season, the bonds between Rory, Eleanor, Jenny and Francesca hold fast. But nothing can withstand the unprecedented onslaught of the First World War – and as the best of an entire generation is extinguished on the battlefields of Europe, a schoolgirl pledge, too, lies broken . . .

WILD YOUNG BOHEMIANS

Kate Saunders

'Hugely enjoyable, glossy, sexy and wittily turned' *The Times*

Melissa Lamb and her cousin Ernestine are at the centre of the Wild Young Bohemians, an exclusive dining club at Oxford for the beautiful and ambitious. Melissa is in the grip of an obsession. Ernestine however, mild and practical, does not see through Melissa's ruthless determination to restore her derelict family mansion – a Gothic legacy of lust, greed and death, with a spectacular secret that has slept for a hundred years.

Melissa will let nothing stand in her way – until a vengeful stranger enters their magic circle. But he is only a catalyst: the seed of evil is already sown.

LILY-JOSEPHINE

Kate Saunders

'I loved *Lily-Josephine*. Kate Saunders is such a wonderful writer . . .' Jilly Cooper

Lily-Josephine had a talent for love. Wilful, enchanting and passionate, she was the centre of a charmed universe – until her foolish, indulgent father married again. Like Snow-Drop in Grimms' fairy tale, Lily ran from her jealous stepmother one idyllic summer evening in 1941. She escaped to find sanctuary but, at Randalls, discovered a love far greater than any she had ever known . . .

A generation later the events set in train that night begin to unravel when Sophie Gently falls in love with Octavius Randall and the bizarre and tragic history linking their families is uncovered.

A SONG FOR SUMMER

Eva Ibbotson

When Ellen Carr, daughter of a militant suffragette and raised to be an intellectual, takes a job in Austria as housemother at the Hallendorf School of Music, Drama and the Dance she simply wants to cook beautiful food. What she finds when she reaches Schloss Hallendorf is an eccentrically magical world occupied by wild children, naked Harmony teachers, experimental dancers and a tortoise on wheels.

Life in Hallendorf seems idyllic, but outside the castle Hitler's Reich is already casting its menacing shadow over Europe and the persecutions have begun. Through her growing friendship with the mysterious groundsman Marek, Ellen encounters the dreadful reality of flight from Nazi Germany, and, on the brink of war, discovers a passion that will shape her life.

SEESAW

Deborah Moggach

Take an ordinary, well-off family like the Prices. Watch what happens when, one Sunday, seventeen-year-old Hannah disappears without a trace. See how the family rallies when a ransom note demands half a million pounds for Hannah's safe return.

But it's when Hannah comes home that the story really begins.

Now observe what happens to a family when they lose their house, their status, all their wealth. Note how they disintegrate under the pressures of guilt and poverty and are forced to confront their true selves.

And finally, wait to hear about Hannah, who has the most shocking surprise in store of all.

CLOSE RELATIONS

Deborah Moggach

Louise, Prudence and Maddy are three grown-up sisters happy to lead very different lives. But when their father leaves their mother, his wife of forty years, they find their own lives too are plunged into chaos. Passions run high as the different generations bicker, fall out, test their emotions and pick up the pieces in this rich and profound novel of generations and family.

Praise for Deborah Moggach:

'Moggach is a skilful narrator, deftly weaving together the threads of each family member's life, creating an instantly recognisable world' *Daily Telegraph*

'Provocative, enthralling, bang-up-to-the-minute . . . Truly, Moggach gets better and better' *Daily Mail*

'A gripping and thoroughly intelligent read' *Evening Standard*

THE STAINLESS ANGEL

Elizabeth Palmer

When wealthy bachelor George Marchant marries the exotic Camilla Vane, while on secondment to Rome, his friends and family are astonished. Camilla's motives are entirely pragmatic: her rising debts and a largely forgotten small son. But to her horror, accommodating George proves stubborn in one thing: he insists they live at his family estate back in England.

From the moment Camilla arrives, nothing at Marchants will ever be the same again. Within the first year one of the family has attempted suicide, one marriage has ended, and one son is dead. As she sweeps through the corridors plotting her return to Rome, Camilla is oblivious to the destruction and heartache she leaves in her wake – but she has not reckoned on the one person who will stop at nothing to save the family inheritance.

PLUCKING THE APPLE

Elizabeth Palmer

A Chelsea dinner party at the home of art gallery owners James and Victoria Harting sets in motion a chain of events that will leave none of the guests unscathed.

Among those assembled is artist Jack Carey and Ellen, his long-suffering wife, who has the job of keeping Jack's mind on the canvas. The evening ends, however, with Jack slipping James's vampish sister Tessa his business card, promising future exchanges of a more intimate nature – much to the despair of Tessa's love-sick husband Alexander.

Casting a cool eye over the proceedings is Ginevra, Victoria's intellectual but plain university friend. Her fathomless eyes absorb the subtle nuances at work under the conversational hum, but not even she can foresee the shocking events about to unfold – and just as well . . .

OLD MONEY

Elizabeth Palmer

Morgan Steer and Tom Marchant are handsome, charming and unscrupulous; each one intent on marrying a fortune. Hunting as a pair they trawl the London social circuit, dining out with all the eligible girls.

But while Tom relishes each new conquest, Morgan cannot forget his first love, Caroline Barstow, long since married to someone else. It is with more desperation than delight that he proposes to the icy, beautiful and enormously rich Chloe Post and takes her up to Northumberland to meet his family. At once passions are rekindled, old jealousies nudged awake and steely determination replaces bitter resignation.

FLOWERING JUDAS

Elizabeth Palmer

Charmian Sinclair runs her own PR firm and a regular series of married lovers, one for each day of the week. Weekends are spent with Giles Hayward in Sussex. It is a rewarding way of life, but when Giles, the only bachelor in her set, falls in love with a country neighbour, Charmian realizes it can't go on for ever.

Charmian's opportunities for reflection are cut short, however, by the news that Oliver Curtis, her brother-in-law, has been brutally fired from his high-powered City job. Outraged by this, Charmian resolves to exact revenge through her own influential contacts – and discovers far more than she bargained for . . .

THE GOLDEN RULE

Elizabeth Palmer

Patience Allardyce, a righteous woman who prides herself on her high principles, is generally – though not universally – regarded as perfect. Perfectly poisonous is another view. Her husband's defection is an unpleasantly humiliating surprise which forces Patience to review her future. But not, however, her own behaviour.

Moving to London, she reinvents herself as a crusading guardian of the nation's morals and marries Hillary Causton, the right-wing media mogul. His newspapers present an ideal platform for her uncompromising opinions, but Patience has reckoned without the ongoing feud between Hillary and his arch-rival Charlie Davenport . . .

A PRICE FOR EVERYTHING

Mary Sheepshanks

Sonia, Lady Duntan, loves the family seat rather more than she does her husband. Archie, however, is adamant: their lifestyle must be preserved and the house must go.

When Archie embarks on an affair with the pneumatic Rosie Bartlett, Sonia is even more determined to thwart his plans. But as her conspiracy widens to include her glamorous but unreliable mother-in-law, a rather sinister bogus monk and the urbane Simon Hadleigh from the company Heritage at Risk, things begin to spiral out of control . . .

In turns hilariously funny and genuinely sad, *A Price for Everything* is a bittersweet novel of love, loss and the art of compromise.

FACING THE MUSIC

Mary Sheepshanks

'There wouldn't be any trouble if only you had a wife,' Lady Boynton had said. But Flavia Cameron was not at all what she had in mind for Gervaise Henderson, headmaster of Winsleyhurst School. Impossibly young, with a musical talent that could have been heard in the concert halls around the world, she was beautiful and sparkling and she swept the Upper Fourth off their feet.

And then Ben Forbes arrived at the school, with a father who saw Flavia not as a prodigy, a daughter or a wife, but, for the first time, as herself. It is a discovery that will throw her life into turmoil.

PICKING UP THE PIECES

Mary Sheepshanks

Kate is in her fifties, recently widowed and coping with the difficulties – and occasional pleasures – of flying solo. Helped and hindered in equal measures by her delightful but wicked old mother Cecily, she finds new strengths and must face undiscovered weaknesses. But it is not until her daughter Joanna's husband walks out and Joanna automatically assumes that Kate will step into the supporting Granny role while she goes out career and man-hunting, that Kate realises it is time to step outside her family's preconceived expectations – with devastating results.

BESTSELLING ARROW FICTION

☐	Night Shall Overtake Us	Kate Saunders	£6.99
☐	Wild Young Bohemians	Kate Saunders	£5.99
☐	Lily-Josephine	Kate Saunders	£5.99
☐	A Song For Summer	Eva Ibbotson	£5.99
☐	Seesaw	Deborah Moggach	£5.99
☐	Close Relations	Deborah Moggach	£5.99
☐	The Stainless Angel	Elizabeth Palmer	£5.99
☐	Plucking the Apple	Elizabeth Palmer	£5.99
☐	Old Money	Elizabeth Palmer	£5.99
☐	Flowering Judas	Elizabeth Palmer	£5.99
☐	The Golden Rule	Elizabeth Palmer	£5.99
☐	A Price for Everything	Mary Sheepshanks	£5.99
☐	Facing the Music	Mary Sheepshanks	£5.99
☐	Picking up the Pieces	Mary Sheepshanks	£5.99

ALL BOOKS ARE AVAILABLE THROUGH MAIL ORDER OR FROM YOUR LOCAL BOOKSHOP AND NEWSAGENT.

PLEASE SEND CHEQUE/EUROCHEQUE/POSTAL ORDER (STERLING ONLY) ACCESS, VISA, MASTERCARD, DINERS CARD, SWITCH OR AMEX.

EXPIRY DATE .... SIGNATURE ....

PLEASE ALLOW 75 PENCE PER BOOK FOR POST AND PACKING U.K.

OVERSEAS CUSTOMERS PLEASE ALLOW £1.00 PER COPY FOR POST AND PACKING.

ALL ORDERS TO:

RANDOM HOUSE, BOOK SERVICE BY POST, TBS LIMITED, THE BOOK SERVICE, COLCHESTER ROAD, FRATING GREEN, COLCHESTER, ESSEX CO7 TDW.

NAME ....

ADDRESS ....

....

Please allow 28 days for delivery. Please tick box if you do not wish to receive any additional information ☐

Prices and availability subject to change without notice.